LIAR LIAR

ONE NIGHT FOREVER

DONNA ALAM

Cover Design: LJ Designs
Image: Wander Aguiar
Editing: Jenny Sims

ALSO BY DONNA ALAM

The following are standalone titles often written in relating worlds.

No Ordinary Gentleman

ONE NIGHT FOREVER

Never Say Forever

LONDON LOVERS

To Have and Hate

(Not) The One

The Stand Out

PHILLIPS BROTHERS

In Like Flynn

Down Under

Rafferty's Rules

GREAT SCOTS

Easy

Hard

HOT SCOTS

One Hot Scot

One Wicked Scot

One Dirty Scot

Single Daddy Scot

Surprise Package

AND MORE!

Solider Boy

Playing His Games

Gentleman Player

This book was conceived in a Canberra hotel bar over a pretty average cheese platter and one or five much better margaritas, but more importantly, with a very good friend who I dedicate this book to.

May we all be swan-like and soar.

(love me some Motivated Mo-Fo's)

Truths and roses have thorns about them.
~ Henry David Thoreau

1

ROSE

MARCH

'IT'S NOT every day you find yourself in an Uber on the way home at four a.m. with a blonde wig in your pocket and a foot-long purple penis tucked into your purse.'

'Yes, because my life is just that interesting,' I find myself muttering.

'You're crazy,' Amber replies through a chuckle.

'Oh, I so am. Crazy broke and crazy tired.' I swap my cell phone to my other hand as I lean down to rub my aching calf. 'And maybe just plain crazy because why else would I be on my way home from a strip joint at pervert o'clock in heels and booty shorts?'

'Because you have excellent morals and a strong work ethic,' she replies evenly. 'Your text earlier said you'd had an awful night. Did Shaun, the shitty shift manager, threaten to dock your pay for broken glasses again?'

'The man's name is Ted.'

'Yeah, but alliteration, babe.'

'Well, there was no broken glassware,' I reply with a sigh.

Thankfully, I've mastered the art of balancing a laden tray since my first shift last month. 'But there are better ways to spend a night.'

'I'm sure you'll find something else soon.' My friend's tone turns sympathetic just as my Uber hits a pothole, jostling me against the back seat. I press my hand to my purse on the seat next to me, the action reminding me of the package I'd collected from the post office this afternoon. *Package* being the pertinent word. A blonde wig might be part of my new waitressing persona, but the purple penis, thankfully, is not.

'I can't believe you sent me this monstrosity,' I murmur, my cheeks heating as I look down at the outline through the thin pleather of my purse.

'Well, it's certainly monstrous,' she replies happily.

'Want to tell me why?'

'I thought you might've forgotten what one looks like.'

'That could be true. I don't recall them being quite so purple.'

'The flesh-toned ones were too creepy,' she offers by way of explanation. 'You might be a little more grateful. It cost me a fortune to mail it from Sydney.'

The fact that she lives in Australia is the reason we're having a conversation at four in the morning. The reason she sent me a sex toy is a little harder to understand. Out of all the things she could've sent—heavenly chocolate-dipped macadamia nuts or even a packet of Tim Tam cookies—I get a stand-in penis big enough to hang a hat on.

'I suppose I should also say thanks for your detailed description on the customs declaration form, too?'

She'd checked the box marked 'GIFT' before spelling out the contents in her neat penmanship. *D-I-L-D-O.*

'I could've written *substitute boyfriend* instead.'

'Lord, please send me wine.' I appeal to the roof of the

Subaru. After a month of waitressing in a strip joint, I have neither the time nor the inclination for men. Or even plastic parts of them.

'Rub it in, why don't you?' she complains. 'I can't believe I have two whole months before I can indulge in a cool glass of Chablis, eat my own weight in Camembert, and tie my own damn sneakers again!'

My best friend happens to be pregnant after meeting the love of her life in Australia while we were backpacking there. Sadly, the only thing I found in Australia was thigh chafe.

'But I called because you said you were having a nightmare night, so now I have my swollen cankles resting on a pillow and a glass of juice resting on my humongous bump. I am prepared,' she declares a touch dramatically. 'You may spill at will.'

I feel a brief pinch of envy suddenly picturing her there in her enormous home. She's so settled and so in love. And she *so* doesn't need the thing I have in my purse. I shake off the thoughts; it's not as though love came easy to her. She deserves good things, but that's not to say I deserved the night I had.

'So, I spent the last five hours avoiding an, erm, older gentleman who insisted on following me around the club. Fun, right?'

'That depends. Was he older in the super-hot *yes, daddy* way?' she asks, her voice soft and breathy.

'Nope. He was older in the creepy-assed retiree way. The man hassled me the whole night to take him into one of the private booths to dance for him.'

'I assume these were requests you politely declined since you haven't mentioned you were fired.'

'I can be polite,' I protest. 'Especially when I need a job. Maybe I should dance. The tips are way better.' There's also

3

less opportunity to be touched, though I keep that to myself. No need to worry her.

'Except customers would pay you *not* to dance.'

'Hey, I've got moves, moves they haven't seen.'

'Oh, you've got moves all right. Moves *I* don't ever want to see again. Did security throw him out?'

'They did not. He didn't touch. He just followed me around.' My eyes fall to my lap as I pluck at a loose thread on my so-called uniform. Black shorts and a white shirt knotted at the waist. The whole ensemble two sizes too small, and not by accident but rather for effect. *Like I need to give men any more reason not to look at my face.*

'With a lolling tongue and clacking dentures?' Amber continues. 'Were his rheumy eyes undressing you through glasses like the bottom of a Mason jar?'

I'm pleased this is amusing one of us.

'They were more like glued to my boobs.'

'While the girls are pretty magnificent, I say unto you, *ew!*'

Ew is right. It's all just so nasty, from my tiny uniform and knee socks to how it's taken for granted I'll sweet-talk the scum they call clientele. How I accept that tips are sometimes delivered to my cleavage because I'm so poor right now, I can't afford scruples.

'Did you whip him with your wig?'

Amber finds it hilarious that I wear a platinum blonde wig to work, but it makes me feel a little better. It's as if I've created a distinction between the woman who allows those kinds of liberties and regular old me.

My work personality is called Heidi. I don't do the accent.

'I did not,' I answer, suddenly finding that the pins fastening up my dark hair are beginning to pinch.

'I know you didn't *bless his heart* because you only do that before you make someone eat dirt.'

'One time—I did that one time! And the fool had it coming to him.'

'Agreed. So, what did you do to the old creep?'

'I used my words. I said to him, s*ir, do you see this tray? This is the only part of my uniform I will drop for you tonight.*'

'While imagining dropping it on his head.' As Amber chuckles, I regale her with the rest of our exchange as I unpin my braids, then tuck them into the collar of my coat.

'*Come on, honey. I'll make it worth your while,*' I intone in some approximation of elderly hillbilly. 'He just kept grinning at me with these teeth that looked like a row of crooked headstones. And speaking of headstones, he ought to be under one. The man was older than dirt.'

'You know what they say; only the good die young.'

'Hell, there was nothing good about him. What part of *no* don't you understand? I almost yelled at him. I told him there were any number of gorgeous girls willing to—'

'Take his money?'

'To dance for him. Why plague me?'

'Because he likes them with a little fight, apparently.'

'Only his answer was much worse.' So bad it made me sick to my stomach. 'He said he wanted me to dance for him—and we both know by dance, he meant strip—*because, honey, you're the spit of my granddaughter.*' Again, I lay on the good ole boy accent thick.

'Oh, my God. That is so bad.'

'No, *that* is my job,' I reply, pretending not to look at the driver just as he pretends not to listen as the car begins to slow. 'But thanks for calling back. For checking in.'

'I'm sorry you're having such a hard time,' Amber answers quietly. 'I wish I could help.' And she would, but for the pesky immigration rules. 'But I was thinking that maybe you could come and stay sometime soon. Maybe when Roman is here?'

'Roman?' I repeat a little incredulously. Her brother-in-law?

'What's wrong with Roman? He's single, rich, handsome, and has the kind of accent that disintegrates panties in a mile radius.'

'All very true. But me and Roman?'

'Wouldn't that be something.'

Roman and I would be something all right. Something ridiculous. I've never dated a rich man. I wouldn't know what to do with one! So even if the theory of a wealthy boyfriend is appealing, I'm pretty sure the practicalities would be a bust.

'Just think about it. Please?'

'Sure, that sounds like a plan.' A pie in the sky kind of plan given I can barely afford this Uber ride. But a girl can dream, can't she? Even if my dreams aren't about dating rich, pretty men but travelling again. It was the most exciting year of my life, even if it does seem like a distant dream now.

A year out of community college, I was interning for a hotel chain when I received an unexpected windfall from a distant relative of my mom's. It came out of the blue, considering I'd been parentless and struggling since she had passed away in my senior year of high school. But I didn't question where or the why because it was my ticket out. I paid off my debts, and I left without looking back. But a girl has to put down roots at some point. In my case, I applied for a job Stateside when funds began to run low. I guess all parties have to end sometime, but some move this turned out to be. I might've graduated to an apartment from a backpacker's hostel, but I'm no further ahead, despite my worldly experiences.

Back to drudgery and the grind.

'In the meantime, maybe you could use my gift to help

you blow away those lady cavity cobwebs.' Amber's words are heavy with meaning.

'You think I have cobwebs?'

'Oh, honey, and dust bunnies.'

'Sounds like you should've sent me a feather duster.'

'What you need is a little fun. And a man. A man who knows his way around a woman. A man with a great big—'

'*And* I think we can stop right there. I'm home now, anyway.'

We say our goodbyes as the car pulls to a stop outside of the reason I find myself waitressing in a strip club right now; 228 S Albany Ave, described *as a charmingly bright and airy two-bedroom, one-bathroom garden unit in the vibrant and culturally diverse Little Village area of San Francisco.* At least, according to the sales particulars on the internet. I suppose it is bright and airy, but only between the months of June and October. It's frigid, dark, and draughty the rest of the year. And what isn't so charming is that I had to sublet the spare bedroom to a stranger after being laid off.

As the car pulls away, I breathe out heavily, my exhalation a puff of white in the night air. At least I have the place to myself this weekend. Sarah, my roommate, has herself a new boyfriend.

With my door keys in hand, I hitch my purse higher over my shoulder as a sudden gust of cold wind blows the sides of my coat open. The cold air reminds me of my tiny uniform, a sudden prickling sensation crawling up my spine from the base. With a shiver, I push the sense of foreboding away, my heels clacking rapidly on the sidewalk on the way to the stairs leading to my second-floor walk-up apartment.

Not tonight, Satan, I silently intone. *Bogeyman be gone! I will not be murdered outside my own home.*

Not dressed like this. What would the neighbours say?

'I'll tell you what they'd say,' I mumble as I lift my foot onto the wooden tread. 'Serves her right, getting herself killed, being out on the street at this hour dressed like a ten-dollar hooker.'

I might be too old to believe in the bogeyman and trolls who live under bridges, but I'm not too old to believe in other monsters. The kind who lurk in dark corners just waiting for a damsel to pass. But right now, I'm more concerned about *this* damsel as a hand suddenly clamps around my elbow, bringing me to a grinding halt. My heart is suddenly in my throat, my thought processes lagging as they struggle to compute this reality.

Things like this don't happen to me.

I am *not* that girl.

Only I am that girl, the kind of girl who whimpers as her legs turn to jelly. The girl who tries not to choke out a sob as panic wells under her diaphragm. But I also happen to be the kind of girl who is practical, who slips her hand into her purse as she turns, bringing out, not the can of pepper spray she was reaching for, but a twelve-inch purple dildo.

A dildo her friend sent to her in the mail this morning as a joke. *She hopes.*

A dildo called the Pussy Pounder 2000 with the kind of girth to make even the gamest of girls wince.

'Hi-ya!'

I'm too terrified to wonder when I turned into Miss Piggy as I whip around and whack my would-be attacker across the side of his head. I take nothing else in, other than he's male and big, but that doesn't mean I'm not stunned as the figure immediately crumples to the ground. But I'm not so stunned that I don't remember I need to make a run for it.

I'm pretty sure my heart is about to break through my ribcage as I struggle with the marriage of key and lock. But sweet mother of Jesus, the door falls open an instant later, and my body with it. Scrambling and scrabbling, I trip over the handle of my purse, scattering my belongings across the floor as I kick the door closed.

'Ohmygod. Ohmygod.' My throat constricts, my whole body trembling as I stand, slamming the bolt into place. 'I'm fine,' I whisper, pressing my back against the door. 'I'm just fine. And I'm safe. I'm . . . fuck. Oh, fuck.'

'Rose! Rose! What's happening? For the love of God answer me!'

'Amber?' I swipe my phone from the floor; it must've dialled her number as it bounced from my purse. 'Oh my God, Amber. There was a man, he tried to grab me—on the stairs. I was so frightened. But I'm okay. I-I'm okay.' My words fall in a jumble as I seek to reassure myself as much as her.

'Oh, my Lord! How did you get away?'

My gaze falls to the purple monstrosity in my hand as though unsure what it's doing there.

'I hit him with your dildo.' I'm too wired to cringe, but for the record, this is a sentence I *never* want to hear again, let alone say. 'I think I knocked him out.'

'Ha! You said dildo. I knew I could get you to say it.'

'I was in an Uber!' I almost screech. 'I wasn't about to publicly discuss the gigantic phallus my best friend decided to send me. But this is neither the time nor the place to be discussing inappropriate gifts. Focus!' I guess I also shouldn't be still staring at it, though it's hard not to. The veins are almost mesmerising.

'Oh my God, you're serious?' she cries. 'I thought you were joking. You need to call the police now! I'll stay on the line.'

'How can you stay on the line while I make another call?'

'Make the call from your landline,' she urges.

'Who has a landline these days?' I ask, looking around for

9

someplace to set down the Pussy Pounder, eventually deciding on the console table where it stands like a pornographic game of ring toss.

'You don't have a landline? What about for power outages? Emergencies?'

'I can't afford emergencies. Besides, can you even be a millennial if you own a landline?'

'Jesus, Rose. Quit arguing. There's a homicidal maniac at your door!'

'For the record, that is *not* reassuring.'

'Can you use the conference call thing?'

I snort in response. Technology and I have never been a thing. We're not even casual acquaintances.

'Or just hang up, call them, then call me back so I know you're okay!'

Hmm. I'm not sure about that.

Hello, I was grabbed by a stranger at my front door.

Ma'am, where is the attacker now?

On the ground. I knocked him out with a massive dildo.

I'm pretty sure that would *not* get a car dispatched.

'Shush.' I press my ear to the door. 'I think I hear something.'

'You think you hear something? Should I record those as your last words? Of course you hear something,' she replies a little hysterically. 'You hear the bad man. I swear to God, if I go into labour right now, I'm blaming you!'

'Hush!' I repeat as I bring my ear to the surface of the door. 'He's groaning.' I realise my fear has reduced to a slight tremor in my hand, curiosity overtaking dread somehow.

'It's just a ploy,' Amber warns.

'He just whispered *please*. I'm almost sure of it.'

'Yeah, please let me in so I can murder you. Or please

come and hit me with your dildo some more. Either way, that is not good.'

'He sounds like he's in pain.'

'That makes two of us!'

'Cut it out.' I pull the phone momentarily away from my ear. 'I'm trying to listen. He's groaning again.'

'He might be a pervert.' My gaze drops to my outfit, the sides of my coat no longer tied, and I consider she might be right. 'He could be jacking off. It might be the old dude from the club.'

'He was too tall to be the old dude. Besides, it's too cold out for al fresco finger fumbling. Those groans do *not* sound like a fun masturbation session. I'm going to have a look.'

'Are you insane?'

'Just a quick peek,' I say oh so reasonably, certain he can't have moved from the bottom of the stairs. Almost certain, in any case.

'You are crazy! Haven't you ever watched a horror movie? He could totally be pretending, waiting to lure you outside.'

'Wait, I have pepper spray,' I announce, dropping to the floor and slipping my hand into my purse to rummage around for the small can I always carry. *It's in here somewhere, I know it.*

'No, don't do it! Don't be the dumb as dog shit girl who always gets killed first,' she wails.

I stand and scan the hallway for a weapon in lieu of the missing spray, my gaze falling to the monstrous dildo again.

I guess it worked the first time . . .

'The noises are too far away to be happening right on the other side of the door. I'm just gonna crack it open a little.'

'You know there's no such thing as just a little dead, right?'

'I promise I'll be careful.' As I say this, I've already tucked the dildo under my arm to gingerly slide back the bolt. My fingers are on the handle, just itching to turn it. 'Just a peek. I promise.'

Ignoring her wailed *noooo*, I press my toes at the bottom of the door and crack it an inch. The bogeyman isn't waiting on the other side, I'm pleased to report back to Amber, whose complaints are still audible as I open it another couple of inches.

There at the bottom of the stairs lies a crumpled heap I assume to be both male and human. He twists a little in his position, his arms suddenly thrown wide as though inviting a hug.

Nope! Not today, bogeyman.

And maybe I am an idiot as I step gingerly down a couple of treads, finding myself jumping as his head falls back, hitting a wooden stair with a dull *thud*.

'I think he's unconscious.'

'This is where he jumps up and shouts BOO!'

'Ouch!' I pull the phone away from my ear with a wince.

'Please, just call the police.'

I meant to reassure her and say I would. Instead, a different declaration leaves my mouth.

'He's cute.'

Though cute is an understatement as a gust of wind whips down the street, lifting his hair and turning it copper in the glow of a nearby streetlight.

A dead ringer for Adonis minus the whole toga deal. But his looks aren't important. The fact that he's hurt *is*.

'You know who else was cute?' Amber hisses back. 'Ted Bundy.'

'He looks nothing like Ted Bundy.'

'And by that, I know you mean he looks nothing like Zac Efron starring *as* Ted Bundy. But that's not the point. The point is, he could be a killer!'

'He has killer cheekbones,' I find myself mumbling, not quite able to bring myself to move closer to him. As for other Zac Efron comparisons, he's probably around the same age, less *High School Musical* Zac and more buff *Baywatch* Zac, but without the bad hair. Dark jeans coat his long legs, and a white T-shirt hugs his broad chest. An expensive-looking leather jacket and rugged, scuffed boots complete the look. He doesn't look like an addict or someone down on his luck. In fact, as he groans and turns his head, he looks more like a victim of some kind of attack—not the whacked by a dildo kind of attack, but the real thing.

'Was he robbed?' I find myself musing.

'What?'

'I said he's hurt.' Unconscious, bruised, and battered by more than a couple of pounds of latex would be my guess.

'Please, please, *please* just go back to your apartment,' Amber begs.

'I can't just leave him here.'

'So call an ambulance. From inside! Why aren't you running for the hills?'

I can't. I'm not the type who could leave an injured dog at the side of the road, let alone a person. And for the record, I'm not dumb enough to be enchanted by his high cheekbones or his powerful physique. I'm not the kind of girl who'd risk life or limb just because the man is a little pretty.

Or even a lot pretty, as the case may be.

I draw closer because he's stopped groaning, which anyone with half a brain knows isn't good. Add to that the shallow movements of his chest and the trickle of blood running from his hairline, and I find I'm whispering into my phone.

'Oh, God. He's bleeding.' I swallow convulsively, trying very hard not to be sick. 'There's blood on his T-shirt.' I step over his outspread arm onto the stair below, gripping the fake penis in my fist. You know, just in case.

'Or maybe it's fake blood, and he's going to shove you in a big hole with a bottle of lotion!'

'Amber, the man is hurt. He's in no state to attack me.' And now that I'm on the sidewalk in front of him, I can say this categorically.

'It's usually the monsters who don't look like monsters who are the ones you need to worry about. Just, *please*, call the authorities. Let them deal with this.'

'I can't just leave him here! Abandon the man bleeding on my doorstep.'

'Abandon the man who, five minutes ago, you were sure was out to attack you?'

'He was trying to get my attention, to get my help.'

'And by calling an ambulance, you will be helping him.'

'Yes, okay,' I agree as the stranger moans once more. 'I'll do that. Let me call you back.'

Without waiting for her response, I end the call.

2

ROSE

'ROSE?'

At the sound of my name, I'm jerked from my microsleep.

'A-yesh. I mean, yes, that's me.' Grimacing at the metallic taste in my mouth, I rub my lips together, rolling my aching shoulders and stiff neck. *Was I drooling?* I wipe the back of my hand across my mouth just in case and straighten from my cramped position.

And there's a nurse standing in front of me . . . why?

'You can go in now. He's in the end cubicle.'

And then it comes back to me; the man on my doorstep. I'd pulled his wallet from his inside pocket as I'd looked for his phone, hoping to find family or a loved one to call. As it was, there was no phone and only a French driving license and a few US dollars in his wallet. *And a couple of condoms.*

But at least it gave me his name.

Remy Durrand.

He'd groaned, his eyes flickering open as he'd grasped my hand. He was still clutching it when the ambulance arrived, and I was mistaken for his girlfriend. I'd decided to just go with it after thinking I'd hate to wake alone. Maybe I'd also need to explain the bump on the side of his head. He was still unconscious when we'd arrived at the hospital where he was whisked off while strapped to a gurney. I was asked a million questions, most of which I couldn't answer, then shown the family waiting room.

Over the next few hours, the nursing staff had kindly supplied me with updates.

Don't worry, he'll be fine, and *he's coming around.*

Then, *it won't be long now*, along with *he's just undergoing a neurological evaluation. He has a nasty concussion.*

And just before I fell asleep in the chair at seven in the morning, I'd received the last update.

He's about to have his wound cleaned. Would you like to come hold his hand while it's sutured?

That'd be a big fat no, actually.

I'd lived in a lot of places, at least ten towns across four states before I turned twelve, but I was born in Kentucky, and my mom used to say Kentucky women have both sugar and fire in their veins. But I guess even women from the Bluegrass State have their weak spots, and mine is the sight of blood. *Or maybe it's a case of a cat being born in a stable not making it a horse.* Either way, if I can see Remy now, the gory business must be over, and I can breathe through my nose again without fear of passing out.

As I haul my tired body from the chair, the nurse's kind smile suddenly falters. My gaze follows hers to where my coat has fallen open as I've dozed.

'Thank you.' I leisurely pull the sides closed, knotting the belt tight as I stride past her into the nearby hallway. She can judge me for drooling but not for an honest night's work. Even if me and my slutty outfit could be mistaken for a hooker.

'Ah, here she is.'

The curtain is open at the end cubicle, and I find myself freezing, not at the sound of the doctor's voice, but because of the man facing me in the bed opposite. His hair is matted and stained russet in parts, his complexion sallow against the stark white of the pillows propping him up from behind. A Steri-Strip bisects one eyebrow, making him look thoroughly dissolute, but even that doesn't detract from how good looking he is. I mean, I'd known he was attractive. Handsome, even. Didn't I say as much to Amber over the phone? But it turns out that good looking doesn't even cover it. The strong line of his jaw is a perfect complement to those sharp cheekbones, the whole effect made more mortal than Greek god by a rasp of stubble. His eyes are the kind of green that speaks of tropical islands that are lush and inviting, but possess an intensity that's almost mesmerising.

'He's looking much better now, don't you think?'

'He's looking good,' I find myself replying in a completely unnecessary tone, as I enter the cubicle, immediately drawn to the side of the bed. I can't say whether it's out of concern or curiosity, or even something else.

'I don't think there's any cause for ordering imaging,' the doctor muses, his index finger tracing across the screen of a tablet he holds in his hand. 'No need for X-rays or a CT.'

'Good.' Those sound expensive.

Wow. He has such big shoulders under that thin hospital gown.

'And even though it looked as though he'd lost a prodigious amount of blood, his head wound was superficial.'

'Good, that's good,' I agree just as pensively, my eyes flicking down to where his long-fingered hands lie over the edges of the blue hospital blanket.

You know what they say about big hands.

'I'm Dr Scott, by the way. One of the emergency physicians here. We were quite concerned when Remy arrived, but his testing has so far been satisfactory. In fact, I was hoping you could help us with his cognitive assessment. . .'

Hands that size would make even my ass feel small.

'. . . by translating for us.'

'Hmm. Yes. I understand.'

'Great. We won't need to involve a translator, in that case.'

'Okay—wait, what?' My head whips to Dr Scott, who is, apparently, serious.

'Well, my French is non-existent. You'd need only to ask him some questions on my behalf,' he reports.

He only speaks French? I find myself looking at him again. *He's French. Ooh-la-la!*

'One of our nursing staff helped out until a few minutes ago,' the doctor continues. 'Her knowledge of the language proved very helpful, but she's been called to another ward. Ordinarily, I'd call in a translation service, but as you're listed as his significant other . . .' His words trail away as, like a bad comedy sketch, my head then whips from doctor to patient, the latter managing a wan-looking smile.

'I'm what?'

'You're noted as Remy's girlfriend. Is that not right?'

Did he say I was his girlfriend? Or did the hospital staff assume, the same as the paramedics? Oh my God, if he has a brain injury, they might have told him I'm his girlfriend, and he might think it's the truth! And if he does have a brain injury, it could be my fault—caused by being whacked upside the head with a monstrous sex toy.

I open my mouth to come clean when the man in the bed reaches for my hand, and a swirl of ink peeks from the sleeve of his hospital gown. *He has tattoos?* My eyes trace up his arm as I wonder what else he's hiding under there. As I glance up at him once again, he shoots me the kind of smile that makes blood hum in my veins.

But it's one thing to have waited around, to let the staff assume, even if my intentions were good. It's another to continue this charade. Except, he's alone, and he's hurt, and I find I can't abandon him. Especially as I might be partly responsible for him being here.

Concussion by sex toy, and not a headboard in sight.

'His girlfriend,' I murmur, almost to myself. And I'm pretty sure he just tried to nod. Though now he's grimacing.

So, was that a smile *yes,* or a grimace *no*?

If I come clean now, I'll look like an idiot. Or worse still, maybe I could be charged with impostor-ing. Maybe even assault.

'If you'd prefer, I can contact the interpreter service?' the doctor prompts.

'No, that's okay,' I find myself answering. Or maybe that should be *absolument?*

And then the magnitude of my mistake dawns on me; of what I've just done.

Not only am I not this hottie's significant other, but I also don't speak French.

3

ROSE

MERDE! Merde on a stick!

I seem to have no issues remembering French curse words.

Je t'emmerde, salope! Fuck you, bitch!

My mind rapidly runs through the snippets of French I remember from a week spent in a backpacker's hostel in Paris, my stupid brain only offering up profanity.

Enfoiré. Asshole.

But what else? There must be other words—phrases? Sensible things to say?

Café au lait, une croissant, un grande vin. Coffee, croissant, and wine; what else does a girl need for a week in Paris?

Casse-toi! Piss off! Now, this I remember came in useful one Saturday night, but it's not helpful right now.

'If we could start by asking Remy if he knows what day it is today?'

'What? Oh, it's—' My mind preoccupied, it seems my mouth seeks automatically to answer him.

'*We* may know what day it is,' the doctor replies tolerantly, 'but we need to know if Remy knows.'

'Oh. Right. Of course.'

My mind continues to race as I draw closer to the side of the bed. His black leather wallet has been placed on the hospital nightstand, a tired-looking masculine watch lying open across it. I begin to wonder how he'll pay his hospital bill, given the lack of bank cards. A translating service would only add to the cost, and I don't want the bill delivered to my mailbox, no matter how pretty he is. The ridiculous thoughts continue to rotate as I attempt to drown out my internal freakout. Why have I put myself in this position? It's too late now to say there's been some mistake.

Well, here goes nothing.

'*Quelle . . . quelle . . .*' *Quelle* is the French word for "day", again? My palms begin to feel sticky. I can't remember being so nervous since a spelling bee in sixth grade. I feel like I'm on stage again. But then in a blinding flash, the phrase comes to me—another blast from my middle school past.

'*Quelle jour il est!*'

'*Quel jour* est il?' the patient repeats in a deep baritone. And with a smirk.

Okay, pretty boy. So your French is better than mine—big whoop.

'*Oui,*' I reply with the hauteur of a Parisienne *grande dame*, earning me the kind of smile that makes me feel unnecessarily giddy.

'*Dimanche.*' The patient's eyes flick briefly to the clock on the wall. '*Non. On est Lundi.*'

I haven't a clue what he just said, but if he says it again, I'm climbing in the bed with him, hospital or not. Why does everything said in a French accent sound so sexy?

'What was his answer?'

I find myself frowning as I glance the doctor's way. How could I forget he was there?

'He said yes. I mean, he got it right.' Hopefully. I think? I turn to face Remy again as I contemplate how I'm barely sure what day it is myself. How is a man with a concussion expected to know in either language? 'Did the nurse ask him how this happened?' I enquire carefully, though he's hardly likely to confess to being felled by a rubber dong. Not that I think I'm wholly responsible for the things that happened to him tonight.

'He fell from a bike, as I understand.'

That makes sense, I suppose, but—

'From a bike? Like a bicycle? Or a motorcycle?'

'I thought he didn't speak any English?' The doctor points at Remy, his expression bland.

'Actually, I was asking you. Last night there wasn't any kind of bike or any evidence of there being a bike—wreckage or helmet—where I found him.' Or where he found me, I suppose. As I speak, Remy's green eyes glitter dangerously, almost as though in recognition. Maybe the word for bike is the same in English, and he's pissed at it.

'A motorcycle,' the doc answers. 'He came off at a very low speed, which would account for the lack of other injuries. He has a concussion and a small wound on his head as a result of hitting it on a metal rail, once he'd taken off his helmet, following a dizzy spell.'

'Is the concussion from the railing?' I ask haltingly.

'More likely from falling from the motorcycle.'

'Could it have been from something else?'

'Like what?' His gaze narrows.

'I was just thinking,' I reply, all wide-eyed and forced innocence. Thinking about the damage I could've done with the dildo and how his head might've met with the railing outside of my house.

Felony by dildo. Would that be a thing?

I glance at the doctor again, my brow furrowed. I'd watched a TV program recently about football players and the risks they face from concussions and traumatic brain injuries. It was pretty scary. 'Is he going to be okay?'

'That's what we're trying to find out.' My frown deepens at his terse tone. 'How do you not know what kind of bike he owns?'

'It must be a new hobby,' I mumble, wondering if I'm imagining how the patient's expression seems to become purposely blank every time the doctor looks his way. Meanwhile, he looks at me as though he's struggling to contain his amusement.

Probably because I wear every one of my feelings on my face.

'If you could next ask him if he knows where he is, please.'

It's a stupid question and one that also happens to be beyond my French-speaking capabilities.

'*Ou es . . .*' where is '*Ou es . . . vous?*' Where is you? That's near enough, I suppose, though I try to mime the question with a flutter of my hands, hoping this might help somehow. It turns out that it does, even if he does look like he's struggling not to laugh. But even the doctor is able to determine his eventual answer.

'*À l'hôpital.*'

'Very good.' The doctor's attention falls to his tablet again as Remy settles his head back on the pillow, his gaze seeming to drink me in. 'Could you ask him if he remembers why he's in the hospital?'

I clear my throat, ignoring Remy's very eloquent expression. '*J'ai . . . mal à la tête?*' Another middle school gem which roughly translates to: I have a headache. Yeah, I know; why would I have a headache when he's the one with the concussion? But I don't know how to turn the statement into a question, which is kind of a headache in itself.

At this, he launches into a litany of Frenchness that would, on any other occasion, have me kneeling at his feet. *And my fingers on his zipper, possibly.* But as the doctor interjects this vociferousness with a dozen questions of his own, cautioning Remy against becoming agitated, along with wondering aloud what on earth I could've said to upset him, I find I'm unable to speak.

The room suddenly falls quiet, two pairs of eyes turning to me.

'He says yes,' I answer, my voice small. 'He also says he has a headache.'

The man in the bed sets off laughing, laughter that turns almost immediately to a groan, and a groan that then turns to profanity.

'*Putain de merde!*' His hands clutch his head. The doctor moves closer to the man in the bed, but it's my hand Remy squeezes as he processes the wave of pain.

'I really don't think you need me to translate *that*.' Because that was clearly an ouch. A big ouch.

As Remy's grip slackens, his features relaxing as the pain dissipates, the good doctor turns to face me.

'I'm beginning to think you don't really speak French at all.'

'Not a lot,' I agree, drawing myself up to my full five-eight high heel-aided height. I cock my hip a little and begin to toy with the end of one of my dark braids, the movement making my coat gape a little at my chest. *Can you say boobalicious, Doctor?* 'You might say our bond is a little less meeting of the minds, and a little more physical, if you know what I mean.'

And judging by the way he blushes, he does.

———

It turns out the French-Canadian nurse is available to translate for the rest of Remy's cognitive testing, testing where Remy insists on clinging to my hand. Gone are the flirty smiles and the saucy winking. Instead, he looks to be in a serious amount of pain.

'Are you sure he doesn't need a scan?' Out of the room now, I drop my purse to the nurses' station, hurriedly shoving the can of pepper spray back as it almost rolls onto the countertop. 'He looks like he should be in the hospital.'

'It's natural to be worried, but clinically, he's fine.' The doctor barely glances up from his pile of paperwork this time. 'Of course, if there's any change in his condition, you're to contact us right away. Here.' He passes over a leaflet. 'Some information on what to expect. What to look out for.'

My eyes scan the text, my heart beginning to gallop quite suddenly.

Head injuries.

Concussion.

The warning signs of mild traumatic brain injuries.

'I think he should be admitted overnight.' He doesn't look up, though his expression ripples with something uncomplimentary. 'I mean it. I'm not qualified to do this.' I say, almost waving the leaflet under his nose. 'I can't even keep a houseplant alive!'

'I'm confident he'll be fine in your care.'

Along with this reassurance, Dr Scott straightens, bestowing me with an empathetic look. You know the look; the one I swear they must teach at medical school. For the record, I don't feel comforted.

It occurs to me that now would be the perfect time to come clean. To admit to the good doc that I'm just the good Samaritan who found Remy on the staircase, and we're not dating. That we're nothing more than strangers. It might be the best opportunity I get to relinquish this responsibility, even if it'd make me look insane, but I find I just can't do it. I just want to make sure Remy is okay.

'You just need to make sure he rests up for the next few days.' The doctor's voice refocuses my attention. 'No strenuous activity. No sport, horizontal or otherwise, for at least seven days.'

I guess I brought that on myself but find myself clutching the lapels of my coat anyway.

'He needs to rest mentally, too. No video games or TV for forty-eight hours minimum. Reading, too. It's all in there.'

I glance down as he taps the edge of the leaflet in my hand, attempting to mentally work out the time in Australia. I'm almost sure that Amber speaks French, and I'm sure she won't mind explaining to Remy what he should and shouldn't do, provided I don't call her in the middle of the night, that is.

'But he'll be okay? He doesn't need any medication?' I want to be sure he has everything he needs before I call an Uber and have him dropped off at his hotel or whatever.

'He'll probably suffer from a headache for a few days, so stick to Tylenol. No ibuprofen.'

'Okay.' A trip to the pharmacy it is.

'And check on him every couple of hours for the next twenty-four, especially if he's sleeping.'

'W-what?'

'Don't worry. It sounds dramatic, but it's standard protocol for a concussion.'

'So I should . . . do what?'

'He should be observed for the next twenty-four hours. Check on him while he's sleeping.'

'So he can't be left alone?'

'That's usually the nature of observation. Is that going to be an issue?'

His tone brims with judgment, and my mind is a riot of thoughts—

I can't have a stranger stay with me, not even if he is as hot as Hades.

I have work later today, so I won't be in any fit state to "observe" him.

I'll be asleep before my head hits the pillow!

Still, I find myself answering anyway.

'No. Of course. It's the least I can do for him.'

4

ROSE

It's the least I can do for him. You know, other than save his hide after he frightened me half to death in the early hours of this morning.

I suppose also the least I can do for him after spending hours in the hospital, hours when I could've been sleeping.

And also the least I can do for him when I'll (most probably) lose my job when I call in sick tonight in order to "observe" him.

At least he's pretty to observe.

Urgh!

But it might not come to that, I tell myself. Surely, he has someplace to go—a home or a hotel? I'll just take him to my apartment, and once Amber is awake in a few hours, I'll call her and get her to speak to him. Once she stops laughing, that is. Or maybe shouting.

It's not so crazy, is it? Taking him home, I mean. I did the exact same thing for that mangey Poodle a couple of weeks ago; I took him to the animal hospital, got him patched up and cleaned, then took him to my home until I found him a forever home.

At least Remy won't need worming or a flea bath.

I study his profile in the Uber on the way back to my place. His eyes are closed, and his head tipped back on the headrest. He appears to be asleep, which is convenient because I can't help but stare at the arch of his brow and high slant of his cheekbone. Or the way his long lashes make shadowy half-moons against his skin. He may not be cute or fluffy, but I still have the urge to reach out and touch him. I blame the other kind of animal magnetism. The very male kind. His large hands rest on his broad thighs, the flat planes of his stomach barely concealed by the hideous pink and yellow aloha shirt he's now wearing. His bloodstained T-shirt was cut from him while unconscious, and this was the only thing the nurse could find that fit because the man is kind of large.

Maybe I should've anticipated he'd feel the weight of my attention, yet I'm still shocked when his eyes flicker open, and he turns to face me.

'*Ça va bien?*' I find myself stuttering. *Are you well?*

'*Bof,*' comes his deep reply, accompanied by a small smile and an even smaller shrug.

I'm unprepared for this response as an answer. *Ça va bien or ça va mal*; good and not so good, I wouldn't be staring at him like this because what the hell is bof? I know what boffing is—sex—but that didn't seem like a suggestion or an offer.

Which kind of seems like a shame.

'This is awkward, right?' I glance across at him when he flashes me the kind of smile that speaks of bedrooms and sighs and unspoken promises, almost as though he'd plucked the thoughts right out of my head. With a jolt, I tear my gaze from his, realising it's only awkward when I remember how long it's been since I last had sex. I'm suddenly very aware of the part of my body just south of my belt.

'This is . . . not good,' I find myself whispering. I slide Remy another look, noting how his eyes rise slowly from where I appear to be flashing a little thigh.

'*Pardon*,' he murmurs, though his gaze bears no hint of that apology.

I am so not sure what to make of that look but as the Uber pulls to a stop, I find myself stuttering, 'L-look, we're here.'

I don't think I've ever gotten out of a car so fast, and while I've bitched and moaned about the number of stairs up to my front door since I moved in, I take them almost at a run. Key in the lock, I virtually stumble through the door, dropping my bag to the thrift store console table, covering the purple penis which a moment ago stood erect and proud. For once, I'm pleased the thermostat is on the fritz because it's the perfect excuse to keep my coat on. Especially when I consider I'm still wearing my god-awful uniform.

Wrapping my coat tighter, I stamp my feet a little as I dig through my purse for my phone when I realise why it's so arctic in here. Remy hasn't followed me in and is standing at the still open door. In our very short acquaintance, I've seen this man semiconscious and vulnerable, watched him bear pain with stoicism while insistent on opening the Uber door for me. He's also, I think, behaved a little naughtily. But as he stands on the threshold of my little apartment, he looks hesitant. Something tells me this is a state of being that's unfamiliar to him.

'Please, come in.' Along with the invitation, I gesture for him to enter.

'*Merci.*'

We get by the next thirty minutes almost as though we're playing a game of charades.

'You can hang your jacket up here.' *Point to the coatrack.*

'Or you can keep it on. I know, it's cold in here.' *Rub my arms.* 'But it'll warm up soon.'

'The bathroom is through here.' *Nope, not touching that one.*

'Can I get you something to eat?' *Cram an invisible sandwich between my teeth.*

'Can I get you a coffee?' *Mimes a dainty cup and saucer, then sips like the queen.*

The last is how we find ourselves sitting opposite each other at my tiny kitchen table as I watch Remy try not to grimace at the taste of the coffee I've just put in front of him.

'It's pretty terrible, huh? Not like anything you'd get in Paris, for sure.' I pull a face as I gesture to my own cup. 'Bleurgh.'

'*Non, c'est très bien.*' Bringing the cup to his lips, he makes a sound of appreciation, the almost sexual noise echoing through the small room. Or maybe that's just my imagination playing tricks on me, pleasantly plucking at my insides.

The man is just being polite, not trying to turn me on.

'Your mother must've raised you right,' I murmur into my cup, mostly to hide my pink face. 'Because this coffee is anything other than *bien*.' Which means good, I know. 'In fact, this coffee is nothing but *bein'* terrible.' I spring from my chair, dumping the contents of my cup down the sink, my gaze on the grey sky beyond the window. 'Something else terrible is the fact that I've lived in this apartment for over a year, yet you're the first man I've ever had here. Well, not *had* here exactly.' Gripping the edge of the sink, I drop my head before I remember Remy's grasp of English is almost non-existent. 'I haven't had anyone anywhere in quite some time,' I find myself adding unnecessarily along with a little giggle. It must be exhaustion, even if it feels almost cathartic to be able to speak without the need to moderate or censor my words.

'In fact, I haven't had *that* pleasure in over a year. Can you believe it? This year has been all work and no pleasure. Well, other than the pleasure I've brought to myself. And I'm sure I don't need to explain what I mean when I say that. Or maybe I wouldn't if you understood what I was saying.'

I press my lips together to halt my sudden stream of stupidity, but it seems I'm on a roll.

'Not that we'd be talking about that kind of stuff if you understood what I was saying. Oh, but that's not why I was carrying that thing in my bag, by the way, if you even remember that, which I truly hope you don't. Either way, I'm sorry for my actions, but you shouldn't creep up on a girl.'

I glance over my shoulder to where Remy's expression remains unchanged.

'You sure do look like you'd know the way around a woman's body with a feather duster.' I turn to face him, pressing my back against the sink. 'Is there anything you want to say? No sense in me being the only idiot here today. Go ahead, say what you're thinking.'

He blinks as though coming back to the moment. *Je suis désolé . . . I'm sorry. I was trying to work out why I would need a feather duster.* His resultant smile could be best described as enigmatic. It just adds to my curiosity. And damn, I wish I spoke French right now.

'Talk,' I find myself announcing. 'I like the sound of your voice. Besides, whatever you say is between you and the Lord.'

Je ne pense pas que le bon Dieu . . . I don't think the good Lord is ready to hear me confess my thoughts right now.

'See?' I find my hands in the air, my smile probably a little manic. 'How easy was that? I have no idea what you just said.

You can say whatever you like, and I wouldn't even be able to guess!'

His fingers unfurl from around the cup on the table in front of him, and he leans back, hooking an elbow around the back of the wooden chair, the picture of manliness and ease. Am I imagining the change in the atmosphere? The way he seems to take up so much space in the room.

'*Rose. Pardonne-moi, mais je parle un peu anglais . . . Forgive me, but I do speak a little English. You might even say perfect English. But there's no sense in spoiling our fun.*'

The way he says my name makes it sound like a whole other word. The rolling, guttural R. The low rumble. It's so damn sexy. And the rest? Swoon!

'Wait, how do you know that was my name? *Comment mon nom?*' Or at least it sounds something like that, I think.

'*L'hôpital?*'

'Oh.' I nod because this totally makes sense.

'*Si je te dis ce que . . . If I told you what I was doing on your doorstep, you might throw me out.*'

My shoulders rise and fall in a tiny shrug. But whatever he said, it sounded so sexy.

'*D'accord,*' he adds in a decisive tone.

'Says who?' I know *d'accord* means okay. But, 'Okay to what?'

'*J'entends que tu me donnes la permission . . . I accept I have your permission to say what I like. I agree to your suggestion to give myself the freedom to say exactly what I think. First, I think I should say that you must be a good person to have brought me here, to have opened your home to me, to have taken care of me as you have. So, I'll try to behave myself.*'

I'm pleased one of us is amused.

'*Mais je ne peux pas non plus . . . But I also can't help but imagine what you're wearing under your coat. Not a lot, as far as I can tell.'* He tilts his head, his gaze wandering down my body, his perusal almost a physical thing. *'Which makes me wonder even more.'*

I'm probably imagining things. Imagining the basis of those looks which, coupled with the deep tenor of his voice, makes every word sound like an invitation to the bedroom.

Or should that be boudoir?

'Je pense que c'est une sorte d'uniforme . . . I think it's a uniform of sorts, rather than something you're wearing for your boyfriend, given your colourful explanation of just how single you are. Merci.'

I know "merci" is thank you in French, so I reply, 'You're welcome,' assuming he's thanking me for my help.

Lord, this conversation makes me feel like a horny terrier. If I don't get laid soon, I might start humping fenceposts. What a shame he has a broken head.

But getting back to our little tête-à-tête, I think he must be asking about my coat. He's probably interested in why I'm still wearing it, judging by the fact that I *am* still wearing it, coupled with the way his eyes swept over me as he spoke.

'It is a little warmer in here now,' I begin to explain, 'but believe me, you really don't need to see what I'm wearing under here. Especially as, when I take off this coat, the girls are likely to make a break for freedom.' If I haven't popped at least one button tonight, I'll be surprised.

'J'aimerais beaucoup voir ce . . . I'd very much like to see what's underneath. The little I've seen so far, including when you embarrassed the poor doctor, makes me wonder if you're some kind of dancer. In a club, perhaps? And speaking of concealment . . .' He taps the tabletop, a smile catching at the corner of his mouth. *'I'm as hard as this wood just thinking about what's under your coat. I did warn you God wouldn't welcome my confessions.'*

Tapping the table? Maybe he's hungry. Any food that's currently in the fridge has a white sticker slapped on it with

Sarah's name scrawled across it. Let's just say I'm not big on grocery shopping, but I know there's a little leftover Chinese takeout he can have.

'I'm sure I can offer you better than this.' I move to the table, leaning across to take Remy's cup when he also grabs for it, which somehow results in him wearing the contents.

'I'm so sorry,' I say as he jumps from the chair, pulling the damp fabric from his skin. I round the table, dish towel in hand, and begin to blot the liquid, following the damp slashes down. 'I told you the coffee was terrible. You could've just poured it down the sink instead of wearing it, you know?' I rub one spot of the garish fabric a little vigorously. 'Do you know what else is terrible? This shirt. And coffee brown does not help its appearance at all.'

My hands still as, under the towel, Remy's body becomes rigid. My head also appears to be level with his junk.

'*Ça n'aide pas mon . . . Your touch doesn't help my hard-on either.*' He catches my hands, stilling them by pressing them against the flat planes of his stomach. '*Would you like to come up here?*' His smile turns mischievous. '*Of course, you're also welcome to go in the opposite direction.*'

I don't know what he said. I only know it sounded sexual. Again. But it's the nature of the French language. 'You could make something as ordinary as ordering a baguette sounds sexy.'

'*Baguette?*' Along with his curious tone, Remy quirks a brow.

Guess where my eyes go.

Yep.

Down.

And he's hard—through the hem of this God-awful shirt, the man has a little French stick action. *Little? He probably needs planning permission for an erection that size.*

35

And yes, my eyes are still glued to his crotch. I'm likely drooling, looking at him like I'd slather his baguette in butter and lick it clean. But in less crazy news, I slide my hands from under his, then straighten and pull away.

'I almost got down on my knees. Praise the Lord, I've been saved!' I find myself waving my hands in the air like a Baptist on Sunday, acting about as crazy as I feel. It defuses the heat of the moment as Remy begins to chuckle. But Lord, even the deep sound of his laughter is sexy. I'm totally having a moment here as the sun streams through the kitchen window and bathes this god of a man in a golden light.

'*Si tu étais à genoux. . . If you were on your knees, it wouldn't be God I'd be praising.*' With a gruff chuckle, his fingers move to the hem of his shirt. '*This isn't an invitation, by the way.*' He flicks a button loose.

And another.

And another.

And all the while, I'm watching. And also torturing the dish towel in my hand.

'*À moins que tu* . . . Unless you want it to be.' His tone is low and husky, and then because God is loving and benevolent, and probably thinks I deserve reward for my ridiculousness, Remy slips the shirt from his shoulders, balling the monstrosity in one fist.

'*C'est trop mouillé . . . It's too wet.*' His murmur is accompanied by an apologetic shrug.

I feel like I should tell him there's no need to apologise, not on my part, but my mouth doesn't seem to be working. Be still my beating heart, the man looks like he should be on the cover of a magazine. I'm thinking maybe *Men's Health* or something like that, though if there's a magazine out there called *Virile and Manly*, Remy could be their poster boy. Or maybe it could be a tattoo magazine, if they do them, because the man is *inked*. Swirls of black and blood red roses, patterns and whirls cover his upper chest, cresting his shoulders and traversing halfway down both arms. He is a study in deliciousness, his body made of strong lines and ridges, and those muscles that look like handles at his hips. *Well, they were sure made for handling.*

He was easy on the eyes fully dressed, but now? This is like being offered a cake with a cookie inside. I can't seem to stop looking at him. But as his fist tightens around his shirt, I find my manners again.

'Your . . . your shirt. Here I am, watching you like a starving man staring at a sandwich, when you're probably worried you'll catch a chill! Let me put it in the washing machine.' I step forward, grabbing the balled-up shirt from his hand when he dips his head, his lips suddenly just a breath away from my ear.

'*Tu es mouillé, toi aussi? Are you wet, too?*'

I shiver as I straighten, something hot and heady suddenly coursing through my veins. 'I'm sorry,' I find myself whispering, unable to pull away. '*Mouillé.* I think you said that twice. But I still don't understand.'

'*Demande-moi . . . Ask me if I'd like to find out. I must've hit my head very hard, Rose, because I'm feeling a little crazed.*'

'I wish I knew what you were saying.' I hear the longing in my voice and feel immediately embarrassed. But not for long, not as he reaches out to take a lock of my hair between his fingers.

'*J'aimerais pouvoir . . . I wish I could tell you. God knows, you are tempting.*'

'Well, it's been a long night,' I begin, stepping away as I remind myself his side of this conversation might not be as inviting as it sounds. Maybe he's complaining. Maybe he's unimpressed. I suppose there's only one way to find out. 'In a few hours, I'll be able to call my friend, Amber. She speaks French. I was thinking she might translate for us.'

'*J'espère que ton amie . . . I hope your friend is broadminded.*'

'Again, I don't know why I'm telling you this. It's not like you understand. Which is maybe just as well, or I might be about to say something completely inappropriate. Something like, I think this is where I get you into bed.'

His response is as slow and as sweet as spilled honey, and I'd be tempted to sell a kidney just to understand his answer.

'*C'est probablement la meilleure proposition que j'ai reçue de toute l'année.*'

5

ROSE

'WHEN YOU SMILE LIKE THAT, it doesn't matter what language you speak. I probably wouldn't hear the words anyway.'

'*Sache que j'ai dit . . . For the record, I said that's probably the best offer I've had all year. So show me the way to this bed, and I will show you anything you like because I liked how you looked at my cock earlier. Did you know you almost licked your lip when you saw how hard I was? I don't like to be boastful, but it's worth taking a look at. In fact, the only thing to make it look better would be to see it wrapped in those pretty lips of yours.*'

'You know, you talk, and it hits me right in the feels. And when I say feels, I mean . . . well, you don't need to know where I mean.'

'*Tu le sens dans ta chatte?*'

Wait, doesn't *chatte* mean cat in French? Does he think I'm talking about a cat? Or, ohmygod, could *chatte* also mean pussy? And if so, is he piecing this together somehow? I take a deep, cleansing breath and push my mind on to more sensible things.

'I think we both need some rest, but you especially. With

Amber's help, we can talk about, well, everything, but later.' But not about pussies or dildos. Never those. 'When we're not feeling so . . .'

'*Excités?*'

'Did you just say excited, or am I losing my ever-loving mind? You know what?' I press both hands to my head as I turn from him, then close my eyes and take a deep breath. 'Don't answer that.' Then as fast as my tired legs will carry me, I leave the room, his deep chuckle following me. 'This way,' I call over my shoulder. Then add in an undertone, 'There's no sense in being ridiculous without an audience.'

'*C'est fermé? It's locked?*'

It doesn't take a French speaker to guess what he's asking me as I rattle Sarah's bedroom door.

'What a bitch,' I grumble, swinging around and giving the door a kick with my heel. 'She put a lock on her door and didn't even ask.'

'*Tu as une colocataire? . . . A roommate? Ah, that makes sense.*'

'It's my security deposit that'll pay for that,' I complain. 'Why'd she need a lock on there anyway? It's not like she could've anticipated I'd be letting a strange Frenchman sleep in her bed tonight, is it?

'It's fine. I'll take the sofa.'

'*J'ai vu ton canapé. . . . I've seen your sofa. No one over three-foot-tall could get any rest there.*'

'I shouldn't sleep anyway. Not if I've got to check on you every two hours.'

'*Tu ferais ça pour moi?. . .You'd do that for me?*' Remy reaches out, his thumb smoothing the crease between my brows. '*I didn't think there were people like you in the world anymore.*' His hand cups my face, those unusually green eyes of his suddenly so intense. '*You take me to the hospital. You stay with* me. *You bring me home like a lost puppy. And now you want to give me your bed? Non, chérie.'*

His words pitched low, and the cadence of his voice is so soft and so sweet sounding, it's all I can do not to lean in to him. Instead, I sort of force my butt along the wall, sliding in the direction of my bedroom.

My bedroom.

Virgin man-territory.

The room. And me, I suppose, since I moved into it. Revirginized, anyway

But then, as we pass the bathroom, a thought occurs to me.

'Douche?'

'J'espère sincèrement que tu me parles en français . . . I sincerely hope you don't mean that in the American way.'

Judging by his expression, maybe that was the wrong word.

'Gel douche? That's shower gel,' I murmur to myself. 'The word for shower is in there somewhere.'

'Tu es adorable . . . You're adorable when you're concentrating, do you know that? You do this thing where you roll your bottom lip inwards, which is not only cute but also very sexy. I think you probably pull the same face when you're touching yourself.'

I stumble backwards a little when I think he might be about to caress my lip. Clutching the doorframe with my hand, I slip into the tiny bathroom, immediately grabbing a fresh towel from the shelf. I drop it over the edge of the tiny tub.

'It's the one thing this apartment is missing. A tub I mean. Well, not the *one* thing. But it's the one thing I miss. *Prendre un douche!*' I announce, the words somehow slotting together in my head.

'C'était une invitation . . . That seemed more like a demand than

an invitation to shower. Is there room for two? Will you'll scrub my back for me?'

'That seemed like a lot of questions.' I sigh. 'I don't know what the answers are, but I know you can't get your stitches wet.' Pushing up onto my tiptoes, I turn and I grab Sarah's shower cap from where she's hidden it before pushing it into his hands. 'Here, you can use this.'

'Trés joli . . . very attractive.' He quirks a brow, his expression painting a thousand words, nine hundred and ninety nine of them unimpressed.

'It's not a fashion show. No one is going to see.'

'Tu ne comptes pas me frotter le dos, alors . . . There's to be no back scrubbing, then?'

'I'm just gonna . . . leave you to it,' I say, sliding between Remy and the basin, then closing the door behind me.

I blow out a breath, long and hard, as I rest my back against the bathroom door. I hear the sound of his zipper, followed by the thud of his boots—one, two—hitting the floor. His belt buckle clangs against the tile and, oh, my, I have a naked man in my bathroom. Naked but for a floral shower cap. But naked—butt naked!!

I slap a hand across my mouth to smother a near hysterical snigger as the shower curtain screeches, the shower squeaking in protest as he turns it on. The next sound is the one that propels me along the hall long after I should've already left. A low groan of appreciation as the water hits him, the tenor almost pornographic.

'I'm not thinking about him,' I mutter, pulling open the hall closet and throwing his awful shirt into the washing machine. I briefly consider slipping into the bathroom to grab the rest of his clothes—and not because I'm thinking about him, all slick and sudsy in the steamy room. Much. 'I'm also not thinking about spying on him. I'm just what you might call a considerate host.'

I decide against the laundry dash, mostly because I'm a chickenshit. Powering on the machine, I exhale a harsh, 'Shit!' at the same time as Remy's yell sounds from along the hall.

'Shit, shit, shit!' The washing machine and the shower do not exist in any form of symbiotic harmony. Quite the opposite, because if the washing machine is switched on when the shower is running, the water feels like it's being pumped from the Arctic.

I hurry along the hallway to shout my apologies when a loud *thud* sounds from the other side of the bathroom door.

Oh my God. He might've slipped and fallen with the shock—please not a concussion on top of a concussion. I'm supposed to be looking after him!

'Remy?' I call, hammering the side of my fist against the door. 'Remy!' I twist the handle, too worried to wait when the door springs wide, and I stumble against an expanse of toned and tan chest. Under my fingertips, his skin is warm and smooth and so very firm.

'Rose?' Did you know you can actually hear someone smile?

I don't look up, and I'm not sure my reluctance stems purely from embarrassment.

'I thought you might have fallen.'

Some nurse I am. I tell myself that I'm just checking on him—that I shouldn't be surprised to see my fingers widen against his pectoral because I'm just making sure he's okay. The motion disturbs a bead of water, my eyes tracking the rivulet with the care of a cartographer as it rolls down the landscape of his broad chest. Though not a very diligent cartographer as I become distracted by the trail of downy hair under his navel to where it disappears into the towel tucked low on his waist.

I realise I'm staring—staring like I'm wearing X-ray specs.

Unfortunately, I'm not wearing them. And I'm happy he can't read my thoughts as he cups my chin, raising my attention to his languid, green gaze. *Does the shade of his eyes change with his mood?*

One hand on my face becomes two as he leans in to press his lips to my left cheek, then my right. His whispered words, though French, are nothing short of perfect.

'*Merci . . . Thank you for worrying about me.*'

I pull away with a sense of reluctance I feel deep in my bones. But this isn't about me and what I want. This is about taking care of the man who's been attacked. A man with a head injury.

Remy follows me to the bedroom, throwing his clothes on the chair next to the door, then dropping his wallet and watch negligently on top. *Doesn't he have a phone? Did it slip from his pocket when he fell from his bike?*

I'd drawn my blinds last night before leaving for work and my bed was freshly made yesterday, which is just as well as I'm too tired to fight with a duvet cover right now. I peel back the bed linens and plump the pillows, savouring the floral scent of my laundry detergent.

'I guess we shouldn't sleep too long, not unless we want to become vampires or opossums or something. Anyway, I'll see you in an hour or two. You know, just to make sure you haven't died in your sleep.' I straighten and turn quite suddenly, the plea of *don't die in your sleep* drying in my throat as Remy stands in front of me, not wearing a towel but rather *holding* it. I mean, he's holding it over his crotch, but what it doesn't hide is the reflection of his ass in my dresser mirror.

An ass sculpted by squats.

An ass which, intriguingly, has no tan lines.

The man lives somewhere sunny, and evidently, near a nudist beach.

'Right, well. Sleep tight!' I move from the room with the approximate speed of a rocket, banishing the thoughts of his ass, though not the image, from my head.

I'm no prude. I consider myself to be very much sex positive, as in I'm positive I really like sex. I like men. And I like sex with men. I've just had a lot to deal with lately. I haven't had the bandwidth to deal with a relationship, not even the fun two hours kind. But right now, none of this means anything. What does matter is the fact that I've been tasked with this man's care, and I'll be damned if I end up banging him into a coma.

I need a shower. I'm still wearing my coat, and I have been for *hours*. Given the temperature isn't too bad inside right now, I'm kind of baking under the thing.

Close proximity to a hot guy

+ a flash of his hot ass

+ coat wearing inside

= Rose needs to shower.

I strip, ready to brave the kind of shower only my washing machine can provide. Hot, cold, then freezing cold. But I've played shower roulette before, usually when I've said something to piss off Sarah. Unfortunately, when I get out, I find my robe isn't hanging on the back of the bathroom door where it usually is, and when I go to pull another towel from the shelf, there's only one lonely hand towel left. *Damn.* Which leaves me the choice of creeping into my bedroom wearing nothing but a tiny towel or my coat. I go with the first option because, *ew.* Also, Remy should be asleep right now.

After a stealthy tip-toeing dash along the hall, it takes a moment for my eyes to adjust to the darkness of my room.

Thankfully, he is asleep. I mean, he looks asleep, plus he's also facing the other way. Which also means he's facing the dresser mirror, and one flash, inadvertent or not, is enough for today.

But is it really, my mind supplies, *because you hardly complained*.

'I'm not about to shove my boobs in his face in repayment for a flash of his ass,' I murmur to myself.

Following some stealthy opening of drawers, I pull out a T-shirt and a pair of shorty pyjamas—the laundry gods are not on my side today—and after some circus-worthy contortionist moves, I pull them on without one towel slip. No wardrobe malfunctions on my watch. Images of his butt aside, a cold shower and the thought of a few cramped hours on the wicker framed sofa is enough to make anyone reluctant to bed down for the night. So I putter around the shadowy room, straightening his boots and picking up the remainder of his clothes to slot them into the washing machine. *Jeans and socks. No underwear.*

He must have chosen to sleep in them.

Hmm. He didn't strike me as the modest type. If you've got it, flaunt it, I say. And the man has it. In spades.

I find myself chuckling as I leave the bedroom, placing his clothes in the washing machine. Then I tiptoe back into the room with a glass of water and a couple of Tylenol, depositing them on the nightstand without once looking at him.

Because looking leads to other thoughts. And looking can also lead to other things.

I make my way over to the 50s era dresser, a fabulous thrift store find, and even in the low light I can see my carefully lined eyes are definitely more panda than feline. I begin pulling the hair ties from the ends of my damp and wilted braids. The relief is instantaneous as I unravel them, and the touch of fingers on my throbbing scalp sheer bliss. So much so that I don't quite manage to stifle a sigh of satisfaction that, on reflection, might have sounded a little bit sexual.

As far as I can remember. It's been a while, you understand.
'Rose.'

I turn my head over my shoulder, the sound of my name in the dark a pull I find hard to resist. 'Sorry,' I whisper. 'I didn't mean to wake you.'

The bedlinens rustle, one muscled shoulder and arm revealed. *'Viens ici. . . . come here.'* His free hand pats the mattress heavily and I find myself moving across the room.

'What is it?' The floor is cool under my bare feet, but the rest of my body is burning as Remy reaches out and takes my hand in his much larger one. I know I should pull away, maybe offer him the water and pills? I know I shouldn't be standing here gazing at him like he's a pastry just waiting to be nibbled. But he just looks so tempting. So inviting. Is he looking at me like I'm looking at him? Like he could do with a little comfort, a little company? It strikes me that he and I, we're alike. Life has treated us harshly, dealt us a rough hand. And maybe we could both benefit from this moment, a human moment of reassurance and faith.

'Viens t'allonger . . . Come lie with me. I promise your virtue is safe.' He tugs on my hand as he moves across the bed, making room. I don't put up much of a fight, crawling in as he pulls back the duvet a little.

'C'est bien . . . That's good. Don't worry, despite my big words, I find I can barely lift an eyebrow. Don't tell. It's a secret. I don't want to ruin the image of Frenchmen everywhere.'

His murmurs are comforting as I settle myself on the pillow with my back to him. And it seems like the most natural thing in the world as his arm wraps around my waist.

'This is nice,' I whisper, resting my arm across his as he pulls me closer still. 'We all need a little hug sometimes.'

'Et parfois . . . And sometimes we need a little more.'

At that moment, I make another discovery. His underwear is neither in the machine nor *on* him.

'Peut-être . . . Maybe in the morning. Sleep well, Rose.'

6

ROSE

You'd think I'd have moved *vite!*

Quickly!

That I'd have jumped out of that bed like a ninja once I realised the man next to me was naked. Not only naked but sporting a little action in his non-existent pants.

Yep, the man had a little wood. A little action in the baguette department.

And oh, I planned on it. I planned on laying very still, maybe allowing myself just a tiny snuggle, at least until he'd fallen asleep when I'd creep out of the bed and move to the sofa. I planned on it, just as I planned on waking him up every couple of hours to make sure he didn't die from a brain haemorrhage or slip into a concussion-induced coma.

I planned, but I failed.

I mean, not entirely. He's not dead. But he is up.

Let me clarify. He's not out of bed. He's just *up.*

And hard. And pressed against me as his mouth plays some sort of enchantment against the soft skin behind my ear.

'Bonjour, Rose.'

If I could bottle his voice, I'd be able to sell it as an aphrodisiac.

'*M-morning.*' I release a long, shuddering breath, absorbing the feel of him. The softness of his lips is contrasted by the delicious friction of the hair on his thighs behind mine.

'*Tu as bien dormi . . . Did you sleep well? Did you dream of me?*'

I exhale a breathy sigh, fighting hard to retain my senses. As if his deep voice and accent weren't hard enough to resist, his touch is nothing short of unravelling.

'*J'ai rêvé que . . . I dreamt I was inside you. Tell me I can make my dream real.*'

'*Yes.*' Yes to all of it—yes to his husky whispers and yes to his lips as I turn my head into the pillow, giving him better access to my neck. The sibilant whisper of the cotton sheets is overlaid by my quiet gasp as his hand slides under my T-shirt to cup my breast.

Yes. Oh, yes . . .

'*Embrasse-moi . . . Kiss me. Give me your mouth, Rose.*' His rasping demands find my ear, his teeth closing on the sensitive lobe and giving it a sharp tug. The pressure resonates between my legs. My body opens, arching into his hand, and the movement earns me a low growl of his approval. '*J'ai envie de toi . . . I want you.*' He grinds against me, his head falling to rest against mine. '*Ta peau est . . . Your skin is so soft. I want to kiss every inch of it. Taste it with my tongue.*'

As his hot breath blows against my neck, the thought arises that what we're doing is wrong. Not wrong exactly, because I can't remember wanting anything like I want this, but it's risky. For him at least. I bring my hand to the back of his head in an attempt to get his attention, tightening my grip on the silky strands in a very poor attempt to stop him.

'We really shouldn't be doing this. Not for forty-eight hours the doctor said.'

And I do get his attention. The kind that makes me feel like I'm losing my mind as he squeezes my ass, sort of low and dirty, settling the hard length of his cock between my butt cheeks

'*Je . . . ta tête,*' I whisper. *Your head.* I'd meant it as a warning. It sounds more like an invitation.

'*Tu es sûre que . . . Are you sure that's what's troubling you.*' A filthy-sounding chuckle reverberates against my skin.

Yeah, I kind of guess where he went with that one. Which head, right?

'But the doctor . . .'

'*Le médecin qui . . . The doctor who looked down your cleavage when your coat gaped? He probably got his degree from a counterfeiter. Trust me, I know what will make me feel better.*'

'We shouldn't,' I whisper as his hand moves down my thigh, his calloused fingers adding another level of deliciousness as he lifts it over his. I find I'm barely able to retain my train of thought let alone try to convey the risks sex might have on his health.

'*J'ai besoin de toi . . . I need you. I can't wait.* His tone is dark and delicious, and it doesn't matter that I don't exactly know what he's saying because my body understands his need, and my ears know praise when they hear it.

His hand slips between my body and the mattress, palming my breast and banding my back to his chest as his other hand slips into my pyjama shorts.

'Oh my God.' My body bows, the sensations overwhelming as his long fingers swipe through the slickness between my legs.

Everything inside me clenches, my heart beating wildly as he begins to pet and tease the buds of both my nipple and clit with the sweetest percussion.

'Tu es si belle . . .You're so beautiful. So wet for me. I can feel you pulsing against my fingertips.'

I'm no stranger to coming by hand, usually by my own hand, but never has it felt so intoxicating. Every swipe and circle, every press and pet makes me feel like I'm being peeled open, my every whimper and tremble exposing me shamelessly.

'C'est bien, ma belle . . . That's it, beautiful girl. Take it. Take it all. I can't wait to taste you.' His voice is so low and his tone fervent, yet I'm unprepared for the intensity as his fingers thrust inside, his thumb unrelenting on my clit.

'Oh, God,' I whimper as I buck up into his hand, chasing the sublime sensation. It's been so long, and this feels so illicit, his hands working under the covers, slipped into my clothes. Sensation layers upon sensation—his accent, his praise. The way I'm captive to more than just his commands.

'Tu entends . . . Can you hear how wet you are for me? How much you want this.'

Sensations swirl and coalesce as I'm driven on by words I don't understand yet recognise, unashamedly grinding against his hand. Elastic snaps against my stomach and his fingers appear above the covers, the evidence of my arousal glistening there.

'Tu es délicieux.'

I need no translation as he brings them to his mouth to lick them clean.

As his arm lowers, he pulls the hem of my T-shirt up over my head, dropping it to the floor and deftly rolling me under him.

'Maintenant,' he growls, pressing himself between my legs. *'Now. I need you now.'*

His body over mine . . . it's no less than perfect. The angles of his shoulders block out the light spilling from the hallway, the weight and feel of his solidness over me.

'*Parfaite.*'

His thumb grazes my nipple, sliding back and forth over the sensitive peak, leaving me a desperate, whimpering heap.

'Yes, perfect.'

We need no common language for Remy to discern the effect he has on me. I tremble as his gaze falls over me. With the barest and most teasing of touches I melt.

Oh, the relief—the absolute relief—as he greedily draws my nipple into his mouth. Matching his hunger, I wrap my legs around his waist, my hands in his hair as my cries ring through the air.

He's touched me, his fingers have been inside me, yet I'm somehow shocked when his mouth meets mine. Maybe my shock stems not from the kiss, but the way that he kisses. The intensity. The sense that he's all power and command restrained, and I know at this moment, he'll fuck like he kisses. There's nothing tentative in his most thorough of applications as he presses me into the mattress. He swallows my carnal groan, everything speeding up in that instant. Hands grasp, tongues thrust, fingers biting skin. Our mouths fused, and our minds deaf and blind to anything but this. But then my body mourns the lack of his as he suddenly pulls back, rising before me on his knees. And, oh my God, is he beautiful. My gaze follows the bold curve of his shoulders down his muscular arm—*deltoids and triceps, oh my!*—my attention drawn to the ladder of abdominals with the movement of his hand. The long powerful line of his thighs and that delicious *V*, lower still to where his cock stands proud. Proud and so vulgar and so beautiful.

And so big.

I don't realise I've pushed up onto my elbow until I'm

reaching for it. He's so hard, like satin over steel as my thumb caresses his silken head, he exhales a wholly masculine groan.

'You're *huge*.' I'm certain I don't mean to sound so awe-filled. This isn't the first time I've had a cock in my hand, but it's easily the loveliest. And the longest. Fullest? To put it another way, this man wins the Rose Ryan Prize for Penii.

'*Ça me plaît . . . I like that a lot. But if you keep doing that while looking at me as you are, we're both going to be very disappointed.*'

'I wish I understood,' I murmur, taking him in my fist. Then suddenly I do as he releases a long, measured exhale, almost arching into my hand.

'Like that?' I tighten my grasp, running my hand from root to tip.

'*Plus fort . . . harder.*' His words are taut, his gaze glued to my bare breasts as he covers my hand with his. But in a sudden fit of daring, I pull my hand from under his.

'Let me watch.'

Head lowered, he stares up at me through thick, dark lashes. My heart moves into my throat. Was that too bold? Too forward? Was it lost in fucking translation?

'*Tu aimes regarder . . You like to watch.*' His sudden smile is a study in sinfulness, and he moves so fast, I find myself squealing as he reaches for the hem of my pyjama pants, whipping them off and leaving me feeling thoroughly undignified with my toes around his ears.

I don't have time to cogitate his expression as, palm flat against the pillow, he presses me back with a kiss. A hungry kiss. A thorough kiss. The kind that fries my brain, melting me across the bed.

'*Touche-toi pour moi, chérie . . . Touch yourself for me, darling. Make yourself come.*' With his words, he lifts my hand, pressing it between my legs as he kisses me again, coaxing my fingers to begin.

My eyes flutter closed. I'm so turned on, I'm almost embarrassed to let him see just how much. But they don't stay closed for long. Not as cool air settles between us as he pulls away. Not as he exhales. Groans. Not as the rhythmic sound of skin on skin fills the room.

Oh my. That looks so at home in his hand.

On his knees between my open thighs, his gaze settles on where my hand rests between my legs.

'*C'est ça. Si belle . . . That's it. So beautiful. I was right about how you'd look touching yourself.*'

His gaze is so focussed and the cadence of his voice so rich and deep, I find myself teasing a finger along my crease. My tremulous whimper joins his praise, the digit dipping inside as I gather my own arousal and roll it across my clit.

If he says anything else, I don't hear it, lost to the sight of him taking his cock firmly in his hand. A vein stands to attention in his forearm, the muscles of his thighs and abdomen taut as his hand moves from root to crown, twisting his fist a delicious amount. Delicious for the both of us. His attention is so focussed, his expression a mixture of agony and relief as his hand repeats the action.

I find myself lost in the moment, my fingers beginning to work slickly. My breathing is rapid and my moans unrestrained as I watch the man above me take pleasure in himself. Take pleasure in watching me.

'You're so big and so hard.' I feel like a goddess under his attentions, my words unrestrained.

'*Tout ça est pour toi . . . This is all for you. To fill you. To fuck you.*'

'I want to feel you inside me.' I roll my lips inward to stem the expulsion of my thoughts. My hips begin to jolt as though electrified as my orgasm builds, teetering just beyond my reach.

'Jouir pour moi . . . Come for me, beautiful girl. Come for me and I'll give you everything.'

'Oh, God. Don't stop—don't stop talking,' I whisper, giving over to the acute surge of my desire. No doubt I'll regret my filthy stream of consciousness later, but for now, I can't stop the words spilling from my mouth as he watches me with an intensity that makes my vision more than a little hazy. 'Yes, don't stop watching me. Don't you dare stop touching yourself. You're so damn delicious, and I'll be so, so sorry if I fuck you to death.'

'Je mourrais heureux . . . I'd die happy,' he growls, his hand beginning to slide faster now.

'Oh, God. Yes! Keep talking.'

'Ce n'est pas . . . That isn't how I want to use my tongue.'

I have no more words as I ride out this ecstasy, bucking up into my own hand.

'Tu vaux la peine de perdre quelques neurones . . . You are worth losing brain cells for.'

His words are breathless and sort of raspy as he drops forward, catching himself on his palms as he puts his mouth and tongue to such wicked use along my neck. The bed creaks as his body lifts from mine, stretched out above me as he reaches for his wallet before returning to me with a sinful smile. He pushes up onto his knees, and with a flash of white teeth, the foil packet is ripped. He sheaths himself with such expertise that my hips begin to twitch.

He takes one deep breath as he secures the latex at the root of his cock, before settling himself between my open thighs. The room is so still and so quiet, an electric-like anticipation binding us together as we watch the channel between our bodies. He glides his crown against me, the breathy sound of my whimper an invitation. He breaches my wetness, my limbs clinging to him like he's my new religion, my head pressed to the pillow as though it could stifle my cry. He groans as he presses deeper, my back bowing in a silent plea. A plea he rewards with one solid thrust as he fills me to his hilt.

'*Mon Dieu . . .*'

He undulates above me, slow and easy, allowing me to adjust to the size of him as his eyes trace my face. Then with a jab of his hips, he drives into me. My whimpers turn to cries of ecstasy as his thrusts become deeper. He fills me, fucking me so solidly.

'*C'est si bon d'être en toi . . . You feel so good.*'

His eyes are almost black, his gaze hooded as he ducks his head, sucking the pebble of my nipple into his mouth once again. I cry out at the tug of his teeth, sliding my hands above my head. I want this. I'll take whatever he can give and leave all thought of consequence to another day. His mouth meets mine once more, our palms pressed together, fingers entwined. Anchored together like this, he changes both depth and pace, surging above me. Hands and hearts pressed together, it's all too much. The ends of this climax are tied so tightly to the previous, making me almost delirious with pleasure.

'*Je te sens jouir . . . I feel you coming so hard, and it is beautiful.*'

I implode. Explode. Come harder than I ever have. His guttural words turn to breathless grunts as he buries his face in the soft skin of my neck and follows me over the edge.

7

REMY

A DARK CAR idles on the road outside. But it can wait. *Wait at my leisure.*

My shoulder pressed to the doorframe of her bedroom door, my gut aches with the desire to go to her. To pull back the covers and slip in next to her, to press my nose to her silken neck and inhale her delicate scent.

I'd wrap her in my arms and show her what my words can't convey.

Make her understand how precious these hours have been to me.

Her dark hair is splayed across the pillow, wild and tangled from the attentions of my fingers. I push my hands deep into my pockets because it takes every grain of my restraint not to give in as she nestles deeper into her pillow, pulling the covers up under her chin, bringing my attention to her soft, pouting mouth.

A mouth that is a temptation like nothing else.

When I left my hotel in the early hours of the morning, I could not have imagined an outcome such as this. I told myself that a bike ride was an expedition to clear my head. An appeal for clarity. Yet how I came to be on this street can hardly be called an accident.

Because I went looking for a girl and found trouble in her place.

I went looking for one girl and found *another* in her place.

One girl who could take from me. Ruin everything.

Another who did nothing but give.

When was the last time someone took care of me? Gave freely without expectation of something in return? The sad reality is I really can't recall. Yet the woman in the bed just a few feet away took me into her home. She gave me her time and her care. She let me take comfort in her body. And she held me there. She gave, and she gave, and she asked for nothing in return.

And that's why I have to leave.

A woman like her can only be hurt by my world.

8

ROSE

MAY

'THAT BABY IS THE CUTEST.'

'That baby has a name,' calls a manly voice from out of range of the camera.

'Yeah, and it's Beryl,' says Amber, kissing her newborn baby's fluffy blonde head.

'We're not calling her Beryl,' growls Australian baby daddy as he appears briefly on the screen of our weekly catch-up call, taking the pink swaddled bundle from Amber's arms.

'We're not calling her Coral or Pearl, either,' she retorts.

'Eish. You guys, those names are *bad*.'

'Byron thinks we should give her a themed name,' she gripes. 'You know; Amber, Pearl, Coral, Amethyst.'

'Where the hell did Beryl come from?'

'It's a kind of emerald,' she says with a dismissive wave.

'It's kind of ugly. A cutie like the peanut deserves better than an old lady's name.'

'I tell you, it's a good thing she is cute because this waking at the crack of dawn part of parenting is already getting old.' Amber's answer is accompanied by a deep yawn. 'Keep me awake. Tell me what's new with you.'

'Well, Sarah finally moved out.'

'Great!'

'And now I can't afford the rent.'

'Oh. Not so great.'

'It'll be fine.' I shrug off her concern even as the familiar roll of anxiety washes through the pit of my stomach. 'Remember Shaun, the shitty shift manager?'

'I thought his name was Ted?'

'Do you remember all the tiny details?'

'Just the interesting ones, like how you got sacked after you spent the night with the mysterious Monsieur Baguette.' On screen, my friend's brows wiggle suggestively, though whether over the terrible way she purposely mispronounces monsieur—*mon-sew-er*—or her taunt, I'm not sure.

'Girl talk secrets!' I protest.

'Relax. Byron has taken Baby Beryl downstairs.' She waves away my concern. 'But the manager?'

'It looks like I'll be dusting off my Heidi hair because he called and offered me my job back.' It seems I'm not the worst waitress in the world, especially when the flu comes to town.

'For a minute there, I had the most awful thought. I thought you were going to say you'd bumped into him at the coffee shop, and he's a whole other person out of work.'

'Urgh, no! Credit me with a little taste,' I complain. 'The man's mother probably still sews tags into his clothes, tags that read *asshole*. In fact, if he was the last man on earth—'

'You wouldn't want to nibble on *his* baguette. Speaking of baguettes, have you gotten any more gifts from the sexy Frenchman lately?'

'We don't know the gifts were from him,' I demur.

'*Mm-hmm.*' Amber's tone and expression are both thoroughly unconvinced. 'I say again, my translation skills aren't as good as you thought they'd be, but I do wish I'd gotten a good look at *Monsieur Baguette.*' This time, her pronunciation is flawless.

'At Monsieur Baguette, or at monsieur's baguette?' The brow move belongs to me now.

'Seen one big baguette, you've seem 'em all. What a girl needs in her life is someone who owns a mighty bread stick and the knowledge to wield it.'

'You've just had a baby. You're supposed to be baguette opposed.'

'I'm more baguette adjacent. At least until the doctor says so. I mean, it's not like *I* have a secret admirer or anything.'

'No, you've got a fuckin' overt one,' comes her husband's deep voice again.

'Don't curse in front of the baby!' she calls back, turning away from the camera for a beat.

'I thought he'd left?'

'Relax, he was just passing by the bedroom door. So, has anything more landed on your doorstep lately?'

'Look, we really don't know where the gifts came from.'

'Do you make a regular habit of rescuing men from the streets? Could there be more men in the Golden Gate City area who've recovered from a concussion by way of the restorative powers of your vagina?'

'You make it sound like I sat on his head.'

'Head. Face. Whatever you did, he obviously liked it. More to the point, he liked you. Come on, Rose. Who else could've been sending you things?'

It's been two months since I found Remy on my doorstep. Two months since I experienced the best orgasms of my entire existence. Yes, orgasms with an extra *s*. As in, orgasms of the multiple kind. The morning after the night before—the night before being when I found him battered and bruised on my doorstep, took him to the hospital, brought him home, and tucked him up in bed . . . then got in after him—I woke to him gone. Gone were his wet jeans from the washing machine, his boots from under the chair, and his body from my bed. Every trace of him had vanished, discounting the faint scent of him on my pillow and the delicious aches he left my body with.

'Sticking around to deliver a personal thank you in the morning would've been enough.' Though my words sound pretty convincing, the fact that he left before I woke did us both a favour. The morning after the night before can only ever be awkward, I think. Especially when you don't speak the language. An erotic encounter turned to lost in translation.

'After the five very personal thank yous he gave you before he left? You're lucky you didn't wake to a corpse! But it's clear, whoever he was, he likes you. What's more, he's been thinking of you.'

What's clear to me is the fact that Amber would like nothing more than for me to declare the series of anonymous gifts I've received over the last couple of months were from Remy. At first, I'll admit I was inclined to agree with her hypothesis, especially as the first gift to arrive was a basket of gourmet French coffee. I'd smiled as I opened it, remembering how awful the coffee was I served that night. It felt like he was teasing me a little, and that the gift was a cute sort of thank you.

I'll admit it made me feel good. Great sex, the decency to be gone before I woke, and the gift of coffee!

But then a fancy-assed European coffee machine was delivered the next day. A three-thousand-dollar coffee machine. I could hardly believe it and left it boxed in case it had been delivered by mistake, especially as it was addressed only to *Rose*. Plus, there was not a card with either of these gifts.

Then the following week, a beautiful bouquet turned up on my doorstep. Dozens of delicate tea roses all balanced on slender green stems. And no card again. I mean, how difficult could it be to pen a quick thanks with the help of Google Translate? Hell, I'd have even liked it in French!

But even without a card, I could believe the bouquet was from Remy. The coffee basket was cute and appropriate. Also, flowers are a perfect way to say thank you—thank you for looking after him, I mean. *Not thank you for the sex.* Plus, one bunch of flowers isn't going to bankrupt anyone, even a bouquet from a fancy downtown florist.

But then another bouquet arrived the following week.

Then another.

Then another, and they were still arriving weekly right up until yesterday, making my apartment smell like a church.

A week after the first bouquet, another gift arrived at my door, and I'll admit I was set to pitch a fit. But then I opened the box to a silk kimono robe from a New York boutique. Blue and green, it was the most beautiful thing I've ever seen, and it makes me feel as regal as a peacock wearing it. Not that I've worn it more than once because it's as ridiculously impractical as it is gorgeous, but also, I checked online, and the thing cost over eight hundred dollars! Eight hundred dollars for a robe!

It's now hanging on my closet door, more artwork than apparel.

But I digress. While the coffee and the roses sort of made sense, an expensive robe didn't. What significance could that have had? None, I told Amber, though I failed to mention that my ratty old cotton robe had gone missing the same night.

Coincidence, I'd thought. Until a few days after the kimono arrived, and I'd found it stuffed down in the back of the hamper. No way it could have fallen there. I'd blamed Sarah for dumping it there, and we'd had a fight. And then she moved out. Which was a complication I didn't need.

I resolved to think no more about it, about the gifts or about him, until a membership in my name arrived to a high-end spa in a hotel downtown. A spa with a beautiful hammam, which is sort of a bathing pool. I didn't even know what it was until I asked! And didn't I tell him I missed having a bath in the apartment?

I love all of my gifts and appreciate every one of them, no matter where they've come from, but this gift is the gift to beat all others. This gift is absolute heaven. Life is pretty tough at the moment, but my visits to the spa keep me going. I schlep on down there with my Gucci knock-off slung over my arm, which probably looks more Forever Twenty-One than designer. *Because that's where I bought it from.* I enjoy a glorious treatment—a massage or facial—then I go soak in the hammam, which is just pure bliss, unlike the bus ride home.

There's no Porsche or Maserati waiting in the parking lot for me. And this is just one more reason I can't see how these gifts could have come from Remy. He was a tourist, maybe even a backpacker. And after spending a year travelling around the world, I know these demographics aren't exactly known for being plump in the pocket or even very considerate. And if Remy was wealthy, how come he came back to my place that night? Yeah, okay, other than the obvious, but that wasn't on the cards when we left the hospital. Or even when I tucked him into bed.

Not that I'm saying the gifts aren't considerate. And he was a considerate bedmate. *Orgasms a-plenty were delivered that night.* Also, he was considerate enough not to die in my bed.

But then he left, leaving behind a lot of unanswered questions. I mean, how did he come to be on my street in the first place? And what about the tale of his bike? I did find a road bike helmet behind the house the following week, but if he'd had an accident, where'd the bike go? And why didn't he have credit cards or even a phone?

'You look like you're deep in thought.' Amber's words pull me from my thoughts, propelling me out of my chair.

'I'm thinking about snacks,' I lie, grabbing my iPad from the kitchen table and holding it instead as I pull a bag of chips from the cupboard.

'But seriously, if you name that baby Beryl, I'll turn up like Maleficent and put a curse on y'all's asses.' I stuff a couple of chips into my mouth to prevent me from spilling the thoughts that seem to continually rotate through my brain.

Remy. Remy. Remy.

Who is he really? What was he doing in my neighbourhood? Why me?

'That was hardly a seamless segue. And y'all's? Aren't we a spitfire tonight?'

'When I'm under pressure, the Kentucky in me always busts out.'

'And you're under pressure because I'm busting your lady balls?'

'My lady balls are safe in your gentle hands. It's just . . .' I should've shoved another handful of chips down. I should've choked on them rather than speak. 'I keep thinking about the gifts.' Why do they keep coming? Why is he making me think? He bailed. Fine. I get it. He had reasons not to stay. But he's now supposed to let me forget how much I enjoyed having him around.

'Are you thinking about selling the coffee machine?'

'No, I already did that.' Desperate times calls for desperate measures and poor girls don't need expensive kitchen gadgets. Besides, I've sort of gotten used to drinking bad coffee.

'So . . . you keep thinking about him?'

The fact that she hasn't referred to him as *Monsieur Baguette* catches me off guard a little.

'I just don't see how the gifts can be from him. The man had calloused fingers!'

'I'm sure there's logic in there somewhere, honey, but I'm damned if I can see it.'

'Rich men don't look like him.' Can't feel like him. 'Hell, working men don't look like him, either.'

'You're going to have to explain this to me. Words of one syllable, maybe add in a little detail.' She adds a roll of her hand to hurry me along, but I don't exactly know where to start.

'The man was ripped.'

'So you said.'

'And though he was very sweet, there was something a little uncivilised about him.' Especially in the bedroom. 'Like he'd be at home wearing a bearskin and bludgeoning his dinner to death.'

'I'm going to refrain from asking if you swung from vines and got up to monkey business and instead ask you to explain *exactly* what you mean.'

'I don't know. I can't put my finger on it.' He was almost a perfect contradiction. 'Anyway, I'm not sure he sent those gifts. He just didn't seem the type.'

'You're saying he didn't seem like the appreciative type? Or do you mean the thoughtful type?'

'What's with the tone?' I ask, frowning down at the screen of my iPad screen.

'I'm just confused. It sounds like you're saying he was

really hot for you but that you want him not to be grateful, or thoughtful, or just decent, maybe.'

'That's not fair,' I protest. 'And that's not what I'm saying. I'm just saying we don't know who or what he is.'

'Yet you still brought him home like a lost puppy.'

'He was hurt. What was I supposed to do?'

'And the fact that he was pretty had nothing to do with you taking him home.'

I don't answer, though I narrow my eyes at her tone.

'Okay. Fine. You took him home because you're a paragon of virtue. It's not your fault it was a cold, cold night, and you got into bed next to him to share your body heat.'

Again, I don't answer. I just deepen the stink eye.

'And it's absolutely not your fault that you rolled onto his dick at some point during the night—fell onto it vigorously. Multiple times!'

'Are you done yet?'

'You know his name,' she says, trying a little stink eye of her own. 'You could google him.'

'Do you think I haven't done that already? A search for the name Remy Durrant offered up a couple of kids on skateboards, one who lives in Toronto and the other in Calgary, plus a middle-aged accountant living in someplace called Clapham in London.'

'You googled him?'

'Didn't I just say so? Why are you looking at me like that?'

'Like what?'

I open my mouth, reflecting some semblance of her expression right back at her. She looks like a guppy.

'Ha. Funny. Is it any wonder I'm a little stunned? You're behaving very un-Rose like.'

'We've laughed and bickered and laughed some more. Sounds like the usual Sunday night call, if you ask me.'

'That's not what I'm talking about. You *googled* him? The man has totally pushed you out of your comfort zone.'

'I don't know what you mean.'

'You never chase after a man.'

'A Google search is hardly chasing,' I respond, but even I can hear how defensive I sound.

'But it shows interest. Even if you don't want the gifts to have come from him.'

'What are you talking about?'

'Because if the gifts didn't come from him, then that makes him thoughtless and ungrateful and possibly broke.'

'Your point being?'

'Which kind of makes him perfectly your type. If he is those things, I mean.'

'That's ridiculous,' I scoff. 'I don't have a type.'

'Oh, sweetie, you do. You only date men who are easy to kick to the curb.'

'That makes no sense.'

'Doesn't it?' she says kindly. 'Even if it means your heart doesn't get hurt?'

Whether from her expression or her words, I'm stopped dead in my tracks. Is that me? Is that who I am? But then a thought strikes me.

'I see a flaw in your hypothesis because even if Remy is rich and grateful, he's not thoughtful. Or else he'd have stuck around.'

'Which means it's safe for you to still be crushing on him. Hence, the Google search.'

'I think pregnancy has made you addle-brained.'

'I think you're probably right. But I have to say, if he sent you gifts, it means he's thinking about you, too.'

'Amber, you're being ridiculous. The man was hurt, and I helped him. We both woke up kind of horny, and we had sex.

The fact that he left in the morning was a blessing. He did us both that favour.' It doesn't make us star-crossed lovers or anything even close to that.

'But he's still thinking about you,' she sort of sings.

'And I think you're a little bit crazy,' I sing right back, even as my heart does a little skippity-skip. *Bad heart!*

'Admit it, you liked him.'

'So, he was cute,' I reply, admitting no such thing. 'And sweet, even though I couldn't understand a word he said. 'And he—' I clamp my lips together, unwilling to confess he held me in his arms all night, let alone that I let him.

'He what?' Amber prompts.

'Was great in bed. But while that's all well and good,' I say, hurrying on, 'the only thing I'm interested in right now is keeping my head above water.'

As Amber's expression falters, my conscience prickles. My troubles are my troubles, yet I had to go open my big fat mouth.

'Sweetie, you know I can loan you some money to tide you over until you get a job.'

'Nope. I'm fine. As Great-Grandma Aida used to say, never a lender or a borrower be.' In the meantime, I'll just keep on clipping coupons and stretching my weekly grocery budget to nine days' worth of meals.

'I'm pretty sure Aida wasn't considering shaking her tush in a titty bar to pay her rent.'

I set off laughing. Only Amber could make that sound hilarious.

'I'll have you know that The Pink Pussy Cat is a respectable gentlemen's club.'

'Sure. And I'm about to let Byron name our daughter after a green rock. But seriously, do you think you might have something suitable coming up, work wise?'

'I have a few irons in the fire.' Unfortunately, I think I forgot to light the fire before putting them in, but I'll keep that to myself. She has enough to worry about without fretting about me. Especially from the other side of the world.

'I wish I could offer you a job,' she says suddenly.

And I wish the Aussie immigration system wasn't so tricky because then she would.

'You'll keep me up to date, right? And please let me know if I can do anything to help.'

'You do help. You helped fudge my resumé, and you help me every Sunday by showing me your sweet, sunny face.'

'Now I know you're taking the piss.'

'Okay, little Miss Aussie-ness. Until next week. I've got to go and launder my tush-shaking outfits for my first shift.'

'You're really going to go back there?'

'It's not that bad.' I'm surprised I don't choke on my own words. 'No booty shaking. Just waitressing and just for a couple of shifts.' Though hopefully more because really, what choice do I have? I'm down to my last couple of hundred dollars in the bank. My windfall is almost completely spent. Next comes living on my credit card, and that is a slippery slope I'll try very hard to avoid.

'Something will turn up soon. I know it will.'

I just hope my responding smile looks less brittle than it feels.

———

Birds chirp, pulling me from my sleep.

Birds in the rainforest?

Am I still in Australia?

Or have I fallen asleep on the spa massage table again?

I hope I haven't drooled this time.

As the irritating cheeping continues, realisation slowly dawns that my phone is ringing.

'Who disturbs my frickin' slumber,' I complain, rising up in my bed with the animation of one of Dracula's brides.

I hate working at the Pussy Cat. *Hate it.* I hate the boss, and I hate the patrons. I hate going to bed when everyone else is waking up, and I really hate eating Cheerios in the afternoon.

Fucking. Hate. It.

But most of all, I hate it when I'm sleeping, and the phone rings, and it's just a stupid marketing call.

Pulling off the satin eye mask, I drop it on the bed. It arrived last week in my little Aussie care package from Amber. I'm only wearing it because she promised that, along with the cream she sent, it'd help prevent fine lines. Honestly, I think it's more likely she's just getting a kick out of me wearing something that's embroidered with the words "dreaming of dick".

'Miss Ryan?' a smoky voice enquires.

'Speaking.' I swing my legs out of the bed and pull the phone away from my ear as I yawn.

'My name is Therese Moore. I'm with Executive Search Recruitment'—I'm suddenly very awake—'I'm calling about a position you recently applied for via our website.'

'Yes?' My voice sounds high, reedy even, and I begin to worry about the impression I'm giving. 'I mean, of course. I applied online and took part in the virtual interview for a trainee position in hotel management.'

Months ago, back in March, I think. As for a virtual interview, what a crock. I sat in front of my ancient laptop and gave *a personal account of myself*, as instructed. I was supposed to inform the robotic voice of a time in my life that I was most proud, and I'd begun to recite the well-rehearsed tale of how

I'd travelled around the world by myself; my one big accomplishment. I'd intended to cover all the interview candidate buzz words—organised, passionate, enthusiastic, detail-orientated, flexible—in an effort to sell those highly valued transferable skills.

Unfortunately, I'd gotten no farther than explaining how I'd worked in hospitality on several continents when the dumb Poodle I was working on rehoming jumped up on my knee, pressing his front paws to my laptop. The interview I actually sent them was of me mouthing "what the fuck, mutt!" along with one final horrified look at the camera as excitable doggy paws hit the enter key, my interview immediately uploading and pinged to the agency. To add insult to injury, he then peed on me. Suffice it to say, I felt pretty downhearted about the whole thing. When I didn't hear back, I wasn't surprised. But hallelujah, it looks like they're desperate, and I'm about to get a second chance!

'I have wonderful news, Miss Ryan.' The woman's forty-a-day voice brings me back to the moment in a snap. 'A position has just become available, and after viewing your interview, our client would like to go ahead and offer you the job.'

'That's . . . that's . . . wonderful.' And as well as so, so strange. 'When would they like to interview me?"

'Oh, there's no need for that. The position is yours. Isn't that wonderful?' she gushes. Yes, gushes. The woman who gave zero fucks when I called to explain what happened during my so-called interview. It wasn't even an interview for an advertised job but an interview to get me on their books, so to speak. And now this?

'Yes. Wonderful,' I answer haltingly. 'But isn't it also a little,' weird, whacky, not to mention downright, 'strange?'

'It is a little unorthodox,' she demurs, 'but hardly unprecedented.'

'My interview recording was a disaster.' I rub the heel of my palm against my eye, not quite believing I'm bringing this up right now.

'Well, what can I say?' she replies, not bothering to hide her annoyance. 'They must've seen the funny side as well as being impressed with what else you had to say.'

'I find it hard to believe you sent it to them.' Especially after not responding to my botched interview. Right now, the competition is pretty fierce in the current job market, as I've found since coming home. Surely, they must have had better interviews than mine.

'Do you want to hear about this job or not? Because I'm sure there are lots of other candidates who would receive this news with much more grace.'

Grace; the thing Southern women are supposed to have an abundance of. That's the whole cat born in the stable thing again. But hell, what am I doing?

'No, of course I'm interested!' I begin, hitting reverse. 'I suppose this has all just come as a shock. I mean, like a wonderful shock. A surprise, in fact!'

'There are more surprises to come,' she adds, a touch inscrutably. And then she mentions a figure that causes me to curse, though I have the decorum to do so silently.

'That's . . . that's the whole package, though, right? The figure? It includes all benefits.' Because ho-lee-hell, that is a lot of money. More money than I ever dreamed I'd earn.

'Oh, my dear, not at all. *That* is the figure of your base salary only.'

My eyes are as wide as saucers in the dresser mirror as she goes on to explain the scope of the position, the opportunities for promotion, and how, with my experience, I'm a great fit for the team.

'My experience?' I halt my happy dance mid-hop. What

experience? The fact that I work in a strip joint? That I serve drinks to men with grabby hands and an obsession for shoving dollar bills between my tits? Amber has a theory. She thinks it's because *they want to shove other things there.* And she doesn't mean Legos.

'Yes. The fact that you worked for Riposo Estates in Australia is of particular interest to them. You began in the vineyard and worked your way to the hospitality arm of the business, according to your resumé.'

My highly inflated resumé that I know Amber and Byron (and their HR team) will help me pull off. I picked grapes, waited tables, and worked the cellar door. None of it was groundbreaking career stuff, but I'm not about to admit so now.

'Ah, yes, well. The Phillips team believe that in order to understand the wine, you have to have an understanding of the land. They take a . . . holistic approach to education and employment.'

Please don't ask me what that means.

'I believe you also worked as a trainee manager in a motel chain after graduating college.' She says "motel" as I imagine she would say "used condom".

'Yes, I did. Well, a mid-priced hotel chain, actually.' Slave labour by any other name is just the same.

'And now you work in hospitality as a waitress, I believe.'

'Yes, that's correct.' If you look at it through cataracts. I might have also fudged my resumé a little here by listing the name of the holding company that owns the club, rather than the club itself. I also didn't include their details under the reference section.

But really, who is going to admit to working in a strip joint while looking for a corporate position?

Yes, I was vice president of the booty shorts, and my boobs are boner-*fide marketing materials.*

'Wonderful. Well, when can you come in and sign the paperwork for your visa and such?'

'Visa?'

'You did say you were willing to relocate for a position.'

'Well, yeah but, as I understood, you deal with employment here in the States.'

'Goodness, no. ESR is an American subsidiary of a worldwide company. In fact, our headquarters are in France.'

'France?'

'Yes, which is exactly where the position is.'

My stomach twists. This *cannot* be another of Remy's gifts.

'But I don't speak French.'

'Knowledge of the language isn't necessary for the role. You'll be working with an English-speaking team and taking care of the needs of the English-speaking guests, on the whole. After all, English is the language of business there.'

'English is the business language in France?' Horseshit. I may not know much, but I do know the French speak French in their own country!

'No, in the Principality of Monaco. You'll be residing in France, on the Côte d'Azure, in fact, but you'll spend a large portion of your working time in Monaco.'

Ooh la la!

9

ROSE

JUNE

MONACO. Visions of Grace Kelly and her European prince. Of casinos and Daniel Craig's James Bond. Of endless sunny days, azure skies, of sand like sugar and a Mediterranean Sea.

Those were my impressions of Monaco without even seeing it. Not that I needed to see the place to agree to work there. I just needed to keep thinking of the zeros on the contract I'd signed in the offices of ESR the very next day. I can only imagine that the agent was promised a sizeable percentage of the finder's fee because she actually sent a car to collect me, while also trying not to imagine what sort of a company would want to hire someone with an interview video like mine. But anything has got to be better than being poor and working at the Pussy Cat.

I gave notice on my apartment, gladly told Shaun, the shitty shift manager he could stick his job where the sun don't shine, grabbed my ticket the agency couriered to me, and got on a plane to France. To the Côte d'Azure!

I'll be working for The Wolf Group who, amongst other things, run a chain of hotels that cater to the rich and gorgeous. And let me tell you, Monaco is a place built for the demographic. Or maybe those demographics. As far as I can tell there are:

Those who are both rich and gorgeous; those blessed in looks and wealth.

Those who are rich and not so gorgeous; more often than not, rich and old.

Those who are just gorgeous; usually draped over the category above.

The city state is a tax haven for the super wealthy, a home for their multi-million-dollar real estate, their super yachts, and their model skinny wives and girlfriends. I'm sure there are uber-wealthy women out here, juggling their money and gigolo men friends, but these are not so visible, as far as I can tell.

Only the super-rich live in Monaco, along with a handful of Monegasques, or Monaco locals. The rest of the people who work there bus, drive, or train in over the Monaco/French border every day. The Wolf Group staff are fortunate enough to have a shuttle service to and from the city of Nice, home of the staff accommodations, along with the salad. *Salad niçoise*. The company houses most of its staff in a couple of buildings on *Rue Arson*, or Arson Street I guess you could say, where I've been allocated a studio apartment. It's anything but spacious or swanky, but it's bright and clean and has a tiny Juliet balcony overlooking the street, so that's pretty cool.

I'd arrived late Thursday night, and the following day, I was taken to the HR department in Monaco. I'd also visited a government building of some sort to arrange my work permit. Thankfully, I was accompanied by someone who spoke French because as it turns out, the first language of Monaco isn't English but French.

Help!

I'm told there's also a local language in Monaco which is a mixture of French and Italian, but I'm not going to worry about that. Instead, I've decided to concentrate on learning French and have spent the weekend listening to YouTube videos, spending my downtime repeating useful phrases, injected with a little Remy-like flair.

Things like:

Is this seat taken?

Can I buy you a drink?

Is that a baguette in your pants, or are you just pleased to see me?

You know, the useful stuff.

Monday morning—my first real day at work—and the blonde sitting in front of me on the bus turns my way with a smile.

'Bonjour.'

I hesitate for a moment not because I'm rude but because my mind freezes. I can say *bonjour* in return, sure, but I don't want her to start babbling in French, thinking I speak the language or anything.

'Hi,' I eventually settle on. I'm a scintillating conversationalist, right?

'What did you think of Monaco?' Thank God, an English speaker! 'I saw you on the bus on Friday.' Her accent is British and her expression open and friendly. 'You must've gone to sign the paperwork for your work permit.'

'Yeah, I did.' After, I had a few hours to kill before being bussed back with the rest of the staff, giving me a little time to explore, not that I went far. 'I think Monaco is beautiful, though I'm pretty sure I prefer Nice so far.' I think I'd eventually end up feeling hemmed in, living in a country that's no bigger than Central Park. 'To be honest, I'm still trying to process that I'm here.'

'Don't worry, it takes time,' she answers kindly. 'I'm Fee, by the way.' She points at her name badge on her blue polo shirt which actually reads Fiadh. 'Ignore this,' she says, glancing down. 'No one can ever pronounce it anyway.'

'Fiadh,' I reply with the correct pronunciation. *Fee-ah*. I also know it means wild, though she looks anything but wild. Her fair hair is pulled back in a neat ponytail, her complexion peaches and cream. Besides, no one who wears a polo shirt could ever be wild.

'An Irish American?' she asks, her eyes sparkling.

'Róisín.' I hold out my hand along with the introduction. Róisín, said *Row-sheen,* means little rose in Gaelic, so I'm told. I have an equally interesting middle name because I'm what you might call a bit of a mixed bag. *Poor Irish Lebanese Kentuckian born little girl.* 'Guilty as charged.' *A little Irish, a little Lebanese. Culturally confused AF.*

'What are the odds!'

'Very slim,' I reply, chuckling, her delight almost infectious.

'I can tell we're going to be firm friends.'

'United by our parents' love of unpronounceable names?'

'Oh, God, never say that in front of my mother. She may have lived in London for thirty years but cut her and her blood will probably run green. Did you grow up hating that no one could ever say your name?'

'Yup,' I agree emphatically. 'There are only so many times you can be called raisin without losing it a little. By the time I turned twelve, I refused to answer to anything but Rose.'

'Raisin? That's hilarious.'

'For the first hundred times, at least.'

'And after that, it's just annoying, right?' I nod. 'I used to get called Fido a lot myself. Or some bloody awful variation.

Fi-dada, Fi-yar-dar. So I put my foot down. Only my parents are allowed to call me anything other than Fee.'

My mother died when I was a teen, so few people know my real name is Róisín at all. But I don't mention any of this. Mentioning you're an orphan, even as an adult, only makes for awkward conversations. Also, my Irish roots aren't so fierce. Not with a middle name like Samira.

'I can't complain about my name being butchered when I'm living in a French speaking country and I can't even speak French.'

'You don't speak French? At all?'

'No.' But by her expression, I'm beginning to think that maybe I should.

'Oh. Okay.'

You know what kind of "okay" that sounds like? The kind of okay that isn't okay at all.

'Do you think so?' I ask, swallowing a little bubble of panic. What if there was a mistake? Maybe they didn't see my ridiculous video interview at all. 'I mean, the agent seemed to think so.' Though I'm pretty sure she'd have sold my soul to the devil to get her hands on the commission. 'It's not like I lied on my resumé or anything.' At least, not about speaking French. 'Do you speak French?' I can't help but hear the note of panic in that.

'Well, yes.' Fee shrugs as though worried the admission might make me uncomfortable. We both fall silent, and I begin to notice how the conversations going on around me all sound like they're being conducted in French.

'I'm sorry, I don't mean to worry you. In fact, I'm sure whatever position you've been hired for doesn't need you to know the language.'

'Do you need to know the language for your job?' Does everyone?

'Well, I work in the health club at *L'Hôtel du Loup*.' Her accent sounds flawless, as far as I can tell. 'The exercise classes I hold are all conducted in French.'

'You're a fitness instructor?' That explains the running pants I'd noticed she was wearing as she got on the bus, along with the kind of ass you could probably bounce coins off.

'Try not to look so worried. You've been interviewed and hired, you've met the HR team and gotten your work permit. You don't need to speak the language for whatever it is you're doing. What is it you'll be doing anyway, your job, I mean? If you don't mind me asking, that is.'

You know what? I have no idea. The job title mentioned on the contract was so vague.

'Customer relations associate,' I recount. Despite my unease, I deliver my title confidently. 'I've got to report to the guest relations department in *l'agence centrale*.' I fight off the feelings of inadequacy trying not to compare Fee's accent to my own. 'That's just the head office, right?'

On Friday, the head office was referred to as the head office, yet the email I received yesterday said *l'agence centrale*. Thank God for Google Translate because one of these things is not said like the other, even if they're essentially the same department.

'Yes. We get dropped off at the hotel employee entrance and the head office is housed in the nearby residence tower, *Tours de Loup*.'

'I don't know what that is.'

'You've never heard of it? Wolf Tower?'

'Can't say that I have.'

'It's owned by by The Wolf Group. You know, *Le Groupe Loup* in French.'

'*Le Groupe Loup*,' I repeat, attempting to inject my voice

with a little French flair. Sadly, it sounds more like I'm saying "Froot Loop".

'So, the place you visited Friday? That was *Tour du Loup*. Or Wolf Tower.'

'Oh, well that makes sense.' Sort of. 'So Wolf Hotel and Wolf Tower are owned by the same company?' Fee nods again. 'These wolfs, I mean wolves, aren't very imaginative.' What's next? Wolf Beach? Wolf Mall? Wolf FroYo?

'So I guess you don't know that Wolf Tower is the tallest building in Monaco, as well as one of the most expensive places to live, given that it's within minutes of the Place du Casino and the port?'

'And the Place du Casino is . . . ?'

'Just the most iconic place in Monaco.' Her words waver with amusement.

'And the port is where the rich keep their toy boats.'

'Something like that.' This time, she can't hold her amusement back. 'Million-dollar toys.'

'Huh. Look at that, I'm learning already.' I'm sure I'll be learning more than just one thing new every day while I'm here.

'The Wolf Group is the biggest player in property development out here. They say the business has doubled in the last couple of years alone. I mean, there's the market for it. There is just so much wealth. Monaco is a little mad at first glance. Just take a look at the cars. Every second one that passes is a Bentley, Ferrari, or a Maserati.'

'Well, they can throw a little of that wealth my way. I won't complain.'

'Oh, most of us aren't going to get rich here, unless we snag a wealthy husband or something. Unfortunately, we're here to cater to the whims of the rich and powerful. Or, in my case, to make the bums of the rich and powerful not jiggle quite so much.'

'A fat ass is about the only thing I have in common with these people.'

'I've got to drop something off at reception this morning. I'll walk in with you, if you like?'

'That'd be great.' My usual go-to or immediate response would be a polite refusal, though it would come from a sense of independence and stubbornness rather than frostiness, but I recognise that not only would her company be helpful, it would also be welcome. I need to start making friends, and Fee seems like the ideal candidate.

I'm grateful for the air-conditioning in the little bus as the sun streams in through the window, heating the side of my face. Conversation flows freely between the two of us, occasionally interrupted by our fellow travellers, not that I understand them, of course.

'They're complaining about the journey time,' Fee says as a dark-haired young man bursts into a voluble explosion of French. 'It usually takes us around forty minutes to get from the apartments in Nice to work, but there are roadworks going west so we have to take the coastal road.'

'*Touristes!*' another complains from behind us.

'This is the touristy route, huh?'

She nods. 'But it's a much nicer view, at least. And a good start to your first day at work.'

And she is right. The view is pretty special. Narrow streets lined with towering palm trees widen to stretches of road with views across the Mediterranean. To the left lies a mountain range, the very top of which is capped by snowy white clouds, even on a sunny blue-skied morning such as this. Through a tunnel and the urban sprawl starts to thicken, signalling we're drawing closer. As we travel, Fee confirms that the company owns several hotels in the tiny principality alone, all catering to an elite clientele. She also says that many of the billion-dollar construction projects in the country belong to The Wolf Group. It seems they're expanding their properties and holdings, not only in the Côte d'Azure area but also worldwide.

Chatter from our fellow travellers is subdued, and though Fee is a good companion, I begin to feel more and more tense the closer we draw to the hotel. Before I can say *sacré bleu*, we're there, and Fee is leaving me in the vast glass and sparkling quartz foyer, a space so bright I almost feel like I need to wear sunglasses.

An attractive twenty-something receptionist smiles, then begins speaking to me in French.

'*Pardon. Je ne parle pas Francais,*' I begin haltingly as I explain I don't speak French. 'My name is Róisín Ryan. I was told to report to reception this morning?'

She nods as she taps away on a keyboard I can't see. I suddenly feel prickly and hot, and I'm so caught up in how silly and inadequate I feel at my lack of French that I almost miss the lanyard and badge she issues me.

'*Bienvenue,* Mademoiselle Ryan. Welcome to The Wolf Group.'

As she slides the badge across the expanse of quartz, I note how it reads *Visiteur*. It almost seems like a bad omen, one quickly pushed to the side as another employee introduces herself.

'Bonjour. I am Alice.' There are so many more syllables in her name than regular old Alice. Al-ee-sss. 'Please, come this way.'

I follow the tap of her heels to the bank of shining elevators.

'That's a very pretty scarf. Do all the staff wear them?' I

85

gesture to the blue and white striped scarf around the woman's neck, noting how the receptionist was also wearing one. Along with a pale fitted shift dress, nude pumps, and a stylish chignon, there's something very "uniform" about their look.

Or maybe cloned.

'*Oui*,' she answers happily. 'It is not, 'ow you say, compulsory but it is encouraged.' *Wow. So many syllables in that last word.* 'This is the company logo, see?' She fans the edges to show the stripes are actually a row of *W's* and *I's* intertwined.

'It's *très chic*.' Argh! I'm such a dork.

Alice smiles indulgently, and as that's about the extent of my French fashion commentary, I step in silently behind her when the elevator doors open. I suppose the scarf must be handy for hiding hickeys, if you're lucky enough to be getting some. But other than that, I feel kind of dowdy standing next to her corporate self. My hair is braided loosely, and I'd chosen to wear my sand-coloured shirt dress and strappy heels. Earlier this morning, I thought I'd looked a little business and a little bohemian, but as I glance down, I realise my dress now resembles a burlap sack.

Linen and bus rides don't make good partners.

The elevator doors open, and I follow her out and along the marble hallway, the joint click of our heels echoing through the space. But then a door slams somewhere nearby, the loud crack making me jump. I tighten the grip on my purse as a man begins to shout, his anger apparent even to someone who doesn't speak the language.

Some lessons are a little hard to unlearn.

'*Il est furieux*.' The woman in front turns her head over her shoulder, shooting me a cautious smile. 'He sounds furious, no? Do not worry. He is not always in a bad mood.'

'Who isn't? I mean, who is it?' I trot a little to catch up with her. Despite working in a strip joint, heels are not my go-to footwear. Slow and sedate is the only way I can move in them.

'Monsieur Durrand, the *prèsident*. CEO, I think you would say.'

A fist squeezes around my heart. *His name was Durrant not Durrand,* I remind myself, not sure if I'm self-soothing or commiserating.

'You won't see him too often,' she continues. 'Though I expect you will remember the first time you do.'

'Because he's so terrible?' I try to keep the derision from my voice. Working within these shiny walls can't be as bad as working in a grimy strip club, where hands wander places they shouldn't, and the soles of your shoes stick to a beer-stained floor. If I can put up with that shit, I can put up with anything.

'*Non.*' The word is more tinkling laugh than anything else. 'That is not it.'

Fine, you be all enigmatic. I don't reply. See if I care.

I guess she must read my expression as she then offers, '*Le petit Loup,* how you say, his bark is worse than his bite.'

Le petit Loup? The small wolf? It's not exactly a recommendation of the shouting asshole, but something is making her smile. Maybe she's one of those girls who thinks any kind of attention is good. I don't ponder it for long as the shouting gets louder and more distinct. Someone is definitely being ripped a new one, and what's more, the dressing down has switched to English.

Another door slams and, all of a sudden, a man appears in front, heading in the opposite direction. There's nothing little about him, which makes me think that Alice means something else. Something a little more personal, like a pet name. Maybe that's why she's smiling. Maybe she's been banging the boss's little loup.

The one he keeps in his pants, I mean.

I rein in my runaway brain as the man draws closer. Head down, focussed on his phone, there's something familiar about him. Which is stupid, I know. Unless he's been near The Pink Pussy Cat in San Francisco lately.

As if, my brain supplies. The Pussy Cat is a million miles away, figuratively and almost literally. It's more spit and sawdust than champagne. Yet something continues to poke at me, tugging the very edge of my attention even as I try very hard not to look at him.

'Bonjour, Monsieur Durrand,' the woman next to me murmurs deferentially.

The asshole doesn't look up.

And the second squeeze of my heart is just as strange, only this time, the fist seems to catapult that muscle to the pit of my stomach, bringing me to a stop at the same moment his shoulder almost brushes mine.

'Remy.' It's no more than a whisper—a whisper of a whisper—a murmur of a denial as I try to convince myself otherwise.

The man's attention lifts slowly from his phone, every moment drawn out, seconds and milliseconds appearing to slow. His eyes meet mine, the jolt of recognition like being plunged into an icy cold pool. His head turns as he moves past me, as though he's unwilling to release my gaze.

My God, it is him.

My heart pounds solidly in my stomach, or at least I think that's what's thrumming down there, as his shoes suddenly scuff against the floor, and he stops, turning to face me.

'I'm sorry?'

This really isn't a question or even an apology from him,

not with such a haughty delivery. Though it is delivered in faultless English. I know somehow I'm looking at the asshole who switched from yelling French to English so seamlessly. My mouth works soundlessly, words failing me because *how? Why?* And *oh, hell no.*

'Alice?'

My spirits sink to my sandals. He doesn't even remember my name? I belatedly comprehend he isn't speaking to me as the girl beside me almost jumps to attention, bullet fast French streaming from her mouth. It doesn't take me long to realise she's offering an introduction as I add one more to the tally of times in twenty-five years that I've been called Raisin Ryan.

'Actually, it's Rose. Rose Ryan.' I smile, and I shrug as though he and I are perfect strangers, and not two people who've tasted each other's genitals. Oh, Jesus. I did not just think that—just like the responding image did *not* just flash through my head. 'No one ever calls me Róisín.'

'Rose.' The way he says my name is like a replay of an aural memory, even if the visual part of that memory isn't quite the same.

He was damn sexy in jeans and boots, and exuded a kind of rugged handsomeness. His charming nature was apparent even through our supposed language barrier. The man standing in front of me has the same self-assurance, minus the playful air. He's made no effort to be charming, and he's barely cracked a smile, but his presence is no less magnetic. He seems more somehow. Older. Harder. Darker. Urbane and self-assured. And the outfit he's wearing the heck out of? It's what the term *suit porn* was invented for, and even his pocket square is sexy.

And I know what's going on underneath. All that swirling ink. From businessman to bad boy in the shedding of a shirt.

Bottom line? Remy version 2.0 is the off the charts kind of hot.

His attention is intense and like a brush of hot fingertips before the look is replaced by a flash of annoyance. His gaze glitters with an almost olive hue, and something in his demeanour changes in that instant. His expression hardens, almost as though he's come to some kind of conclusion. A conclusion that becomes perfectly clear as he turns and walks away without a backward glance.

10

REMY

'I DON'T KNOW. Just get in here.' I drop my phone to my desk and tear off my jacket and begin pacing once again.

What is she doing here?

This can't be happening.

It just can't. Because that would mean . . .

Non! I refuse to fucking allow it, whatever this is.

And what it appears to be is the fuckup to crown all fuckups—the kind of error that should bring a grown man to his knees.

'You took your time.' I swing around to where Everett enters the office almost silently.

'I've got feet, not wheels.' Closing the door behind him, he pushes his hands into his pockets as he saunters farther into the room. 'What's with the pacing? A new addition to the repertoire of angry arsehole mogul?'

'The girl,' I begin immediately, pushing aside his taunting reply. I'll admit to sometimes feeling like I'm still struggling to adjust to the role my father's death has cast me in, but that hardly signifies right now. 'The girl,' I repeat. 'She's here.' My pacing halts, one display of my discomfort exchanged for another as I rake my hands through my hair.

How the fuck can this have happened?

How could we have gotten this so wrong?

How could *I* have made such a mistake?

'So? That was the plan, wasn't it?' His lack of concern is jarring. I watch him stroll across the room, pausing at the concealed bar behind my desk. 'Because if it wasn't,' he adds, sliding the panel and pulling a glass jar from the shelf, 'we went to an awful lot of fucking trouble to get her out here.'

I glance down at my feet, not sure whether the impulse to move is for the purpose of crossing the room to punch him or to flee. This . . . this is not me. Not how I operate. I fight. I scheme. I tear down the competition to build up the Durrand name. I will not lose my peace over a girl.

A woman, my mind corrects. *A goddess.*

I grit my teeth, forcing my mind in the opposite direction. A girl. A piece of skirt. A one-night fucking lay.

'No, not that girl,' I reply, my voice icily calm. 'The other girl.'

Even as I say this, I know in the pit of my gut they're one and the same.

Mon Dieu. What have I done?

'The surveillance photographs show her as blonde,' I grate out. 'She isn't.' Photographs I'd given only a cursory glance, less interested in who she was than why she was set to intrude on my life.

'You don't need to be Sherlock Holmes to work that out,' he answers. 'I told the private investigator the images weren't exactly stellar, but even the ones taken in that dark shit hole of a club, you could tell she was wearing a wig. She was no fucking Heidi,' he asserts with a wink.

'What's that supposed to mean?' My response is almost a growl.

'You don't find many good girls working in strip clubs.'

I take a deep breath in an attempt to calm myself and tamp back this wave of anger that I don't quite understand. He's talking about an anonymous woman who means nothing to him, not the woman with the tender heart who looked after me. Surely that's the definition of good. *Not that she wasn't good in other ways.*

A good girl. A piece of skirt. A one-night glorious lay.

Not now. I cannot think of that.

'What about the interview? Didn't you say there was a recording?' I think this is what he would call clutching at straws.

'Not one that I looked at.' His answer is dismissive, the task below his pay grade.

'In which case, there is a girl, here in this building, who we went to much trouble and expense to employ, who isn't who she is supposed to be.'

'They rarely are.'

I take a deep breath before continuing, resisting the urge to blame him for the magnitude of my mistakes. 'For one minute, could you stop being so fucking obtuse? I've just met her. She's the same woman who took me to the hospital the night I was attacked in San Francisco.'

That girl—*non*, that woman—the one I'd been looking for, she wasn't supposed to be brunette. Not that the colour of her hair can be encompassed in that bland word. Rich, like mahogany. Strands of amber and red gold, silky to the touch.

When I woke in the hospital, I thought Rose was a neighbour, or perhaps a roommate of Róisín, the woman I was looking for, investigating, but not hoping to meet. *At least, not yet.*

If I'd known, I never would've—

I cut off the thought. As much as I don't want to believe it, these women are one and the same. Confirmed by her introduction. *Roísin, but no one ever calls me that.*

Confusion and frustration morph into a volcano of thoughts; discomfort, disquiet, and fucking dread. But none of these encompass how I feel, none even touching the magnitude of this fuckup.

'Say that again?' From across the room, Rhett's attention appears to be only for his afternoon snack.

'The woman we had investigated, the woman I have employed; she is the same person who looked after me the night of my accident.' The memory of her under me that night rises before me like an apparition. The dark, silken waves of hair in my hands, her eyes like melted honey. The taste of her tiny gasp as I'd slid into her.

Was she a taste of the forbidden?

I push away the thought because only madness lies there.

'The woman you screwed, you mean.' With a grin, he pops off the lid, throwing a protein ball into his mouth—the mouth I suddenly want to fill with my fist. 'They're good, these. Does Amélie make them for you?'

I glower his way without answering his asinine question, a look that would turn a lesser man to dust. But not him. We train together and spar regularly. We both live clean and fight dirty. And while he is the ex-Special Forces head of my security team, this doesn't keep me from eviscerating him. What does is the fact that he is my friend. A very annoying friend, yes. But he's probably the only person in the world I truly trust.

The thought is followed in an instant by another. Perhaps less thought and more a memory, two voices almost floating from a grave. My childhood long dead, my father also passed.

Remy, when you grow up, you will be respected, revered, like the son of a king. People will seek to flatter you, but remember, they bring you close for only one reason. And what is that reason?

For the opportunity to stick a knife in my back, Papa.

Two years and the man is still haunting me. As for treating me like a king, he himself treated me as though I was begotten on a kitchen maid. When he said the business would never be mine, I thought he meant it as a punishment. But not so. As the adage goes, all war is based on deception, and he set me up to fail.

'The woman who was kind to me,' I correct. The woman who doesn't deserve to be brought into my fucked-up world. Yet, she's here anyway. Here within reach, a fact that should not bring any comfort.

Rhett's expression darkens. I know he still blames himself for what happened that night. But this is no one's fault but my own. It was midnight. I couldn't sleep so I had gone out for a ride. Is it any wonder I found myself outside of her house? She was, after all, the reason we were in the city.

Investigation only, I insisted. No contact to be made.

An obvious mission failure.

'The one who picked me up off the street after I fell from my bike,' I add, rubbing a little salt into his professional wound. A low blow, but as I said, we both fight dirty.

'I told you I should've gone with you,' he replies obstinately, turning to place the jar back on the shelf. 'If you'd woken me, none of this would've happened.'

And if I'd woken him, I wouldn't have found *her*. Like an angel brought to earth, she saved me that night. She didn't save me from the claws of death but rather my faith in humanity.

'As for falling off your bike, I still don't buy it. This has been a theme of Everett's since I'd called him while Rose was sleeping—called him so I could leave without waking her.

Not cowardice. I sought to protect her.

'We've been through this so many times already.' I try not to let my irritation seep into my tone. 'It was an accident.'

'An accident during the middle of the night on an abandoned street? You've been riding since you were old enough to get a license—*before* you were legally of age—and not one accident. Do you know how rare that is? An accident at your age and experience is more likely to be the kind that's life changing.'

Life changing is right. I've thought near constantly of Rose since I left her house that night. Thought of her kind heart and her consideration, of her soft lips and lush curves. I've remembered that night more times than can be regarded as healthy.

As the aphorism goes, you should be careful what you wish for.

'And when I say change your life, I don't mean for better.'

The censure in Rhett's tone pulls me back to the present. I make my way across the room to him, laying a hand on his shoulder as I bring my gaze level with his.

'There really is no other answer.' I woke on the side of the road, my head feeling as though it had been split with an axe, and the bike nowhere to be seen. 'I skidded or fell or had a minor accident, or else I was robbed.'

'Remy, a Ducati Panigale—a bike worth eighty thousand —would've stood out like tits on a bull. It's not the kind of machine that can be sold without notice, not without it coming to the notice of the authorities.'

'Maybe it's in a shed somewhere. Maybe it was taken out of the state. What does it matter?'

'It matters because it's my job to make sure these things don't happen, and I wasn't there.'

'My fault, not yours. Stop beating yourself up about it.'

'It's not me I want to beat up,' he replies meaningfully, while also fighting a smile.

'I think the bike did a good enough job for you.' I run my finger over the small scar bisecting my eyebrow. It was either the bike, the road, the curb, or possibly something purple.

Purple? Why does that suddenly seem probable?

'I could've wrung your neck myself for putting yourself at such fucking risk.'

'Ah, you could try, I suppose.' My answer is flippant, though I tighten my hand on his shoulder, an action meant to reassure rather than exacerbate.

'There's just something not right about the whole deal.' His brows draw together over brooding dark eyes.

'You're right. But the thing that isn't right is that there is a woman in this building that shouldn't be.'

'Or there's a woman in this building who you shouldn't have been *in*.'

Immediately, my temper flares.

'*Sortez votre tête de vos fesses et écoutez-moi!*'

'Touchy,' he drawls, his hand pushing mine from his shoulder. 'I think you'll find it's not me who has his head up his arse, especially if you don't remember how getting her here was all your plan.'

'This is not a matter to joke about!'

'Apologies. Am I interrupting?'

Both our heads turn to the voice at the other side of the room.

'Ben. Come in.' I direct him with a wave of my hand, ignoring his obsequious tone. 'Everett and I were just discussing our training plans for tonight.' Ben, or Benoît as he prefers, is my cousin as well as a member of the executive team for The Wolf Group, the company my father founded. The company that passed unexpectedly into my hands on his death. *Damn the old bastard and his twisting, underhanded ways.*

'All right, Benny?' Rhett offers with an annoyingly wide grin.

'My name is Benoît, as well you know,' my cousin retorts imperiously. His airs are often so high-handed, I sometimes think he forgets exactly who's in charge. Which, I suppose, is not so very difficult to understand given he was always more involved in the business. And, much like myself, he was deceived in how things would eventually play out.

'You prefer Benoît, do you, Benny?' Rhett's brows retract to his hairline as though this is news, rather than one more thing he can do to irritate the man he likes least in the whole of Monaco. 'Well, blow me. *Not* an invitation by the way.'

'Not an invit—are you suggesting I am *homosexual?*'

'*Du calme,*' I interject. I could well do without the whole pistols at dawn scene. 'Rhett isn't suggesting anything.'

'No offence, man.' He grins, juggling the spherical snacks between his hands. 'Here, Benny. You should try these. I guarantee these are the best tasting balls you'll ever have in your mouth.'

'*Arrête.*' *Enough.* One glance at Rhett's supposed innocent expression makes me shake my head. What can I say? Rhett is Rhett while Ben is an uptight, supercilious pain in my ass. But he's also family, and unlike my father, I intend to make that count. 'What is it you wanted?' I slip my hand around his shoulders, directing our footsteps in the direction of the door.

'Your mother wanted me to remind you to sign off on the security for the foundation benefit ball.'

'She has already. You know she can use email? She has even mastered the art of the smartphone. She also has a full-time assistant on staff. No need to offer your services as messenger.'

'I was merely being courteous. Tante Josephine is not the sort of woman you can ignore.'

This might be true but that's not why he's here. No, not at all.

'Also, my assistant tells me there is some confusion in one of the departments. HR, I believe. It seems some idiot has taken on a new hire who can't speak a word of French.'

And there we have it. For a company of this size, very little gets past Ben.

'Why is that a problem?' I ask evenly. 'The team speaks many languages. We have clientele from over thirty countries. And though you and I may be French, we are not speaking the language now.'

English is my preference, as well as my custom when Rhett is around. In fact, I've been speaking English so long, I no longer dream in French. Ben, meanwhile, prefers to speak in riddles, mainly to ascertain information; information being the currency he thrives on.

'Yes, but The Wolf Group is a French company—in France.'

'I'm almost certain Prince Albert would have something to say about that.' Prince Albert being the country's monarch, and Monaco being a small city state and a country all of its own.

'Monaco is a French-speaking country,' Ben retorts, the edges of his exasperation showing. 'That is what I mean. You can't work in Monaco if you don't possess the language.'

'There are many residents without command of the language,' I argue reasonably.

'The wealthy, yes. Monaco is a tax haven for those rich enough who may not care to speak French. But the ordinary working man?' He shoots me a triumphant look. 'One must question why they are here in this case.'

'What about you, Rhett?' I ask without turning to look at him. 'Why are you here?'

'To keep your arse out of trouble,' comes his response. 'And funny, here I thought I had a pretty decent command of the language.'

'If a little butchering,' I throw over my shoulder. 'Have this woman sent to my office,' I direct Ben.

'Who said it was a woman?' Ben turns to face me as we reach the door.

'Come, now. You expect me to believe it was a man who caught your attention?'

Ben's gaze slides to Rhett, and with eyes narrowed, he responds, 'You know me well.'

'I like to think so.'

'She's a very pretty girl,' he accepts as his attention returns. 'And Remy, I saw her first.'

It's an assertion I'll allow him to keep on believing. For all of us.

'I'm not interested in making a conquest of a new hire. Have her sent to my office. Let me get to the bottom of this.'

Ben frowns, then consents with a perfectly Gallic shrug. The door is no sooner closed behind him when Rhett speaks again.

'Must be the only bit of her you haven't had.'

'*Ta gueule.*' *Shut it*. 'Also, leave.'

'What, and miss the fireworks?'

'I don't know what you're talking about,' I answer, my tone bored.

There will be no fireworks. The plan mustn't change. Rose might not be the woman I thought she was, but whatever has passed between us, she's here at my behest. And here she'll stay until I discover why my father sought to involve her in our family politics.

'You think you're confused?' Rhett answers with a bark of a laugh. 'That woman out there has travelled six thousand miles for a job to find she's fucked her new boss, the same boss who's been sending her creepy gifts—'

'A coffee machine isn't creepy.' This is possibly not what I should've responded with. But I also suppose I should not be surprised he knows exactly what gifts I've sent. The why he can't possibly understand because I'm not sure I understand it myself.

'A coffee machine isn't very sexy either.'

'It wasn't meant to be sexy.' Especially now. 'I was just showing my appreciation.'

'Appreciation? Well, she's out there now wondering if you've brought her here to gift her something else.' As though there might be the slightest possibility I mistake his meaning, he palms his crotch.

'I thought your right hand was your girlfriend, not your left.'

'Better to fuck my hand than fuck my—'

'I did not fuck Róisín Ryan,' I retort angrily.

'What do you call it? Keeping it in the family?'

11

ROSE

'WHY DO I need to see him?'

'I do not ask.' Alice throws this terse reply over her shoulder as she steps from the elevator onto, what is, I understand, the executive floor. 'I only know, he says leap, I ask how high.'

'And why did you call him *Le petit Loup*?' I ask, trying to keep up with her as she darts along the hallway as though escaping the police. 'Loup is wolf, right?' Remy wasn't predatory, not as I recall. It can't have been a cute name for his dick, not the size of that thing. Unless she means it ironically. I glance her way, and I decide she has no knowledge of Remy Durrand's mighty baguette because if she did, she wouldn't be looking so disconcerted.

'His father was the wolf; he is the wolf cub. He is, *la rusé*... what is the word in English?' she muses as we turn a corner. 'Cunning! *Le petit Loup*, the young wolf is cunning.'

Was it charm or cunning that led him to my bed?

I know which I'd like to think it was. I'm also not sure I'd be right, not after this morning.

We enter an airy reception, a verbal exchange taking place between Alice and a woman acting as sentry behind an imposing industrial design desk. With the hauteur of a queen, she gestures us to a butter-soft leather sofa where we wait. And wait.

An older man is admitted to the double doors, exiting a few minutes later without the paperwork he'd carried in. Another man leaves, but not before perching his ass on the corner of the older administrator's desk and beginning to speak to her in French—French with a clearly British accent. A one-sided conversation too, as the woman just swats his arm with a folder, turning her attention back to her computer screen.

'We won't be long here, will we?' I whisper to Alice.

'Have you got somewhere to be?' the man asks, amused.

My cheeks begin to sting, and I begin to stammer an answer as the older woman seems to take pity on me, gesturing us toward the imposing double doors.

One quick rap and Alice gingerly pushes the door open.

'Entre,' comes the commanding reply in a voice I still seem to summon in my dreams.

She pushes the door wider as I consider her earlier words about his bark being worse than his bite. If that's the case, why does she look like she's entering the wolf's den and worried she's about to have her head bitten off? Whatever, she might be the appetiser, but something tells me I'm about to be his entrée.

And not in the fun, sexy kind of way, either.

Remy Durrand not Durrant. Not so hard to confuse.

Maybe if I'd have paid more attention, I'd have googled him more successfully. And then I would've learned the job I'd been offered was working for the man I'd had the sexy times with.

What I still don't understand is how he looked so surprised.

And so pissed.

And why the heck did he storm off instead of looking pleased his nefarious plan had come together?

Has jet lag made me lose my mind?

The first thing I notice is the size of the room. It's huge, double height, and filled with light thanks to the wall of glass providing breathtaking views over a marina filled with million-dollar yachts and farther to the Mediterranean Sea. Would these be multimillion-dollar or billion-dollar views?

A dark table dominates one side of the room, a dozen classic white Swan chairs clustered around it. Blue marbled panels stand sentry behind an imposing modernist-era desk; the chair behind it unoccupied. The same for the black leather and chrome Le Corbusier lounge setting placed in the middle of the room. Despite the light and space, the room is decidedly masculine. Not least of which is the man standing on the far side of it, his broad shoulders framed by a sea of blue.

'You asked to see me?' Alice's voice wavers ever so slightly. I find I'm almost surprised she'd spoken in English, considering how in the elevator on the way up she'd mumbled in nothing but French. And let me tell you, none of it had sounded complimentary. It wasn't just her tone which made me think I was in trouble because I'd also spent two hours in an office where the people around me murmured frantically while trying—and failing—not to send their troubled glances my way. I gather my employment is an issue. That no one knows what to do with me. That no one seems to know why I'm here.

I also gather Alice doesn't intend on taking the blame.

Oh, I've been treated well enough, and I was even taken to

the staff restaurant for lunch, which was pretty swanky. But I haven't been issued a desk or a locker and not once has anyone mentioned my job.

Like the lanyard hanging around my neck, I feel like a *visiteur*.

'*Laissez-nous.*'

I don't need to understand French to know he just issued a dismissal, confirmed as Alice darts from the room.

'*Bonne chance.*' Her gaze darts my way as she passes, shooting me a brief grimace of a smile. The door then closes with an ominous *clunk*.

I don't move, at a loss what to think or say. Why am I here? Why in the world would he set up such an elaborate second meeting? This isn't about sex, that much is clear. Not the way he looked at me earlier in the hallway. Not the way he's looking at me right now.

My goodness, the man is like an artisan chocolate; mouthwateringly tasty and wrapped to appeal, but with hidden layers of delicious his outer coating doesn't reveal. I wish I could say the same for my outfit as I twist the belt on my dress, silently cursing its resemblance to a sack as, without officially acknowledging my presence, Remy strolls to his desk. With his back facing me, he begins sifting through a folder.

'Róisín Ryan,' he announces without turning. Points to him for making my name sound less like raisin than Alice did. Also, minus points for the low rumble of his voice that reminds me of that night. Like I need that kind of aural memory.

'Born June twenty-ninth,' he continues in that delectable accent of his. Despicable; I definitely meant despicable. '1994, in Knoxville, Tennessee, to the late Nora Ryan, nee Awad. That's an Arabic surname, right?' With the question, he turns his head over his shoulder, glancing briefly my way.

Okay, handsome. So we've established my ancestry is a little hodgepodge; a little Irish and a little something else. And while I don't know what I was expecting, I'm certain it wasn't this.

'Do you investigate every girl you've slept with?' I fold my arms across my chest, my hip seeming to cock with an attitude all on its own. 'Send them weird gifts afterwards, too?'

'Weird?' He turns to face me then, negligently arranging himself on the desk, one leg bent, the other out straight. If you can't man-spread in your own office, where can you? But this isn't about his comfort. This is a declaration of strength, of dominance. He's the big cat in the room. Or wolf, as the case may be.

Got it.

Loud and clear.

But, be warned, this little mouse also has sharp teeth.

'A coffee machine?' I reply derisively, fingers fluttering in the air, matching the inconsequence of my words, as though I'm used to receiving much more suitable gifts from my hordes of admirers. In truth, I appreciated every one of the things he sent, including the coffee machine, which I sold to help make my rent. 'And now the weirdest of all, a job.'

I hope to high heavens that I'm not right about this.

I deserve a break. I need the money!

'Am I to surmise you liked your previous position waitressing?' He says "position" like it's something dirty, and my spine stiffens instantly. His eyes dip from my face to my chest, and just as I think he's about to twist the knife by making some comment about my boobs, he adds, 'I much prefer your hair that way.'

What way? Like in one braid instead of two?' Or could he be talking about my blonde wig? The wig I *wasn't* wearing the night I met him. Could he have visited the Pussy Cat? I push aside the unpleasant thought. He can't have, I know. I'd have noticed someone like him in there, and if he'd called on one of my nights off, it would've been marked on the board in the dressing room. There are always customers to be wary of, and the dancers in the Pink Cat would make sure everyone knew who to be cautious around. Often, the board would mention other customers of note.

Brad Pit lookalike. Handsy. Stingy. Not worth the time.

To be avoided at all costs.

Harold. Looks like a hobo, tips like a king.

Smart to show the man a little attention.

I try not to think what the board would say about Remy, mustering a reply instead.

'Whether I liked waitressing or not doesn't matter.' My heels click angrily against the highly polished floor. 'Because I lost my job the night I decided to play nurse to you.'

Why did I move closer? I could've pointed my finger at him from the other side of the room. Maybe because I wouldn't be standing this close to him, remembering how good he smells or noticing the tiny scar through his eyebrow. I don't need to be this close unless I really intend on slapping him, which isn't me at all. I don't let men get under my skin, not the cute ones and definitely not the expensive and dangerous ones. All I know is none of this reality makes sense, yet I draw closer still. From slapping distance to the almost kissing kind.

'I didn't know,' he answers, sounding almost sincere. *Almost.*

'I might've been born at night, but it wasn't last night.'

His eyes narrow, verdant green turning almost black. 'You don't believe me?'

'Put yourself in my place. And you'd better believe I wouldn't be standing here if I'd known from the start this was some kind of game.'

'I play no game.' Annoyance flickers to life in his expression, fading just as fast.

'I find that hard to believe. But what do I know? I thought you only spoke French.'

'An assumption.' His lips quirk in something that isn't quite a smile. 'After all, you never asked.'

'I was *told* by the hospital staff!' I try to temper my response without much success. 'Hospital staff *you* lied to.'

Ah! This is why I needed to be close—so I could poke him in the chest. His broad, firm chest that I know to be the colour of caramel and covered in dramatic swirls of ink.

In an echo of that first night, Remy catches my finger, pressing my hand to the centre of his chest, and covering it with his own. Ridiculously, I wonder if Alice knows what's lying under his shirt. How warm his skin is. How beautiful he is.

'You'll remember I had suffered a blow to the head. I probably came around speaking French. It is, after all, my mother tongue.'

The mention of his tongue in that stupid accent of his makes my blush deepen.

And yes, it *is* a stupid accent.

Stupid sexy.

'I did not lie. You, on the other hand . . .'

'What?'

'Shall we start with your name?'

'You are unbelievable,' I mutter, pushing my hand solidly

against his chest as my cheeks begin to prickle with annoyance.

'Unlike you, who even made the doctor blush.'

'It was necessary at that point.' I glower back at him, his own gaze dancing merrily in response.

'It was a nice touch to the story,' he purrs, 'but what reason would you have to embellish? To lie? Then to go along with it afterwards?'

'Wouldn't you like to know.' There's no way I'm admitting I felt sorry for him being all alone in a foreign country. Or that I just wasn't ready to let him go. *Because that's just hilarious, right?* 'You could've mentioned at a later point that you spoke English. You know, when you remembered,' I retort snarkily.

'Perhaps I was saving your blushes. Do you make it a habit of confessing your innermost thoughts to complete strangers?'

It's clear he's not saving my blushes right now as I open my mouth to respond, finding no words within reach.

'What was it you said? You hadn't had the pleasure for over a year? Was that true?'

Sweet mother-of-pearl, the man is as hot as he is annoying. And the fact that he is annoying is the reason I won't mention that, up until just now, I was sure the sex we'd had back then would be enough to tide me over for another year.

Now, standing this close to him, I'm not so sure.

'I'm not sure I mentioned sex,' I reply evasively.

'I'm pretty sure the *only* thing we spoke of was sex.' His tone is even, but there's a glint of provocation in his gaze.

I find myself inhaling audibly as he reaches out, drawing his forefinger lightly down my cheek. Heat blooms deep inside me at the touch.

'That's not fair.' I'm not sure if I mean his words or his touch. I wet my lips, telling myself that my voice is suddenly husky because my throat is dry, and that it has nothing to do with thirsting for him. 'You deliberately kept me in the dark.'

'It was for your own good.'

'No man gets to decide what's right for me. If there's one thing my mother taught me, it was that.' Even if I came by that lesson watching her mistakes.

Whether my mulish reply is responsible for the change in his demeanour, or the mention of my mother, I'm not sure. He might not physically withdraw, but it's almost as though a barrier has fallen between us. But if I'm sure of one thing it's that the man in front of me isn't the light-hearted tourist I found on my doorstep that night. The real Remy seems calculating, mercurial even, as his attention moves to the manila folder to the side of him.

He flips it open, sifting through the sheets of paper inside.

'Your mother, Nora?' His eyes are shrewd as they meet mine.

Her name was Noorah, but he hasn't earned the right to that information.

'What of her?' I draw myself to the full extent of my five-foot-seven height in heels, determined not to be caught off guard by his change of pace.

'On your medical insurance application, it states your blood type is AB positive. Is that correct?'

'Last time I checked,' I answer facetiously as he reaches out and grasps a silver Mont Blanc pen. He turns the page and begins jotting notes. 'Just like my personality. A be positive person.'

It's a dumb joke, as well as a stretch right now, but as he doesn't acknowledge my answer, it definitely falls flat.

'Do you happen to know what blood type your mother was?'

'I do.'

His pen poised over the page, he turns his head, his eyes flaring angrily, his words staccato. 'This is important.'

'Jeez, chill out. Fine.' I'm pleased my response sounds so unaffected. It's so jarring to feel like I know him when I don't really know him at all.

'Well?' His expression is unchanging.

'I guess your parents deserve a refund from that charm school of yours. My mother was the same as me. AB positive. What's this about, anyway?'

'You're sure?' His eyes appear suddenly darker, and there's an intensity in his gaze that's a little unnerving. This isn't the playful or languid gaze of the man who crept from my bed while I slept. And I'm sorry to say that it doesn't make me want him any less.

There, I admit it. At least I kept it to myself this time, English or otherwise.

'How sure are you?'

Can you simultaneously want to wrap yourself around a man while also wanting to wrap your hands around his neck?

'I spent two years of my childhood caring for her while cancer ate her from the inside out. I'm pretty sure I know her blood type.'

There is so much of this time marked indelibly on the walls of my brain. Her diagnosis, our tears, our denials. Clinic visits. Chemotherapy. Radiotherapy. The way she cried in my arms as the so-called love of her life bailed on her following her diagnosis, but not before he'd emptied the little she had in her bank account. The last in a line of men who promised her the earth and delivered nothing but dirt.

The death of a parent is the natural order of things, so they say. But no kid needs to see their mother wasting away.

'I'm sorry.' His words are delivered with a softness that contradicts his firm expression. 'I don't mean to be unfeeling, but this is important.'

'I don't see how. I also don't understand why I'm here.'

'That makes two of us,' he murmurs, turning away and jotting something down.

I can't have heard that right, can I?

'What are you doing?' I try to get a glimpse of the notes he's jotting down when he suddenly flicks the folder closed.

'What I'm doing is thinking.' He drops the pen to the desk, his head suddenly bowed. His hands grasp the edge of his desk, his knuckles so pronounced I wouldn't be surprised to see the glossy wood snap.

'It looked like you were doodling to me,' I find myself babbling. 'Are you one of those people who draws little hearts and stars in margins while you're thinking?' I know I am, though I'm more a flower-doodling girl. 'Or maybe you're nervous about something?'

'No,' he answers, laughter lightening his voice. 'Why, should I be?'

And oh, my God, for the first time since I walked into his office, I get a glimpse of the man I found on my doorstep that night. A flash of white teeth. The playful grin.

'What I am,' he says as he begins to loosen his shirt at the cuff, 'is relieved.' A silver cuff link drops to the desktop, and he begins to fold back the brilliant white fabric.

I feel like I'm watching something intimate, something that should only be available by pay per view.

'Is that supposed to be reassuring?' I'm not sure if I mean his verbal statement or the shirt folding one, or even the way he's looking at me like I already belong to him. My gaze falls to the watch on his wrist, the same one he wore that night. The weathered leather strap, the scarred masculine face. It's at odds with the rest of his appearance, yet it's somehow completely him.

'Oh, sh—sugar!' I find myself grabbing his forearm in both of my hands, staring at his watch. 'I've got to go.'

Before I can pull away, his fingers loop around my wrist, drawing me closer to him. 'We are not done.'

'Aren't we?' I tug against his hold. 'I have five minutes to get to the staff bus before it leaves without me.' And it'll probably take me all of those five minutes to find my way out of this labyrinth of a building. Fee said the staff drivers are ruthless when it comes to the timetabled pickup times.

'The bus?' he replies, his brow creasing.

'Four wheels? Takes multiple passengers, usually for a small charge? Maybe you know it better as the peasant wagon?'

'I'm aware of what a bus is,' he replies silkily, resisting my second tug. As his thumb feathers the underside of my wrist, I find I'm not struggling anymore. 'Your heart is beating so fast.' His eyes rise from where our skins touch, his expression almost provocative. 'Why is that, do you think?'

'Because I'm about to miss my bus.'

'*Non*. I don't think so.'

'I have no idea how I came to get this job, but I'm pretty certain you're going to explain it to me sometime.'

'Is that a fact?'

'Yes, it is. But for now, I have a bus to catch. A bus I can't afford to miss. For one thing, I don't even know where I live.'

'I'm sure I can find you a place to stay.'

'Oh, I don't think so.' I find myself chuckling at the man's audacity.

'I could make a call. Find out for you.'

'Knowing where I live isn't going to get me there.'

A tiny breath catches in my throat as he lifts my hand, pressing it to his lips. It's not a sweet gesture, not by any stretch of the imagination. Not the way he watches me. Not as liquid heat courses through my veins, answering the almost magnetic pull of him.

'I don't want you to go, Rose.'

My name is a temptation, and his lips so sure and so firm and little more than a breath away. I try not to stare as I wonder if Remy would kiss me differently in this alternate reality. Would his kiss be more, here in his natural habitat? Would it be harder? Commanding? Would he hold me tight against him?

Would I even let him kiss me right now?

Like that's even a serious question.

'Do you know Emile Durrand?' he asks, the question jolting me back in place.

'As in, Emile Durrand, the founder of The Wolf Group?'

His thumb resumes its feather-light caress. 'You've met him?'

'Only between the covers of the company magazine.' Emile Durrand founded the group. He's also Remy's father, according to the articles. 'I read the back catalogue while HR was deciding what to do with me. I guess you don't offer many of your so-called conquests jobs, given how they struggled to keep me occupied. Should I be flattered? Because, honestly? I'm just confused.'

'Conquests?'

'So-called,' I correct. 'One night in my bed doesn't mean you own me.'

'What about one night in *my* bed.' His fingers tighten, his expression shuttering quite suddenly. 'What do you think that would earn me?'

Probably a stalker, I don't answer.

'You say you've never met him?'

'I have not met your father,' I reply imperiously. 'And, according to those magazines, I'm not likely to now.' Unless I'm living in a bad telenovela because Emile Durrand died over two years ago.

'*Non*,' Remy replies, this time making me roll my eyes. *Sexy French accent be gone.* 'I didn't think so. He liked them *un peu dociles.*' He holds his thumb and forefinger a pinch apart.

'Whatever.' I glance away. No way I'm touching that. And to hell with docile. 'I've probably missed my bus now.'

'Do you know your eyes turn gold when you're annoyed?'

'It's my special superpower.'

'I disagree. Your talents lie elsewhere.'

'I think I preferred it when I didn't understand what you were saying.'

'You don't like my voice?'

I don't answer. I like his voice plenty, especially when it's addressing me in that low, bedroom-y tone with the hint of his accent rounding the words.

His hand trails up the inside of my arm, the pads of his fingers heating my skin. I find my nipples standing to attention under the thin layers of my dress and hope he doesn't notice.

'Rose.' He elongates my name almost chidingly as he lifts my chin, turning me to face him. 'We both know you appreciate the things my mouth can do.'

Oh, my. He is relentless.

I know I should come up with a rebuttal, some kind of put down—and maybe I would if my head was on straight. I should resist the pull of him, deny his arms as they slide around my waist, but I find I can't. Even if, at the last minute, I turn my head.

'I'm not the kind of girl who kisses the boss.' Even if as his lips brush my cheek, my body cries out with the memory of his.

'I'm not your boss.' His words are barely a whisper yet they still make me shiver.

'I also don't kiss my boss several times removed.'

I feel the smile he presses against my cheek. 'What if I promise I didn't bring you to Monaco to fuck you?'

'That's not good enough. You need to tell me why I'm here.'

'You're here because I want to know who you are.' His voice is suddenly rough, and I can feel the heat coming off him in waves.

I make as though to push him away—I swear those are my intentions—because I won't be played with a second time. Instead, his eyes dip to my mouth, and I have no idea who moves first. All I know is my fingers are pulling at him, wrapped in his shirt, and not for a little leverage to knee him where it hurts. And then I'm noticing how his lips are so soft against mine, not hard like I'd imagined and not at all tentative. His touch skates up my spine, clasping the back of my neck as though to hold me in place. I've little intention of moving, not as his mouth plunders, his kiss deepening and coaxing mine to return the change of pace. I need no encouragement, my hands questing and greedy, my will bent to his. Tongues tangle and teeth graze, his shirt not the only item of clothing between us gripped and tortured as his big hand cups my backside, his fingers as unforgiving as his lips.

'I've dreamed of your mouth.' Oh, God. His husky admission and the feel of him hot and hard pressed against me makes me *ache*. 'Tell me you've dreamed of me.'

'Only in my fantasies.'

Breath catches in my throat as he twists my braid around his fist, his words growled into my neck.

'*Je veux te baiser.*'

'You know I don't understand.'

His response is a silky chuckle as he begins to gather my dress in small increments against my thigh. 'I said I want to fuck you.' His words bloom and burst in my belly. Is it his lips at my ear that make me shiver, or is it the way his accent thickens, his words sounding more promise than threat?

'Not exactly subtle.' Hell, was that a reprimand or a compliment? I can't be sure, not as his fingers brush lightly between my legs.

'I want to put my mouth here. Do those words work for you?'

'They're a little better.' Not to mention a little knee weakening.

'Good. Because I also plan on fucking you with my tongue.'

Oh, my God. Where do I sign up?

'Do you kiss your mother with that mouth?' I manage to say instead.

'*Non.*' Remy spins, and suddenly, I'm the one resting against the desk, his mouth on mine and his hands everywhere. 'This mouth is for kissing you. And I want to kiss you everywhere.'

12

ROSE

THIS MOUTH IS for kissing you.

I want to kiss you everywhere.

'Are you okay?'

'Yes.' I glance across the darkened car, managing to shoot Fee a tight yet grateful smile. 'I'm fine. I suppose it's just been a long day. Thank you so much for picking me up. I don't know how I'd have made it back without you.'

She waves away my thanks. 'I don't mind driving around town out of peak hours. It's actually quite therapeutic.'

I could be lying across a desk right now being kissed everywhere. But that would be wrong, no matter how much I wanted it.

'Still, thank you. You should be at home with a glass of wine, not driving across the border to pick up stupid people.'

Wine, yes. Thank God I picked up a couple of bottles over the weekend. I can't afford to get shit-faced tonight, but I need a little something to take away the mortification.

'You're not stupid,' Fee replies with a tinkling laugh. 'You're just new here, which is exactly why I'm surprised no one gave any thought to you getting back to the accommodation block on your first day.' She follows her words with a disparaging click of teeth and tongue.

'It's not so surprising really. He didn't even know there was a staff bus.' The words are out of my mouth without thought. I fight to keep my eyes straight because I can't afford for her to read my expression. In fact, there's no way I'm ever telling anyone about the compromising situation I put myself in.

'Who didn't know about the bus?'

'The man I was shadowing this afternoon. I can't remember his name.'

I hope the same can be said for whoever interrupted us just as Remy's hand was about to slip into my underwear. I'd stiffened at the sound of the door, Remy's mouth rising slowly from where he'd been whispering in very explicit terms how much he wanted me. My wide eyes had shot to his, trying to convey my panic. My first day at work, and I'd been discovered under the boss—way to go, Rose.

'*Your timing, as always, is impeccable, Everett,*' he'd murmured. It wasn't the response I was expecting as, still shielding me, his fingers had unhurriedly refastened the buttons he'd worked loose as he'd pressed a petal-soft kiss against my cheek.

It was probably for the best that we were interrupted, but that doesn't mean the asshole should've taken a seat on the sofa behind him.

'*You said six o'clock,*' the man replied. An English accent. The same guy who annoyed Remy's secretary, maybe? Whoever he was, he was definitely amused.

'*Ta mère,*' Remy drawled without heat.

'*Sure,*' he'd drawled in reply. '*But if you've the energy to fuck my mother after you've finished here, you're doing something wrong.*'

Remy continued to shield my body and held out his hand

to help me down from the desk. I couldn't look at him, utterly mortified as I was. As I still am. When he'd turned to address the man fully, growling a catalogue of French insults, I'd taken the opportunity to tiptoe across the room before slipping out of the door.

Fleeing the scene of the crime, so to speak. Head down, I was too ashamed to even glance at the woman at the desk outside his door, even as Remy's footsteps followed me out, then again into the hallway as he'd called my name. But I didn't wait, and I didn't look back. I'm not ashamed to admit that I hustled, moving as fast as my spindly heels would allow, putting distance between me and that man, distance between me and my bad decisions, while also not moving so fast that it looked like I stole something.

I don't ever want to be that girl, the one who listens to her heart rather than her head. The girl who gives it up to her boss on his desk. And yet, not two hours ago, there I was, ready to give him anything he'd wanted.

Any way he'd wanted.

I'd managed to slip into the elevator before he could reach me, my heart beating frantically as I'd willed the doors to close. Then he was there quite suddenly, his long legs eating up the space between us, his expression piqued.

Okay, pissed.

He said my name, his delivery making it sound like a reprimand. I felt like my poor overworked heart was about to burst from overload because if he reached me, I wasn't at all sure what would transpire. Would the security cameras record him kissing or killing me? Or would it be the other way around?

He caught the doors with his hand as they began to close, a strange mixture of fear and elation taking over me. I'd pressed my back against the elevator walls, expecting him to step in.

'You didn't have to run.' His tone was even, despite his frown, but he didn't step any closer. I couldn't discern whether I was relieved or disappointed about that.

'That—that was wrong, Remy. What we did. I work for you now. My first day and I can't keep on my underwear?'

'You were still dressed. Mostly.' He smiled quite suddenly, though tried to conceal it by rubbing his thumb across an unfairly lush bottom lip. The way his eyes drank me in felt like a remembrance.

'That's not the point. Who was that anyway?' I threw out my arm in the rough direction of his office. My fingers were trembling.

'Someone who won't speak of this to anyone.'

'Good.' My gaze fell to my shoes, and the next words out of my mouth were the truth delivered without thought. Without grace. 'I need you to leave me alone.'

'You don't mean that.' The doors tried to close once more, but he held them back.

'I have to.' I couldn't look at him. 'Please let me go.'

His arm dropped, the doors reacting. The last thing I registered was his forbidding expression as they slid fully closed.

I'd escaped into the twilight and took refuge in a nearby café until Fee arrived. I'm so grateful she'd suggested I take her number this morning, or I don't know what I'd have done. She offered to come and get me, which I'll admit, was enough to make me tear up from sheer relief. I also feel like a total turd for lying to her, but she could do without being embroiled in this.

'What an arsehole,' she mutters, glowering out of the driver's window, and for a moment, I think she means the motorcyclist who'd just undertaken us instead of responding to my half-truths.

'Yep, asshole,' I agree. A sexy, maddening asshole who seems to have plans for me. Or maybe that's just wishful thinking.

'Next time,' she adds, 'be sure to tell him you need to leave. Some people are just so bloody inconsiderate.'

Inconsiderate isn't the way I would've described him back in March. He was certainly a considerate lover. Considerate and gifted. But now, I just don't know. He's got that whole downtown vibe about him. You know the one; I'm master of everything I touch, of all I survey.

But I don't think he brought me here to get me into bed. I mean, it's hardly like he fist-pumped the air when we passed in the hallway earlier. He looked more annoyed than delighted. And he didn't behave like a man desperate to get into my panties when I walked into his office. At least, not until the end of our heated exchange.

Something tells me he didn't bring me to Monaco to screw.

But did he bring me here to screw me over?

The sweet man I met in March? I say no.

The demanding business mogul from this afternoon? I really don't know.

13

REMY

Róisín Ryan. Rose Ryan.

The same person.

But more importantly, no relation to me.

Let me go back to the beginning. To that night. I'd initiated an investigation into Róisín for some time after the reading of my father's will. He'd left her a bequest, the kind sizeable enough to invite question. *To invite investigation.*

Who was this woman he left provision for? A bequest with strings, the knowledge of which is at my discretion until she comes into her inheritance at the age of thirty. It will leave her a wealthy woman, eventually, as well as involve her in Wolf affairs. It's only natural I jumped to conclusions; conclusions cemented when I discovered he'd also sent her money two years prior while he was still alive.

Gifting money was a little unorthodox for him. The women in his life, his mistresses, usually received much less liquid assets in exchange for fucking him. *Art and property. Sometimes investments but never cash.*

Everything about it felt off. To leave such a substantial amount to someone not family? Why? Who was she? A little investigation into Róisín Ryan revealed a girl who graduated from a no-name college and was waiting tables in a strip club.

There were only two ways my mind could go. She was either fucking him or was the result of his fucking. And back before I'd met her, I feared it was the latter. A long-lost sister could certainly complicate things for me and the company. The board had already suffered the shock of finding Emile's so-called playboy son installed at the helm. A drawn-out court case and subsequent power struggle could return us to a position of precariousness. Harming our investors' confidence so soon again could, quite simply, be disastrous.

But as she is not the daughter of Emile, she has no claim to that other than the provision made for her in his will. Her shares in the company, once she inherits them, won't be enough to harm us in any way. And as she is not the blood daughter of Emile, she's no sister to me. And for that, I am eternally grateful.

Which leaves the second hypothesis: she's someone he'd fucked.

After she'd sped out of my office, I'd spread the photographs out on my desk, along with the information gathered by a private investigator in the States, now even less convinced. Though capricious by nature, Emile had a definite type; early thirties, sophisticated, someone adept at the game, someone who knew not to make waves. A young girl from the wrong side of the tracks didn't seem like his MO. My opinion was only strengthened now that she was no longer just a name, a collection of images and intrusive facts. As Róisín, she was too young, too unpredictable, and too blonde, or so I thought at that point. As Rose, she was too good for him to have ever laid his hands on.

She isn't to inherit as the result of a casual weekend fuck.

And if I'm right, the question must be asked: then why is she?

———

'I still say she might've been a little holiday strange.' Rhett stares down at me, his face upside down as his tall form blocks out the light from above.

'Yes, because San Francisco is the kind of place Emile would've chosen for a vacation.' Despite being thirty minutes into our workout, I'm still pissed at the way he'd interrupted earlier. Angry and biding my time for a little retribution from the cock-blocking *imbécile*.

'So, he was in town, on business, and decided to treat himself.'

'It's a blessing I don't pay you to think,' I grunt, tightening my hands on the barbell above my chest.

'I'm just the idiot hired muscle now?'

'Delicacy has never been one of your strong points.'

'Don't pout, boss man. If you didn't want anyone to walk in, you should've locked the door.'

'Most people knock as a courtesy.'

'I'm not most people, though, am I? Besides, the door bitch wasn't at her desk, so I snuck in.'

'Maybe I should be paying Madame Bisset to protect me. And Paulette is my executive assistant, not a door bitch.'

'Assistant, bitch, dragon.' He makes a weighing motion with his hands. 'She could start her own company. Gargoyles R Us. But you'd have to be sure to tell her you don't want to be protected from girls with willing mouths.'

'That isn't what you walked in on.' I don't like where this conversation is going as I tighten my fingers, and with a grunt, I push the barbell above my chest, beginning the next set.

'Bastard.' Arms straight, my chest immediately stretching and burning from the effort, feeding the nature of the beast. The more it hurts, the more I want it.

'Touchy,' Rhett taunts in return. 'And also not true. I know who my father was.' I roll my gaze upwards to where he's spotting me with the addition of an annoying smirk. 'He was a right bastard, though. So you're not far wrong. Anyway, it's not the willing mouth that's a worry. It's her backstory.'

'And what exactly is her backstory?'

'You know what I think.'

'And you're wrong. Two years ago, she was working in the kind of hotel Emile wouldn't have subjected his luggage to, let alone his person.' It was a mid-range place, not exactly the kind that rents rooms by the hour, but the man was an elitist snob. 'Besides, she isn't—wasn't—at all to his taste.'

'It's all relative.'

'Meaning what, exactly?

'Sometimes, you crave fillet mignon, and other times, you fancy a cheap burger.'

'I suggest you refrain from telling me which you think Rose is.'

'Before you stick that barbell where the sun doesn't shine, you mean? Seriously though, I wouldn't have thought she was to your tastes, either. But you know what they say, the apple doesn't fall far from the tree. Stands to reason you both had the hots for the same type.'

'And I thought I was an equal opportunity lover.' I am not my father's son in that respect. Also, I have never paid a woman for the pleasure of her company, neither in cash or kind.

'And I thought you'd put those days behind. You know, since you took over the company.'

I suddenly want to wipe the smirk from his face. 'Meaning?' I grunt, lowering, then raising the bar again.

'Remy, mate. You know who I'm talking about. Come to think of it, she also happens to fit the other end of the spectrum of your old man's preferences. Blonde. Refined. Knows the difference between a Picasso and a pisshead.'

'You forgot gold-digging, demanding, and a bitch.' I'm not sure if my head or my biceps are most likely to explode as it strikes me that there is more than one way to pay for sex. Something I've somehow chosen to ignore. 'But we aren't talking about either of those women right now.'

'Even if my steak and burger analogy stands. Don't fucking glare at me—I'm not saying your girl is cheap.'

'Then what exactly are you saying?' My question is expelled through gritted teeth and a strained breath.

'Just that good girls don't work in strip clubs. Good girls don't have lips like hers.'

'Say another thing about her, and I'll rip off your balls and feed them to you.'

'It's what had you shitting bricks,' he insists. 'But tell me, was it the thought of losing half of your wealth to your long-lost sister, or the fact that you might've fucked said long-lost sister that had you looking the colour of oatmeal yesterday?'

'I'm not going to answer that,' I retort through another grunt.

Rise and repeat. Again and again until my muscles scream.

When I saw her yesterday, I'll admit I was terrified I'd had carnal knowledge of my sister, no matter how unwittingly. And now that I know I haven't, that knowledge is like a weight lifted from my very being. Only a degenerate would lust after their sister, unwittingly or not. And God knows, I've hungered for her. Many a night since March, I've woken from dreaming of her, my cock rock hard and pounding, the phantom wisps of her hair dragging across my chest.

And then she came to life, and in that hallway, my world fell away.

I thank God and all the saints that a lesson of high school biology had come back to me as I'd looked at her paperwork on my desk. Her application for medical care. Mention of her height, her weight, pre-existing conditions, *nil*, and there in one column in neat, black penmanship, her blood type.

AB+

I don't know about *be positive*, but my heart had suddenly jolted in my chest cavity. I saw my younger self in the biology lab at boarding school in Switzerland, jotting down blood type charts, learning about alleles.

Without even realising it, I found myself flipping over the sheet and plotting my father's blood type against hers. You can determine the chances of a child's blood type by examining those of the parents. And while you can't guarantee parentage by this method, you can, in some cases, eliminate it.

And Rose's blood type was one such case.

'I take that back. Emile would never have let anyone know what he was thinking.'

'You have no fucking idea what I'm thinking.'

'Don't I? You're, what's the word? *Énèrve*. Pissed off. You're also thinking about ripping my head off when you're finished here.' His hands hover under the bar as I lower it to the frame this time. 'And yesterday, you were shitting bricks. I thought you were going to hurl all over your shoes. But tell me again how she can't be your sister.'

Metal clunks against metal, and I twist on the bench, rising to sit.

'AB+ and O blood types can't lead to a child with AB+

blood.' My heart and head pounds, and though I owe Rhett no answer, I long to repeat the science and speak the truth. 'There has to be a commonality in the alleles. Her father can't be mine.' As I wipe the sweat from my face, I send another thanks to the heavens. 'I'll confirm it, of course. But these things take time.' Even though DNA will confirm what I know in my gut to be true.

'Had she fucked him, though? Before he died?'

'She's hardly likely to have done so afterwards.' Elbows on my knees, I drop my head between my shoulder blades.

'You know what I mean.'

'You really want this, don't you?' I turn my head to look at him. Really look at him.

'Fuck, yeah. A bit of humility could be the making of you.'

'I'm sure you'll learn to live with the disappointment because she doesn't know him. She never met him.'

'Or maybe she just doesn't want to admit to it, admit to selling herself to him. I'm not judging. Poor girl, a rich man, and a chance of escape. It's just the way the world works. You know it's true. *What though the Rose have prickles, yet 'tis pluck'd.*'

I stand from the bench and languidly stretch, before I twist from the waist, swiftly and violently planting my right fist into Everett's gut.

'You won't speak about her that way again.' *Shakespeare or not.* My hand on his left shoulder, my warning is a growl in his ear as he tries to catch his breath, not that it stops the *foutu connard* from wheezing out his retort. *Yes, stupid bastard.*

'Getting information out of you is like getting blood out of a fucking stone.' His smile is more grimace than smug. Regardless, I wouldn't chance punching him again. 'I shouldn't need to goad you into a grand fucking reveal. You could've just said you were into her.'

'Who says I am?'

'My mistake,' he says as he straightens, stretching the kinks out of his neck. 'You must've lost a contact lens this afternoon. Did you find it in her throat or her underwear?'

'*Casse-toi.*' *Piss off.*

'Such fine words from a man defending a lady's honour.' With a flutter of his lashes, he fans his face like a debutant.

'If you mention this to anyone . . .' I let the threat hang in the air.

'You'll what? Throw me off the top of Wolf Tower?' His eyes drop to where my hands are balled into fists by my sides. 'How long have I worked for you? No, how long have we been friends? You should've told me, Remy. If for no other reason than because your enemies become her enemies, too.'

'There was nothing to tell. Not until this afternoon.'

Even as the words leave my mouth, I recognise them as lies. I'm drawn to her. I have been since that first night. No matter what transpired before or even after, I know the true Rose. The woman who opened her heart to me, as well as her door. I know her beyond the feel of her under me. My recognition of her is soul deep. Rose with the soft skin and generous lips. She is made of the tears of those who both built and broke her somehow. The sum of her parts, brittle and battle worn.

I know this about her. And I'll know more.

'What about Ben?' Rhett's question pulls me back to the moment. 'You heard him—he saw her first. He's not interested in her as a bit of skirt. He knows there's something going on.'

'I'll find something to distract him.'

'Are you going to tell her about the money?'

'I will. When I'm ready.'

'And you say you're not like him,' he scoffs, shaking his head.

'Few sons are like their father,' I retort as his head comes up fast.

'Many are worse.'

'A few are better.' I keep my words mild.

'That's not how it goes. Not according to Homer.'

'Stick to the fat yellow man, Rhett. Leave the dead philosophers to someone else.'

'Fuck you,' he retorts, throwing his sweaty towel at me as we exchange places.

Few sons are like their father, I intone silently. *Few are better. Many are worse.*

With regard to the business, I'm well aware I'm no facsimile of my father. Despite being christened *the wolf cub*, since I took over the helm, I'm much worse than a pup. I am much worse than my father.

But with Rose, it remains to be seen if I'll treat her better or worse than my father has.

14

ROSE

'H-HELLO?' I pull myself upright against the upholstered headboard. My voice sounds like I've taken up smoking in my sleep and leased my mouth to a hamster colony. It can mean only one thing. I polished off a whole bottle of red last night.

Smooth, Rose. Real smooth. At least you didn't have an ex to call and abuse. Not one in the same time zone anyway.

'Miss Ryan?'

'Speaking.' I try not to rustle the bedlinens as I pull the phone away from my ear to have a look at the time. 6.25 a.m. Holy moly; my alarm hasn't even gone off! Urgh. Waking up still drunk is so much more fun than waking to a hangover. 'Can I help you?'

'This is Madame Bisset,' says a French accent and imperious tone. 'I am assistant to Monsieur Durrand.' Oh. The regal looking silver-haired keeper of his calendar I sorta-kinda met yesterday. Well, smiled at, more like. 'Monsieur has asked me to call to convey to you to pack up you sings.'

'My sings?'

'*Oui.* Your sings. *C'est quoi le mot pour bagages?*' she

murmurs to herself. 'Ah, luggage!' she adds in the vein of someone hitting jackpot.

'I-I have to pack up?' Something flutters painfully in my chest. I'm leaving? Because I let him grope me on the desk or because I didn't hang around to put out? Or was it because he was the almost-ex I called last night? The ridiculous thought is followed by the realisation that I don't have his number, let alone the right to call him an ex.

'Yes. You should be ready for . . .*à quelle heure?*' There follows the sound of a keyboard being tapped. 'Seven o'clock.'

'That's only thirty minutes from now. And where exactly am I going? Don't I have to sign paperwork or something first? And there's the matter of my ticket. I don't even know what time my flight is!' I push my hand through my hair, my mind running in a million different directions. I don't have anywhere to go. I don't have a job, and I barely have any money. I am so, so very screwed.

But am I screwed because we didn't screw or because we almost did?

'Flight?' she repeats, sounding just as confused. 'You are new to the company. It is too soon yet for a 'oliday.'

'So I'm not going anywhere?'

'Yes—this is what I am telling you! At seven o'clock, a car will pick you up and take you to your new apartment. The key is with concierge, the department you will be working from today. They will expect you to report to the desk later at . . . *le midi* . . . Ah, at noon.'

A new apartment? A new job. What the hell is going on?

'So, I'll be working at the concierge desk at the hotel? And where is my new apartment?'

'Not at *L'Hôtel*. You'll be working and living at the residence—at Wolf Tower.'

Three hours later and I'm at Wolf Tower and I've wandered around my new home approximately eleventy-billion times. I could walk around it eleventy-billion more times and I'd still have trouble believing I live here now.

I have three bedrooms—three! For one person. Unless I'm getting roommates, not that this is the kind of place that looks like it allows roommates or subletting or any of that kind of stuff. Almost every room has a view over the Mediterranean Sea. Even the master bath has a sea view!

From a front door opened by a digital key, the small entrance hall leads into a living area large enough to hold a game of tennis. A gourmet kitchen overlooks the dining room, lights like crystal flowers hang stylishly low over a long refectory-style table.

With seating for eight.

I don't even know that many people here!

The place is light and airy and furnished with such care, and everything is brand new, from the hotel-style linens on the king-sized beds to the artwork hanging on the walls, to the silverware filling the kitchen drawers, including a set of tiny three-pronged cake forks in the kitchen. Who the fork owns cake forks!

And best of all is the balcony that wraps around the space. It's not wide by any means, but it's big enough for a lounger or two. Sunbathing, here I come!

Or maybe not as I plant my butt on the corner of the sectional and place my face in my hands as I begin to cry. I hate that I do—hate that the passage of tears gives way to hiccupping sobs, but I can't seem to help it. I can't seem to stop. I feel so conflicted. This place that's to be my new home, and it's so gorgeously stylish, so tempting, so unlike any place I've ever lived. It's mine, but at what cost?

I feel like my eyelids have swollen to Grinch-heart proportions. I haven't cried like this since my mom died, and I really don't know if I'm crying because I feel wretched or because I feel a sense of relief. The last year has been tough, the years before I went travelling tougher still. And now this? I have a job that pays the kind of money people would kill for in a place very few people will ever experience living. But then there's also the man. The man I feel inexplicably drawn to, despite the fact that he isn't who he pretended to be—a lie is a lie, isn't it? I shouldn't feel this conflicted, but I do.

I liked the carefree tourist enough to take him to my bed.

The powerful businessman, I like him less.

But want him more.

What's with that?

And the way he looked at me, he seems to be suffering the same symptoms. As though he's drawn to me against his better judgment.

But to what ends?

What is this all about? What does he want me here for?

It's not just to get into my panties, I'm sure.

I sit straight suddenly, drying my eyes with the backs of my hands. This is not me. I don't wallow, and I don't feel sorry for myself. I'm a survivor. I do what needs to be done. Fancy job and apartment or not, it's up to me what I choose to do from now on.

Resolved, I roll up my damp sleeves and throw my suitcase onto the biggest damn bed I'll ever have the pleasure of sleeping in and begin to unpack my clothes. I don't know how long this ride is going to last, but I may as well enjoy the benefits.

I'm just arranging my toiletries on the marble bathroom

vanity when I hear my phone begin to ring with a FaceTime call. Making my way back into the bedroom—my bedroom!—I swipe up my cell from the bed.

'You're in trouble!' sings the Phillips collective as the screen fills with the eager faces of Amber and Byron's children.

'Auntie Rose, do they eat frog's legs in France?' asks Matty as he pulls a face of disgust. 'And do snails taste like snot? Auntie Rose? I can see right up your nose.'

I begin to chuckle but don't get a chance to answer his question as his sister, Edie, almost climbs over his head, eager to speak.

'My turn! My turn!' she sings.

'Oi, get off, Edie.'

I see nothing but the blur of the white ceiling as the pair fight over the iPad. A beat later, the screen is filled with a close up of Matty's face again.

'*Daaad!*' His mouth opens so wide that I can almost see his tonsils. 'Edie's being a brat again!'

'Anyone would think you were both kept in a cage,' Amber grumbles, her face appearing on the screen, albeit briefly.

'They should be kept in a cage,' gripes Byron, their dad from somewhere beyond as the iPad is passed to Edie.

'Am not a brat,' she retorts, her fair brows pulling in. 'I just have a joke for Auntie Rose. Can I tell it to you?' Her blonde curls bounce as her head nods eagerly.

'Sure, honey. I could use a laugh.'

'Why do French people eat snails?' she asks immediately.

'I've no idea.'

'Because they don't like fast food!' She barely takes a breath before asking, 'I don't like the taste of snots. Do you?'

The iPad changes hands yet again, Amber's unimpressed expression my next view.

'And now I know what the row of green pebbles on Edie's bedroom wall is.' She screws up her nose. 'Remember me?' Oh no. She's wearing her mom expression; pursed lips, eyebrows riding high. You know the one, *I love you, but I'm disappointed*. 'I'm the person you promised to call.'

'Sorry. Things have been hectic. I had jet lag, so the times between us were off, then I had to get my visa and stuff. Plus, I've moved to two separate apartments since I got here.' All true. All also excuses. Truthfully, I forgot I'd said I'd call once I got settled. And I'm not. Settled yet, that is. How can you feel settled or secure in the middle of a whirlwind?

'Good for you I'm a forgiving friend,' she answers, 'I'm extra specially forgiving after I googled Monsieur Baguette.'

'You did. What?'

'I spelled his name right, for a start. I have to tell you, if that man were a fruit, he'd be fineapple. Pick of the crop.'

'What does that make me?' calls Byron out.

'You're more like a coconut, babe.'

'Because I'm hairy, meaty, and milky?'

'Are you trying to traumatise the children?' she asks, turning her head.

'I'm more like a cumquat,' he adds. 'Want to know why?'

'No,' she replies in a bored tone before she begins to giggle as he appears on the screen behind to whisper something in her ear. 'Urgh, get off, you Neanderthal!'

The pair tussle for a moment, Byron's gaze wicked as he tortures her with kisses and tickles and stubble rubs, and she's still holding the baby who continues to sleep undisturbed. Meanwhile, I experience a pang of longing. I want this. The relationship. A man who'll love me and tease me and exasperate me in equal turns. A man who'll take a chance. Who'll turn his life upside down for me all because he wants to love me like I'll love him.

'You are such an ass.' Her complaining yet smiling face turns back to me, her expression morphing from playful to concern almost immediately. 'What's wrong? Why are you crying?'

Urgh, not again! I bite my lip and shrug in response, fighting the welling tears.

Jesus H. Enough with the waterworks.

The phone muffles for a minute. Her baby daughter whimpers as she's passed to her father's arms. An instruction is issued for all and sundry to eat their carrots under threat of no dessert. A door closes. Footsteps echo along a wooden floor, and then she's there again, my best friend's face filling the screen of my phone.

'Tell me.' It's not a demand but a permission to let go.

Despite feeling bad about interrupting her family's meal, I do.

'Speaking of Monsieur Baguette.'

'The man you nearly killed with your dildo.'

Despite my blubbering, I chuckle at her description. 'That sounds so much worse than what actually happened, even if he did end up with a concussion. You make it sound like I badly used him.'

'Okay, the man you whacked with your dildo, not ravaged via the butt. The French hottie,' she prompts, cutting off my protestations. 'I get it. You're hearing nothing but sexy French accents, and you realised you suddenly miss his ass—though not to badly use. With said dildo.'

God, this woman makes me smile. 'Not even close.'

'Spit it out. Or am I supposed to guess?'

'He's my new boss.'

'No way.' Eyes wide, her answer is awe-filled.

'Well, my boss's boss's boss. Several times removed, probably.' He owns my ass? My work ass, maybe.

'How? Why? Oh, my God. Did he think the coffee machine wasn't enough?' Amber doesn't bother to hide her disbelief. And why would she? I'm having difficulty believing it myself. 'Is this why you're upset? He's got you there under false pretences?'

'No, these are just pre-period tears.' Hormones and overwhelm, I guess. 'As for this job, Monaco is full of women who look like models. Why would he go to such huge amounts of trouble just to get me out here?'

'Yeah, I see your point,' she agrees. 'Especially as you have a face like a dog butt.'

'I'm not saying I'm ugly,' I protest. 'I'm just not in the supermodel league.'

'So true. All that luxurious hair, that face, and those boobs. You definitely don't look like a cross between Sophia Loren and Gigi Hadid or anything. Add in your heinous personality, and I'm surprised Monsieur Baguette, MB now that you're very particular friends, didn't pay to send you to outer Mongolia.'

Everyone needs a friend like Amber. A friend who'll talk you up and talk you out of the biggest funk, even when you know you look like you *ate* Gigi Hadid.

'Thank you, my cheer squad of one. But the fact is, I could be the embodiment of Gigi or a young Sophia, and I'm not sure that would've been enough to induce him to bring me here. Not the way he looked at me when I bumped into him yesterday.'

If our first meeting had been in the office, I might've thought differently. But the way he looked at me in that hallway . . . eesh.

'First of all, this happened yesterday, and you didn't call? And what do you mean *the way he looked at you*?'

'He didn't seem pleased to see me. In fact, he looked mightily pissed.'

'Okay. I can buy that. He's probably still having nightmares about purple dildos.' She doesn't bother to hide how hilarious she finds this, even going as far as making herself go cross-eyed as she mimes hitting herself on the head with an invisible dong.

'And that's not even a little bit funny.' I pinch my forefinger and thumb to show exactly how unfunny I find her suggestion, even as I smile at her ridiculousness. 'I didn't cause his concussion.'

'I'm sure you didn't help it, babe. But *anyway*, it sounds like your new job isn't an elaborate ploy. So that's good, right?'

'I don't know. Something is off about the whole thing.' I don't mean my panties yesterday. *Much.*

'Maybe he was embarrassed to see you? You know, after the whole smash and dash.'

'The smash and . . .?' Got it. 'Never mind.'

'Yep, you saved his life, and he repaid you by ejaculating before evacuating,' she continues unnecessarily. 'The old hit and quit.' She throws her thumb over her shoulder.

'I wouldn't have put it quite like that.'

'Even if it made you smile?'

'I'm not smiling,' I protest, doing exactly just that. 'And I'm not sure he was embarrassed,' I add as our exchange in the hallway flashes in my mind. The dark suit jacket that hugged his broad shoulders, the leather belt around his trim waist. His stupid pocket square and the fact that I'd noticed his hair is a little shorter than it was back in March. Alice's reaction as she'd stood next to me, her words breathy and her cheeks coloured pink. He didn't look like a man who felt any kind of remorse for his actions; for leaving me that night. Neither did he look like his nefarious plan had come together seeing me there. 'But he was definitely annoyed.'

'So maybe seeing you tweaked his conscience? Made him feel bad. But I agree, if MB looked angry, rather than whipping out his *saucisson,* at first sight, the chances of you being sexed and hired by the same man have to be slim. Hired on purpose, I mean.'

'Maybe.' My response sounds unconvinced. But really, what do I know? Except that baguette is a better descriptive; *saucisson*, or sausage, really is selling him a little short, pardon the pun.

'It sounds as though you're communicating with your clothes on this time.' Amber's eyebrows wiggle suggestively on the screen, but I'm not in the right frame of mind to be cheered.

'Communication is not an issue. It turns out, the man speaks perfect English.'

'Oh. Bad Monsieur Baguette. Did you ask him why?'

'Not yet. I'm still smarting over here. I feel like a total idiot!'

'Come on, Rose. No one could take you for an idiot. Don't pull that face. The man sent you flowers—expensive gifts! That doesn't sound like a man who thought you were just a piece of ass. He sounds like a man who maybe felt a little bad about not being one hundred percent truthful with you.'

I frown back, unconvinced, also realising how mad this makes me right now. He completely bamboozled me. Why? To what end?

'I'm reserving my judgment until I ask him.' Probably on the twelfth of never.

'See, every cloud has a silver lining. Now at least you'll get the opportunity to ask him why. A chance to speak with him, right?' she adds optimistically.

'I liked him better when I didn't think he could speak English.'

'Of course you did. Because there was no future in it. The truth is, the fact that he wasn't there when you woke back in March makes no difference. It just saved you from throwing him out.'

'So?'

'So, now here he is again, in your face. And I think you've been crying because the rich man kissed you.'

'I didn't say that.' My protest is immediate. Maybe a little too immediate. But how could she know? It's my eyes that are a little swollen, not my lips!

'The rich *hot* man kissed you, and you liked it. I sense fireworks. Pheromones flying, fire—panties flying through the air.'

'Well, there was fire,' I admit, glancing briefly to the window and the brilliant views.

'I knew it!'

'But he also acted pretty weird. He was hot and cold.'

'And then he was just hot.' On screen, Amber fans her face before becoming serious once again. 'He was probably conflicted, which is understandable. He didn't expect to see you again, yet there you were. The woman he's been thinking of. For *months*.'

'Yeah, but he asked me some weird questions about my blood type and stuff, and then he yammered on about our parents.' God knows why.

'Rich people are allowed to be weird. Only it's called eccentricity when you have a big bank book. Who knows, maybe he's thinking about you as a long term prospect, and that's why he got a little personal?'

'I might not know what it was, but I know it wasn't that. Just don't go buying a hat yet. I almost feel like he was expecting someone else.' My voice sounds small as though admitting this aloud might somehow make it real. 'But then he kissed me.'

'If he was expecting someone else, he wouldn't have kissed you. Was it just a kiss,' she asks a little more eagerly, 'or is there more to this tale?'

'It almost went further. But we were interrupted.' My stomach twists uncomfortably. All I need now is news of this to get out, then I'll be that slut—that friendless floozy that fucks the boss to get ahead! 'And now he's moved me out of the company accommodation into this palace!' My gaze roams the room again, and once again, it takes my breath away.

'Are we talking the kind of palace with towers and dungeons, and not the good kind?'

'The good kind?'

'You know, the kinky kind.'

'No! There isn't any kind of dungeon here—good, bad, or kinky.'

'So it's just a palace. Like, somewhere nice?'

I feel the tension leak from my body when I realise what she's trying to convey. Is what I'm complaining about really so bad?

'Yes, very nice. And very fancy. An apartment in the swankiest building in Monaco, the kind with million-dollar views.' I throw out my arm as though inviting her to look, which is a little stupid, considering she's not physically here.

'Has he suggested he's expecting repayment? Like, not rent. Payment in kind?'

'No.'

'Has he made any kind of demands?'

'He's bossy as fuck, but no.'

'But if it's upsetting you, then you're worried he might?'

'No. At least, I don't think so. I haven't even spoken to him about it. It was more like a decree from his assistant. But Amber, I kissed my boss—at work!'

'Yeah. Me, too.' She shrugs, her expression unrepentant.

'This is different. I got caught.'

'Same. We were busted by his mom, and there's no beating that in the embarrassment stakes. I'm going to suggest something to you, but you have to promise not to blow up or even interrupt, all right?'

'You think I should leave,' I reply immediately. 'I knew you'd think that was the right thing to do.'

'No interrupting, Rose.'

'Fine.' On my screen, Amber's lips purse. 'I said fine!'

'I think you're frightened. I think the reality of him is scaring you. He's not a backpacker or a tourist or a deadbeat—'

'I do not date deadbeats!' I protest. I learned to spot these before I was twelve years old. Learned to spot them. Learned to avoid 'em.

'You're right. You date pricks. Men who are emotionally stunted, which suits you just fine because you don't want them to stick around. And now that you've found someone who might be a little more serious. Someone who is financially stable—'

'Financially stable? The man is as rich as Croesus!'

'And your point is?'

'Rich men are dangerous, and I don't like them,' I reply mulishly.

'Byron is rich. You like him.'

'I like Byron for *you*.' I don't mention that if she wasn't such a great friend, I'd probably hate her. Her life looks so great. 'I can't see me becoming a rich man's plaything.'

Amber bursts into laughter, and though she seems

amused, I begin to worry I've upset her. I don't have to worry for long.

'Well, I tell you, it's not exactly what it's cracked up to be. Diamonds can be pretty hard to sleep in. So lumpy.' She wiggles her shoulders as though recalling that exact discomfort. 'And many an evening, I've thought I should've married a man who came home stinking of sweat and beer rather than success.'

'Hardy-har,' I reply, unimpressed. 'The difference is, you're his wife. Byron has always been respectful of you.'

'You weren't there when he got handsy in the laundry room back when I was the nanny to his poor motherless twins. And you weren't there when he was looking at me like he was trying to make my clothes disintegrate. Of course, he respects me. Always has, always will, if he knows what's good for him. Rich or poor, there's nothing wrong with a man who wants to treat you right.'

'Treat me right so long as there isn't a desk around.'

'There's more space on a desk than a washing machine.' From the other side of the world, she sends me an eloquent look. 'What is it exactly that you've got against men with money?'

'Honestly? I don't know. Maybe the imbalance of power?'

Even as I say this, something tweaks at my memory, my mother's caution almost curling around my ear. *All men will take you for a ride if you let them, sweetie, but the fall is harder when you're dropped by a rich man.* A speculative opinion, I guess. Mom never had any luck with men. I don't remember many of them holding down a job, let alone them having a little cash in their pocket. *You can't rely on anyone but yourself.* Now, that was the truth.

'Honey, an imbalance of power sounds like the difference

between dating a rich guy and a rich asshole. Different animals, different experiences.'

'Then I don't know what it is.' My tone is borderline defensive.

'I do. You're scared.'

'You haven't seen the size of this apartment. I feel like I'm being groomed!'

'Really?' she deadpans. 'Has he asked you to call him daddy? To sit on his knee?'

'No.'

'Don't knock it until you've tried it.' Her words sound serious, her expression something else entirely. 'Look, if you're unhappy, you can always go home. Or maybe you can take my advice.' Her gaze is almost dancing.

'I think I'm frightened to ask.'

'I was going to say wait to see how things go, but it occurs to me that I have something better to say.'

'Now, I'm officially terrified.'

'I think you should pull up your big girl panties and ride that man like the stallion he is.'

'How do you know he's a stallion?'

'Because you kissed and told about the baguette.' She pulls an unremorseful duckface. 'But use condoms,' she adds as somewhere in the distance, a baby begins to cry.

'A baby named Beryl?'

She nods. 'We still can't agree on a name. But hark,' she adds, cupping her ear with her hand, 'from yonder window, the fruit of my loins is playing my song.'

'You are such a dag,' I say, using an Aussi-ism I know she'll appreciate.

'I feel like a dag, but that's sleep deprivation for you. Unless you want to look like this,'—she points at her face —'bulk buy prophylactics.'

146

After we say our goodbyes, I pull myself together for my first afternoon of work and basically get over myself. So it's not an ideal situation, but it could be worse. Much worse. My new boss isn't demanding I be his personal sex slave. Plus, he's super easy on the eyes. *Maybe I'll make him my sex slave instead.*

I snort at the ridiculous thought; I can't see the man taking orders from anyone. Not even if I whip out my trusty purple dildo and hit him upside the head. Which, by the way, is still in my case. Don't judge—it was a gift! It has sentimental value as well as being lightly used. In fact, it's been used only once. On a sexy French tourist, who later turned out to be a man in a suit so sharp, it'd probably eviscerate his enemies on sight.

First a snort, and now I'm smiling to myself? I must be going soft in the head. Which is probably why I keep thinking about him. He was cute when he didn't speak my language, but out here in his element, the man is dynamite.

As in, dangerous to handle.

I can't help but think of what that very proper exterior conceals.

And I'm not just thinking about his ink. I'm also thinking about his mad sexy-times skills.

I drop my low heels on the bed, swiping my lightweight jacket from the back of the elegant chair, the tactile fabric just calling for the brush of my fingers as I pass. I slide the doors to the balcony open just to breathe in a little of the scant breeze. The sun is shining, and the air up here sweet. All is right with the world, or as right as it can be for a woman in my position.

Stepping back into the bedroom, I shake out my jacket and slip it on. This fine Tuesday sees me swapping my braid for loose hair and my Mango linen shirtdress for a pair of black pencil pants and a sleeveless cream shell. And the jacket, of course.

I slip on my shoes and study my reflection in the mirror.

It's just a job, I intone, pulling on my lapels. Whatever today brings, it has to be better than waiting tables at the Pussy Cat any day of the week. It's not like I'm doing anything critical. I'm not brokering peace in Yemen, for goodness' sake.

'I can do this.' My reflection looks back at me, unconvinced. 'I have a super-hot boss that I've had sex with. Things could be worse.'

15

REMY

'Why don't I just bend over for you? Right here over this desk. We'll just get it over and done with here and now, and you can just shove it hard up my ass.'

Stifling a sigh, I allow my eyes to wander around the room. The panelled walls. The elaborate drapes. The mid-century decanter sitting on the credenza near the door. The glass that has already been used today. My gaze slides to my watch. *Barely ten o'clock.*

'Because, let me tell you, by my age, I ought to know the difference between being on the receiving end of an enema and being royally fucked over.'

'Monsieur Hayes, please.' Pelletier, the newest member of my legal team, uses a conciliatory tone, unused to the brash address of a man on the edge. 'There really is no need for such vulgarity.'

'Fuck off and fuck you,' the American retorts. 'This is my office, and I'll say what goes in here. Anyway, I'm not talking to you. I'm talking to him.'

I bring my bored gaze back to the men sitting at the head of the table. The grandson being groomed to take over looks like a Californian surfer. The other points an arthritic finger my way. 'There's no way you're getting your hands on this company. I'll raze it to the damn ground before it comes to that.'

'*Mr* Hayes, I understand your frustration. You requested finance, finance that has been denied to you, and now your operation is in dire straits.'

'Because you're in cahoots with the bank!'

To a certain degree, this is true, not that I'll admit it. 'I am the solution, not the problem.'

'You're a parasite—'

'Grandfather, stop.' His hand grasps the older man's arm, his eyes burning with contempt as his gaze swings my way. *Contempt and revenge.*

'You should listen to Hayes, the younger.'

'And you should kiss my ass. You chop up companies and feast on their bones before swallowing them down. And for what? Just to say Remy Durrand owns the South of France?'

Why stop at just the South of France?

'You don't have the funds to pay for the shipment of steel,' I continue, examining an invisible tear in one of my fingernails. 'Your workforce is about to put down their tools and walk away because they know, as well as you know yourself, as well as the industry knows, you will struggle to pay them this coming Friday. The media will circle like sharks. Your share price will plummet and along with it, your good name.' A good name with a dirty past. A past that is entwined with my own, as it turns out.

'We only need a couple of million to see us through 'till the end of the month and your friends at the bank have nullified our line of credit. You're strangling us, Durrand. I hope your father is turning in his grave.'

'I hope so, too.'

'We were friends, him and me!'

'I very much doubt that.'

Carson Hayes is proof that God has a sense of humour. Wizened and bent, the man is riddled with cancer and has been for years. Yet my father, as fit and as sleek as a racehorse, was struck down by a common illness in his prime.

I'm sure God is the only one laughing.

'We had an agreement.' The old man's voice shakes with ill-suppressed anger. 'We shook on it.'

'I also shook my dick last time I took a piss.' Next to me, Pelletier stiffens. 'It doesn't mean I'm making friends. And then there is the matter of the documents I have in my possession.'

'What documents?' His grandson's gaze volleys back and forth between us, though neither of us pay him attention in return.

'Photographs. Unsavoury photographs, along with a video, I'm told. One from my father's vaults. It looks like it was recorded sometime in the late eighties. Maybe the nineties?' My attention swings to his grandson. 'It's hard to tell from hairstyles alone. There wasn't a lot to go on in terms of fashion, if you catch my meaning.'

'What's this about, Grandfather? Blackmail? What does he have on you?'

'That snake. He gave me that film, and I destroyed it, but not before I paid him well for it!' His grey eyebrows pull down as his grandson's hand retracts slowly from his arm.

'Tell me what he's talking about,' he demands. But the older man doesn't respond. He has eyes for no one. No one but me as I sit on the opposite end of the long table with my legal counsel, who has no idea what I'm talking about but the good sense to pretend otherwise.

'Those things happened a long time ago.'

'Did they happen before Monaco created laws? No, I didn't think so. Pelletier, the paperwork.' I'm already pushing back my chair as I reach in to the inside pocket of my jacket for my phone. As I leave the room, I spare no time for the thought of the poor girl in the video, splayed out and comatose under a younger version of the old man. Not because I'm heartless but because it happened a long time ago.

Your wealth was built on her suffering. I acknowledge the thought as something beyond my control, pushing it away clinically.

Tell the steel company they can call off their dogs, I type out. **Hayes Construction belongs to The Wolf Group now.**

D'accord, Everett types back. **Congratulations on eviscerating another of the competition**. His sarcasm rings loud and clear. He liked the idea of blackmail much less than myself and would've preferred to hand the evidence of the young woman's abuse over to the authorities. But men like Carson Hayes rarely face justice, especially thirty years after the fact. And while I would welcome any attempt to expose my father as the conniver he was as opposed to the paragon of success and philanthropy he sought to portray, blackening the Durrand name would not serve my purpose. Ruining the Hayes company, absorbing it into my own, does.

There's something poetic about it.

And the girl? Hénri, my security for today, holds open the elevator door and I step in.

Correctly, Rhett intuits the topic has moved on. **Already situated on the twelfth floor, according to the dragon.**

Good.

You must feel like the dogs bollocks manipulating two people before lunchtime, eh?

What can I say? Today already feels like a good day. I'm just about to slip my phone back into my pocket when my gaze happens on Carson's grandson and his haughty disdain. Once upon a time, I might've been like him. Entitled. Wet behind the ears. Possibly feral. The difference is, I knew what my father was capable of.

Carson Hayes' grandson, I type out as the elevator doors close. **Get me all you can on him**. Just in case.

16

ROSE

THINGS COULD *NOT* BE WORSE.

Tuesday of the following week and I've yet to set eyes on Remy—seven whole days and not one peep from him! What kind of fuckery is this? I mean, is he trying to make me expire from sheer suspense? If that's his endgame, then all I can say is, *well played, sir. Well fucking played.*

Or maybe he isn't playing games at all. Maybe he's placed me in a box marked *strictly business.* Maybe employing me was just a mistake, and now that I'm here, he no longer thinks about me. Maybe he feels that, in giving me a job, his debt is complete, so he doesn't need to concern himself with me anymore. And if that's the case, why am I thinking about him? *Gah!*

Oh, my God. I've been ghosted!

This is why I don't do relationships—the lesson I was supposed to learn from watching my mother! Relationships are a balancing act of power, and in thinking about him, obsessing over him, I've handed control over to him. Not that he knows it. Because he's not here! Gah!

'*Ça va*, Rose.'

'Oh, hey, Charles.' I glance up at my co-worker and force a smile. *Ride that man like the stallion he is?* I don't know about that, but I'd sure like to hogtie and whip him. Show Remy exactly how much I've missed him. *Missed him so much, I'm not crazy.*

'Why are you making the face?' I look up once more to find Charles pouting. And that's not Charles with a *Ch* but Charles with a *Sh,* or *Shaaarles* as he corrected me on my first day.

'This is my thinking face.' My *thinking I'd like to strangle Remy* face.

'*Non*. It is your angry face.'

'How are you?' I ask, moving on to Charles's favourite topic. Him.

'I would like to say *bien*,' he says, dropping his Louis Vuitton messenger bag to the desk and almost knocking over the framed photograph of Loulou, his precious pet spaniel. 'But living with the man you love, 'oo no longer loves you, it makes my 'art 'urt.'

It takes me a moment to discern his response, though the way he dramatically clasps his hands over his 'art, I mean, heart, helps.

'Rough weekend, huh?' We both worked Tuesday through Saturday last week, and while Sunday and Monday aren't technically a weekend, it was *my* weekend. Two mornings of late wake-ups and *café au lait* and croissants on the balcony while staring at the gloriously blue sea. And two days of mooching around Monaco, doing touristy things. I visited the port at *La Condamine*, people watched from a café at the marina before visiting an old church, the name of which I forget.

'*Ouais*,' he affirms with a nod. 'Philipe, he spurned my advances again. I want the makeup sex, but he said no.' He pouts like a child denied dessert, his oddly cherubic features marred by a frown.

'That sucks,' I reply, taking my empty cup for a refill. While French coffee, not to be confused with the much less delicious French roast we get back home, has become my unofficial addiction, I stick to jasmine tea while at work. My mind is already working like a squirrel on speed, no thanks to being ghosted by the man who brought me here.

'*Non*—there was no sucking! This is the problem!'

'Yeah, because you dumped him on Friday, right?' It's like *The Bold and the Beautiful* around here.

I slip out of my jacket, which was a mistake for this time of the year. Draping it over the back of my chair, I then ease my index finger between my throat and my company-issued silk scarf to loosen it a little.

'Because I see him making eyes at the lifeguard. Like this!' He blinks rapidly, his perfectly curled silky lashes like the wings of an angry bee. '*Fils de pute,*' he spits.

I open my mouth to ask him if it's Philipe or the lifeguard who is the son of a whore in his estimation, finding myself asking instead, 'Are you wearing fake lashes right now?'

'Pfft!' He gives a perfectly Gallic shrug as if to say *what do you think*? I think yes, yes he is. 'I just curl them and wear a little mascara sometimes.'

'They must rub the lenses of your glasses.' And annoy the heck out of him.

'I do not want to talk about this. I am *énervé*—how you say, pissed! I 'ave my revenge on 'im.'

'Oh, dear.' With an indulgent shake of my head, I splash some hot water over my teabag. 'Can I expect a visit from the police today?'

'I will not kill him! I still love him!'

'Okay, so you don't need help disposing of the body. Good to know. Hey, do you think the prison in Monaco is fancy?'

'I do not know, and I do not wish to find out.'

'*O-kay.*' Someone has their panties in a wad today. 'If you didn't kill him, what did you do?'

'Philipe 'as no work today, and I begin late, so I made an offer to make *le bacon pour le petit déjeuner*—bacon for breakfast, yes?' I nod. I both understand and agree with bacon. Bacon beats Cheerios any day for breakfast. '*Bon.* I wipe a little grease on the power *bouton* of his Xbox.'

As he describes his not so dastardly deed, he's carefully tidying his hair using his reflection in the glass cabinets.

'Oh, good one. I'm sure he'll be mildly irritated when he goes to switch it on and finds he has bacon grease on his finger. *Zut alors!*' I exclaim, examining my hand in faux horror.

'No one says this, Rose,' he chides. 'Not in France and not in Monaco.'

'And in America, we're more likely to take a baseball bat to someone's car as revenge. It's a much more effective way to express yourself.'

'I think he will be totally pissed when he is playing *le Xbox* and Loulou keeps sniffing the button and turning it off.' I snigger as Charles pauses, pulling out his chair, then in a change of direction, asks, 'What does *le livre* have in store for today?'

'So far, the total of today's requests could pay off the debt of a third world country.'

'This is *le livre*.' Charles shrugs as though to say "whatcha gonna do?" Only with a little more French flair.

Le livre, or the book, often referred to in the most hallowed of terms, is actually an online diary pertaining to the residents of Wolf Tower's needs. Each apartment comes with a tablet linked to the concierge department computer system, and if they're away from home when a need arises, well, they can just use the handy-dandy app they can download onto their phone. Anything they need help with, be it a maintenance issue or an item they need sourcing or a reservation they'd like made, they can just pick up their handy tablet and pass the job to someone else.

Pass it off to me, in fact. Or Charles. Or whoever else is on shift. And the concierge desk aims to meet those needs 24/7. And I don't mean their very ordinary needs, like bread and milk and eggs. I'm almost certain the people who live in Wolf Tower think the food they eat just magically appears. *Those who look like they know what food is, I mean.* But those items, the most basic of necessities, are usually ordered via the apartment's housekeeping tablet by their personal housekeeping staff.

The concierge desk deals with a whole other level of needs. We're told that the most precious commodity available is time, and apparently, this is even more so for the uber-wealthy. And here at the concierge desk, our sole aim is to protect the time of our residents.

We help them get back precious time without the aid of a time machine.

If you ask me, the whole concept is hokum because most people who live here don't appear to work. Or if they do, they don't seem to work more than a couple of hours each day. I know this because I spend most of *my time* on the phone with them or answering their hundreds of demanding and whiny emails. As I see it, my job is to help the rich to spend their vast amounts of money.

Need a last-minute anniversary gift for the wife? Or an *I'm sorry I can't screw you this weekend because it's my anniversary* sweetener to your bit on the side? Then you just pick up the phone to contact me, give me a ballpark figure, and I put in a call to *Zegg et Cerlati* or maybe Cartier. Or I'll take myself for a walk along the *Place du Casino* and do a little window shopping in the high-end stores, and because I'm wearing my natty Wolf Group scarf, me and non-couture clothing won't be sneered at in my Zara dress or my Gap pants. I might not be shopping for myself unless it's an apple from Condamine Market, but I'm still shopping. It's also a little time out of the office where I get to wander through streets, soaking up the sunshine as I people watch the portly Midwesterners rubbernecking at supercars to James Bond lookalikes who step from them. It's kind of like a tourist to trillionaire tour.

But my job isn't all shopping for the tycoon who needs time like he needs air.

Need a last-minute private jet to take you to Paris for the weekend?

Then I'm your (wo)man.

Desperate for front row seats to La bohéme in Milan instead?

How about a helicopter ride there?

Your wish is my command.

Or maybe it's a table at the Ivy when you're in London next week?

Consider it booked.

Or else I might consider joining the unemployment lines. At least, according to Olga, head of the concierge department.

Speaking of which.

'Charles, you already see to the Petrov's dog?' The woman herself strides into the office in her skyscraper heels. And what a delight she is. She never smiles, probably because her lips have so much filler, she can barely close her duck bill, I mean, mouth. Which I suppose is efficient because she never stops complaining—usually about me. I don't know why, but I am *not* her favourite person, yet I have no idea what I've done to deserve her ire. Although, come to think of it, yesterday she was slightly less caustic after lunch. She must've had champagne with her food. Or maybe edibles.

'I *engagé* a new dog walker.' Charles doesn't move his attention from his computer screen. 'A *male* dogwalker,' he adds meaningfully. 'Per'aps Alexi can keep on the trousers this time.' The latter he adds in an undertone.

'It is not for the likes of you to comment on how our clients spend their time.' Someone ought to explain to Olga that *Ice Blonde* is just a hair colour, not a personality type. I'll bet she was really pretty once, before the intervention of Botox, fillers, and silicone. Other than the flotation devices disguised as breasts, she's tall and willowy and looks like she'd snap in a strong wind. But her appearance belies a caustic tongue and a will of steel.

'Wasn't she paid to walk the dog, not run around the kitchen island fighting the owner off?' I ask, referring to the highpoint of last Friday afternoon. A distressed dogwalker and the millionaire Russian pervert—excuse me— businessman who both descended to the concierge desk, one in a dreadful panic, the other bullish. 'I think he's lucky she didn't call the police, oligarch or not.'

'That would not happen at the Tower. At Wolf Tower—'

'Discretion is everything.' Neither me nor Charles is enthusiastic in our recital of the concierge dogma.

'*Bon*.' With a decisive nod, she turns to her own office leaving her minions to run the show. 'I forgot.' She pauses at the doorway without bothering to fully turn, her hand on the frame. '*L'hôtel* requires assistance in the catering department this afternoon.' Her smile is a touch malicious as she adds, 'I have told them that you will help, Rose. I believe you have experience waiting tables.'

Anger burns like acid in my veins immediately. She's been digging through my resumé and googling my previous places of work? But then I remember I'd listed waitressing as one of my duties while working at Riposo Estates in Australia, Byron and Amber's place, along with a very vague description of my duties at my last job.

If she thinks she can embarrass me, the woman needs to think again.

'Waitressing? Sure, I have experience. I can work a function like nobody's business, from casual drinks to silver service good enough for a queen. Hell, I can even do it in heels and booty shorts,' I retort with a slap to my ass.

'*Cherié,*' Charles sniggers as Olga's office door slams, 'you have, how you say, pissed on her fireworks.'

'I tell you, Charlie, I thought about adding in a slut drop, but I was worried I'd rip my pants.' I twist at the waist, trying to get a better look at my butt. 'They're a little tight. I'd better lay off the croissants.'

'Pfft! You eat like a bird.'

'Yeah, Big Bird.'

'And I don't like Charlie,' he says, pronouncing it, surprise surprise, as *Sharlie,* which sounds kind of silly.

'Hey, but does this happen often? Being called to the hotel, I mean?'

'*Non.* But waiting tables might be better than dealing with Alexi when he finds out his new dog walker is an amateur boxer.'

17

ROSE

I'm NOT until I'm making my way across to the hotel, and my stomach starts to fizz that I consider I might somehow cross paths with Remy. And if I do, how would I greet him? How would he greet me? Would he ignore me after what passed between us last week? Could I be civil to him knowing just a few days ago he had his hand in my panties? My nipple in his mouth? No, probably not. Not when my head tells me I need to stay away from him. *Against the better judgment of my body.*

I'm directed to the kitchens, though they aren't in need of a waitress and have no idea what I'm talking about, even after finding someone who speaks my language perfectly. Calls are made as I wait, and I'm eventually directed back to Wolf Tower to report to the kitchen there. *Who knew there was a commercial kitchen there, too.*

When I finally find where I'm going, I'm chastised by the chef for being late, I think. One of the few perks of not being proficient in the language. I'm then pointed to a room service cart covered with a white starched cloth. As he returns his attentions to his minions, I take a peek under the cloth to find a prettily printed china tea service, dishes covered with silver tops, and on the bottom shelf, a hot water urn along with a bottle of champagne in a silver bucket.

I guess it must be for a meeting somewhere.

'*Vite!*' I drop the cloth quickly, startled by the chef's bellow from the other side of the gleaming kitchen. 'You are late. Take the envelope. Use the service *élévateur.*'

With a nod, I pick up the printed directions and wheel the trolley out, *tout de suit.* What is it about men who cook? The short-order guy at the Pussy Cat was also an asshole. If they don't like their jobs, they should find something else to do.

I use the smart key in the envelope to access the lift, pressing the button for the forty-seventh floor. I use the key again at the door to the room, though it's not quite the room I was expecting. It's not a meeting room. At least, not the kind with a smartboard, or a table and chairs, but rather an apartment. More to the point, the penthouse—it's so large and so stylish it makes my new place look like a broom closet!

'Hello?' My voice echoes in the cavernous space as I linger in the entryway. 'Hello?' I pinch my lips together to resist adding 'housekeeping!'

Who the hell gives a stranger a key to their home? I wonder, glancing once again at the printed instructions, then again at the open door.

Seems I'm in the right place.

'Hell.' The wheels of the trolley squeak as I wheel it across the onyx marble floor, glancing around as I wonder where I'm supposed to set this all out. I start by unloading it onto the twelve-seat dining setting, relocating it to a low coffee table between two modern sofas as the covers come off, and I realise this is an afternoon tea for two, complete with two dainty silver cake stands, which I have to assemble before filling with goodies. Tiny fancy iced cakes and finger sandwiches with the crusts cut off. A chest with a selection of teas; Darjeeling, oolong, lapsang souchong, and a selection of herbal and fruity teas. And champagne.

Once satisfied with the position of the china, silverware, and napery, I wonder what comes next. I mean, I guess I'm supposed to wait. Maybe serve? After standing around for a few minutes, I decide to investigate. Not investigate investigate; I don't want to be caught rifling through bedroom drawers or anything. But I take a wander around the living space. I gaze at the modern art on the walls, stormy, and sort of masculine. Run my hand over the velvet sofas and leaf through the coffee table books; mostly architectural and art. Then I take a peek at the kitchens, yes, plural; one Calacatta marble and high-end units, the other commercial grade, and probably for the use of the chef. There's a silk-covered cocktail bar that would look more at home in a fancy hotel, a small library with a pair of very slouchy yet very uncomfortable looking leather chairs. And, no surprise, staff quarters. Two rooms, you know. Just in case you need more than one person to pick up after you.

How the other half do live with their mezzanine floors, which, if I stand on my tiptoes, I can just about see the floor of. Beyond the wall of glass lies a resort-style pool area with loungers and a table setting or two, plus an inviting infinity-edge pool, providing views to the horizon, I'll bet.

Back in the living area, I poke one of the dainty sandwiches, wondering how long before the bread starts to curl. Dipping forward, I inhale the delicious aromas; the almond marzipan coating the petit fours, the zesty lemon iced cakes, and the glaze of chocolate on the tiny cream-filled eclairs. My stomach rumbles, and I'm tempted to help myself to a piece, my hand hovering over a succulent looking sugar dipped strawberry.

'Fruit, as if,' I snigger, popping a pistachio-encrusted chocolate square into my mouth. The burst of flavours is glorious. Butter and chocolate and sugar and nuts and just the best thing I've tasted in ages! 'Oh, my stars,' I mumble, swallowing it down. Of course, like Noah's Ark, these treats come in twos. Which means I have to hide the evidence of having already eaten one . . . by eating another one.

Who says crime doesn't pay? Not me.

'Ventre affamé n'a point d'oreilles.'

You know that saying, I almost jumped out of my skin? That's pretty much what I do, my body springing immediately straight, my hand retracting to my hammering heart, but it's not just the fact that I've been busted helping myself, it's more who I've been busted by.

'Jesus, Remy! You scared the tar out of me.' I press my hand to my chest, the sensation beneath my palm like runaway hooves. Only, I'm not sure it's entirely shock. It's almost as though my body remembers his.

'Désolée.' I'm sorry. 'I thought you heard me come in.'

That voice.

Rich, warm. Seductive.

That accent.

Just kill me now. Preferably by orgasm overload. Or pistachio-coated chocolate.

That tone.

So not désolée at all.

And don't get me started on the view; his suit, impeccably cut and the colour of midnight sins. The contrast of his brilliant white shirt, open at the neck to expose the caramel of his skin. His hair is stylishly tidy, his cheeks smooth. He looks almost edible in whatever he chooses to wear, but something tells me he's made a little more of an effort today.

I tamp back the hope the effort could be for me.

'But perhaps you were too busy enjoying your cookie to hear. *Ventre affamé n'a pas d'oreilles.* A hungry stomach has no ears.'

I can literally feel the blood rushing to my cheeks—and my poor maligned ears.

'Okay, so you caught me.' I fold my arms across my chest. Or under the girls, at any rate. I swear I don't do it to get his attention, but it goes there anyway. When his attention rises, I'm wearing an expression I like to call, *buddy, my face is up here.*

'Rose,' he says, sliding off his suit jacket and dropping it carelessly to a chest that must surely be a Japanese antique. 'With you, a man is spoilt for choice where to look.'

I note the lack of apology or discomfit as his gaze roams over me, even as I kind of enjoy it, too. 'Yeah, well, my boobs are like this fine china here. They only come out for special occasions.'

'I don't know about china, but they're certainly fine.'

'What are you doing here, Remy?' If this sounds like an accusation, I'm sure it's because it's meant to. I mean, where the hell has he been for the past week? Not thinking about me, that's for sure.

'What am I doing here? I happen to be looking at my lunch.' I'm pretty sure my heart skips an excited, horny little beat. Could that be me? 'My late lunch.' I find myself glancing down at the afternoon tea, my sense of exhilaration dipping along with my gaze. He arrived after me. If I'd been invited, wouldn't he have said "my lunch date".

Tea for two and guess who gets to play waitress?

'I guess this must be your place then, huh?' I try to keep

my voice light as I glance around the room. No way I want to look at him, especially not as I experience the unexpected prick of tears. What did I expect? He's not interested in me. At least, for no more than a cursory boob browse.

'In a way,' he agrees, sliding his hands into his pocket and sauntering farther into the room. 'What do you think of it?'

'I think it looks expensive.' But I'm no longer looking at the penthouse. 'The views are great.'

His gaze is soft yet challenging as he comes to a stop in front of me. 'Personally, I find the view entrancing.' He reaches out, tugging lightly on the scarf around my neck, his gaze dipping to my mouth and lingering there. Everything south of my navel clenches, the way he's looking at me seeming to make perfect sense everywhere but my head.

'What are we doing here, Remy?'

'Talking,' he answers simply.

'After a week of nothing?'

A shadow of something crosses his expression, but it's gone just as quick. 'You asked me to stay away from you last Tuesday. I promised myself I would.'

'Oh.' I swallow over the sudden lump in my throat. A whole week and I've only myself to blame? I've been cursing myself for thinking I was a rich man's plaything when, in fact, he'd behaved honourably, abiding by my wishes.

But if he'd felt the same about me, wouldn't he have—

'At least, I tried. I did keep away until Wednesday, at least.'

'What?' I find myself shaking my head a little. This doesn't make sense. But in the midst of such confusion, why when he's near does this all seem possible?

'I stayed away from you until Wednesday.'

'But I didn't hear from you then—I haven't seen you all week.'

I know, I know. It's all my fault.

'I requested a delivery over the concierge booking system. When it arrived without you, I thought perhaps you were still angry.'

'I didn't see your request.' It certainly didn't come to me, because if it had, I'd already be familiar with the butterfly wings beating in my chest, encouraging that overworked muscle to take flight.

'I tried again on Thursday. Then Friday morning. Once more on Friday afternoon. Three times on Saturday. I've acquired a lot of things I don't require, yet I'm very sorry to say that my needs have gone unfulfilled.'

'Maybe you should lodge a complaint.' I chew on the inside of my lip, though I'm sure it barely conceals my relief or my giddiness to see him smiling back at me.

'I gather someone in your office was eager to take care of me herself.'

'Tall, blonde, and Polish?' I ask with no little chagrin. 'Lips like a duckbill? But you know she works for you, right?' *So you can kick her ass anytime you like. Figuratively, at least.*

He inclines his head, seeming to weigh up his words. 'I felt the path of least resistance would be one you'd prefer. You value your privacy. It's what made you run from me last week, what made you tell me to stay away. You should know that Everett is the head of my security team and very discreet.'

'Thank you,' I answer quietly. 'That helps.' Helps to confirm I'm not the topic of gossip, though I kind of worked that out for myself.

'And while I apologise for putting you in that position, I won't say sorry for wanting you.' *Oh my.* I try to will my pulse to slow and not react to his words. Words that seem to hint at very big things. 'I almost knocked on your door more than once.' His voice is low and husky, his fingers suddenly warm against my face. 'But I didn't want you to think I'd moved you to the building for convenience.'

'Why did you? What am I doing here?'

'Indulging a selfish man. That's why I thought we should keep our first meeting professional.'

'Is that what this is?' I glance behind me to where I've laid out the items from the trolley.

'What does it look like to you?'

'Borderline diabetes?'

His laughter is deep and rich, like a vintage Bordeaux. *And just as intoxicating.* 'It's afternoon tea,' he says, a ghost of a smile lurking still.

'Isn't that more a British pastime?'

'*Non.* It's a very civilised pastime, and the French are nothing if not civilised.'

'And I suppose the table and hot water aren't there to make sure you behave well?' Despite my sparring response, something inside me turns instantly to goo. When was the last time someone did something like this for me? Well, maybe other than the heap of gifts he sent, which suddenly seem to make more sense. This is what Grandma Aida would've called courting, though I'm not sure she'd say the same for what happened in his office last week.

Would that have been a little heavy petting back in her day?

'I think you secretly like me when I don't behave well.'

'Do you?' My arched tone matches my brow.

'At the very least, I hoped I could persuade you to stay.' He seems to temper his expression; from provoking to penitent. I'm not so easily fooled, though I certainly appreciate the effort. 'If all else failed, I plan to get you drunk and take advantage of you.' I find myself laughing, feeling all kinds of giddy inside as Remy's expression firms. 'You told me to stay away. And I did. But it was never going to last very long. I want to get to know you, Rose. I want you in whatever capacity you'll have me.'

The butterflies turn into tiny bursts of fireworks, though I'm able to keep my tone cool and my voice even. 'Even if that capacity is just as my boss?'

They're just words, I tell myself. Words from him to me and right back at him. I don't have to read too much into it, do I?

'You know that's not going to work for either of us. Not while there are desks in almost every room of this building.'

'Are there? In every room?'

'If not, there will be soon. A desk in every room to remind you of what you do to me. To remind you of what I want to do to you.'

'What happened to whatever capacity I want?'

'I'll abide by any rules you instigate. Outwardly, at least.'

Oh, my Lord, could the guy's smile be any more enticing than it is? Any more inciting? And who was it again who said the man was cunning? Alice from HR, I think, when she called him the little wolf. She might be right, not that it matters, because you know the heart eye emoji? That is currently me. I'm bursting with joy and relief—relief that this hasn't all been one-sided. That his abandonment of me is all in my head. I don't pretend to understand exactly what's going on here, and I know this goes against everything I've ever done to protect myself. Told myself. But I can't help it—I don't want to help it.

I just know I want to give in. Give in to it. Give in to him.

'Well,' I begin, unable to move my eyes from his. 'I suppose we should . . . drink tea.'

'Or you could let me kiss you.' A dare glitters in his gaze.

'I don't remember you asking last time.'

'That was before you told me to stay away.' Even as he

answers, he's cradling my face in his hands, slanting his head. Parting my lips with his tongue.

I find myself sighing. It's as though every fibre of my being has been tight, or tangled like a woollen ball and now? Now I'm unfurling in his arms, undone by this man, by his tender lips and the subtle strokes of his tongue.

As he pulls back, his eyes are darkly dilated, more midnight sky than lush green. 'This mouth was made for kissing,' he murmurs, his thumb skimming my tingling bottom lip. 'I've thought about this mouth for so many nights.' He presses a kiss to the corner, his lips grazing mine. At the tauntingly sweet brush of his tongue, I push up onto my toes, aching and desperate for more. 'So greedy.' The heat of his words whisper across my lips as I reach for him, but then he grabs my wrists, shackling them in his fingers.

'No one likes a tease.' My words sound hoarse as he lowers my arms to my sides.

'You know that's not true.' His words, like his kisses, are soft but insistent. Petal-soft brushes, a lick, a graze and he continues to tease. 'You like me ... very ... very ... much.'

Oh, my God. What is he doing to me? I mean, apart from shackling my hands while he tortures me. Is it the suit that makes him like this, or is this how he really operates? You know, when he's not pretending to be a helplessly cute tourist. I've never experienced this kind of need. Never felt the slow burn of a glancing, dancing tease. It's quite literally making me dizzy. Dizzy with need.

'Please, Remy, kiss me. Kiss me properly.'

The voice is mine, but it doesn't sound like me as, with each press of his lips, I become a little more needy, a little more desperate, until his tongue brushes my own, and I'm suddenly moaning into his mouth. In that instant, everything changes as he pulls me closer, his mouth suddenly urgent and greedy. It's all so familiar yet also new as he begins to manoeuvre me backwards across the room. It isn't just the press of his freshly shaven cheek that's different; it's in the subtleties of his touch. Or maybe that should be the lack of subtleties as his hands slip to the hem of my top, pulling it up and over my head.

It drops to the floor, my white flag of surrender, his gaze devouring my skin.

'You like me so much you'd even beg.'

'That wasn't begging. That was asking. Nicely.'

'Very nicely.' His hands slide around my hips, the span of those long fingers making me feel tiny for a change.

'Where are we going?'

'Somewhere more forgiving than the desk.' Though playful, there's an edge to his words.

'I didn't mind the desk,' I rasp as we reach the bottom of the sweeping industrial-style staircase

'We'll add it to the list. My desk, the piano, the cinema room. Out by the pool under the moon. I want it all. I want you everywhere.' My attention moves to the wall of windows. Does he mean everywhere or *everywhere*? 'What do you think?' he almost taunts, reading my expression. 'Don't worry.' His lips finding the sensitive spot behind my ear. 'I'll be good. For a little while, at least.'

Oh, my God. Why does that excite me? And which is it . . . that he'll be good for now, or that he won't be eventually? All I know is I feel hot, literally, and figuratively as I reach for the edge of the scarf at my neck.

'Leave it. For now.'

'Because then no one looking in can say they saw me truly naked?'

'You're forty-seven floors up. No one is going to see you come. No one but me.' There's both promise and command in the husky timbre of his voice, one that explodes inside like a dozen tiny fireworks. My hands in his, he drapes them around his neck before he brings our bodies together, wrapping his arm around my waist. I've never felt so delicate as he lifts me quite suddenly, whispering words of adoration as he begins to climb the stairs. The man is barely affected by his exertions as we reach the top stairs, immediately entering casual living space, suffused by the afternoon light. The soft furnishings are modern and masculine, the air cool.

'The view from here is heavenly.' From the direction of his gaze, he's not talking about the brilliant blue of the Mediterranean but rather my breasts, currently balanced under his chin in a pretty cream lace bra.

I don't have time to register much more as Remy carries me through a nearby open door.

His bedroom.

My feet touch the cool floor in the shadowy room, dust motes dancing idly in a gap in the drapery, the silvery voiles otherwise providing a twilight feel. A huge bed dominates one wall, the linens stark white against the blue-black walls behind as a dark velvet bench hems it. Nightstands of black stand sentry either side of the bed, a large gothic-looking mirror leaning in one corner. A pair of wingback chairs occupy another, a matching table between stacked with leather-bound books. Wood and velvet, silk and steel; every item in the room seems to have been chosen to complement a darkly sensual look.

'You don't have a TV,' I murmur as he lowers my feet to the Persian-looking rug, turning ostensibly to take it all in. In truth, a spike of nervousness takes over.

'This bedroom is for only two things.' Reaching out, he takes my hand.

'Sleeping and ... ?'

'Fucking you.' There's something about that word in his accent, which seems to magnify it somehow, the fluttering inside turning to a swoop as he cups my face to kiss me again.

'Yeah, sure. I bet if that bed could tell tales—'

'It would have none to tell. Not before today. You don't believe me?'

'I—' I don't know what to say. I've never had a man respond to me as he does. Never had a man *look* at me as he does. I've always thought only the naïve take what lovers say at face value, especially during sex, but something inside me tells me what he's saying is true.

About this bed, anyway.

'This is just all so unreal.' The way we've come together, the way he makes me feel.

'Perhaps if you need a little more convincing.'

Lust instantly blooms deep inside as he lifts my hand, pressing it over his cock. The lightweight wool of his pants moulds to him instantly, the rigid outline of him visible.

'You're so hard.'

'I seem to have been in this state since you left me last Tuesday.' His voice is a touch strained as he rocks into my hand,

'Poor Remy's baguette. Would you like me to kiss it better?'

'Baguette?' His eyes almost sparkle with mirth. 'If you mean my cock, then my answer is an emphatic yes, though I don't remember you being quite so coy our first time. Or would that technically be the first five times?'

'What I said back in March doesn't count.' I dip my gaze, hoping the weight of my hair will contain the smile I can't quite restrain.

'That can't be true, not when you begged so prettily. When

you looked at my cock as though you might die without tasting it.'

'I might die from embarrassment right now.'

'Rose.' My name from his lips is like a curl of smoke. 'I've never been so hard as I am when I'm next to you. Never feel too embarrassed to tell me what you need. Now, let us give this bed some tales to tell.'

18

REMY

'*J'AI ENVIE DE TOI,*' I whisper against her mouth, not able to stop myself from kissing her but needing somehow to express what she's doing to me.

'You're so sexy when you speak French.'

'Only when I speak French?' I tease, though, in truth, I hadn't realised I'd switched languages.

'*Especially* when you speak French. You could recite the phone book and get me hot.'

'Are you fetishizing my accent?' I growl, caging her with my body. 'Because go ahead. I like it.'

'You're crazy.'

'Crazy hard for you. I want you—*j'ai envie de toi*—I want so badly that I ache to be inside you. I am desperate to fuck you.' French is all well and good, and it might roll off the tongue, but there's nothing quite like the use of *fuck* to get your point across.

'I take it back. A phone book won't do.' She sighs as my teeth graze the sensitive lobe of her ear, the challenge in her stance melting. 'How come bad words sound so much sexier said by you?'

176

'Maybe it's the man, not the words.'

'Oh, it's definitely the man.' Her response is pure encouragement, an invitation to reveal.

'A man who has thought of these. Imagined these.' My voice is hoarse, and my accent thick as I cup her full breasts, my thumbs gliding back and forth over the sensitive peaks. She sighs as I lower my head, teasing her over the lace, rendering her lacy bra almost transparent. 'A man who wants to fuck these.'

'Even mildly pornographic sounds better from your mouth.'

'There's nothing mild about my plans for you.' I continue to torture and tease until she's pressing herself against me, whimpering for more. 'We're going to play a little game called make Rose desperate for Remy's baguette.' I'm surprised I can keep a straight face, yet at the same time, I'm endeared by her ridiculousness.

'Okay, you win. Give it to me.'

I find myself chuckling. 'Oh, I will. Over and over again until your legs are shaking, and the neighbours know my name.'

'But you don't have any neighbours.'

'When I'm finished with you, *your* neighbours will know my name. No more confusion this time. No talk of baguettes, no whispered words you can't understand. I'll keep to English.'

'Killjoy,' she whispers as she begins to pluck at my belt.

'Except,' I bring my mouth to her ear and whisper huskily, 'for the words I whisper between your legs.'

'Promises, promises.' Her words are a sultry whisper, her gaze burning bright.

'I promise not to stop until I've made you come a dozen times.'

Her smile is pressed against my cheek before she uses her teeth, part playful, part serious. She peppers my jaw with teasing kisses, my abs flexing and bunching under her questing fingertips . Together, we pull my half-unbuttoned shirt over my head.

'Take off your pants.' My voice is husky, my need immediate.

She does as I demand, barely stepping from the pool of them when I spin her around, gathering her hair in my fist. It takes her a beat to notice the mirror in front of her as, her head turned over her shoulder, she fights to reach my mouth.

'Look at how beautiful you are.' She follows the direction of my gaze, my larger body framing her lush form, her hard pebbles through the transparent lace of her bra. She is Venus. Juno. Made of the kind of hills and valleys and curves that would make an artist weep. Her eyes dark and her lush lips inviting, Rose is a prize I don't deserve. But I'll have her anyway.

'I can see how wet you are.' I tighten my grip on her hair, her body yielding. 'I can almost taste your arousal.'

'Remy, please.' More moan than words, her body gives at the graze of my teeth against her shoulder as I devour her satin skin. I want to inhale her—consume her whole. What is it about this woman that makes me so reckless? Makes me forget all the trouble she could bring to my door.

Makes me long for something more.

'Please what, *ma Rose*. Do you want me to taste you?' I flick the clasp of her bra, trailing it down her arms until it drops to the floor. *Dieu,* the sight of her before me, her breasts so full and round and spilling from my hands. 'What would you do for me in return? Would you get on your knees? Would you touch yourself?'

'Yes, anything.'

I pull her against me, letting her feel the hard outline of my cock through the fabric of my pants as those eyes of melted honey find mine in the mirror, the truth of her longing shining there. I'd tried to tell myself that she wouldn't be the same woman as she was in March. That a one-night stand brings its own kind of desperate reveal. But that isn't so. She's even more open now, her body arching, her nipples hard. I can't wait to taste them, to tongue them, to feel them harden in my mouth as she writhes under me. But for now . . .

'Oh!' Her breath hitches as I press her forward, and she catches herself against the heavy mirror, her palms spread wide. My body mourns the loss of hers, but the sight of her makes up for the loss. The slope of her shoulders, the flare of her hips, and those delicious indents at the base of her back. Her hair is wild and her body bare but for the tiny scrap of her underwear and the last vestiges of her uniform tied around her neck.

She is *irrésistible*.

'Oh, God.' This is more a sound of appreciation than a plea for clemency as I slip my hand under the elastic of her underwear and cup her pussy. Her body responds instantly, writhing against me—against my cock and my hand— begging for relief.

'You know what the French language doesn't have?' I part her sweet flesh, swiping a finger through her wetness to gather it against the part of her that throbs. 'It doesn't have enough words for this.'

'Remy, please.'

'This piece of heaven. This little bit of paradise.' My words are a rasp of appreciation as I begin to love her clit; to pet and circle and tease, to paint the throbbing bud with her own arousal. Her breath hits the air in a series of tight gasps, her eyes rolling closed as her body begins to undulate, riding my hand. 'This sweet, sweet pussy.' My fingers still inside her, I twist the scrap of lace at her hip until it snaps.

Her eyes fly open, her movements fuller, her breath coming faster as I torture her a little more until she's crying out and coming against my hand, her cries heightening as tiny spasms wrack her body as she tries to escape my hand.

'Please, no,' she pants. 'Remy, please, I can't.' She drops her head, the curtain of her hair shielding her face, her body sagging with relief as I pull my fingers from her. I gather her hair over her shoulder, pressing a kiss to her cheek. Her shoulder. The top of her spine.

'*Je veux te goûter.*' At my rasping words, her eyes flare. 'I want to taste you . . . just so there can be no confusion.'

I drop to my heels, dragging the remains of her underwear with me before burying my head between her legs, making this piece of paradise my very own.

One swipe of my tongue, and she cries out. Two and she's pushing up onto her toes, the tension in her body. My third swipe is a teasing caress to her inner thigh that makes her mewl a protest.

'I can't,' she protests, even as she begins canting her hips, the threads of her building orgasm tied so tightly to the other, her mind and body at war.

'Yes, you can. There can be no such thing as too much pleasure.'

'There can be if it kills you,' she whimpers. But then she complains no more.

The sounds of our joint pleasure begin to fill the darkened room; wet sucking, slick fingers fucking, my whispers of encouragement and growls of pleasure and those heady cries of hers that drive me fucking wild.

She undulates, chasing my touch as my hand slips away as I stand. The mirror was for her benefit—for her to see herself as I see her—but I find I can't get close enough for satisfaction. I can't feel enough, taste enough, see enough of her right now.

Her gaze is darkly dilated, her heavy lids widening as I feed those glistening fingers into her mouth. But she makes no protest, instead lapping and sucking the digits with a filthy kind of reverence that makes my cock ache.

I spin her to face me, pressing my lips against hers. The taste of her arousal from her own mouth is a turn-on like nothing else. She's like a drug, an obsession, and I'm afraid I'll never have enough. With the realisation, the moment turns fierce, my desperation to own and possess her growing as I push my tongue into her mouth. My cock grows harder at the way she accepts it. Sucks on it. Entwines it with her own. The way she moans as I find her clit, slippery and swollen, and her head falls back along with her moan.

I press her nakedness against the cool mirror, her gaze falling over my tattoos, her fingers teasing the trail of hair that dips into my open pants.

'Your tongue is diabolical and your whispers divine.' Her husky words echo under my lips as I kiss her again, working lips down her neck before using my teeth to pull her scarf loose.

'What about my cock?' I ask, unravelling the silk from her neck and wrapping it around my fist.

She tilts her head, mischief making her eyes glisten. 'I don't know if I remember. Maybe you should remind me—'

I cut off her words with a slow, sensual kiss, grinding my hips against her nakedness as I press my hands to the mirror on either side of her head.

'Is it coming back to you yet?'

'I think I need to take a quick peek. Just to be sure.' Her hands reach for my pants when I cover them with my own.

'Be sure of what, *ma Rose*?'

'Be sure it's as pretty as I remember.'

'You can't call my cock pretty, not without there being consequences.' This woman. Just her. I don't care what follows. I care for nothing right now but having her.

'Oh, no,' she purrs. 'However can I make it up to you?'

Before I can say another word, she drops to her knees, lifting me free from the confines of my underwear. She lowers her gaze demurely, her fingers warm on my scalding skin. Her nails are painted pink, and her hands small and dainty. I can't help but be struck by the contrast between her softness and my rigid cock, the veins bulging ruddily.

I gather the mass of dark waves to better see, hissing out a breath as the soft brush of her hair draws my abs tight. My body bowing forward as she places a tender kiss to my crown, my knees almost going out from under me as she then inhales me almost to the back of her throat.

'*Fuck . . .*'

'You're so hot and hard,' she whispers, her eyes almost coy as they flick up to me. But coy is a ruse, coy is a deception, as her tongue flicks out, tonguing my head, my slit, licking my aching length, her attentions blowing my mind.

'*Ta langue est diabolique.*' I use her earlier words against her, *your tongue is diabolical*, the delivery a rush of air. It's a praise that seems to please her, judging by the way she begins to work me faster. Her hand is firm at the root of my cock as she twists and jacks, her mouth alternating between tight and messy until my mind is blank of all thoughts but one.

'*Suce-moi,*' I moan, my words hoarse, my eyes glued to the delicious slide of her lips. My pulse pounds, and my thighs tremble as she moans the most encouraging sounds, the vibrations like a drug hitting my veins.

'*Tu vas me faire jouir. You're going to make me come.*'

My balls draw tight; I'm close to coming, and though the room is cool, my skin feels as though it's been pierced by a million hot pins, the sensation of fire expanding under my skin. I crave this release, but I don't give in. Not at the sight of her naked and on her knees. Not as her gaze meets mine full of heat and unspoken promises. Not as her languid gaze grows dark, her mouth full of me. Because I need more.

'*Viens ici.* Come here.' It takes every grain of my restraint to encourage her to leave me with those few remaining brain cells. I pull her up, pull her mouth from me as she tightens her lips, releasing me with a smacking kiss.

I waste no time pressing her back against the bed as, between us, we work off the rest of my clothing. Her hands reach for my shoulders as I press myself between her legs.

'I want to feel you, skin to skin,' I whisper, pressing kisses to the silken column of her throat as my fingers find her still plump and swollen. 'I want to feel you pulsing around me.'

'Yes. Let's do it,' she whispers, her hips tilting in invitation. 'Let's have babies. Let's have dozens of them.'

I halt, my brain lagging behind my willing body. Before I've even processed her response, she begins to shake under me.

'God, your face,' she laughs. 'You looked like you were mentally reciting a pros and cons list.'

'You . . .' I narrow my eyes, unable to complete the rest of that sentence without spoiling everything. *You are exceptional. I don't care who you are, and I don't care the lies I'll have to tell to keep you here.*

'Are joking!' she brings her hands to her face, finishing for me. 'And I'm on the pill. I don't sleep around.' *Do you?* Her enquiry goes unspoken, but I hear it anyway.

'The last woman I slept with was you.'

And then there are no more words as I kiss her again, her

hand reaching between us to feed me inside. The sensation is sublime, her soft slickness cradling me. I grit my teeth against the sudden desire to give in, to let her pull me under, my eyes rolling closed. As I fight the moment, I almost miss her reaction. Which would've been a shame worth crying over as she inhales a sharp breath, her words falling in a rush as she adjusts to my thickness.

'I forgot how big you are.'

'You're about to get a reminder.' I almost smirk, reining it in at the last minute for a modest smile. 'Feel free to tell me how big my cock is anytime.'

As she giggles. *Oh, mon Dieu*, the sensation.

'I've been dreaming of this since our first time.' Unable to resist, I rotate my hips, my pelvis brushing her slickly swollen clit. As I pull back almost to the tip, she makes the most wonderful sound, her pussy clenching around my retreat, her hands tightening on my shoulders as though she fears I might remove myself completely.

As if that is even possible.

'*Mon Dieu*,' I growl. 'You are perfect.' My hand skates down her body and behind her knee, her body opening for me like a hothouse flower.

'Oh, Remy, that . . . that feels so good.'

At her tone, my brain all but shuts down. I'm almost certain my eyes roll back in my head as her hot walls squeeze me again, a throbbing sensory memory of our first night. The night where it all began. I might have released her from my arms. I might've climbed out of her bed. I might then have turned my face from her, but she never once left my head.

My body undulates against hers, and she is the most beautiful thing I have ever seen as she writhes against me, taking her relief. I slide out and push back in, rotate my hips, then repeat the process until she's whimpering. I begin to drive inside her again and again until her whimpers turn to cries, her fingers beginning to score the skin of my back in a kind of torturous encouragement. Unable to get close enough, I cup her backside in my hands as I whisper a liturgy of filth in her ear. I feel the moment when it arrives, the moment her world comes undone, her pussy bleeding me of all I am worth. And, my God, that isn't very much as everything narrows, my movements frantic as I try to fuck my madness and possession into her. I want to be deep inside her, own her. Leave my mark. I want to keep fucking her until all that remains are our empty husks. The intensity builds with the collision of skin, growing and expanding until there is nothing but this—this moment.

This joining in all its head emptying, muscle twisting glory.

This exquisite and yet torturous release.

19

ROSE

The following morning—the morning following the afternoon spent in Remy's arms, christening several surfaces including the piano (lid down after my butt played a few discordant cords) his pristine and tidy desk, the shockingly cold kitchen worktop, along with a little fooling around out by the moonlit pool—I feel the most content I can ever remember being in quite some time. I mean, it's not like I'm one of those people who live for misery, the kind who looks on life as a glass half empty. But for the first time, I feel like my glass is overflowing.

The morning sun shining through the drapes gives Remy's bedroom a silvery, almost ethereal feel as I slip from his enormous bed and pad over to the adjoining bathroom to brush my teeth, once again grabbing Remy's discarded shirt to cover my nakedness. I'd more or less made the garment my own late yesterday, though as I press my nose into the collar, I realise with a tiny burst of pleasure that it still smells like him. *Rich and sensual, like bergamot, spice and the heady scent of his skin.* It doesn't, however, look quite so pristine, stained, and crumpled as it is in my reflection. My hair also looks like an opossum has nested in it overnight and I am definitely going to make use of my company scarf for the coming week. But those aren't the things that catch me off guard because, as I close the bathroom door behind me, I realise I'm smiling.

Smiling!

Before seven a.m.

On a workday!

And ducking my smile into Remy's shirt only makes me smile harder because it just smells so heavenly.

I make my way to the bathroom, avoiding the crushed cookies and strawberry stems discarded from our midnight feast. An empty bottle of champagne lies on its side, a small sticky puddle forming under it from where it'd been knocked over, not during the throes of passion, but when he'd begun to tickle me in retaliation for something snarky I'd said. I find myself blushing at the memory of how, as I'd laid back against the pillows to catch my breath, he'd reached for his glass, splashing the cool liquid between my breasts. I'd gasped in shock, everything inside me drawing tight as Remy bent forward, his tongue following the trail of the liquid . . . until he wasn't following it anymore. Even now, just thinking of it, I almost melt into a needy puddle.

I take care of business in a bathroom fit for a five-star hotel. Marble and chrome, dark cabinetry. The tub is matt black and big enough for a family, the double shower unencumbered by such trivialities as glass. It's the kind of bathroom that has never once been offended by the sight of a greying washed-out towel, let alone run out of toilet tissue. I wash my face, then spread a little paste on Remy's toothbrush, figuring I've had more intimate possessions of his in my mouth over the past eighteen hours. My own toothbrush isn't too far away—just a few floors below—but I can't wait that long. I give my hair a quick finger brush before deciding it's too painful and giving up. Then I give my reflection a silent pep talk.

I resolve to take this experience for what it is; to stay in the moment and let the future take care of itself. I'm in Monaco, in a hot man's apartment—a hot man who has the hots for me. So. Much. Hot!

Because for the first time in a long time, I have no prickling urge to creep out before my gentleman caller (*ahem*) awakes. Though I suppose I'm the "caller" in this scenario. A caller who isn't ready to leave, let alone run far, far away.

As I rinse, my mind slips to the day before and Remy's description of how he'd tried to reach me, along with his sensitivity in the task—the way he'd considered how it might look to my new colleagues, and my reluctance to become the topic of any kind of office gossip. Colour me a little moved and impressed. Seriously, I find myself touched by his care and thoughtfulness. I realise I'm content, that my psyche isn't preparing for any kind of internal freak-out. Our differences in station, income, or background don't seem to matter right now. I mean, I'm not about to choose flowers for my bouquet, but I feel content in enjoying what this is, for however long it might last.

It's enough for now.

Or so I tell myself.

In the mirror, my cheeks appear flushed. *My cheeks aren't the only place blood has pooled to.* But I have to work today, so I don't have time to indulge myself. I also don't have time to indulge myself in the real thing either, and hope Remy is still asleep. Yeah, okay, that's what I should be hoping for because I really do have to make it back to my apartment to get changed.

As I open the door, I hear his voice before my eyes feast on him lounged across the bed. One hand mindlessly traverses the prominent ladder of his abdominals as the other holds his phone to his ear. His smile is almost infectious as he turns to me.

'Who are you calling?' He holds up his index finger, beginning to speak again, this time in English.

'Ah, yes. Bonjour. Am I speaking to Olga?'

My heart plummets, despite the worst rendition of an American accent I've ever heard. 'What are you doing?' I'm not sure if it's my question or the frantic manner it's delivered in that he finds amusing, though it's not so hard to tell that he appreciates the sight of me wearing his shirt if the way his eyes keep dipping to the hem proves anything.

'Ah, yes. Hello. This is Rose's uncle—Rose's uncle Fred!' he adds, clearly pleased with his character's name while also turning kind of British in his diction. 'I'm afraid she'll be coming in a little late today. I arrived in town last night to surprise her—an agreeable surprise, I should add. And well, let's just say following our reunion she's has some internal issues overnight.'

'Remy!' I hiss. No mean feat, considering I'm also smiling and also trying to steal the phone from his hand unsuccessfully as he holds me at bay with one hand. One *tickling* hand.

'What kind of issues, you ask?' *And he's back to the terrible American accent again.* 'Well, ma'am, I don't like to say. Really? Oh, I see. Well, between you and me, she said it feels like her internal organs have been rearranged.'

'Remy!' I protest again without volume. I mean, he isn't lying, but that isn't the reason I drop dramatically to the bed. 'Kill me now! Being fired isn't enough to escape this embarrassment.'

His gaze cuts my way. One eloquent eyebrow raised, his way of reminding me he's the boss, I suppose. Oh well, no need to worry about being fired, just dying from mortification, I guess.

'I'll be sure to tell her that, though it does seem a little unfair. In fact, I think I might need to mention your thoughts to the folks at the top. Come to think of it, I met one of your top guys last night. What was his name again? Let me see. Jimmy something, I think. Jimmy? Timmy? I'm getting there—there's no need to take that tone with me. Ah, Remy! Remy Durrand,' he says, mispronouncing his own name. *Doo-raand.* 'Seemed like a decent fella. In fact, he said I could just go on ahead and call his personal assistant, Miss Bisset if I needed anything.' *Miss Bee-set.* 'Well, that's mighty good of you. I'll be sure to pass on your words to my squeeze, I mean, my niece. You have yourself a nice day.'

'I'm dead,' I groan, crossing my hands across my chest as though a corpse, only to throw them up in the air almost immediately. 'Oh my Lord, what even was that?'

'That was your line manager, not God, *ma biche.*'

'Did you just call me your bitch?' I lift my head from the mattress and glare at him. I'm nobody's bitch. Unless I say so.

'*Biche*,' he corrects in that sinful accent of his. 'It means doe. It was meant with affection. Like honey, or sweetie, or babe.'

Worst. American. Accent. *Ever.*

So long as he's not calling me dough-y, not that this is the only potential issue here. 'Speaking of line managers, did you not think to ask my opinion before deciding I'd play hooky?' My gaze flicks to my thighs poking out like undercooked sausages from the bottom of Remy's shirt.

'You're perhaps less doe and more leonine, especially the way you're glaring at me.' His darkened gaze rakes over me, the brush of his gaze almost a physical thing.

'Except you're not looking at my eyes.' Maybe he's right; my response is more purr than reprimand.

'What do you think has my attention?'

His question strikes a sudden chord within me. What is it exactly that interests him? Is it the sex? Is it the novelty? Could it really be me?

'What are we doing here, Remy?'

'We are . . .' A suggestive smile plays in the corner of his mouth. 'Enjoying ourselves.'

'No, really. We're enjoying ourselves—enjoying each other. But what about tomorrow, and the day after that? Will you go back to ignoring me in hallways?'

'I preferred getting you hot on my desk.'

'And afterwards?' I sit quite suddenly. I turn to face him, curling my legs as I pull the hem of his shirt down my thighs. 'What happens when things start to wane between us?' And what if it's his interest that begins to fade first? Which would be worse; losing my job, or staying to watch him move on? I grit my jaw, refusing to give in to the emotion welling inside me. So much for staying in the moment and enjoying this for what it is.

'You don't think very much of me, do you?'

'I barely know you.' My gaze falls from his with this truth, a truth my head and body seemed content to ignore a few hours ago. I knew what I was getting myself into—I knew the score—but I have to be woman enough to say what I feel as I force myself to meet his eyes once more. 'And you barely know me, or you wouldn't have rung Olga without clearing it with me first.'

'Point taken.' He inclines his head, almost as though he thinks I'm being cute. 'I'll try to restrain *some* of my urges around you.'

'Try or will?'

'What do you think?'

'That's just it. I don't know what to think, beyond the fact that I'm here by some kind of cosmic accident after what happened between us back in March. But as for what happens now.' My words dry up, my mind beginning to race.

'Why are you thinking about this ending before it has even begun?'

'Maybe I worry that this is what you do. That you'll creep out again when I fall asleep.'

'You forget, this is my bed.'

'Figuratively, then. You don't really know me, and I don't know you, and we're both from such different places. Maybe this was a mistake. Maybe it shouldn't have gone beyond that night back in March.' As I'm saying this, that emotion welling? It turns to anxiety, to fight or flight. And guess whose legs are sliding from the bed . . .

Well, not mine as he lunges for me, and I find myself almost instantly under him, the change of position so fluid it's almost as though it's part of a choreographed dance.

'Neither of us are going anywhere.' His shoulders are so wide and so strong, his body bent over mine like an arc of sunlight spilling across the room.

'For now.' Why do my words sound like a dare?

'You're right. You don't know me because if you did, you'd know how hard it was for me to leave you that night.' My intake of breath is sharp, his body meeting mine, his weight balanced on his forearms. 'You were so kind to me,' he murmurs, pushing away my hair to cradle my face. 'Kinder than I can ever remember anyone ever being. But I was only in town for that week, so it seemed kinder to leave that way. For one of us, at least.'

'It was almost as though you'd been a dream.' My heart rises to my throat along with the admission.

'A dream. I like that. A dream made real once again.'

As his head dips, my response is almost a whisper against his lips as I try not to let myself get swept away. 'If you'd stayed, I would've at least made you coffee before kicking you out.'

'Not the coffee.' His expression turns almost pained, though I'm pretty sure my giggles are more relief than amusement. *Relief that he hasn't challenged the way I try to protect myself.* 'I think we both recognised, even back then, that the night was special. But I promise it wasn't disinterest that made me leave. It seemed so impossible. And you're correct. I don't lead an ordinary life. I decided you didn't deserve to be dragged into it.'

'Yet, here I am.'

'Yes. Here you are.' The green of his gaze is so vivid as it roams over me with a belly-licking kind of warmth. 'And now that the gods and the cosmos have intervened, I'm not letting you go.'

'You know what I think?' I press my palm against the centre of his chest as he lowers his forehead to mine. 'I think you're kind of sweet.'

'Sweet?' he repeats, though his tone isn't the same.

'Kind of,' I correct. No need for him to get a big head.

'I don't think anyone has ever referred to me in such a way.'

'Not even your mom?'

'Especially not her.' There's a story, though not one for today.

'Well, I think you're sweet. Especially when you're pretending not to know people who pass you in the hallway.'

'It wasn't my finest moment,' he agrees. 'Forgive me, I was shocked.'

'I think the word you're looking for is asshole.'

'I thought I was sweet.' His words are delivered in a whisper to my neck. *A whisper, a lick, a graze of his teeth, the kind of attentions that make me tremble under him.*

'You are sweet.' I swallow deeply at the feel of his body pressed against mine. 'You bought me a three-thousand-dollar coffee machine. A beautiful robe, which I now have the perfect apartment to glide around in while wearing it. And such beautiful flowers, and coffee, and a spa membership, which I hope you've gotten a refund on. But what I don't understand is, why you thought to do all this for me? To send me these gifts.'

His eyes are darker as his head appears above mine. 'Because I wanted to thank you for looking after me. For giving me that night.' I inhale sharply at the flex of his hips. 'And because I couldn't get you out of my head. Perhaps I wanted to make sure you wouldn't forget me.'

As if that were even possible.

'I'm nothing special.'

'You're ridiculous. And ridiculously beautiful.'

When was the last time anyone but Remy said that to me? I mean, I know the things said during sex only contain about five percent truth; five percent truth and ninety-five percent gibberish. But he's the only man who has made me swoon in a long time. That's not to say I haven't been paid compliments from time to time.

I love your eyes. You're hot.

That ass is like the North Star. Can you blame me for following it?

Girl, you've got a rack to die for. Feel free to smother me with those things anytime.

But nothing with such sincerity. Such beauty. Such promise.

A realisation washes over me, my skin immediately cold

yet clammy. Oh, man, I'm not worried about losing my job. I'm worried I'll fall for him. Fall hard.

'You don't like compliments.' His expression is playful and completely oblivious to this insane internal chatter.

'Who doesn't like compliments?' I retort, my mouth working of its own accord as he suddenly cages me in with his body, his lightly furred legs on either side of mine and his hands at the sides of my head.

'People who don't know how to receive them.' His words take on that velvety quality of his, the inflection of his accent only adding to the aural thrill. 'I could paint you in such adoration.'

His thumb finds my mouth and strokes my bottom lip, my panic ebbing away. He dips, pressing his lips to mine once more, turning my insides molten as his hand moves between us, reaching for the buttons of his shirt. One, two, three tiny hindrances worked loose, he pushes the sides of his shirt open, exposing me to his trailing fingers and his gaze.

'*Tu es très belle,*' he whispers, his words pressed to my lips. 'Once in English. Once in French, because you deserve to hear it twice. You are very, very beautiful.'

'You can say that to me in any language you like.' My words are just a rush of breath as I absorb the weight of his body over mine and the feel of him pressed between my legs.

'*Mmmm.*' The vibration is more growl as his mouth engulfs my nipple briefly, his words whispering against my skin. 'You know, that could be dangerous.'

I push up on my elbows, watching as he works his way down my body. Circling my navel with his tongue, a sucking bite pressed to my hip, his hand sliding under my thigh. We've been in bed hours, kissing, tasting, fucking. Surely, he isn't going to—

'What are you doing?'

There's a challenge in the way his eyes rise to mine. '*Je veux te bouffer la chatte.*' Even with my very little understanding of the language, I know instinctively what he just said.

I don't need a translation, my body surging from the bed with an inarticulate sound as Remy's fingers part my oversensitive flesh. As he sucks my clit into his mouth, I'm sure the weight of him over me is the only thing stopping me from floating away.

20

REMY

'REMY.' As I turn, a hand is proffered along with my name. 'Long time, no see, man.'

'Gunnar. How are things?' As we shake hands, the man shrugs and smiles the kind of smile that still makes him sought after to grace magazine covers long after his football career is over.

'Can't complain. I haven't seen you around lately. What can be keeping you away from these things?' He gestures to the melee going on around us. *A charity function.* Though there was nothing charitable in the look of a thirty-something passing blonde as her gaze lingers over me. Nothing charitable and nothing subtle, because she's still giving me the eye as she reaches the side of her elderly husband.

'You know how it is.' I take a sip from my glass, pleasantly surprised by the quality of the wine on offer this evening. Usually, it's as insipid as the company, most people in attendance using this type of event as a means to be seen.

Wine. Champagne. Canapés. The yacht show. The Grand Prix. Art showings. The opera. Charity auctions. Corporate functions. Night after night of double air-kisses, tinkling laughter, and pleasure as faked as the orgasms they make for the benefit of their husbands. As the head of the group, my attendance is sometimes necessary. As a man, I'm so fucking bored of it all.

And I can't believe I gave up a few hours with Rose to be here.

'So, what's been keeping you away? The lure of your yacht and the Caribbean, or the willing arms of a certain someone?'

'Just the usual,' I reply, lying through my teeth. 'Work, work, and more work. I'm sure that's a familiar refrain.' Though I'm not truly sure he does; what exactly does a Portuguese football player retired at the height of his fame do when he moves to Monaco? Apart from fuck around and set up a charity, I suppose. *Merde.* 'This is his function?' I hiss to Everett as Gunnar turns to greet someone else. 'How the hell could I have forgotten that?'

'Probably because you're functioning on about three hours sleep a night.' He's right; I can't get enough of Rose. Even when I'm with her, I can't get close enough. I feel like I want to be under her skin.

'I see Carson Hayes is here.' He tips his head inconspicuously to the space behind me. 'Boring holes in the back of your head.' He raises his glass to his mouth, then asks, 'Did you read the file I sent on him?'

'Ex-military. Only came into the business when his father died.'

'The older Hayes is as hard as nails. And about as crooked as one pulled from a lump of wood.'

'He would be, as a long-term friend of Emile's.' I use the term *friend* loosely.

'And that's why another one bites the dust, right?'

That's not quite what the takeover was about. Or maybe it was. Partially.

'It was a mistake moving her into the building,' Rhett adds in an undertone that I'm certain I'm meant to hear, but his attempt at nonchalance falls flat.

Not only does his feigned disinterest fall flat, but he's also wrong about Rose. While she'd made it abundantly clear from the start that she didn't want to risk being seen out with me—she doesn't want to be judged by her colleagues and is obviously wary of our relationship's life expectancy—our living arrangements suit me very well. They provide for complete privacy. No one would think anything of seeing either of us in the building and no one but Everett is aware of our relationship. And that's the way we'd like it to stay. For now, at least.

I look down at the glass in my hand, absently rubbing my calloused finger against my thumb as a snapshot of last night flashes in my head. I was lying on my back with Rose half draped across my chest, her hair wild and her fingers linked with mine.

'You must be the only billionaire I know with workers hands.' She'd lifted our joined hands closer, rubbing a long-ingrained callous on my index finger.

'Do you know many billionaires?'

'Not personally, but I have passed all manner of shopping and gifts into the lily white and manicured paws of many a Wolf Tower resident.'

'Mere millionaires.'

Pressed together as we move, her laughter vibrated through my body pleasantly. 'I *do* beg your pardon,' she'd replied, her accent modulated and drawn out for effect. 'But even the peasant millionaire classes don't have hands like these. Or a watch that looks like it needs retiring.'

'Are you insinuating I have ugly hands? And an ugly watch?'

'There's nothing ugly about you.' Dark hair fell across her brow, and I smoothed it back. 'What's with the sad smile?'

Nothing but my soul, perhaps. If she knew about the lies I'd told, she wouldn't be looking at me as she did. 'This watch belonged to my grandfather.'

'I'm sorry.' Her voice was suddenly as soft as her gaze.

'Don't be. I never met him.' But by all accounts, he was a good man. 'It's an Omega, though not very fashionable or worth a great deal. I only began to wear it to annoy my father. A habit that seems to have ingrained itself.'

'Wearing the watch or annoying him?'

When I didn't answer, she turned her attention back to our hands. 'Well, this is not an ugly hand. But it is a hand that's seen manual labour.'

'Subtle, *ma Rose*.'

'So sue me.'

'I'd rather screw you.'

'What, again?' She'd lifted the sheet lying low on my waist, peering beneath it comically. 'Hmm. Not yet.' She dropped the sheet. 'In the meantime, you can tell me why the richest man in Monaco has the hands of a carpenter.'

'Maybe I have a hobby.'

'I thought your hobby was sexing me?'

I laughed. 'You're not a hobby.' *You're an obsession*. I caught myself before adding that. 'This life, this role of CEO wasn't always mine. My father made it very clear that I wasn't up to the job and that the business would go to my cousin. When he died, I think we were both heartily disappointed at how things turned out. I was enjoying myself, living a life with no responsibilities and no consequences.'

'Were you one of those international playboys? Yachts and Cristal, girls in bikinis and partying like you were Jay-Z?' she'd teased.

Little did she know that's exactly how I spent my years post university. My father supplied the money, and I just lived for ruin.

'For a little while,' I'd answered eventually. 'Well, for long enough to make myself sick. Bored with my own company. I sold the yacht for something a little less ostentatious, then navigated my way to Indonesia where I bought a little bit of paradise.'

Her hand paused in stroking my chest as her head lifted. 'So they're sailor's hands, not carpenter's.'

'They're hands that have seen a little bit of everything.' Hands that find a little heaven in you. 'I designed a house and set to work building it.'

'By yourself?'

'No.' I'd laughed. 'I was a spoiled rich kid with no skills. But I learned on the job, so to speak. And yes, I developed a taste for carpentry. You might say I'm good with wood.'

'Tell me something I don't know.' Her smile was reluctant.

I'm losing my mind over you, I almost replied.

'All that stopped when Emile died suddenly two years ago.' I was devastated, though not about my father.

'If you didn't want the business, why come back? Why put yourself through it at all?'

'Sometimes, I ask myself the same question.'

'Do you ever find the answer?'

'He said I'd never amount to much. He was a self-made man, and never shied away from proclaiming it. He came from nothing and pointed out often that I had everything— everything given to me on a silver platter, yet I'd never be the man he was.'

'He sounds like he was an unhappy man. Jealous, even.'

'He loved Monaco, yet it has never felt like home to me.'

DONNA ALAM

'Really?' She pushed up on her elbow and stared down at me. 'Because, to me, you look like you own it.'

'I was bundled off to boarding school at the first opportunity and was never in any hurry to come back.' I'd sighed and dragged my hand down my face, almost as though cleansing myself of the memories. 'Listen to the poor little rich boy complain.'

'No, don't do that. Don't depreciate your experiences. You can be rich in the pocket and poor in other ways.'

'What about you, Rose? What were you poor in?'

'Cash,' she replied with an unhappy laugh. 'Permanency.' My conscience tugged at me. Not because my existence was more than hers but because of all I've hidden from her. Here she lies in my bed, counting her blessing of a job and stability when what's due to her is so much more. 'But my house, my home, in whichever apartment, town, or county we were living in at the time, well, it was always rich in love. More so when there was just the two of us together. When she wasn't dating, I mean.'

'And your father?'

'He died before I was born. It was a whirlwind romance followed by a pregnancy and a hasty court-house wedding. It probably never would've lasted, but Mom's Irish bad boy was killed in a car accident before they had a chance to find out.'

'I'm sorry.

'Thank you.' She sighed deeply, her chest expanding against mine. 'You never miss what you never had. But being a single parent couldn't have been easy on her. She always seemed to be looking for a man to give her stability.' Her attention turned inward before she seemed to rouse herself. You know what my home was rich in?' she'd added, angling her head. 'Ass whoopings.'

'Were you a naughty girl?'

'Ha! You wish. But we were talking about you and your workman's hands.' She'd reached for me then, intertwining our fingers once more. 'And how you were going to prove your father wrong.'

'He's dead. He doesn't get to see what I've become.' My words were intentionally dismissive, but dismissive was better than betraying my annoyance.

'Maybe. Maybe not. But the world does. They say The Wolf Group has almost doubled in size in the past two years. Since you've been in charge, right?'

'I do what needs to be done,' I responded, silently adding my intention to discover exactly who the woman was in my arms. The woman I'd become so dependent on, the woman with no idea of the depths of my need. *My need for her. My need to know where she's come from.* I'd started on a path there was no return from.

'I'm sure your father would be proud. I mean, I haven't been here long, but it looks like you own kind of a lot of Monaco.'

'We do have a number of projects,' I'd replied.

'I heard they crowned you the king of the South of France.'

'It sounds like someone is trying to get me sent to the Grimaldi dungeon.'

'What's that?'

'Grimaldi? The name of Monaco's ruling family. Prince Albert being the head of it, and the ruler of Monaco.'

'You know there's a *t* on the end of that guy's name.'

'Not in France, there isn't.'

'Yet his mother was American. Al*bert*.'

'More and more, it sounds like you want to get me in trouble.'

'Ha! The authorities would take one look at my google

history before deciding I framed you.'

I tilted my head. 'You've been googling me?'

'Here, let me help you scratch that big head of yours,' she retorted, her words dripping with faux irritation as her fingers wiggled in the air at least a foot from my head. 'It was an article about you in the local newspaper, if you must know. I was trying to better my language skills. I hate not understanding what people are saying around me.'

'Hmm. That is a shame. Especially as you missed what I said when you did that thing with your tongue. I could translate, I suppose. All in the interests of educating you.'

'I think you've educated me plenty.'

'I do what I can,' I replied, rolling her underneath me once again. 'It's time for a little woodwork again . . .'

With memories like these, who would fault me for agreeing we need total privacy. Can I be blamed that privacy also provides me a shield? I want her more than I've wanted any other woman, but I'm still cognisant of the fact that I still don't know how she comes to be in my life. Or why.

Digging into someone's past takes time. Meanwhile, Rose and I don't dine out, and we don't attend public functions, which means there is neither sight nor sound of our relationship beyond the four walls of our respective apartments. A state of affair that suits both our purposes. But that's not to say we haven't had fun. What we have is more than just sex.

We might not have dined out, but we've dined in, our meals prepared by some of the leading chefs in the region. We've watched movies and gotten a taste for the other's likes and dislikes, and it turns out we're both a fan of thrillers. Rose loves a jump-scare, and I enjoy how they result in her almost always crawling onto my knee. We've indulged in cocktails out by the pool and champagne under the stars, talking about everything and nothing. I know she worries about our differences in station, and the fact that I'm her boss. I know she has little more than a few hundred dollars in her checking account without her ever saying so. She worries she's walking a fine line between affluence and poverty; if only she knew the truth. I suppose I should feel some form of guilt for not telling her she'll one day be a wealthy woman in her own right. But I can't allow myself to feel those sentiments because if I do, if I tell her before I'm ready, then this will be the end of things between us.

When we're together, there is nothing else but us.

It's when she's not around that my mind begins to wander.

Who is she? What is the damn connection? It's like a puzzle I cannot fix.

She told me once she has trust issues. If only she knew what that really feels like.

'No news from the investigator yet?'

I'm pulled sharply back into the present, to murmuring voices, the delicate chime of glasses, and to a voice that isn't hers.

'You're here on your own tonight?' I turn to the sound of Gunnar's voice, my mind a step behind his question, occupied by other things.

'I'm his plus one tonight,' Rhett says, beating me to an answer as he holds out his hand for the other man to shake. 'All the gorgeous women in Monaco and he has my ugly mug trailing him around.'

'He must've been wicked in a past life.' Gunnar's eyes gleam over the rim of his glass.

'Past life?' Rhett scoffs. 'He's a bastard now.'

'I know just the thing to redeem him,' the other man says, reaching out for a glass from the tray of a passing waitress. '*Merci.*'

'I suppose that would be a donation to your charity,' I interject, mentally increasing the size of my contribution. Manners cost nothing, yet the rich don't often use them.

'It couldn't harm.' Gunnar grins widely. 'It's for the kids.' His accent is a mixture of Latin lover and London lad, according to Everett, as a result of learning to speak English while playing in the English football league. Hence the name; Gunnar for the club he captained all the way to the top. *The Gunners, not Gunnars, but who am I to comment?*

'Jesus, don't let him drag out his evangelical soapbox. You know who you're like?' Everett asks with a vague wave of his finger. 'Fucking Fagin. Well, except for the whole pickpocketing thing.'

'You've met Everett, I see.'

Gunnar nods. 'We play five-a-side soccer on Sunday.'

'Football,' my companion corrects. 'Soccer is for the uninitiated. He's French,' he adds, directing his thumb my way, 'no need to explain it to him.'

'I'm honoured. As you must be on Sundays.'

'Ha. He was a shit centre forward when he played professionally,' Rhett grumbles, 'he's only gotten worse since.'

'That must be why my team wiped the floor with yours last week.'

'Yeah, well, I couldn't see for the fog of the female spectators' sighs.' With a sly smile, Rhett turns to me. 'He still draws a crowd. He broke more hearts than he kicked footballs in the last year of his career.'

'You're just jealous because my legs look better in shorts. What exactly does this man do for you, Remy?' He says "man" like you might carbuncle.

'Everett is the head of my security team, or so they tell me.'

'You're expecting trouble?' Gunnar asks, one dark eyebrow raised like a question mark.

'Nah. He only keeps me around to make his face look prettier. Sometimes I get to beat off the ladies with a big stick.' As he says this, his gaze is scanning the crowd, the results of my recent accident still making him paranoid. 'You know how it is with you good-looking, rich types.'

'You'll have to excuse him. He doesn't get out much. He's not what you'd call socialised.'

'You mean, give him a chance, and he'll start humping my leg?' Before either of us can answer, his name is called from the other side of the room, the voice high-pitched and excitable. 'I don't suppose you want to come and beat some off for me,' he murmurs, watching the crowd of people part like the Red Sea.

'Nah, you're not my type,' Everett answers with a grin as a diminutive brunette comes barrelling towards us, waving manically to get Gunnar's attention.

'Monsieur Gunnar,' she calls. '*Bonsoir!* Hello, it is I! Princess Mariella!'

'A princess,' Rhett scoffs. 'You're moving up in the world.'

'Piss off,' he retorts as he turns. 'She probably just wants to talk about the donation she's making.'

I doubt it, though I keep the thoughts to myself. These European minor royals usually think charity begins at home and often struggle to keep the heirloom Bentley on the road.

'I reckon she's looking for a deposit from you. A personal kind of deposit, if you know what I mean.' Everett smirks as the matronly princess appears in front of the retired athlete, staring up at his face with wide-eyed expectance.

'We shall leave you to it,' I murmur, drawing away.

And this is what I've exchanged a night with Rose for.

I must be crazy.

21

ROSE

'Mon Dieu!' my dinner date announces, sliding aviator sunglasses to the top of his head. 'The sun is so bright today that it is burning my rectums!'

'Charlie, what the hell?' I splutter through the mouthful of water I've just ingested, though manage not to expel it over the little wooden bistro table.

'What? Did I not say this correct?' He frowns, pulling out the chair opposite but not yet seating himself. 'It is still bright outside. This is why I have my sunglasses.' He places them on the tabletop between us, running his hand down the front of his tightly fit shirt. The rest of his outfit is very him; baby blue chinos that look like they've been sprayed rather than pulled on, a skinny navy leather belt to draw the attention to his trim waist, and matching Gucci penny loafers.

'What do you think?' he says, doing a little twirl.

'*Très chic*. I also think if your *rectum* is burning, you're wearing your sunglasses in the wrong place.'

His expression seems to turn inward as he lowers himself into his chair. After considering his reflection in the smoke grey lenses. 'Les yeux. The eyes,' he begins to muse aloud.

'Les rétines. Retinas. Le rectum . . . Oh!' He titters. 'I think that would be one way to bleach *l'anus*.'

'No. No, I don't think it would be.' Covering my mouth with my hand, I try to keep from giggling myself.

'Maybe with a little lemon juice,' he adds with a one-shouldered shrug.

'*Limon jooz?*'

'Bah! You can't make fun of *my* accent.'

'I can try.'

'Not the way you butcher *la langue française*.'

'That's fightin' talk!'

'Bon. Then it shall be handbags at dawn!' He tightens his fingers on the strap of his invisible purse, one eyebrow incitingly raised.

The waiter arrives, and Charles suggests we order a bottle of wine, and I agree while also hoping he orders a cheap one this time because funds are getting low. I don't get paid until next week, and I'm currently living on bread and cheese when I'm not with Remy. Bread and cheese might sound kind of fancy, especially considering where I'm living. It's not because I'm not eating the fancy stuff, but the carrot-orange processed yuck. My diet is a little more balanced thanks to the contents of the fruit bowl kept on the concierge reception desk, which I think is mostly for show, but provides at least one of my 5 A Day, the number increased by a liberal consumption of grapes. In liquid form.

Still, it beats living on ramen and cups of watery coffee to fill my stomach. It sounds like a poor person cliché but, if you ask me, the unfortunate thing about clichés is that they are all too often true.

When I am with Remy, which has been a lot these past three weeks, but not every night—because, hello, no one likes needy—I eat well. Like amazingly well. It blows my mind that he has the kind of influence that has brought some of the best chefs in Europe into his kitchen. Last night, for instance, some Michelin-starred dude flown in from Sicily served a melt-in-the-mouth arancini that was so delicious, I'm pretty sure I could live on just that for the rest of my days. It was followed by a pasta dish that I was initially certain I could live without ever seeing again because it looked disturbingly like a bowl of black worms. It turned out to be squid ink pasta and equally as tasty.

We drank cocktails poolside watching as the sun turned molten, dusk then turning to dark. The weather was so beautiful, we decided to eat outside. At the end of the meal, the chef was presented at the table, still dressed in his whites, and Lord knows why, but I was surprised as Remy began to thank him in perfect sounding Italian.

Is there anything this man is bad at? Except maybe riding motorcycles.

But I teased him anyway.

'I think your Italian mustn't be as good as it sounds,' I'd said, hiding my smile behind my wine glass.

'What makes you think that?' His purring expression should've warned me I was heading into a trap.

'Oh, just the way the man turned pink in the middle of your conversation. You must've mispronounced something, making it sound dirty.'

He'd tipped his head back and smiled up into the star-filled sky and laughed. A slight breeze in the air ruffled his hair, and I'd curled my hands into fists against the urge to reach across the table and run my fingers through it.

'No, ma Rose. He turned pink because I told him you made such enthusiastic sounds as you'd eaten your entrée that I thought I was going to have to cut the meal short and take you to bed.'

'You did not!' I'd squealed, but he'd just inclined his head and said my rapture belonged to him now.

When we're not being fed by the best in the business, Remy's housekeeper isn't averse to rustling up a delicious dish. She—and I'm assuming she is a she, which isn't very modern of me—cooks a mean lasagne and her salads are to die for. A couple of evenings we've even cooked together, though nothing fancy because neither of us is particularly housetrained. What we haven't done yet is eat out, like in a restaurant or café. In fact, we haven't been anywhere together in public, and the truth is, I'm not ready to be seen with him. When I'd explained my fears to Remy, how I worried it was too soon, that I'd be gossiped about and not taken seriously at work because people would probably assume he'd brought me out to Monaco to bone, he said he understood. In fact, he was very sweet about it.

And to think I was worried there'd be some sort of power imbalance ebbing involved with a rich man. Maybe Amber was right; maybe power issues are the difference between dating a rich guy and a rich asshole. Remy is no ass. In fact, he's probably one of the best men I've ever met. When we're together, everything is so normal—we talk about everything, but I never wanted to fall in love with him. Hell, I never wanted to fall in love with anyone. Love leaves you vulnerable. Leaves you wanting. It makes junkies out of mothers and relegates children to the sense of never being quite enough. Yet, each time we get together, he steals a little more of my heart.

But I'm happy to exist in our little bubble for now because I know once we step out in public, all that will come to an end. Aside from how I'll be viewed at work, there are other concerns. Will I be accepted into his world? Would he make a place for me there? Also, it seems the richer you are in

Monaco, the more appealing you are as society pages fodder, which is more than a little freaky. Think TMZ but a little classier, because paparazzi aren't allowed to follow the rich and fabulous in Monaco, by order of the Crown Prince.

Remy doesn't get to keep me all to himself every night. He has his social obligations, and I have mine. Like tonight—dinner with my new work friends!

'What's up, bitches!' Fee arrives at the table wearing a cute pink dress that shows off her toned arms and her golden tan. Charles rises to greet her, and double air-kisses are bestowed to each of us, as is the custom out here.

'Your tan is great,' I tell her, taking in the golden glow of her arms as they retract.

She looks down, then holds her arm against mine to compare. I'm olive skinned while Fee is fair, though after spending this morning at Larvotto Beach together, we're both a little tanner than we were. Charles refused to come with us for fear of premature sun-induced wrinkles.

'I thought for sure I'd be sunburnt after we laid out so long.' I'm pleased to report I did not. I'd also began topping up my tan last weekend by spending a little bikini time out in Remy's penthouse pool in the sky. And now I know why the man has no tan lines. And the view. It was good.

'You look *tres* glamorous, my darlings,' Charles offers with a pout.

'Well, you look super glamorous, too. And I see you started without me,' she quips as the waiter arrives with our bottle of Pinot. Before he leaves, she orders herself a vodka tonic.

'You could have a glass of wine with us,' I suggest. 'Especially as you're our best *biche*.'

'*Biche?* You mean as in doe?'

I nod. 'Are you impressed? I'm working on expanding my

vocabulary.' Thanks to Remy mostly. 'Though much of it isn't appropriate for the ears of polite company.'

'Then it is a good thing you choose us as your friends.' Charles inclines his head in the manner of one all-knowing, reaching for his empty glass. 'We can teach you all the good sex words.'

'I didn't say they were sex words. I've been learning some pretty good insults, too. You know, so I can mutter them under my breath when one of the residents says he needs to find someone to fill his bath with jellybeans or something equally ridiculous.'

Charles puts down his glass and brings his hands to his shaking head. 'This has happened to me when I worked in Paris. Worse, I had to pick out the red ones. I never want to work in a 'otel again.'

'I'll drink to that,' Fee agrees. As her vodka hasn't yet arrived, I reach for the bottle intending to splash a little into the spare glass.

'No, thank you. I can't have a wine hangover tomorrow. I'm leading a spinning class at seven a.m.'

'On Sunday?' I splutter a little incredulously. 'First of all, what kind of person exercises on Sunday, and second of all, who the hell is out of bed at that time?'

'*Mon chère,* you live in Monaco now,' drawls Charles.

'People be cra-zy!'

'Monaco is the home of the rich and the cra-zy,' adds Fee.

'No doubt 'zis class will be full of trophy wives and girlfriends.' Charles wrinkles his nose in distaste.

'While that's not necessarily untrue, I do have some men who attend regularly.'

'Gay men,' he asserts, 'because *le cyclisme* is good for le buns!' He lifts a little from his chair, tapping his own ass.

'The only buns I want to see at seven on Sunday are the

kind that are filled with chocolate. Seven a.m.,' I repeat with a dramatic shiver. 'No thanks.'

'I've always been an early riser,' Fee answers mildly, watching as Charles fills our glasses—finally!

This isn't the sort of restaurant where hovering waiters wear a uniform of black or pristine white aprons, rather it's a little place off the beaten path where the clientele is mostly Monégasque; those native to Monaco. In other words, the ordinary folk, not the uber-rich. The décor is less fancy and a little more hodgepodge with scarred bistro tables and leatherette booths. The walls are painted magnolia and covered with framed prints and old photographs. There's a garden seating area outside for those warm summer nights, or for when you don't mind your hair growing in volume due to the humidity. Tonight is not one of those nights, and the tables are free of linens, napery arriving in the form of red and white chequered napkins. The food is hearty rather than fancy, the wine mostly French and the beer Belgian, and importantly, all are reasonably priced. In short, I'd recommend!

'As my dad likes to say,' Fee continues, 'the early bird catches the worm.'

'Ah, but Rose already has a worm in her bed—one that keeps her up all night!' Charles titters. 'That is why she is reluctant to get out of bed, *n'est-ce pas?' Right?*

'Really? A worm?' I echo, though not in the same tone.

'*Non.* Not a worm. *Plus gros!*' he amends, miming like a fisherman describing the one that got away.

'You mean a snake,' Fee adds, raising her glass. 'Here's to huge trouser snakes!'

'I drink to that,' replies Charles, clinking his glass against hers. 'And I will buy champagne if Rose tells us about her mystery *lover.*' He annunciates the final word ridiculously, all teeth and lips, his lashes fluttering manically.

'Ah, but then it wouldn't be a mystery,' I hedge. 'And what would we have to talk about in the office, then?' And by talk, I mean gossip.

'Bah! I don't need mysteries. I need tales of hot men!'

'Then get your own hot man.'

'I am living with one! But 'e is still angry with me.' He pouts ridiculously.

'You're so lucky to find yourself a man out here.' With her elbow on the table and her hand cupping her chin, Fee takes a sip from her newly delivered glass. 'My love life has been like the Sahara since I got here. And I don't mean hot and vast.'

'How can that be? Just look at you, babe-a-licious. If I had an ass like yours, I'd be wearing booty shorts all day every day.'

'Squats,' she says by way of explanation for booty deliciousness. 'Swap you for boobs?'

'This conversation does nothing for me,' Charles sniffs.

'You must be the one gay man who isn't fascinated with boobs.'

'They are interesting,' he replies with a disinterested shrug. 'But like a fluffy tail on a rabbit. That is all.'

'What about man boobs?' Fee asks. 'Are you into those at all?'

'Yeah, breasts,' I add with a giggle as Charles deigns not to answer but rather glares. 'You probably like the moobs on a male gym bunny, though, right?'

'I prefer the ass.' He sighs, glancing at the retreating form of a passing waiter.

'Yet, my ass does nothing for you,' I quip. 'And Lord knows, I have enough of it.'

'Whatever,' Fee scoffs, dipping the rim of her glass in my direction. 'It's working for you. Out of the three of us, you're the one who's—'

'Getting some,' interjects Charles.

'I was going to say *found someone.*'

'I wouldn't say that exactly,' I demur, my mind rapidly scanning and rejecting ways to turn the conversation from me. I don't want to talk about Remy now, and I can't afford to drop my guard three glasses in. I like Fee and Charles—I like them a lot. But we don't know each other well enough to establish any great degree of trust.

'But she is the only one getting some,' Charles huffs mulishly, crossing his arms. Charles is a sweetie, and he's been super helpful during my first few weeks on the job. But he's also a gossip, as well as a tiny bit catty.

'Yeah, but it's not like we've made any declarations or anything. For all I know, he could be seeing other people.' Even as I say this, I know this isn't true, unless Remy is sexing someone between the hours of work. At least, those hours he's not calling me to his office with his ridiculous demands.

Ridiculously sexy demands.

It seems Olga has somehow gotten the message that messages from the resident of the penthouse suite aren't for her sole attention. I'm not sure what exactly has been said, and by whom, but I only know it's resulted in her treating me with a cool sort of reserve.

'I imagine dating in America is a bit like back home in the UK, and I have to say, dating French men isn't the same. Here, it's almost as though exclusivity is implicit. That is, unless it's been addressed as otherwise, I suppose.'

'This is not a conversation we've had,' I admit, reaching for my glass.

'Except if they're rich. Normal rules don't seem to apply to rich men.' My heart sinks to my strappy sandals, but I remind myself this conversation is purely academic. She doesn't know Remy. Maybe she's working on second-hand data. Maybe she's never dated a rich man out here, or anywhere, for that matter. 'Especially out here,' she adds.

'You really think it's worse in Monaco?' My tone is a little sharp, though I don't mean it to be so. But I could tell them some truths about the men. Men who trailed in and out of my life, those I was supposed to call *uncle*, one or two of them *dad*. Men my mother trusted. Men who were no good. I could regale them tales of the men from the Pink Pussy Cat—sons, brothers, fathers, husbands. Bad men. Grabby men. Men who have no respect for women at all. Except I've left that all behind. Plus, I don't really know my new friends. New friends who look a little shocked. 'I'm sorry,' I begin a little more reasonably, 'it's just, as a child, I moved around a whole bunch of times. Then a couple of years ago, I took off on a trip around the world. It seems to me whether you're in Kansas, Kuala Lumpur, or Kathmandu, you will always find assholes without looking too hard.'

'Yes, but people with this,' Charles replies, rubbing his thumb and fingers together in the universal sign for money, 'are the biggest ass'oles of all. They think money makes them untouchable. Also, they are like God's gift or something.'

'People are people,' Fee says, making me think she might be the peacemaker of our trio. 'But while money might make the world go around, it certainly seems to make for bigger arseholes.'

'Enough!' Charles decrees, reaching for the wine bottle. 'We are here to have a good time. Money is not everything. But I say a little prayer of thanks that we get our salary next week.'

I do a little internal squee at the thought of my first pay

cheque. It's so exciting! I can't believe I've been here almost a month already.

'Pass me the menu, would you?' asks Fee. 'I'm so hungry, my bum is eating my knickers.'

'You are so very English.' This from Charles doesn't sound like a compliment.

'You're not allowed to order salad this time,' I say. 'You make me feel guilty just looking at my plate of carbs.'

'Just because Fee means fairy in French,' adds Charles. 'It does not mean you should eat like one.'

We eventually settle down to a mix of pizza, salad, and pommes frites, which are just french fries outside of France. *And Monaco, I suppose.* More wine is ordered, more shit is talked, before Charles seems struck by the most amazing thought.

'Oh! I forget!' Despite being a little wine pickled due to our second bottle, he becomes very animated. 'I have a surprise tonight.'

'You're not going to flash us again on the way home, are you?' I run my finger through a smudge of Chantilly cream, the only evidence remaining of the portion of Tiramisu we've shared three ways. Which doesn't constitute much of a treat, as far as I'm concerned.

'Leave 'z pattern on the plate.' He slaps my hand away. 'And I did not flash,' he scorns. 'My pants make a rip. I was saying . . .' He cuts an unimpressed glance my way. 'A friend 'as 'ooked me up with a special treat.'

'What kind of treat?' Fee asks suspiciously as Charles practically shimmies with excitement in his seat.

'Guess!' he demands, his eyes comically wide.

'You've been comped something, haven't you?' I might be new to the concierge business, but I'm learning quickly, and discovering it's a culture where one hand washes the other, so to speak. Your Russian billionaire client wants to hold a birthday party for his daughter's thirteenth? All it takes is for you to push the twenty-thousand-dollar budget in the direction of one venue over another, and you've earned yourself a favour.

'*Peut-être.*' He pouts saucily.

'It's Friday night, I've had almost a bottle of wine, and my head hurts. '*En Anglaise, s'il vous plaît.*' *In English, please.*

'I said maybe. Also, your accent is atrocious.'

'And the more wine you drink, the meaner you become,' I retort, sticking out my tongue.

'So, you don't want to go to Shimmiez, then?'

'*Ner-ner-na-ner-ner,*' I taunt right back, using the same sing-song delivery, but we're not being serious. Charles is becoming the gay brother I never had. Or even knew I wanted.

'Wine makes you both perfectly obnoxious,' Fee interjects airily. 'And Shimmiez will be a nightmare to get into tonight. The Cannes Film Festival was last week, which means the place will be overflowing with rich creeps. Rich creeps with massive—'

'I am in!' Charles holds up his hand.

'Entitlement complexes,' Fee finishes, sending Charles a little side-eye.

'Also, there will be famous people,' Charles adds, oblivious. 'J-Lo is in town.'

'Oh, well,' I add, 'think she'll have space for us at her table? Maybe Charles can sit on her fiancé's knee.'

'I won't need to. I have a table tonight. And drinks —*gratuit*! Free!'

THOUGH I HAVEN'T BEEN HERE long, I've been here long enough to know that the legendary Shimmiez is one of Monaco's premier hangouts and the place to be seen. More than that, it's an icon of the Monaco nightclubs scene, having been open since the nineteen seventies. But most of my knowledge is academic, gleaned from googling Monaco before moving out here. It's definitely been on my list of places to visit, but I thought I'd have to wait longer than this, especially as I'd read of the ridiculous prices. I've heard it costs the equivalent of thirty dollars for a beer, and if you want to reserve a table, try multiplying that by ten!

But, as Fee and I almost skip along the pavement, arm in arm, following our fearlessly (camp) leader, tonight none of this is my concern because we have a table reservation confirmed for midnight, along with free drinks for the remainder of the night!

Hell to the yes!

'Your outfit is so cute.' Without relinquishing my arm, Fee dips forward, glancing down at my legs. 'You really caught the sun today.'

'And I'm making the most of it,' I agree as our heels clip against the sidewalk. I'm wearing shorts tonight, along with a silky vest and a slouchy blazer, an oversized clutch folded under my arm. I'm feeling pretty good, despite our earlier carbs and wine, though it could be argued that what I'm feeling is drunkalicious.

'Are those shorts Balmain?'

'Nope,' I scoff. 'They cost me twenty bucks from H & M, and I'm pretty sure fifteen bucks worth is currently stuck up my ass.'

'Shhh!' scolds Charles, turning with a fearsome look.

'Do you think it was the price of my outfit that's offended him?'

Fee drops her voice. 'Darling, if it's not Gucci, it's not Monaco!'

We turn into Avenue Princess Grace, not too far from the beach where we'd hung out, and see the entry line snaking in front of us. But Charles doesn't tarry, walking confidently past people lining up, straight to the front. He murmurs something into the door bitch's ear, a door bitch flanked by two fearsome heavies, one of whom doesn't so much have a forehead as a five head, the thing is so prominently huge.

'I wouldn't mind that full of wine,' I whisper to Fee, who tries not to giggle.

'You're awful,' she says as our invite is verified.

'Yeah. Awful nice,' I correct as the door bitch beckons us in and we cut ahead of the line, people complaining in our wake.

Look at me, living large—in Monaco!

As we descend the wide staircase, the thud of bass begins to vibrate through my soles. And then we're there—in Shimmiez—the place to see and be seen! Techno blares, arrhythmic lighting filling the space, bouncing off surfaces, the floor, walls, the glittering disco balls shaped like skulls.

'It's like Alexander McQueen and RuPaul had a baby,' I shout over the music, pointing at the twinkling ceiling skulls.

'I suppose you want one of *those* full of wine,' Fee calls back.

'No, I want one full of champagne!'

There's something very luxe about the place; it could be that it's filled with beautiful people, or it could be the décor, which is modern yet a little feminine with pink and purple accents. The place is buzzing, though not so busy we can't make our way around without feeling claustrophobic.

'Where are we going?' Like a camel train, Fee is still holding my hand as I follow Charles.

'No idea,' I call back over my shoulder. 'But he seems to.'

'Look, there's a VIP section.' She points over my shoulder to a raised area, sectioned off by a red velvet rope. Through the twinkling beaded curtains that look suspiciously like the ones I had on my bedroom door when I was twelve, the area seems packed. 'Can you see J-Lo in there?'

'Nope!'

It's not until we've traversed the circular dance floor, bypassing the bar area, that I realise Charles is following an employee of the club out to the terrace. As we step outside and into the warm evening air, we find ourselves in a club-like oasis filled with mood lighting and greenery. Soft pink illuminates the curvature of the building, following the flow of water that eases around the space like a tropical lagoon.

'There's a pool?' Much to Charles's annoyance, my words are a little incredulous. Yep, don't look now; my hick is showing.

'*Not* for swimming in,' declares the host, haughtily.

'I'm glad I didn't bring my swimsuit, then.' The music is more subdued out here so I don't need to shout to be heard, but I feel like I need to be snarky anyway. I also feel like asking, *girl, what's with the attitude? You work at Shimmiez. You don't own the place.* But I won't because anyone who disrespects their server deserves whatever extras they (won't) find floating in their drink.

Fee chuckles as Charles shoots me a look that conveys he finds me *très* embarrassing, rattling off something that sounds obsequious, even in a language I barely understand.

'You are in the premier club in Monaco and you are acting badly,' Charles hisses as he takes a seat in a circular pod-looking thing. Fee shuffles in after him, and I take a seat on the other side.

'Charles, you're what my mum would call all fur coat and no knickers,' Fee counters happily in my defence.

'This is true,' he agrees. 'Because I cannot wear what you call "knickers" in these tight pants. Also, this is not Gstaad. It is too warm for fur in Monaco.'

'I'm gonna need another drink after that,' I chortle, 'because I did *not* need to know you've gone commando tonight. Better stay out of those strobe lights if you don't want anyone to know what side you dress on.'

'It pays to advertise,' he answers airily, reaching for me. 'Come give papa a kiss, and all will be forgiven.'

'Ew, no. Boy cooties!' I reply, fighting off his playful kissy face.

'Even worse,' he retorts. 'I 'ave the gay cooties!'

Around us, what looks like olive trees are dotted about, though underlit with pink lights, they almost look like cherry trees in full blossom. A couple at a table to our left are smoking an apple-scented hookah, to our right, others are quaffing champagne while, over the lagoon, we have a direct view into the club. Bodies writhe on the dance floor; women in tiny dresses and men in tight shirts and pants. The number of women here seems to outstrip men, which is usual for a nightclub, I guess, but what's different here is that there are more older men than there are young. Pretty young things and older men might be the way of the world, but it's not usually the way of a nightclub.

My musing is interrupted by the arrival of the waitress, just as blonde and snooty as the hostess, as she delivers a bottle of Grey Goose vodka and a bottle of Sakurao gin. Each is placed in an oval container of ice and surrounded by mini bottles of tonic and other mixers. Before I can reach for either, another member of the waitstaff deposits a champagne bucket next to the pod containing a bottle of pink Dom Perignon, no less! I'm beginning to wonder who Charles has been blowing as, with a flourish, she pops the cork then begins to splash the contents into three flutes.

'Compliments of Monsieur Lorenzi,' she says, placing the bottle back.

'You dark horse,' I accuse, turning to Charles. 'That's the guy on the twelfth floor, isn't it? The one who had a problem with his air-conditioning last week.'

'*Oui*,' he replies airily. 'It was so hot in his apartment we had to strip. And then I found I had to rub him down.'

'Vigorously, no doubt!'

'But I thought you were still living with Philipe?' Fee asks as our dirty sniggering laughter dies away.

'Philipe is moving out,' he says, eyes glittering angrily. 'For that *fils de pute* lifeguard.'

'I'm so sorry, Charlie.'

'I am not,' he declares immediately. 'There are many extra seamen in the ocean.'

224

'Sure, though I'm not sure that's the right metaphor.' I pat his arms consolingly. 'See any seamen you'd like here tonight?'

'I think I am otherwise engaged this evening.'

'Oh? What makes you say that?'

'*J'ai du nez,*' he replies, tapping his nose knowingly.

'Fine. You be all mysterious, then. See if I care.'

'How do you say . . . someone is giving me the eye already. *Non,* don't look!' He reaches for my arm, his expression a mixture of alarm and delight. 'Oh! He's coming this way. Act normal. Quick, someone say something!'

'What's long, hard, and full of seamen?' Fee's words are accompanied by a wince as, like a manic, Charles throws his head back and laughs unreservedly.

'I thought you said act normal,' I utter from behind my champagne. 'She hasn't even gotten to the punchline.'

'Was that too much?'

'It was about as natural as a three-legged man.'

'My favourite kind of man,' he answers gleefully, his eyes sliding away.

'You don't want a three-legged man. You want one with a foot-long, you slutty little man,' I say with a snigger, my gaze following his. It's hard to tell who he's looking at because so many people are milling about. Drinking. Swaying. Having a good time. My heart feels light, and it's not the wine or the champagne. It's been so long since I've had a night out on the town, even if Shimmiez is so different from my previous experiences. I have friends, a gorgeous place to live, a man who treats me well. Pinch me now—tell me this is all real.

'Bah! He has stopped to talk to someone.' Charles then glances my way. 'Why would I want a man with another foot? Especially a long one?'

DONNA ALAM

Oh, Lord. I find myself shaking my head. 'I can't . . . you know what? You stick with your tripod.'

'And you.' Charles slips his hand along the sofa, curling his fingers around Fee's shoulder. 'I did not know you were such a dirty girl.'

'It was a joke,' she protests, turning red, or rather a deeper shade of pink under the rosy lighting.

'*Non*. Long, 'ard, and full of semen sounds like 'ow his ass makes me feel.' We both follow his attention to where a man stands chatting to the group seated at a nearby pod, his back to us. How can we tell who's caught his attention this time? The guy is bending over.

'You said to say something,' Fee demurs. 'And I said the first thing that came into my head.'

'What's long, hard, and full of semen?' I recount. 'So, what's the punchline?'

'A submarine,' she answers with a weak smile. 'Terrible, right?'

'It reminds me of the time I was hit on with the gold standard line of: *Damn, girl, did you start a Navy? Because you're about to be full of semen.*'

'Please tell me it didn't work,' she says with a grimace.

'My reply went a little like this. *My.*' I bring my fingers to the middle of my chest and flutter my lashes a little. '*You must be a sailor. Because I do declare your eyes are as blue as the ocean I just dumped my last boyfriend's lifeless body in.*'

'That was a little less Scarlet O'Hara and a little more Scarlett O'Savage,' Fee replies with a giggle.

'That's what I was aiming for. I want smart and sincere, not smart-ass. But riddle me this,' I say, turning to Charles. 'How come there isn't one average-looking woman here tonight? Note I don't include the men. Hot butt aside, there

226

are lots of average-looking men here. And there are lots of men who should be tucked up in bed with a cup of cocoa. So also, I guess, what's up with that?'

'Rich men are their own attraction,' Fee asserts with a careless shrug.

'Really?' My head swings her way, the motion unintentionally exposing my disgust.

'Well . . . yes. There have been studies, haven't there? All this,' she says, gesturing to the people around us with her glass. It's evolutionary psychology. Men seek out mates with youth, which is linked to fertility, and with youth often comes beauty. Women don't seek out mates that have a pretty face. They want security.'

'Yeah, but you're talking about a time when men wielded cubs and looked good in bearskin.'

'It's still the same for some now. They might not need someone to stand at the mouth of their cave but crave the security money brings. It's a thing, especially out here. A beauty-status exchange.'

'Being rich doesn't make you a catch,' I counter, trying hard not to sound prickly as I smooth my hand through my dark hair. The evening is balmy, which doesn't bode well for my sleekly hot ironed look. And getting irrationally angry won't exactly help.

'But money can make you beautiful,' Charles says, his eyes still glued to the guy with the ass.

'You mean they can see beyond skin deep? Probably through wallets, too. Right to those black Amex cards.' I snort as I struggle out of my jacket, feeling hot.

'*Non*. Wis plastic surgery.'

'I don't want money or looks. I just want a man who treats me nicely.' Her voice wistful as she sits forward, resting both hands on the table. 'Anyway, it's probably worse because the film festival lot are in town,' Fee adds.

'You mean, the place is full of actresses and stuff?' I don't recall seeing any famous faces when I was looking for J-Lo on the way in.

She shakes her head. 'Monaco is currently full of fashionistas and the super wealthy. Oil tycoons, minor royals, and medically enhanced socialites.'

'Ah. People who don't have real jobs.'

'Exactly.' She makes a triangle around her glass with her thumbs and forefingers, her attention turning inward almost. 'I'm sure if you happen to be in Ibiza next month, you'll see all the same faces. They're like nomads, but instead of trekking from camp to camp with camels and tents, they use private jets and stay in their vastly expensive holiday homes or ridiculously priced hotel suites. Royal Ascot, next on to Wimbledon, followed by a week in Venice for the film festival, then back to Monaco for the yacht show in September. Art Basel in December, New Year's Eve in St Barts right before heading to Dubai for the races in the spring, then on to the Kentucky Derby.'

'Some people have all the luck, right?'

'I don't know. The same places and the same beautiful faces month after month.' She picks up her glass, seeming to come back to herself. 'I think it sounds like a complete bore, personally.'

'How do you know all this?' Though I keep my tone neutral, something tells me this isn't just an observation or second-hand information from her.

She smiles, but it almost seems tense. 'I hear the wives and girlfriends talking after classes. Complaining, mostly.'

Hmm. I don't think so.

'You forgot about the other beauties.' Charles inclines his

head, his raised glass indicating a group of women crowded around the man Charles thought was about to hit on him. Standing straight now, his face in profile. Tall, dark, and handsome, as far as I can tell.

'Yes,' Fee agrees. 'One of those things is *not* like the others.'

'Because one of them is male?' I'm confused because they're all tall and dressed well; him in dark pants and a fitted shirt, the girls with their long tan legs running up to their chins and tiny dresses sparkling like candy wrappers. 'He must be real entertaining the way they're hanging on his every word.'

'I think you'll find *they* are the entertainment,' Fee murmurs, her tone dropping.

'*Non*. It is 'is wallet they find entertaining.'

'I think someone might be selling sex. Hint: It's not the one wearing pants.'

'I've never seen a working girl look like that.' I glance back at the group. 'Every one of them looks like a freaking Victoria's Secret model!'

'That's how they can charge so much.' She glances knowingly my way. 'The rich nomads follow the events, and the girls follow them.'

'Some even travel with them,' Charles says. 'I understand rich Arabs 'ave their seasonal favourites.'

'What, like a blonde for summer and a redhead for fall?'

'Who knows. You could argue some cultures have arranged marriages, I suppose. Anyway.' Fee sighs, reaching for her glass. 'I guess for a lot of men it's easier to pay for a relationship. Less risky to their billions.'

'What about their hearts?' I find myself asking.

'I dunno.' She shrugs. 'I'll let you know when I find a man with one. A straight man,' she amends as Charles opens his mouth to protest.

'What makes someone as pretty as you be so cynical?'

We all turn to the deep voice to find the working girl's entertainment—*or was that the other way around?*—standing at the side of our booth. I was right; he is good looking. He's also French, though his accent is a lot less pronounced than Charles's. My final observation? Judging by his languid expression, this is a man who has no trouble with self-perception.

'Did anyone ever tell you it's rude to listen to other people's conversation?' I answer when it appears my companions have been struck mute.

'Yes, my mother.' He shakes his head in the vein of one who knows he's a trial and is pretending to give a damn about it. 'I am a grave disappointment to her,' he adds, sliding himself into the seat next to me.

'Sit down, why don't you.' I sneer, wriggling my butt closer to Charles, who, in turn, shimmies closer to Fee while looking like he's ingesting prunes.

Charles, my friend, I think your gaydar needs a reboot.

'My mother also taught me that beautiful girls have sharp tongues,' the stranger says. 'But I find that just makes them all the more fun.' His gaze is bold as it sweeps over me. I find myself glancing at my friends, sure my expression reads *can you believe this dipshit?*

'I'm Benoît, by the way.'

'And I'm not interested,' I retort, my tone flat.

'You prove my point for me.' He looks up, shooting Fee a cheeky wink. 'Your friend doesn't like me.'

'Oh, I'm sure it's not that,' Fee answers with a brightness that seems almost brittle.

'Benoît.' He holds his hand out across the table to her, half standing, repeating the process with Charles. I'm just about to ask why they get the polite version, and I get hit on when Charles, his hand still in Benoît's, speaks.

'We know who you are. We work for The Wolf Group. All three of us.'

'You work there, too?' I ask, turning my head his way.

'Don't sound so excited about it. I should tell you, the meaner you are to me, the more I like it.'

'There are names for people like you,' I mutter, meaning asshole over masochist.

'Yes, names *like boss*,' Charles murmurs under his breath, covering his next words with a cough. *'Also owner.'*

My head swings Charles's way, a denial on the tip of my tongue.

'I wouldn't expect you to be nice to me just because I own a little of the company.' Something tells me that's exactly what he would expect, cemented by his actions as his arm feeds along the seat behind me, his thumb lightly brushing my spine. It's such a light touch but somehow intimate. And unwanted. 'It's the weekend, and you're not working now. Have you ever been in the VIP suite?' Benoît directs his question to Fee, who shakes her head.

'This is only my third time here,' she answers.

'What about you?' This time, he directs his question to Charles.

'*Non*, but I have heard they serve nothing but Dom Perignon. Is this true?'

I can feel Benoît's gaze crawling over me, though I refuse to return it.

'In the VIP suite, you can get almost anything you want.' Was I the only one who caught that tone? 'You should join me,' he adds quite suddenly, as though the idea has only just occurred to him. *Yeah, right.* 'All of you.'

'That's very kind,' Fee protests. I wonder if she's reading my expression or if she has her own reservations. 'But—'

'But we're waiting for my boyfriend,' I interject.

'Then he should come, too.' He stands and pauses briefly. 'I'll leave your names at the door and see you there soon, I hope.' And then he's gone.

'Dammit,' I announce as soon as he's out of earshot. 'I thought that would've put him off. No way I'm going to hang out with the creepy boss.'

Fee grimaces. 'He's not really creepy . . .'

'Oh. My bad. He's just a douche.'

'I know. I'm sorry. God, he was a little intense, wasn't he?'

'If by intense, you mean creepy, yes.'

'Maybe he's drunk?'

At Charles's interjection, I turn to him. 'How did you not realise you were staring at our boss?'

'I don't have in my lenses,' he protests, holding up his hands.

'What?'

'I wore my new sunglasses earlier. Remember? They are prescription!'

As an explanation, I find this baffling.

'So, what, when it got dark, you decided you didn't need to see? How does that even work? Well, I'm not going in there,' I add mulishly. 'The dude has my creep-o-meter going off.'

'But Rose.' Fee reaches over the table to take my hand. 'How can we not?'

'We just don't go. He's partying. His eyes were glazed, so he's probably on something. He'll probably forget he even asked us.'

'And if he doesn't?' she asks carefully. 'And we see him at work, and he remembers we ignored him?'

'Okay, so we'll go and dance. He'll never find us on the dance floor. He'll think we've left.'

'Even I cannot dance all night,' grumbles Charles. 'I think we go. Just for a little while. I, for one, do not want to be fired.'

'How could he fire us for not wanting to party with him?'

Fee's fingers tighten on mine. 'Do we really want to find out?'

23

ROSE

So we go. We leave our drinks, and we leave our table on the terrace to go back into the club, though I do so with the protest that I'm only doing it for them.

Because they don't have a Remy in their lives.

As this thought strikes, I wonder what will happen when I no longer have him. When our relationship runs its course, will I still have a job? I push the thought to the back of my mind. Living day to day, living for now needs to become a way of life for me.

There's another heavy at the velvet rope at the entrance to the VIP suite, and I seriously hope we'll be turned away despite the potential embarrassment. And there would be embarrassment because people seem to look as we approach that hallowed space. But no such luck. The rope is unhooked, and we're ushered through the twinkly crystal curtain.

'Leave our names at the door, my ass,' I complain, following my friends. 'What door.'

Inside, the space is dark and intimate, the décor echoing that of the main club. Black interspersed with pink and purple as the skull-shaped disco balls glittering above, the lights from the dance floor catching the tiny mirrored tiles. And Charles was right; behind the bar is a wall filled with bottles of Dom Perignon champagne.

'My friends!" Benoît approaches us with his arms held wide. 'No boyfriend?'

'He'll be here later.' I twist my lips in an approximation of a smile.

'Then let me get you a drink.'

'I'm good,' I answer as my friends follow his direction to the bar. I flop onto the nearest seat, placing my purse next to my thigh as Benoît lowers himself to the seat opposite.

'Help yourself to the champagne.' A silver bucket sits between us on a tiny black table.

'Like I said, I'm good,' I repeat, folding my arms and deliberately ignoring him. But as I glance up, I notice Fee and Charles eyeing me warily. Their anxious looks remind me of what they perceive as a precarious situation. So I toe the line. For their sake, forcibly turning up the corners of my mouth as I add, 'Thank you.'

'A smile? I'm honoured. *Femme qui rit, à moitié dans ton lit.*'

'Yeah, sure,' I answer with disinterest, wondering why Charles chuckled and why Fee is now frowning.

'Let me introduce you to a few people.' He stands, people nearby gravitating towards us almost as though by prior instruction. Charles is immediately drawn into introductions, but Fee hangs back.

'It's okay,' I assure her, pointing at the small group of people behind her. 'Go mingle. I'm pretty sure the guy in the black shirt was on the front cover of Vogue last month.'

'Rose, *femme qui rit, à moitié dans ton lit.* It means make a girl laugh, and she's halfway in your bed.'

'That's what he said?' She nods. 'In his dreams.' I huff unhappily. 'Honestly, it's all good. *I'll* be good. I mean, I promise not to strangle him or anything.' Or laugh at him, never mind *with*. 'You can keep an eye on me just as well from over there.'

It's not that I feel the need for supervision. I'm pretty sure I can shoot the man down just as effectively whether she's nearby or not. But maybe it's best that I'm the only one making possible enemies right now.

'If you're sure . . .'

'What I'm sure of is, out of the three of us, Charles is the one who needs watching most.' She follows the line of my gaze. 'If he gets any closer to that redhead, there's gonna be a little snake on snake action for sure, and I'm not sure this is the kind of place that would take kindly to that.' *Also, maybe he's not a redhead. Maybe it's just the pink lighting giving his hair that hue.*

'I'll be sure to tell him this is a no-bone zone,' she says, her attention turning back to me briefly, her smile almost reluctant.

She's no sooner gone when Benoît slides into the seat opposite.

'How do you like Monaco so far?' he asks, sitting back in his seat, one long leg crossed over the other.

'How do you know I haven't been here for a long time?' I counter, adopting a similar pose, though without crossing my legs.

'Well, now,' he begins, almost as though he's a little shy. I'll admit, he's pretty good at this even if we both know this is just an act. 'I have a small admission to make. I saw you on your first day. The walls in the office are mostly glass,' he says, almost by way of explanation. 'You were in one of the meeting rooms filling out forms, I think. You looked a little like, what is the saying? Like a fish out of water?'

I try not to bristle at the implication, pushing away the

residual sense of confusion and worry I'd felt that day. 'Doesn't everyone feel a little strange on their first day at a new job?'

'It looked like more than that.' Sitting forward, he pulls the bottle of champagne from the bucket and begins unwinding the foil. 'You looked vulnerable.'

I snort unhappily. You are barking up the wrong tree, friend.

'*Pardonne-moi.* I don't mean to offend you. I was simply intrigued.' He pops the cork expertly and begins pouring the effervescent liquid into two glasses, passing one over the small table with an inciteful look.

'Well, as you can see, I survived.' I take the glass from his hand because champagne is champagne. Besides, I need something to take the taste of this exchange out of my mouth.

'*Non.* You have thrived.' He raises his glass in a toast.

How am I supposed to refuse that toast? So I don't, the crisp bubbles dancing on my tongue.

'Where did they eventually hide you?'

'Hide?' I roll my lips together, savouring the flavour as I place my glass down. Okay, I'm stalling for time, trying to work out what his angle is.

'No one seemed to know where you'd gone to. The beautiful girl with the luxurious dark hair? *Très exotique.*'

'Someone needs to book you some sensitivity training,' I mutter under my breath because exotic is not a compliment.

'I began to think I'd imagined you.'

'Oh, boy. You're really laying it on thick. Did you forget already that I said I'm involved with someone?'

'Ah, the boyfriend.' His head drops between his shoulders, but his smile is still visible. 'Someone snapped you up so quickly.' As his head comes up slowly, his smile almost

wolfish. Though a pale imitation of the wolf himself. *Of Remy.*
'I could be good to you.'

'I think you should stick to neutral topics if you want the pleasure of my company.'

He nods slowly, seeming to consider my words. 'How do you find Monaco?' A change of direction.

'I like it so far.'

'Two square kilometres. More billionaires than anywhere else in the world. Super cars. Super yachts. Supermodels. You like all this?'

'I like my friends. I like my job. I like the scenery.'

'Yes. I can appreciate that.' My skin prickles under the weight of his gaze. 'And you like a man. So, where is this boyfriend of yours?'

'If he has any sense, he'll be tucked up in bed.'

'If he had any sense, he'd make sure you were tucked up next to him. He neglects you, my dear.'

'Is this a speciality of yours, hitting on women who aren't interested? I guess you like them a little hard to get, huh?'

'Hard to get but not impossible.' The final word is wholly French and wholly provocative.

'I don't know, I have to tell you, Benny,' I reply, pressing my elbow on the table to cup my chin in my hand. 'The longer I speak to you, the worse your odds become.'

'*Non.* You like to spar with me. I think you and I would make a fire between the sheets.'

And I think you're not only annoying but deluded, too.

'What a shame I'm not into flammable nightwear.' I make as though to rise, dipping to grab my clutch.

'I'm sorry. Please, at least, finish your drink.'

A quick look at my surroundings tells me neither Charles or Fee are in view. I lower back into my seat reluctantly because I can hardly leave without them.

'What do you think is the item most sold in Monaco?' he asks quite suddenly.

'What?'

'A change in the topic of conversation,' he answers airily.

'I don't know.' Truly, I don't. At work, hundreds of thousands of dollars run through my fingers on any given week, at least figuratively, as I purchase trinkets and experiences. Or time, as the concierge bible goes. But surely this isn't indicative of the whole of Monaco? Just then, an older man swaggers past the velvet entry ropes; you know the type, a balding head, a sizeable paunch, looks like he has a mohair sweater growing out of the neck of his shirt. But this troll, pardon, man has a beautiful woman tucked under each of his arms. Women young enough to be his daughters, though fathers don't, as a rule, feel their daughter's asses.

'Viagra,' I answer impulsively, my attention caught by Benoît's soft chuckle. 'Am I right?'

'A good guess. Should we find a pharmacist to ask?'

'If you don't know, why ask the question?'

'Oh, I know what the answer is.' He sits forward quite suddenly, taking my hand. I try to pull away, but his fingers tighten, his other hand coming to cover it. To those looking on, it must look like a tender moment, not one where his grip is almost punishing. 'The answer is sex. Sex is the commodity traded most here.'

'I'm not sure why you're looking at me like that. I'm not for sale.'

'Oh, I think you are, though perhaps your rates have risen now that you no longer work at the Pink Pussy Cat.' My stomach sinks at the utterance, a sudden flash of strobe lighting turning his features demonic. 'I might not have found you, but I found your file. I also discovered that when you noted you had worked for Highland Holdings, you were actually working at a strip club.'

'Gentleman's club,' I find myself countering ridiculously.

'There are no gentlemen in a place like that.'

'Something you'd know all about?' As his fingers tighten, I try not to wince.

'Clever of you to name the company rather than the name of the place.'

'So you found my resumé.' I'm almost surprised my voice sounds so normal because inside, I'm quaking. I haven't lied on my resumé. Not exactly. Anyone who cared to dig a little would've found what he has. 'I worked as a waitress. I served drinks. I don't see how that's the same as selling sex.'

'While dressed as a schoolgirl, you sold watered down, overpriced drinks to men who wanted to fuck you. Such moral high ground,' he taunts. 'But I do wonder if that's the only thing you sold.'

I find myself leaning forward, peeling his fingers from mine. 'Fuck you.'

'I thought we'd already established I'd like to. Just name your price.'

'Fuck you and the deaf, dumb, and blind horse you rode in on. If you don't let go of my hand—'

'You'll what? Cause a scene? Go ahead. I think my reputation can survive it.'

'I'm sorry to interrupt.' Fee's voice is like sweet relief. It seems his reputation might survive a run-in with me, but not in front of another Wolf employee, and that fact would be kind of interesting if I could gather my thoughts. But I can't right now. I'm too shaken up.

That's kind of interesting. 'Rose, our cab is here.' She turns to Ben almost apologetically. 'It was pre-ordered. You see I have a spinning class at some ungodly hour in the morning, and Rose is helping me.'

'Well, I guess we'd better get going.' As I stand, I find I can pull my hand from his now. I don't spare him a glance as I tuck my arm into Fee's as we hurry to our phantom cab.

24

REMY

ARE you joining me for lunch?

Monday, eleven in the morning, and I've yet to hear from Rose. It's not a huge concern but rather an irritating niggle, especially as it's become our usual manner to have exchanged at least a couple of texts by nine. It should seem a little hypocritical to be suspicious, considering I'm the one keeping secrets, but nevertheless, there it is.

When I don't receive a response, suspicion turns to concern, concern that I brush aside as I decide if anything untoward has happened, I'd already know. Whether I think I'd know instinctually or from the position as her boss, I don't care to examine as I pull up the Wolf Tower concierge app on my phone and place a request. Or rather, an order. An order that's denied immediately.

I go directly to the instant message function.

Rose, my request for lunch was returned with an error code. Any idea why?

Restart the app. That's what we usually advise, comes her immediate response. It's hardly flattering that she'll ignore my texts but answer my questions regarding the app. I consider the fact that I'd intervened with her line manager, who seemed hell-bent on catering to me herself. *Catering for me in kind like she did my father, no doubt.* I told the woman in no uncertain terms that I wanted the newest member of staff to attend to my app requests, the implication being that the least experienced member would be the weakest link. She took the bait, insisting that all members of her team were trained to the highest level. That I would find no fault.

But it was just a way to get her off my back, perhaps getting Rose onto hers. The thought makes me smile because that has yet to happen in my office. Rose is particularly conscientious of what occurs during her hours of work. But back to the app, all enquiries are time-critical and monitored, response times part of the staff key performance indicators. Poor response times to initial enquiries count against both the team and the individual and count towards a financial bonus scheme. The result? Rose might not answer my texts this morning, but she'd protect her colleagues.

Restarting the app is not something I have in mind.

Perhaps you should come and show me how to do that.

Sure. I mean, it's not like I have anything more pressing to do among the other hundred requests that have come through this morning. Whoever said words on a screen come without emotion never took part in this kind of exchange. **You're not the only resident I attend to.**

Care to rephrase that?

Fine. You're the most demanding of my patrons.

And you're trying to make me angry. Why would she phrase it this way? I'm not her patron—that's not the kind of relationship we have. I can barely get her to take a thing from me. She didn't want the membership to Papaya Beach on Saturday, preferring to slum it at the public beach.

How would I explain that to Lea? she'd asked. Or was it Tee?

I can't remember, but I do remember a pinch of annoyance that she was happy to keep things between us secret still. Which is ridiculous, considering the secrets I'm keeping myself.

Can it be she has changed her mind about us in this short time? I push the thought away in favour of another. I'd offered to buy her a watch she was admiring online last week when she went a little crazy, insisting she was looking at it for a client.

Why won't she let me look after her?

See? Demanding, she retorts.

Says the woman who begged me for my cock on Friday when I'd scarcely cleared the front door.

REMY! This is a work app. Do you want to get me fired?

What I want is to see you this afternoon. Why is she fighting this?

Give me until about twenty-five o'clock, and I should be through.

I think I take precedence.

Think? To hell with that. I know I take precedence.

Because you have friends in low places?

Ma Rose, you have that the wrong way around. You are a highly esteemed friend who I happen to like to take low places on occasion.

Again. Work app!

She's certainly making me work for it.

Remy, I'm swamped, comes her response this time. **Try Deliveroo or UberEats. Or whatever the Daddy Warbucks Monaco equivalent is.**

I stare at the phone in my hand, wondering where the resistance is coming from. I haven't seen her since Saturday morning when we parted with plans to catch up on Sunday, plans that didn't come to fruition because she said she wasn't feeling up to it. Was she lying then? Now? Is she too much of a coward to say we're through?

Through? Fuck through. We haven't even started.

My stomach twists, but I push away all analysis, typing out my reply. If she won't accept an invitation, I can always issue a command.

I'm not sure who Daddy Warbucks is, but if he lives in Wolf Tower, he'd use the concierge service, which I believe is you today.

You know, none of the other residents has their lunch delivered to them by us.

Good. As the owner of Wolf Tower, I think I should be the only one. An abuse of power? Who gives a fuck.

Fine, I'll deliver your lunch, but I can't stay. As I've said, I'm super, super busy today.

I'm sure I can persuade her otherwise once she's here, even if sex is off the table.

And if it is off the table, then I'll just have to make sure it's on the desk, conscientiousness be damned.

Resisting the urge to adjust the flicker of interest in my pants, I put down my phone and return to the mound of documents to be signed and begin skimming through them. We've recently broken ground on a development that will become a boutique hotel just outside of Menton Old Town on the edge of the Côte, the first of its kind in decades. Pen poised over the contracts, I consider taking Rose on a trip down there sometime. Nestled between the mountains and the Mediterranean, the little town has a charming old-world feel and is full of buildings from the Belle Époque period that almost seem to turn rose gold at sunset.

Maybe she'd like to go to the lemon festival next spring?

The thought is like a dart to the psyche because spring is months away—next year, in fact. I'd be a fool to think this thing between us could carry on as it is now. The secrets between us can only fester and gnaw, and when the truths eventually surface, could I forgive her if our positions were reversed? Forgive her for hiding the truth from me, for intruding on my past by paying for an investigation. For keeping the balance of power in her favour and forcing me to continue to work for *her* when I'd already be rich in my own right.

At least this I know the answer to.

'I wouldn't—couldn't—forgive her,' I recount quietly, pen still in hand, my gaze unseeing. In the same breath, I know I'm not prepared to let her go. The past three weeks have been unlike any other time in my life and Rose unlike any other woman. She requires nothing but my attention for the time we're together, yet she invades my mind continually.

'*Fuck,*' I exhale, dropping my head into my hands.

'What's wrong with you?'

My head jerks up, swinging sharply to Rhett. What I'd prefer to be swinging is my fists.

'Don't you ever knock,' I complain, looking down at the annotation I'm supposed to initial for at least the third time.

'The dragon said I could come in.'

'You're talking shit again.'

'She did, honestly. She said, Everett, my boy, go right on in because God knows when you'll see him next.' In the periphery of my vision, he folds his arms across his chest, leaning his thigh against the table at the centre of the room. 'You missed a meeting last Friday, I hear.'

'Madame Bisset—'

'Paulette, to you.'

'Madame Bisset would no more tell you I missed a meeting than she would flash you her underwear.'

'I think I just vomited in my mouth,' he says with a

grimace. 'Never, ever say the word *underwear* in relation to your assistant in my hearing again. They're probably like . . . huge, grey tents.'

'The woman is the size of a sparrow.'

'With the viciousness of a pterodactyl, but she's old.'

'And?'

'It stands to reason she wears ugly underwear.'

'I can't believe we're having this conversation.'

'You started it. You and your malingering ways.'

'Even the chairman of the board is entitled to take a few hours off.'

'Yeah, but you're not by yourself, are you? You can't entertain yourself for that length of time.' No need to ask what he means by that as he unfolds his left hand, beginning to shake his curled fist in the air.

'Don't confuse my free time with yours,' I answer witheringly.

'They seek him here. They seek him there. Those Frenchies seek him every-fucking-where.'

'You're not French.'

'I don't go looking for you. I know where you are when you're not with me. If they'd picked up the phone to me, I would've told them.'

'Which is where?'

'With your latest squeeze.'

'Jealous, Rhett?'

He chuckles unpleasantly. 'Not a fucking bit. You're tying yourself up in knots so tight it's only a matter of time before you come a cropper. Or as my delightful niece would say, before you get *effed* in the *a*.'

'You don't have family, do you? I thought you were made in a lab somewhere.'

'No, I think you're confused. What I said was that my mother is a bitch, that she's more pitbull than *Lab*.'

'I sometimes wonder why I keep you around,' I find myself grumbling.

'Maybe because I can kill a man with one hand without spilling my pint. Or maybe because of my sunny temperament and my charming personality.'

'You wouldn't know charming if it bit you on the head.'

'Speaking of heads, your problem is that your little head has been getting all the action, but it's your big head that's suffering. You know there's such a thing as thinking too much, right?'

'An affliction you don't suffer from yourself.'

'What's to think about? The way I look at it, you've made your bed, you've just got to lie in it now. Or shag in it, as the case may be. Make the most of it, mate, because it's only a matter of time before she finds out the many ways you're a total bastard.'

'Don't let me stop you,' I drawl, sitting back in my chair. 'Please, educate me on my failures.'

Why indulge him? Because introspection is something I'd like to be distracted from. Because he's right, though he probably doesn't realise quite how right he is. But the more time I spend with Rose, the less I want to give her up. And the less I want to give her up, the more I complicate things. I'm so fucking aware that I could lose her the minute I tell her the truth. Would she do something rash for revenge when she knows the whole sordid story, like run out and marry the first man she meets to get her hands on her shares so she can be rid of me?

'Nah. What's the point? You know you're fucked.'

With a final withering look in his direction, I return my attention to the paperwork in front of me. Maybe if I ignore him, he'll leave. I initial the page and flip to the next when the door to my suite of offices opens again.

'Does no one in this building knock these days,' I find myself roaring.

'Hey, you called me, not the other way around.' Rose stands on the other side of the office with an unfamiliar scowl painted across her face. One hand pressed to her cocked hip, and in the other, she holds a brown paper bag.

'Rose, you're early.' I begin to stand as she walks a little farther into the room, dropping the paper bag to the boardroom table on the opposite end of where Rhett lounges.

'Yeah, I know. I guess you can always call this brunch instead of lunch, but it's the best I can manage.'

As I draw closer, the scent of hot grease seems to permeate.

'What's in the bag, Heidi?' She presses her lips into a flat line at Rhett's goading enquiry, an uncomplimentary look gliding his way.

'What it is is not for you.'

'Is . . . is that MacDonald's?' The question is barely out of his mouth when he almost launches himself across the table. Meanwhile, I can feel my lip curling in disgust.

'That's what it says on the bag, doesn't it?' She whips the bag away before he can reach it.

'MacDonald's?' I repeat, my response oozing with disgust. Disgust that goes unheard as the pair begin to bicker over the contents of the trans-fat filled bag.

'I didn't bring lunch for you,' she says, holding the brown paper bag tighter.

'Heidi,' he says, infusing this with what I imagine sounds like charm to him. 'You know you're asking for it.'

'*Ta guele,*' I snarl. *Shut it.*

'Relax,' he replies, unmoved. 'Mickey D's milkshakes bring all the boys to the yard.'

'Yeah, well, this milkshake isn't for you,' she retorts.

'You can't get a boy all raring to go and expect him to turn it off like that. Not when there's a Big Mac on offer.'

Chin high, she swings the bag behind her. 'A lucky guess. And why do you keep calling me Heidi?' Though her voice is strong, the high colour of her cheeks gives away her disquiet.

'The braid and the scarf thingy in your hair,' he answers without missing a beat. 'You look like you should be running through meadows with a St. Bernard at your heels.'

Rhett is usually pretty good on his feet, but it's fortunate that she's wearing her hair as she is, or perhaps fortunate that he chose to say it within her hearing today. Heidi isn't meant as a compliment; it's just a way that he gets to goad me. Remind me of where this all started. The knots he's convinced I'm tying myself in. The fact that she worked in a strip club. *Like I even give a fuck.* 'Come on, love,' he resumes. 'Give up the chips.'

'No *fries* for you. Is he telling the truth?' She angles her gaze my way, seeking my reassurance. This doesn't come as a surprise. What does, however, is the sudden prick of conscience I experience.

One more lie I'm complicit in.

'Would I lie to you?' he asks, hands out like a priest giving a sermon. 'Yesterday, you looked like a sexy assassin. You had your hair poker straight and tied up on top of your head. You know what I called you then?'

'No, and I don't think I want to.' Despite her cool tone, he answers anyway.

'Villanelle.'

My mind is still whirling that he called her sexy, though I somehow register his response. 'Like poetry?' Why does it feel worse to me that he thinks of Rose as poetry over sexy? Why? The man can barely recount a limerick.

Rhett glances my way, looking as confused as I feel. 'Poetry? It's a program on TV. Fuck hot Russian assassin? Lesbian undertones?'

'Well, this has been . . . real.' Rose shakes her head like a horse shaking off flies.

She dumps the bag on the table again as Rhett dives for it, sliding into the chair at the head of the table with a triumphant, 'Yes!'

'There's a Big Mac, fries, and twelve chicken nuggets,' she says, rubbing her hand against her forehead. 'I didn't know what you wanted—'

It wasn't greasy fast food, and I'm sure my expression conveys this perfectly. The only thing I had any intention of eating this afternoon was her.

'—but maybe you can share or something.'

'I don't want fast food.' I'm aware how petulant I sound, but this isn't faked disappointment. Fast food or a slow screw —or even just a few minutes with Rose in his arms—which would any man choose?

'Yeah, well, I don't want to spend today pandering to rich people, but here I am anyway.'

'That's your job,' I point out, none too nicely, I fear, judging by her expression. But the way she's looking at me doesn't keep me at bay.

'Lucky me, huh? I get to nanny for babies in grown-up bodies. Babies in control of a large portion of the world's wealth, yet they can't even order a salad or a sandwich for themselves.'

'You don't have a dog and bark yourself.' That was an unpleasant analogy and one I wish I could inhale, dispel, but fuck it, this isn't how I planned my day to go. She said she was too tired to spend time with me Sunday and can barely look at me right now. And now I'm being a bastard to her when all I want to do is take her in my arms and kiss the hurt from her face.

'Rose—' Even her name doesn't sound as gentle as it should.

'No one could ever accuse you of having a silver tongue,' Rhett mutters. 'Ignore him. He must have low blood sugar.'

'I do not need you to make excuses for me.'

'Your funeral. You can't help some people.' He holds up the flaccid looking burger as though in thanks. 'If you ever want anyone killed, Heidi, just give me a shout. Anyone but him,' he amends as her eyes flick my way again.

'Everett, get out.'

'No, you stay. I'm out of here.'

'You're not going anywhere,' I growl, grabbing her arm as she turns.

Her gaze flicks pointedly down to where I've creased the sleeve of her dress. 'Let. The. Fuck. *Go.*'

'Everett,' I repeat.

'Got it.' He begins to gather the grease-stained burger bag in one hand, the half-eaten burger in the other. As the door closes behind him, I unfurl my fingers, almost surprised she hadn't pulled away.

'I am at a loss to explain what just happened,' I begin as the blood in my veins seethes. 'But this isn't about lunch or the way you wear your hair, or your terse texts.'

'*My* terse texts?' she retorts, folding her arms. 'Let me tell you, yours were hardly a barrel of laughs to read. Demanding and childish and—'

'Let me finish.'

'Was it one woof for yes and two for no?' Her response is

sweet yet full of malice, but I brought it on myself. And I won't be baited.

'I'm sorry, that wasn't what I meant.' Her lips purse, but I carry on. 'But I was provoked.'

'Pretty sure that's the excuse all bullies use.'

'I was provoked, and you are doing the provoking,' I continue, not rising to her tone. 'But more importantly, you've been avoiding me.'

'I am not avoiding you,' she replies immediately. 'I told you, yesterday I had a headache. I was tired.'

'That's not it.' And I feel it in my bones as I step into her, forcing her to tip her head back to look at me. Is that confusion in her eyes or regret? 'Friday was, as always, wonderful. Yesterday? Today? You're not the same.' I wrap a wisp of her hair around my finger as she angles her attention away. 'What's going on, Rose? Are we done here?' My words are cool, yet my insides burn. I both desire and dread her answer as something inside me screams that this isn't the end. *It isn't over because I'm not ready to let go.* 'Tell me what I can do.' To make this go away. To make you look at me like you did before the weekend.

'I've done something.' The words fall in a rush, her eyes rising slowly to mine, this time full of tears. 'I know everyone does it sometimes, but it doesn't stop me from feeling terrible.'

A fist suddenly twists my innards in its grip. 'Tell me. What did you do on Saturday?' As my hands grip her shoulders, I'm surprised my tone sounds so even given the sudden eruption of violence bursting in my head.

Has she—I can't contemplate it.

Whoever it is, I swear I will fucking kill them—I'll make her watch as I ruin them.

'Saturday?' A tiny line forms between her brows.

'Tell me,' I grate out, my grip tightening as I ignore the hypocrite I am.

'But what has Saturday got to do with anything?'

'*Remy. Avez-vous . . .*'

At the sound of Benoît's voice, Rose springs from my arms and moves toward the wall of windows as though she's discovered something of great interest there.

'No, Ben, I don't have a moment. And I don't quite know why my office has suddenly become la Gare du Nord!' With each word, my voice becomes louder until the name of the Paris train station roars across the office.

'My apologies. But your assistant isn't at her desk,' he offers, unmoved by my outburst. 'And I did knock. Perhaps you didn't hear it.' His eyes move to Rose; a silhouette in the window. 'Perhaps you were busy.'

I'm going to have a better lock put on the door. One that engages immediately upon closure. 'I don't have time—'

'Rose?' Benoît fills her name with such surprise. 'What a place to find you!'

She stiffens, though she begins to slowly turn.

'Where did you disappear to on Saturday?'

She raises her chin, her arms still folded, and I notice how her fingers make deep indents in the sleeve of her dress. 'I went home. With Fee. You remember Fee? And Charles?'

As her attention moves to me, I bite back the torrent of recrimination forcing it back down my throat. I don't give a fuck who she was with—who will swear blind she had nothing to do with him. I refuse to have this conversation with him here, though I will have answers. She's done something. *Something everyone does.* I know deep in my gut that my cousin is involved somehow, and nothing good can come from that.

'I do remember them. Such a shame we didn't finish our talk.' He's all agreement and openness; an act he's thoroughly perfected. 'Remy, you remember when I said there was a beautiful new member of staff?' His attention skates back to Rose, to where she stands as still as a statue. 'I think someone has been hiding you. What department do you work in, *chérie*?'

'This is my office, not a coffee shop,' I bark, my hands gripping the back of the chair. 'Pick up girls elsewhere unless you want to find yourself facing a sexual harassment suit.'

'Elsewhere or someone else,' he murmurs, his expression like a hyena sniffing for a weakness. 'I'm sensing a lot of tension, *cousin*.'

'You will be sensing the arrival of my fist if you don't get out.'

'Really, Remy? You can't have all the toys.' Our eyes lock, and I feel my lip curl, seconds away from forgetting we were friends as boys.

'I'm no one's plaything.' Rose's voice rings out across the room. Though I hear the waver in it, I can't look at her. Not when I know where this is going.

'You haven't told her, have you?' His voice is pitched lower, but the triumph in it is detectable under the sham.

'Told me what?'

Benoît's shoulders sag with a sigh, his head dropping between his shoulder blades. At least, that's what the outside world would see. But I know him, and I saw the flickering of delight in his gaze. When he looks up again, his expression is one of contrition. My gut tightens again, this time my fists, too. What is the bastard up to?

'I'm sorry, Remy. Seeing Rose here made me lose my train of thought.' *A lie on top of other lies.* 'I came to tell you that Amélie's car is in the parking lot. I thought you'd want to know.'

This . . . is not a lie but perhaps the Fates dealing their

hand. I thought I could ward this off without lowering myself. Ward off the lies and twist it into a truth that didn't need to be heard by her.

'Who is Amélie?'

Neither of us answers, though Ben's barely concealed delight seems to ask, *do you want to tell her or should I?*

It should never have come to this. I should've come clean from the start—but where would I have started? I've built a lie upon a lie until I'm sitting behind the walls of a fortress of falsehoods, first driven by mistrust and then by fear.

And now? Now I risk everything. I risk her love.

'Amélie is . . .' I cannot stop him. I can no longer hide. 'How do you say *femme à être*?'

Though directed at me, I don't answer, just glare. Glare hard enough that he should at least have the decency to turn to salt for looking back.

'Rose.' I've done something. A hundred somethings. But the words won't come because where do I start?

'What is it?'

I curse, this time at the door. The blood in my veins turns to ice water as it opens, a sultry purr preceding her appearance. Her. Amélie. The first of my pigeons come home to roost.

'Bonjour, mon amour. Did you miss me?'

Her eyes remain on me though she reaches Benoît first, languidly grazing his cheeks with air-kisses. *Like recognising like, no doubt.*

'Bonjour, Amélie. Remind me, what is the English for *future épouse*?

Her hand slips from his shoulder, her sights set on me. 'It means wife-to-be. Hello, my future husband. Did you miss me?'

25

ROSE

FOR A MOMENT, I think I've misheard because that just doesn't make sense.

Wife-to-be? Her future husband?

It's almost laughable. Isn't it? It has to be. Except I'm not laughing as he allows her to slide her hands around his neck. As he accepts the kiss she presses to his cheek.

As he refuses to look at me.

Oh, God. I think I'm going to be sick. And not because of the lingering smell of McDonald's but because it's all true.

I'm a fool, and he's a lying, cheating . . . heartbreaking tool.

'If you'll excuse me,' I find myself uttering, not sparing a glance for anyone as I move in the direction of the door. My legs are unsteady, and the phrase *heartache* is suddenly something very real. Like it's being torn apart, the pain of it a scream choking in my throat.

'Allow me.' He's at the door, pulling it open, allowing me to pass through—not the him I want but the other sleaze. The one I left on Saturday night. The one who almost forced me to confess I'd lied on my resumé today. I was so determined that I wouldn't tell Remy I'd worked at a strip club, concerned what he'd think of me. He was right, I was avoiding him. I knew I'd have to tell him, but I didn't know how.

I made myself ill just thinking about it.

What a fucking joke! And I am that joke.

How dare he question me. How dare he look at me with such betrayal when the man has a wife!

To be.

Semantics.

All the same, he's been stringing me along. And how!

Yes, how? Exactly how? Hasn't he spent almost every moment with me? How can he be promised to another when he looks at me like he does?

I stumble past the bank of elevators, pulling open the door to the stairs no one ever uses this far up. The door clunks shut as I press my forehead to the cool concrete wall and choke back a sob of hysteria. My entire body shakes as the result of this emotional tsunami, a situation coming out of nowhere; unforeseen, uninvited, unbelievable. *But I won't cry. Not here. He doesn't deserve my tears. He doesn't deserve the steam off my piss!*

Amélie. Even her name is sexy. She sounds like a sex phone operator and looks like a gazelle—a really good-looking, caramel-toned, shiny gazelle. One with really expensive shoes and a Chanel handbag dangling from her arm.

Do gazelles come with thoroughbred pedigrees?

I bet this one does.

And he didn't even look at me.

'That fucking *fuck!* Ow, that hurts.' I stare at my reddened palm, the wall no worse for my anger-fuelled slap. 'At least I haven't broken a toe.' Along with the inane whisper, I sink to the stairs and push my head into my trembling hands, taking a series of deep, shaking breaths.

Breaths over broken glass.

I swallowed tears like salt on an opened wound.

The door creaks open. I stop breathing, not daring to hope, not daring to think yet doing it anyway.

'There you are.'

The voice is deep and the accent French, but the intonation, the person, isn't the same.

Ma Rose.

Ma fucking douchebag.

'I'm sorry you had to see that.'

'Yeah, sure.' My words tremble with contempt. Contempt for him. Contempt for the situation of Remy's making.

'You think I orchestrated it?' His arm bumps against mine as he sits next to me. 'I'm not to blame. I didn't know you'd be in his office. I didn't even know you and he were—'

'We're nothing!' I spit, my gaze rising to his. Nothing at all.

'I don't think that can be true, but I am sorry you had to find out that way.'

'Why are you being nice to me?' An accusation, not an enquiry.

'Because I'm sorry. And because I owe you an apology for Saturday evening. I wasn't myself. I'd been drinking and . . .' He vacillates a moment and I instinctively know what's coming next. 'I'd had a little coke. You didn't deserve my mind games, and you didn't deserve this. My cousin has always had many women—'

'I really don't want to hear this,' I utter, planting my face in my hands again.

'—not since he and Amélie announced their engagement.'

'Please go away.'

'I can't. I can't leave you like this, not when I feel so responsible for you finding out this way.'

But there's only one man responsible, and he's not here.

He didn't come looking for me.

I guess that's it. No explanation. No apology. Maybe even no job.

He can shove his job up his—

'I feel so terrible for my part in this. Can you at least forgive me for Saturday? For behaving so terrible.' *Terr-e-b-la.* Urgh. I suddenly hate the French accent as he hurries on. 'I won't tell him about your job in the—your waitressing job, I mean.

As if that matters now.

'Whatever.' Like I care. Who worries about stubbing their toe when they're bleeding out? 'So you found out I worked in a strip club,' I say, suddenly sitting straight. I'm a little lightheaded, and the heat in the stairwell is suddenly stifling. 'I only waited tables, not that it matters. I've got to get back to work.' Pressing my hand to the warm concrete, I stand, Benoît following suit and suddenly reaching out to steady me.

'*Non.* Not work. Let me take you out for a drink.' As I shoot him the stink eye, he holds up his hand as though to ward me off. 'Only to talk. To gather your thoughts. You have had a shock.'

'So I shouldn't drive or operate heavy machinery. I think I'm fine to work a laptop.' Even if the last thing I need is to go back to the office. I haven't the bandwidth to deal with the wrath of Olga or the concern-cloaked delight of Charles, who loves a hot topic of gossip twice as much as the next man.

Come to think of it, the last thing I need is to lose my job. But that might happen anyway, now that Remy's dirty secret is out.

Oh my Lord, I realise with a sickening lurch. His dirty little secret is me.

'You cannot work like this, Rose. Please let me help you. My assistant will call your line manager and tell them I have need for you today. One drink. A coffee, or perhaps a brandy for the shock. Then you go home, okay?'

I don't want to work.

I don't want to be alone.

I don't want this to be the shoulder I cry on.

But I also didn't want to discover that the man I'm falling for belongs to another, and look how that worked out.

'I will tell you about Remy.' He sighs deeply, as though it pains him to offer.

'One drink.' Was I always such a sucker for pain, I wonder as I hold up a finger as though to convince him? Or maybe myself. 'But a drink, not brandy.' Brandy can kiss my ass. When you're looking at a breakup, there's only one thing for it, and it starts with a *te* and ends in *quila*.

'Bon.' His hand grasps my elbow. Maybe I look as fragile as I feel. 'Something else. Something strong for shock.'

'Just don't get any ideas.'

Is it wrong that his scoffing nonreply isn't exactly music to my ears? I mean, I don't want him to think he has even the slightest chance with me, but come on, give a discarded girl a break!

'I will tell you this. I looked for you after seeing you in the office your first day. But Remy found you first.' *Much earlier than you think, I almost say.* 'This complicates things too much for me. But perhaps we can be friends.'

Is it a line or the truth? Who the hell knows. It'll be some time before I can trust myself again.

'Café?' Ben asks me as the waiter approaches the table once more.

'What did I tell you about coffee, Benny?' One eye closed, I try to focus on the man in front of me.

'That it does not help heartache,' he says with a wince. I think it's the name I've christened him with rather than his fear of catching feelings.

'What else?'

'Tequila does. But this is too much.' He gestures to the scarred wooden table between us, littered with tiny shot glasses and my abandoned lunch. I've stacked some of the glasses into towers and placed a napkin over the sandwich because the smell of the accompanying fries made me feel ill.

If I'm lucky, maybe I'll never eat a fry again.

'Hey, you helped,' I protest, sitting straighter. *Whoa. Woozy head.* And a flat butt and sore back after sitting on this damned bistro chair for too many hours.

'What do you want?' he asks again.

To be loved. To be held. For Remy's head to explode. Any of those. Instead, I order the damned *café*. 'With milk. And sugar. And in a big mug,' I call as the waiter withdraws. 'Oh, dear god. I feel so messy right now.' Too much tequila and heartbreak will do that to a girl.

'You look fine,' Ben answers, though he's not looking at me but studying his glass of wine. Probably regretting he said he'd bring me to this café, the kind that has penny-sized tables and spindly chairs that look like they might break at any minute and waiters who've taken classes in Gallic-style insolence.

'Sure, that's the kind of compliment I need.' The apathetic kind. The uninterested kind. This Ben is different from Saturday Ben, but that doesn't mean I trust him; mood-altering substances or not. It just means he's the only one in this country I can talk to about this. Which also means he's also one of the few who know I've made such a fool of myself.

I can take some solace in this, I guess. When I get to that point. But whatever, it's kind of convenient that he isn't interested in me, or else I might be feeling spurned for a second time in one day.

'We have decided to be friends, no?'

'No. I mean, yeah. I suppose.' But the friend I need is currently on the other side of the globe. Unlike Benny, Amber would know what to say. We'd probably be at Remy's apartment, cutting the sleeves off his shirts and shoving shrimp into the hem of his drapes. We'd be singing Lily Allen at the top of our lungs, *fuck you very much,* then she'd get me so drunk that I couldn't possibly feel sad any more, before holding my hair and wiping my tears while I puked, trying to purge him from my system.

'At least you're fulfilling the drink part of this,' I mutter, pushing away the shot glasses to make space for my mug as the waiter returns. 'When life gives you lemons, break out the tequila.'

He turns a little in his seat, crossing one leg over the other before picking a little invisible fluff from the knee of his pants. 'Ask me about him,' he murmurs without looking my way. 'I know you want to.'

'Fuck him. He's an asshole.' A traitorous, treacherous, heartbreaking bastard and I never want to hear from him again. Except, I want to hear all the things. About his past, his relationship so I can slot away the tiny details to obsess over later, to torture myself. But I won't ask because I'm not sure I can keep the desperate hope from my tone.

'Yes, an asshole. But not as bad as you think.' I think we're having a staring competition until he blinks.

'You don't even like him.' That much was clear in Remy's office.

'He's family.' He shrugs as though this is explanation

enough, but then he smiles the kind of smile that looks like it belongs on a serial killer. 'You're right. I don't. But I think that's natural, no? We are ... rivals.'

I ignore the way his eyes linger on me. 'Here's not to liking Remy Durrand.' I hook my fingers through the tiny handle of my cup, tapping it to the edge of his drink.

'He's a man. He's made mistakes, but you mean something to him, I can tell.'

'Why are you telling me this? Here.' I pick up the knife from my abandoned sandwich, offering it to him handle first. 'If you want to hurt me, go ahead. Just start poking holes.'

'And I thought the French women were *dramatique*.'

I spin the knife in my hand, pointing it at him this time. 'Want to say that again?'

'I think he might even love you.'

'Sure,' I scoff. 'That's why I was the one who left his office. That's why he came running after me. Oh, wait. He didn't.' Not that time, at least.

'In his own way. As much as he is capable, I suppose. But the more I think about it, the more I am convinced he was protecting you by reacting as he did.'

'What reaction? There was none.' He didn't even respond to her kiss. He didn't turn his head, his hands staying straight by his sides. I look down at my own hand as it begins to smart and see tiny half-moon indentations from my nails. 'Go home, Benny.' I bring my coffee to my mouth. 'You're drunk.' And then I burn my tongue.

'Let me tell you about Remy.'

'I think I'd rather have a pap smear,' I murmur, beginning to doctor my molten beverage as a thought hits me. A similar procedure might not be too far away in my future because Remy and I didn't use condoms.

I want to feel you skin to skin.

The last woman I slept with was you.

Lies again.

Tears prick my eyes like glass. I trusted him with my heart and my sexual health. So help me, if anything is wrong . . .

'Rose?' Ben's concerned expression hovers in the periphery of my vision.

'I don't want to talk about him anymore,' I say, dashing away an escaped tear. 'Let's talk about someone more fun. Like Genghis Khan.' My words are more brittle than bright even as my greedy heart wills him to go on.

'It's not a love match.'

'It sure looked lovey-dovey to me.' I make a tiny whirlpool in my cup as I stir in the sugar, wondering if that's really true. He looked dumbstruck, sure. Then emotionless. He didn't reciprocate her greeting, her kiss, none of it.

Or maybe I'm just seeing what I want.

'How often have you seen him?' Ben's prodding brings me back from someplace painful to somewhere equally as agonising. 'How many times each week?'

'We've seen each other quite a bit,' I concede. Just call me Rose, the side ho.

'He's obsessed with work. Obsessed in making The Wolf Group bigger and better than it was under his father. But I've noticed he's been available less since you arrived. No working dinners, no weekend meetings. And I heard he moved into the Tower.'

'You mean he didn't live there before? Oh, my God. They were living together!' My entire body burns with indignation.

'Bedrooms as separate as their lives, I'm sure. The only thing that keeps them together is a mutual love of money, as I understand it.'

'Well, I don't understand *it*.' Do I believe it? He seems pretty calm about the whole thing. Besides, what reason would Ben have to lie to me? He might have seemed interested on Saturday night—not to mention creepy—but right now, he seems genuine. If he wanted me, wouldn't this conversation be different? Wouldn't he keep all this information to himself?

My head aches with the weight of it all, but I know at the very essence, the possibility that this relationship isn't real means nothing. It changes nothing. Remy has had a hundred opportunities to tell me. To explain. He hasn't, and I'm not sure what that says about me.

Was I not worth it?

'Remy wasn't supposed to inherit his role, you know. Money, yes. Control, no. He didn't even live in Monaco. When the details of his father's will were made public, shares nosedived. The board tried to block his appointment. There was almost a corporate coup.'

'Why?'

'Because he was a playboy. Inexperienced in the world of work, let alone a billion-dollar business. He knew what to do to court a headline or a girl, but not to inspire the confidence of investors.'

'I still don't see what this has to do with his . . . *with her*.' Something inside me curls up and dies. *My self-worth, maybe.*

'He didn't follow you out of the office as Amélie need only complain to her father and you would be deported. He's very high in the principality government, you see. The family has influence but not billions. Remy has billions, but at that time, he had no influence. So he proposed to her.' His head tilts, his expression twisting a little. 'Perhaps "propose" is a little too evocative. He brokered a deal. Her father's support for his cash.'

'And the hand of his daughter in marriage.'

'It would never have come to that, even without you. The

pair are not well matched, though I believe he tried. Amélie is
. . . spoiled, selfish, and quite frankly, a bitch.'

'Maybe those are admirable qualities in the wife of a
billionaire.'

I guess I'll never find out.

26

ROSE

It seems liquor doesn't agree with my stomach tonight, despite my best efforts. Ben left earlier. He might have said he felt responsible for what happened this afternoon, but not enough to ruin his whole evening.

Whatever. I don't need his company. And at least he paid the bill.

I find myself wandering along the marina and farther to the shorefront where there are fewer tourists, and certainly no one lingering. In the early evening humid air, I sit at the base of the cliffs overlooking the water. As the waves crash against the rocks below, I pull the monogrammed scarf from my hair and contemplate letting it go fluttering out over the sea. I end up stuffing it into my purse instead; this isn't a Hallmark movie. There will be no happy ending for me. Plus, I only have one scarf, and I still have a job. At least, so far.

I watch the setting sun touching the horizon with golden fingertips, the clouds backlit by a light that's almost celestial. I'm still sitting there as dusk turns to dark, the evening breeze bringing with it a slight chill and making me wish I'd brought a jacket.

I can't stay here all night, but as I leave, I stand and lean over the concrete parapet, but I can't see the waves below. I'd read somewhere years ago that most ills could be cured by salt. *Sweat. Seawater. Tears.* Well, I'd taken a walk, and I'd be walking some miles back to my apartment, plus I'd spent more than an hour listening to the waves. I'd even had salt with my tequila, but I'd yet to try crying with any real depth to release the tightness in my chest.

I guess it's time to give that a shot.

It's gone eight when I get back to my apartment. I kick off my shoes and drop my keys to a dish not picked out by me, sitting on a table that I like, but I also didn't choose. Bypassing the living room, I make my way to the bedroom, intending on hitting the shower for my epic cry fest. It seems as good a place as any to give it a try. One hand works a few buttons loose, the other reaching for the remote to close the automatic blinds when, in the reflection of the darkened window, a looming figure appears. I choke back a cry, my mind processing the data on slow-mo. There isn't someone at my window, not twelve stories up, but there is someone standing behind me. I stumble deeper into the room, my hands blindly scrambling for something to hurl.

'It's not really my size.' Remy stands at the doorway to my bedroom, holding the nude heeled pump I'd just thrown at him. 'You really should let me buy you a new pair of these,' he murmurs in that stupidly deep voice of his as he glances down at the worn heel.

'What are you doing in here?' I grab the matching shoe, launching it at him.

'I have your key.'

'That doesn't mean you get to use it. Not after the shit you've pulled! Get the hell out!' Excess adrenaline rushes through my veins as I frisbee a small, square pillow from the end of the bed at his head. Hurt and offended—fucking furious, and though I've used that word before, probably hundreds of times, I now know I haven't been using it right. My head throbs with violence, my ears ringing with his untruths, my chest filled with this all-consuming rage where my heart used to exist. And to add insult to injury, that goddamned pillow just didn't cut it. I grab a small decorative box from the dresser and an almost empty bottle of perfume I really don't want to see wasted yet really do want to see smash him in the face. I don't know what's come over me. I can and will always stand up for myself, but violent tendencies aren't really my thing.

Or they weren't.

In an effort to avoid the perfume bottle, his head connects with the doorframe as it glances off his chin. My joy blooms and shrivels. How can I want to hurt him and regret when I do?

'Rose, stop.'

'You don't get to tell me stop. You don't get to tell me anything!' Next, it's a book, followed by a tub of moisturiser, each aimed at his heads, plural. The book to his head on his shoulders, the heavier tub to the baguette, which he catches with a reflexive smile. My head feels like it's about to explode as I launch myself at him, fists flying like hammers to his chest. 'I never want to see you again!'

'You don't mean it,' he answers, stumbling backwards against the bedroom door, his fingers like manacles clamping around my wrists. I fall after him, landing on his chest, half in and half out of my bedroom, my body pressed to his. 'You wish you meant it.' His gaze is full of something I don't recognise. 'But you don't. You can't.'

'Don't you tell me what I mean! You're a lying, cheating bastard.' I try to punctuate my words with my fists against his chest, but he holds my wrists too tightly. I don't think I've ever hit anyone since I was in third grade. I guess I never felt like I needed to before now. I might not have my fists, but I do have my knee. As I raise it, he twists, and I find myself suddenly pinned under him—pinned like a butterfly on a piece of felt. He holds my wrists on either side of my head, pressing his right thigh at the very apex of my legs.

'Ma Rose. You fight dirty.' His expression is provocative and sardonic and infuriating, and I hate every atom of him, yet as he brings his thigh higher, my traitorous clit reacts with a solid pulse. 'I prefer you didn't.'

I tell myself it's my body answering his, that the reaction not at all brain-based. Nothing at all to do with jealousy or the sick sense that I still want him.

I lift my head from the floor to get in his face using the pause to untangle my suddenly thick tongue. 'And I'd prefer not to have been the silent partner in a love triangle.'

His laughter sounds unkind, but what do I expect from a man who would string two women along? 'There is no love triangle. There is just you and me. I have not been unfaithful, Rose.'

'Please don't insult me by saying you have an understanding fiancée.'

'We're engaged only on paper.'

'So Ben said.' And though I'm not sure I one hundred percent believe either of them, it hurts a little less to think so.

'Ben?' Shock hits his expression. First, fury then flashing across his face. 'What were you doing with him?' I'm tempted to make him suffer. Not just because he's the off the chart's kind of sexy when he's angry, his accent thickening, his green eyes glittering, and not because of the way he presses my wrists to the floor, the solid weight of him pressed against me, his body over mine casting me into shadow.

'That's really none of your business. But before you start throwing your big dick around, he did what you should've done already. He explained.'

'I find that hard to believe. If he touched you—'

'We might be even,' I retort.

'Don't,' he growls. 'Don't even joke about that.'

'You don't get to tell me what to do.'

'No?' His thigh presses harder, my body working against him of its own accord, and I bite back a whimper. 'Maybe you should tell me what you'd like me to do.'

'I'd like you to get *off*.'

'Get you off?' His smile is beautiful and cruel, and though it makes no sense, I want to lick the salt from the hollow of his neck, press my teeth into the cording standing taut at the sides, and bite until he bucks into me with a cry. 'Relationships come in many forms, Rose, but that one was purely business. I swear to you on my mother's life, we have never been emotionally involved. I haven't been intimate with anyone but you since March.'

My mouth snaps shut as I process the implication before my brain processes another wave of hurt. 'But you have fucked her.' The woman who looked like a supermodel. How can I compete with her?

'Yes, but it was a long time ago.'

'I don't know why I asked because it doesn't matter.' It shouldn't matter.

'You ask because you care. You ask because you're hurting—'

'Because *you* hurt me. You took me for a fool. You lied to me, and I hate you for it.' My chest heaves as I pant, my nipples still pebbled by the brush of him.

'If I could take it all back, make it better, I would. But what you saw was smoke and mirrors, not the truth. You have to give me a chance to explain.'

'I don't have to do jack shit,' I grate out, angry with him, angry with myself, and angry with my faithless body. I know it would take nothing to raise my face to his, to kiss him, to have him kiss me. To slide my legs around him as we tousle and tangle, thrashing out the confusion and hurt. But what would that make me?

Weak. Wrong. Faithless. Heartless. No better than him.

'Get off me.' I try to wriggle away, to twist from under him because my arousal has been burned away by my anger.

'I'll let you go when you listen to me, and when you stop behaving like a brat.' He presses my wrists flat, his dark hair falling over his brow.

'This brat that wishes she'd hit you harder back in March!' I continue to rail at him, shaking my fists to the best of my abilities.

'You hit me? You made me come off my motorcycle?' His words are sharp and more than a little ugly, finger manacles tightening.

'Yeah, sure. I saw you whizz past and launched a purple dildo at your helmet, just for the hell of it. It was four in the morning, you idiot. You crept up on me! You're lucky it was the dildo I grabbed and not the can of pepper spray.'

'Then I have to ask. Why were you carrying such a . . . deadly weapon in your bag?'

'Don't you laugh. It came in the mail.'

'It *came* in the mail?' As he begins to chuckle, I drop my head back against the tile.

'Not even a little cute. And not like that. It arrived . . . it hit my mailbox. Urgh!' This is a minefield of innuendo. His pickle might be tickled, but I'm just annoyed. Trying again, I utter the words through barely moving lips. 'My friend sent it

273

from Australia as a joke. I'd collected the package that day on my way into work.'

'I suppose I should be grateful she didn't send you a cricket bat.'

'I have different feelings on that, obviously.'

'Ma Rose, there's nothing obvious about you.' From harsh words to soft, his smile spreads slow and sweet.

'Meanwhile, you're no different from a thousand other men. A million of them. Maybe you do have an agreement. Maybe you have some kind of open relationship. I don't care. You lied to me.'

'I'm sorry,' he says, all traces of his smile and mirth wiped from his face. 'I never meant to hurt you.'

Isn't that what they all say?

With one last tiny throb of connection, he releases me, blood rushing back to my wrists. He sits, pressing his back to the wall, his arms draped across his bent knees. Even in the cramped corner between my bedroom and the lounge, he has the bearing of a prince. A prince who has taken liberties where he ought to have not.

'I should've told you before now. I thought . . . I didn't think it would come to this. I thought I could arrange things so you wouldn't be hurt. So you wouldn't think badly of me.'

'So you wouldn't have been caught. Caught hurting two women.' Because after her display earlier, I'm pretty sure Amélie doesn't know about me.

'There is only you.' His head rises, the light spilling from the bedroom, casting his high cheekbones in stark relief. 'With Amélie, it's been a business arrangement since the start. The only thing she'll mourn is my credit card.'

My feckless heart gives a little leap.

'It's you I want. I'm done with keeping secrets, and I'm done with feeling like your dirty little secret.'

'I played right into your hands with that, right? Super convenient for you.' Stupid, stupid, Rose.

'No, that's not true. I was ending things with her. Ending the arrangement between us—the business arrangement. I spoke the truth when I told you there had never been another woman in my bed.'

'I guess that's the kind of thing all cheaters say.'

A muscle in his jaw clenches. 'Whatever you think, whatever I've done, I have not been unfaithful to you.'

'So you just cheated on her?'

'You can't cheat in business. My mistake was waiting for us both to be in the same country for me to finish things.'

'If it was purely a business arrangement, you could've told me. You might've warned me. You might've—' At the first sign of a warble, I clamp my lips together, dropping my head again as I pretend the leaking at the outer corners of my eyes is rain.

Indoor rain. Nothing wrong with that.

'I'm sorry, truly sorry, but none of this changes how I feel about you. I cannot be without you.' I hear the determination. Feel his words. But it takes two to make a relationship, and while he might not have broken Amélie's heart, mine currently needs a baggy and a tub of glue.

'I need you to leave,' I whisper as I finally stand and brush the hair from my face and straighten my clothes, trying to retain the last threads of my dignity as I begin to move. I don't get far as he gracefully rocks to his feet and takes my shoulder in his hands.

'Let me go, Remy.'

'I can't do that. I know I've hurt you, but I'll make it up to you, I promise.'

'Just . . . just go away. I can't deal with you or your lies.'

'I won't let you go.' His hands cup my face, his words softly determined, and I wish I could harden my heart to him.

'But the choice isn't yours.'

'If I can't deal with the thorn, I don't deserve the Rose.'

'I guess you've already proven both of those. I need you to leave me alone, Remy.'

He whispers my name as I walk away, but we were a lost cause before we even began.

27

REMY

'You're still awake. Good.' I'm sure some would say I deserve to go to hell for leaving one woman only to join another, but I've never cared for the opinions of others. Besides, I should've done this long ago.

'Jet lag.' Her attention moves from the open Gucci suitcase on her bed to shoot me a tight smile. If she has any thoughts about me appearing at the threshold of her bedroom, she doesn't share them as she turns away again.

'Where have you been again?' I'm not sure why I ask. A prelude to an awkward conversation?

'Remy, why are you being like this? You know I went to a spa in Florence.'

'For almost three months?'

'Well, no. I hitched a ride with Serge to Paris then on to New York. I would've been back sooner if you'd let me use the Gulfstream.'

That's what it always comes back to with her. What she can get out of me and how. There was a time in the beginning when she'd tried to use sex, but I don't respond well to manipulation.

'Are you ready to tell me who that was in your office now?' Her words are pitched lightly. Deceptively so.

'No.' As I answer, I slide off my jacket and throw it over the back of the ridiculous Bibendum chair. A chair that will be, no doubt, piled high with clothes before long. Because why unpack your case properly when you can have the maid do all the hard work in the morning?

She turns her attention back to her case, her trim frame encased in pastel pink yoga wear, her expensively highlighted hair—for which she engages a full-time stylist, paid for by me —is fashioned into something that looks like a donut. Why was I stupid enough to become engaged in the first place? Why did it have to be her?

The answer is the same as always: I'd have done almost anything to better *him*. And I have. The Wolf name was always highly regarded within the region, but since his death, we're revered. *Feared.*

I press my hands to my hips and drop my head. We've both played our parts. It's time to move on. 'It's over, Amélie.'

She snorts, swinging around to face me. 'What, again? Because I didn't call you from New York? Or is this because I spent over the limit of my credit card again?'

Again with the delusions. I note the transatlantic twang she's acquired since she started spending time with the rich and useless, and women who live by the outmoded maxim that you can never be too rich or too thin.

'When have I ever given a damn how much time you spend out of Monaco with your stupid friends?' As for the credit card, yes. We've had arguments about her spending. The woman has a problem, and it's not the usual sort for a woman of her station; exercise, plastic surgery, champagne, or cocaine. She's addicted to shopping; addicted to impressing her so-called friends. 'We knew this would end sometime. Quite frankly, I'm surprised we've managed this long.'

'This is about her, isn't it? The heavy girl in the office.'

I stare back, my expression blank. My answer, when it comes, is so cold, it makes her visibly flinch. 'When have I ever involved you in my private life?'

'Remy, you and I, we're the same.' A change of tone and a change of tact; her expression desolate, her tone needy. Amélie is the type of person able to convince herself of anything, and if she's convinced, she assumes the rest of the world is, too. 'You need me, and I need you.'

'You need me to bankroll you, perhaps. But not in your life. And not in your bed. I hear that's reserved for someone in a boy band these days. I hope he's legal.'

She reacts to my words like a slap, but I neither wonder nor care who she's fucking. Our arrangement was we live our own lives; discretion the key to our union.

The kind of discretion that led me not to tell Rose the truth? Not even I can use this as an excuse because it was greed and hubris. The need not to be caught out. I acknowledge the thought, but don't accept it for how things are now. The way I feel about Rose bears no relation to the way I'd felt about her before. Yes, I wanted to possess her, and now I know why. Because I love her. Yes, I love her. And it has taken this fuckup for me to realise. I think before, it was a little like being in front of something so large I couldn't really see it.

'Peu import,' Amélie spits—*whatever*—throwing down the scrap of silk that I assume is a dress. 'You need me to keep you away from gold-digging whores—women who are only interested in your money!'

I'm not sure how she can't see the similarities. Perhaps a

professional gold-digging whore might cost less than her. *While Rose might cost me everything.* But I no longer care. Seeing her so upset, so angry . . . tore me apart. Watching her leave the office so pale and so despondent, yet knowing if I followed her, I'd be playing into Amélie's hands. It's time it all came to an end. I'm not proud of my mistakes. Of hurting her and of thinking I could somehow make this right without her ever knowing.

Amélie stomps around the room, muttering insults to my parentage as I consider how different the two women are. Contrary to current appearances, Amélie is cold. She cares for nothing and no one but herself. Rose, by contrast, is full of vitality, and though it's a cliché, she truly has a heart of gold. While Amélie behaves like an overgrown child threatened with the removal of her most useful possession, Rose behaves like a woman who has had her heart broken.

Her. Heart. Broken. Which means she loves me. Which means I have a chance—I can make her heart whole again.

'There will be a settlement, as we agreed in the beginning. You can use the house for the rest of the year and keep the credit card.' For now, at least. With a cast-iron spending limit.

'I am not moving out,' she replies with the hauteur of a duchess. 'I have spent time and money renovating this old place. And for what? So you can move your fat little girlfriend in?'

'Carry on,' I answer blithely. 'I had forgotten how ridiculous you are. And yes, you spent money, lots of *my* money while an army of decorators spent months catering to your every whim. Where were you again? Gstaad, Milan, and God only knows where else. The settlement will include an apartment. There's no need to worry about returning to your parents.'

Her expression hardens. She knows this isn't what her

father planned. He may have offered up his daughter like a suckling pig, but he expected her to turn our contract into wedding vows.

'For your information, I had my own apartment before I moved in with you.'

A rental, the size of a postage stamp, and subsidised by the government as her family is Monégasque; native to Monaco.

'Regardless, you can't stay here.' My tone is one of abrupt finality, feelings, thoughts, and sentiments riot through me, and not one gram of them centred on her. I was wrong. I'll do better. Her anger will burn away, and I'll make it up to her. 'I'm selling the place.' And with that, I grab my jacket, leaving her to both her tantrum and her unpacking.

'That's fucking classic!'

'I'm pleased you're amused. I can't say I felt the same sentiment,' I murmur, initialling plans for the land reclamation project for a hotel and residential complex.

'You can't be surprised. Two women on the go at the same time?' Everett asserts gleefully. 'You were bound to get caught with your trousers down at some point.'

'I hardly, as you so eloquently put it, had two women on the go. I had one.' One I don't intend on letting go. 'The other was a decoy for the board.'

'And kept around far too long.'

I shrug. He's right.

'*Tu as les yeux plus gros que le ventre.*' His accent somewhat butchers the words but not so much as I can't understand.

'My eyes are bigger than my belly? Really?'

'I don't know how to say you're a glutton for punishment.

Man, I wish I'd been here to see the bitch's face when she walked in on you with Rose.'

'You were too busy eating trans fats and chemicals, pretending to be a potato.'

'Give me a girl who'll bring me a burger anytime.'

I frown before my gaze cuts to him. He's certainly singing another tune, and I don't think it's purely the result of yesterday morning's greasy offering. 'It didn't happen like that.' I decide not to mention that Ben was in the office, or how I mishandled Amélie's arrival because I've fucked up enough. 'You know you just said something nice about Rose. What's going on? I don't think you've said anything complimentary about her since she arrived.'

'I haven't said anything bad about her, either. Well, not much. But I'm team Rose if I've got to be team anyone. I'll even get the T-shirt and the hat.' His smile is despicably cheery as he adds, 'Because I'm not the one that has to worry about her hiding things.'

'I'm not worried. In fact, I no longer care.'

'Your fucking funeral, mate.'

'I don't think so. The PI has come back with nothing. There is absolutely nothing to tie her to Emile.' Nothing that interests me. 'He has examined her work history, her family, her relationships all the way back to high school. Also, she says she has never met him, and I believe her.'

'Oh, well. That's it then.' There isn't so much a hint of sarcasm as a deluge.

'*Oui.*'

'So she'll get part of your inheritance? When you choose. The inheritance she knows nothing about. That'll be a fun conversation. *If* it comes.'

'I'll tell her,' I grate out. 'Why would I not?'

'The small fact that she might take her money and piss off.'

'*Non.* That will not happen.' Though I've considered it myself. I'll make sure of it. I know she loves me. I just have to make her admit it. And then? Then I'll spend my days making her happy. The end—a happy ending.

'She's not gonna make it easy for you. You know that, right?'

'And that is why you are team, Rose? You want to watch from the sidelines.'

'Nah. If I want to watch you get battered and bloodied I'd get you into the boxing ring again. I'm team Rose because I never liked Amélie.'

'That, my friend, makes two of us.'

'Ah, but she didn't try to make you trot behind her like a fucking dog. Or carry her shopping.'

I put down my pen. 'So that is relief I detect in your tone? The wicked witch is gone?'

'What, me?' He spreads his hands out on the arms of his chair as he leans back, making it bounce. 'I don't have an opinion. You pay me not to have one.'

'I couldn't pay you enough for you to keep your mouth closed. But I have a thought.' I link my fingers at the back of my head. 'If you'd fucked Amélie, she might not hate you so much. She might not have tried to belittle you at every opportunity.'

'First of all, she didn't belittle me because that would mean I gave a fuck. Second, she was mostly civil to me after the time I left her beautifully glossy, designer-labelled shopping bags at the café where she'd insisted I procure a frappe. But most importantly, how did you know?'

'That she'd propositioned you? Call it a hunch.' And call

her vindictive after she discovered she was no longer welcome in my bed.

'Yeah, well . . .' He grimaces and tugs his earlobe. 'No offence, but I wouldn't fuck her with your dick.

I drop my hands and flip the folder closed. 'Let's go and get—'

'Blind drunk?'

'Dinner,' I correct wearily.

'That was gonna be my second suggestion.' A smile catches in the corner of his mouth as he stands.

We make our way over to the hotel, opting to eat at Le Grill where I pick up the threads of our abandoned conversation.

'I would've been very disappointed if you'd taken her up on it, you know.'

It takes him a moment to determine what it is I refer to before answering. 'Not my style.' As I cut into my steak, my gaze lifts but not my head. 'I know you had an open relationship, but don't laugh, it would've felt like *I* was the one doing the cheating.'

'I'm honoured, I think.' I begin to chuckle which, by his expression, he doesn't appreciate. 'But you're wrong about the relationship being open. I just didn't care what she was up to beyond the first few months.'

'Why keep her around at all? Once you were in power, I mean.'

I place down my silverware and lean back in my chair. 'To begin with, it suited my purposes. I know. Her father desired that the engagement be fulfilled.'

'You mean, that you'd marry her?'

'He hoped she'd be able to bring me around, like a dog, I suppose. That was never going to happen. As to why it's gone on for so long, it was beneficial to have a member of the board side with me. Especially in the earlier days.'

'Especially when you started tearing the competition apart. But you don't need their permission these days.'

I nod in agreement. I suppose I never saw the need to rock the status quo. Amélie lived her life, and I lived mine. Occasionally we came together for some company function to put on a united front, but that was the extent of our dealings. I never felt the need for companionship, consumed with making the company something bigger than *him*, bigger than us both, one obsession turning to another when faced with the intrigues of his will. And at the time, I thought perhaps I was looking for a ghost when, in reality, she was travelling the globe on the proceeds of a windfall, courtesy of Emile.

I felt no remorse or guilt after I slept with Rose in March. I didn't feel the need to repent. Nevertheless, the experience changed me. She reminded me that there is good in the world and that not all people seek to benefit themselves. But I put all that aside when I returned to Monaco, still hell-bent on finding out who this woman was my father sought to benefit —who she was and what she was to me.

And then she arrived, and I have not been the same since.

'Well, whatever the reason,' Rhett reasons, 'all I can say is, I doubt I could ever get hard enough in Amélie's presence to even hate-fuck her.' My chuckling turns to a belly laugh because I can empathise completely. 'I don't know what you're laughing about. You're the one whose life is a mess. It's a fucking joke, man.'

'I don't know. I think my life is pretty good.' Or it will be once I win over Rose. Once I get her to understand that nothing matters beyond her.

'Not from where I'm sitting. First, you get saddled with a business you never wanted or expected any part in. Then to get your hands on the reins, you ditch the image of the playboy son, an image you'd cultivated so very hard—'

'I hardly promoted myself as a hedonist. I just lived the life I wanted.'

'Those were some good times,' he says, tipping his head back as though appealing to the midnight blue ceiling for a recreation of a time gone by. 'And we cultivated hard, didn't we?'

'Partied hard.' And Rhett was an unlikely companion, but one I'll be forever grateful for finding.

'Same thing,' he replies with a sniff. 'But then you go and spoil it all by saddling yourself with a business you don't really need. The money would always have been yours.'

'Precisely why I need to attend to it.'

'You had no interest in the business and no interest in the woman you tied yourself to.'

'A necessary evil,' I interject, brushing the topic aside.

'Those are her middle names, right?' He sits straight, bulldozing on. 'And next, you discover you might have a sister before finding out she's probably some girl your dad has—'

'*Ta gueule,*' I reply in a thoroughly bored tone. *Shut up.* Delivered without a hint of malice and received by his mocking salute.

'But then . . . instead of steering clear, you decide to fuck her. Then bring her here.'

'The first was a mistake, yes. And the second . . . a case of mistaken identity. But I regret nothing.'

'*Je ne regrette rien?*'

'If you start singing, I will murder you and feed your corpse to the fish.' I pick up my glass and bring it to my lips.

'You don't regret anything because you're in the middle of winning her fucking back.'

'You say that as though it were a bad thing.'

'Isn't it? You really don't want to know who she is?'

'I no longer care.' And that's the truth. But I will have her.

'Lord deliver me from lovesick fools.'

'You'll manage,' I murmur, turning my attention to my plate. 'Besides, there won't be much romance at the start.' Battles, yes. Verbal combat. Stolen kisses and vicious skirmishes if last night was anything to go by.

And I look forward to it all because as every seasoned campaigner knows, to the victor go the spoils.

28

REMY

I NEED you to leave me alone.

It isn't the first time she'd said these words to me, but never were words uttered with such meaning. Not that I'm deterred, though for the last few days, I haven't sought her out. I haven't turned up in her apartment, and not out of fear that she'll start throwing things again, and I haven't used the concierge app. Yet. At least, not since I'd requested her as my permanent contact, not that she's aware, though engaged the services of one of her colleagues for a few days. Following, no one else will see to my concierge needs; no one but her.

But up until now, I've left her alone, as she asked. And quite frankly, it's killing me. To know that she's so close, yet out of reach is torturous. I can barely think, let alone run a business. Things can't go on this way much longer. In fact, they won't if things go to plan.

I want you to leave me alone.

And I want to take her words and twist them into something pretty.

I never want you to leave me alone.

'*Mademoiselle Ryan pour toi.*' My assistant's voice drifts

288

from the intercom, bringing my musings to an instant halt. My stomach twists, and my heart thunders.

'Ask her to wait, please.' My response is terse, not because I mean it to be but because I need her here with me. *Need but cannot yet have.*

I switch the intercom to video mode. It's a new system that was installed just last week, along with a new lock for my office door. Some mistakes you just don't want to repeat. In the reception area, Rose frowns, hearing my response. Exactly what I was aiming for. She turns to the couch, she trips on the edge of the area rug, glaring back at it as though it had done so on purpose. She drops a multitude of wrapped packages and shopping bags to the cushions and, if I'm not wrong, suppresses a small growl before turning swiftly once again.

'Excuse me, but do you know how long he'll be?' She smiles tightly, her hands balled into fists by her sides before she slides them behind her back.

'*Non.*' Paulette's attention doesn't deviate from the screen. She's already expressed her displeasure, but as she was also my father's assistant, I think she has seen much less worthy appointments.

'It's just, I have other appointments today.' Paulette doesn't answer. 'Does he have someone in with him?'

Fishing, ma Rose?

'Monsieur Durrand is always busy,' comes a very professional non-answer. 'Very busy.'

I find myself smiling as Rose makes her way back, dropping to the couch with a huff. I'm still smiling as I turn from the screen to open the concealed bar behind my desk to pour myself a drink. An odd sense of satisfaction settles around me, a buzz of anticipation tightening the muscles in my stomach. I often feel like this on the precipice of a new deal or the start of a new project. When I'm about to build something up. *Or tear someone down.* I take my drink to the windows to admire the view. My enjoyment isn't derived from the ocean or the cloudless blue sky but rather from a moment. An extraordinary moment. One Rose cannot possibly anticipate.

I finish my drink, and on my way back to my desk, I pick up, then examine a small box from the credenza I haven't noticed before. I make a couple of slow laps of the room to finish my drink, of course, then place my glass back in the bar, close it, and take my seat behind my desk. Cuffs straightened, I pick up my pen and glance at the video intercom. Her chin resting on her fist, her thumb scrolls rapidly through her phone as her foot bounces in the air, taut like the string of a bow.

Excellent.

I press the buzzer.

'You can go in now,' Paulette murmurs, disabling the door's automatic lock.

It takes Rose a moment to work the dozen or so handles over both wrists, then she grasps the remainder of the packages and strides purposefully in the direction of the door. One sharp knock for courtesy and she barrels in; all guns blazing, is I believe the idiom.

'Rose. What can I do for you?'

I purposely don't look up. Not even as the packages and bags hit my desk and overflow, though I do move a small box aside as it hits the document I'm purportedly examining.

'I guess first you can tell me what all this is.' In the periphery of my vision, she folds her arms across her magnificent chest. With any other woman, I might assume this was a calculated move. But not with Rose, confirmed as I look up and notice the angry finger tattoo tapping against her upper arms.

'It looks like shopping. Business or pleasure?'

'What?' Her eyes flare. *The mention of pleasure?*

Capping my pen, I sit back in my seat and raise my gaze. My God, she is beautiful. Is it because I haven't seen her for days that makes her seem much more so? And she's wearing my favourite dress of hers; the linen one that makes her look like she's stepped out of a Sophia Loren remake. *Maybe* Boy on a Dolphin. I know if she stands in front of the window, the thin linen will reveal her glorious shape. But I'm not in the mood for schoolboy thrills. There are bigger things at play.

'Well, these are clearly shopping bags.' I poke them with my pen. 'Chanel, Dior, Gucci, and is that something from Piaget?'

'Are you telling me you don't know anything about these?'

'I know they're expensive?' I offer, leaning back in my chair.

'You're fucking with me.'

My cock flickers to life as her teeth graze her full bottom lip; the words enunciated angrily. Angrily or not, it still turns me on. God, I've missed you, ma Rose. 'I'd like to.'

'Stop it. You stop that right now!' Her eyes narrow and blaze gold. 'Your sexy little half smile and Frenchy-French accent won't get you anywhere with me today.'

'How about tomorrow? Can you fit me in your schedule then? I'll bring the accent. And the tongue.'

'You—'

'Fit me into your schedule, Rose. I'll fuck you whenever. Wherever.' My eyes drink her in, every inch of her. 'However.'

'Urgh!'

Wide eyes and pink cheeks tell me she caught my underlying meaning perfectly.

I aim to own her everywhere.

For a moment, I think she might stamp her feet. Kick my

desk? I love that she has such a temper. I look forward to reaping makeup benefits for many years to come. Because, yes, that's where I am right now. This thing between us is going the whole biting, scratching, fighting way. Such making up sessions we'll have.

'You don't get to say these things to me.' This time, her eyes flare as I push from my desk. She looks up and up again as I straighten to my full height and begin to round the edge of it. 'I told you to stay away from me.'

'And I have. But you're in *my* office. You sought me out.'

'Because of these,' she says, throwing out her hand as she steps backwards, creating distance between us. I don't want her to go too far away, so I perch myself on the edge of my desk.

'The shopping?'

'The shopping *you* bought.'

'Did I? How can you tell?'

'Because they're all in my size—'

'I am well acquainted with the shape of you.' My eyes wander and deliberately linger, a bloom of colour rising high on her cheeks in response. 'But I'm sure there are other girls in Monaco with similar figures to you.' Lies. All lies. There isn't another in the world built for my hands. Of that, I'm sure.

'And I guess you'd know,' she retorts. 'But the watch is the exact same Piaget as I was looking at online before . . . before . . .'

'Before you told me to stay away?'

Her hand slices through the air. 'Stop. Just admit you bought these things for me.'

'I'm sorry.' I rub my jaw rather pensively because tactics without strategy are just another word for defeat. 'I'm afraid I haven't been shopping lately.'

'The last time you showered me in gifts was because you'd lied to me then, too.'

Denial appears on my tongue immediately, but I swallow it back. The situations aren't the same, despite her insinuations. I'm not in the habit of buying gifts for people I lie to or manipulate. If I were, my business rivals would be decked out in diamonds and furs. I am, however, manipulating her. But it sounds much worse than it is.

'Okay, so maybe you didn't buy them personally, but you ordered them, just like before, only you used the concierge system.' She leans forward, brandishing a forefinger I'd like to bite, her eyes narrowing to slits. 'I know you did.'

'Remind me of the concierge motto again?'

'Discretion is everything,' she recites unenthusiastically, almost rolling her eyes.

'So, how can you possibly know if the concierge department guarantees privacy?' Her eyes are all pupil as I push up from the desk, but she doesn't answer, pursing her lips instead. 'Unless there's something you'd like to tell me.' Which, as I push my hand into my pockets and saunter past her, I know there is. I'm not quite sure if it's endearing or maddening that she'd protect one of her colleagues because, yes, the shopping is mine, and her colleague, Charles, was charged with keeping my part of the deal secret. Which I knew he would be unable to. 'Well?' I ask, swinging around to face her.

'I know these were to be delivered to me because I saw my name on the trolley.'

'Maybe there's more than one Rose Ryan in Monaco. Who knows?' If there is, I'll bet my fortune she won't be as beautiful.

'Goddammit, Remy!' she suddenly yells, the words almost

exploding from her mouth. 'Why are you being such a pain? I told you to stay away from me—'

'And I have done as you asked.'

'You can't buy me.'

'I know. Even I don't have enough money to cover your worth.'

Brushing my words aside, she carries on. 'You ordered all that stuff for me. You gave Charles carte blanche to buy anything he thought I'd like or want or need.'

'Not the watch, or the underwear.' Definitely not the underwear. 'Or the shoes. Those I ordered myself. He just had to collect them.'

'I knew it! I knew you were responsible,' she yells, throwing up her arms as she appeals to the ceiling for deliverance. 'Do you know what you've done?'

Yes, I do. And I think it's all going according to plan, though I reply instead, 'Something tells me you're about to enlighten me.' She starts, suddenly realising I've stepped into her space and steps backwards, holding her hand up as though to ward me off.

'You set this up. You purposely told Charles to buy stuff for me from *you*. And in doing so, you swore the most indiscreet member of the concierge team to secrecy, which is about as effective as using a colander to hold water.'

'I'm not sure what you're most annoyed about. That I bought you gifts or that Charles is the conduit.'

'I'm not annoyed—I'm angry—apocalyptically angry! Still! Again. Because the man can't keep a secret. By the end of today, the whole of The Wolf Group will know what has happened between us.'

'You mean they'll know I love you?'

'What?'

'They'll know I've lost my mind over you.' I almost

chuckle as she realises I've manoeuvred her against my desk. 'We're almost where we started, Rose.' She was like an angel the first time I set eyes on her, even in that shapeless coat in the harsh hospital lights, and she has only become more beautiful. I want to feel her blossom under me again, lush and ripe. Watch her attention turn inward, her eyes unfocussed as I drive her to the place where she grips my shoulders at the same time as she lets go.

'But this time, it won't end the same way.' No, ma Rose. Not this time because . . .

'No, this time, it ends in Charles losing his job.'

'No!'

'I can't condone indiscretion.'

'That's rich coming from you.'

'Heavy is the head that wears the crown,' I murmur sadly, dragging my fingertips from her knees to her hip, two pairs of eyes watching them traverse.

'You can't fire him. Not because of me.'

'I think you'll find I can. Misconduct is misconduct, after all.'

'Don't be a hypocrite.' Her laughter is hard as she stills my hand.

'We can't help being the things we were born to be.' Blood will out and all that.

'Remy, don't.'

'But this is who I am. What I do. How can I expect to be different without you?'

'Oh, so it's emotional blackmail now?'

'No. Not *just* emotional blackmail.'

'I don't know what you mean?' She looks wary. She should be.

'You don't want Charles to lose his job, but what I'm wondering is, what is it worth to you?'

'What?' Was it shock, horror, or perhaps a little excitement that crossed her face?

'You heard me. What is my discretion worth to you, Rose?'

'What do you want?' she asks suspiciously, pressing her palm to my chest, stilling my descent.

'I want you to understand how much I miss you.' With her hand trapped between us, my lips coast the shell of her ear. 'It takes all of my willpower not to kiss you.'

'You can't fire him,' she asserts, turning her head. 'Or if you do, you'll have to fire me, too.'

'I think HR will disagree.' Especially when I tell them to.

'Not when they find out I lied on my resumé.'

I know, I almost answer, awaiting her confession, as something inside me cracks, cool and sweet like a watermelon. I don't deserve her, I know. This woman who is good and kind and honest and true—everything I don't deserve. I'm having her anyway. I just need to persuade her that she needs me, too.

'I didn't work in a restaurant in San Francisco. I worked at a strip club. I got this job under false pretences, so if you want to fire anyone, go ahead and fire me.'

'How about I just kiss you instead?'

I hadn't meant to but find myself dragging her against my chest, banding my arms at her back as though she'd escape. *She could try, I suppose.*

'I worked at a strip club. Are you listening to me?' She shoves at my shoulders, and I pull back with a reluctance I feel in my bones.

'I heard you, and I don't care where you have worked or where you have come from, or even why you are here. You're not going anywhere because you mean everything to me.'

She shakes her head as though refusing to intuit my words. 'I can't trust what you say. Not when you've lied to me.'

'So, we make a good pair. I'm a liar, and you're a thief.' Her shocked expression is almost comical though the fun quickly dissipates

Never give anyone power over you. Don't offer love. My father's words rise as though from the grave. As though I'd ever listen to him.

'You're a thief because you've stolen my heart.'

29

ROSE

'WELL, THAT'S NOT GONNA WORK.' I put my iPad down on the sofa without logging out of my banking app, then yank out my employment contract from under it. 'Dammit. I need to learn to read the small print.'

Small print like he loves you and wants you to stay.

I swallow the thought, push it down and stamp on it, but it floats to the top anyway.

Maybe it's Monaco I shouldn't want to leave because to do so would mean going back to clipping coupons and slapping away wandering hands. To cold winter winds and wearing outdoor clothes to bed just to keep warm.

I flip over the paper to examine the rows of numbers I've scribbled in an attempt to understand my finances. I shouldn't stay, but I must. I should leave, but I can't. At least, not yet. Because it costs too much. If I leave before the end of my probation period, I have to pay not only for my return flight—my repatriation—but also for my original flight out. There's also a daily charge for my accommodation I'll accrue if I leave before then. And it gets better; my probation period is six months.

Six months!

My little row of figures confirms what I already know. I'm going to be here for at least that long. Here, working out of the same building as Remy, maybe even still living here. Maybe there's a chance I'll be able to get a transfer to one of the hotels on the Riviera, or even just move back to one of the little studio apartments in Nice. Because the more I'm around him, the closer I am to my resolve dissolving like the sugar in a hot drink. It's been two weeks, and every day gets a little harder. Every day I get closer to breaking down. To giving in. To admitting I feel the same way about him.

He says he loves me but how can he?

But I'm not going to think about that right now as I make my way into my bedroom to tie up my hair, trailing my fingers over the cashmere throw draped over the bottom of the bed as I pass. A couple of months ago, I wouldn't have even known it was cashmere without reading the label, but so much has changed since then.

I glance around the room. I'll probably never get to live anywhere like this ever again. I'll probably never meet another Remy, but that should feel like a good thing, right? I try to ignore the shiny stack of bags and boxes in the corner of the room; the designer clothes and gifts, also known as items of manipulation. As I tie up my hair, I refuse to indulge in the game of *how much money would selling these gifts net* and decide that as Charles is still showing up to the office every day, I guess my dramatic parting shot of *I'll never forgive you if you fire him* must've worked.

For now, at least.

What was that even all about? Was he using Charles as a bargaining chip?

I really don't know.

Back in the living room, I shove the tablet and paperwork

in the drawer of the coffee table as the doorbell buzzes. Speaking of Charles, I've invited both him and Fee over because I cannot work another day in that office without answering at least some of Charles's questions after Remy gave him the hard sell and a grain of truth. I also thought I'd tell Fee, presuming the news hasn't already reached her. I'll need all the allies I can get for when people start chanting *ho bag* as I pass.

'*Bonsoir!*' Charles practically vibrates with anticipation as I open the door. '*Ça va?*'

'I've been better,' I complain as he presses a kiss to each of my cheeks.

'*Salut.*' Fee is a little more tentative as she pulls me into a hug to accompany her quick *Hi.*

'I brought *la medicine*,' Charles sings, brandishing a bottle of red.

'Come on in. Let's get this over with.'

'You don't have to tell us anything.' Fee tugs on my arm as Charles wanders deeper into the apartment, *oohing* and *ahhing* at the space.

'It's fine. Better you hear it from the horse's mouth, I guess.'

A few minutes later, I'm curled at the end of one sofa, Fee and Charles sitting much more primly on the sofa facing me.

'So.' I take a long pull of the wine Charles had poured, then set it down. 'What do you know about the torrid story so far?'

'Torrid?' Fee's gaze slides Charles's way. 'He made it sound sweet. Ow!' She rubs her arm, glancing to the side once more, but this time Charles refuses to meet her gaze.

'She 'eard nothing from me.' I imagine my expression tells him I know otherwise. 'I just tell her you have a rich boyfriend.' Nose in the air, his gaze makes another inspection of the living room. 'A very rich boyfriend.'

'I must say, this is such a beautiful flat.'

'It is not 'oo you know, but 'oo you blow, right?'

'Charles!' Fee chastises, shocked.

'I make a joke only!'

'Cut it out, Charlie, or I'll dangle you over the balcony. Now, tell me, what do *you* know?'

'I only know what 'e told me.'

'Hang on. Who is *he* in this instance?' Fee interjects.

'The rich boyfriend!'

'I don't have a boyfriend, rich or otherwise.'

'Bon. I will have him then.'

'Charlie, you really do put the *ho* in homosexual.'

'Thank you!' He sends me a beatific smile.

'It wasn't a compliment.'

'Not to you, per'aps.'

'Can someone please tell me who this rich boyfriend is?'

'Remy Durrand,' he replies with a waggle of his eyebrows.

Fee's eyes are suddenly the size of dinner plates. 'Durrand? Not *the* Remy Durrand?' Though her eyes dart back and forth between us, I neither confirm nor deny. 'Oh my . . . wow. Just wow! How? When? But isn't he engaged?'

'He was.' The admission still makes my spine stiffen, but I try to push all that away. He says he didn't make an adulterer out of me, so if he doesn't feel bad, why should I? But it goes deeper than that. It wasn't an oversight that he didn't tell me; a lie of omission is still a lie.

I pause, picking up my glass because I've no intentions of telling them about March, or even how I didn't know about Amélie. I don't want to add *idiot* to *ho bag* when the gossip machine starts to blacken my name. *Stick to the plan*, I silently intone. *You don't owe them all the things.* 'Well, you see—'

'I want to say!' Charles claps his hands together like a performing seal, bouncing in his seat. 'Monsieur Durrand, *il s'est confié*—he confided in me. I need to say before I burst! Also, the man is not so scary as his reputation.' He presses a hand to his chest and sighs like a teenage girl with a crush. 'The words 'e say? Such love 'e feels!'

'Well, this should be interesting.' It seems this might be a night of many mutterings as I take a deep swallow because, as it turns out, Charles *is* that teenage girl. A better analogy might be that he's Pepe le Pew. He thinks he's crushing on another skunk, when in fact, Remy Durrand is a whole other animal.

'He told me that Amélie broke off the engagement before she went travelling last. Zat he'd fallen 'ead over 'eels in love with Rose.'

'Oh, that's so romantic!'

It's so something, all right. So not true, at least in parts. It's also confusing because even though it makes me smile, I also want to cry because Remy can't be trusted.

''E loves you—why are you not smiling?' Charles's tone is more than a little piqued and—oh my God. That's why he told Charles—he was playing with me, yes. But more than that, he knows his big mouth will blab. But now he's going to blab *his* version of events, which doesn't paint me as the woman who puts the *ho* in *ho*mewrecker, but someone who he loves. *And not at all a liar, either.*

'So this is why you moved to this place?' Fee's gaze immediately drops to her glass, her expression aghast. She'd make a pretty poor poker player.

'I didn't ask for this.' I can feel my expression twisting. If Fee's thinking it, others will, too. 'The truth is, I didn't get a choice. Not that anyone will believe I'm dating my boss for anything but the perks.'

'*Oui*, the man, he has many, many perks.' Like an old-time game show hostess, Charles uses his hands to mime a prize like Remy. The curve of his bicep, the handsomeness of his face, and the depths of his pockets. Unless that last mime was a reference to the baguette.

'Of course people won't say those things,' Fee protests, indignant on my behalf despite her assumption about this apartment. 'And if they do, well, you know better.' She nods decisively, as though that's the only thing that matters.

'When I first met him, I didn't even know who he was,' I complain, swinging around to face Charles. 'I swear to God, Charlie, if you tell anyone anything about this—'

'I say nothing!' he retorts, his eyes as wide as dinner plates, his little flounce one of outrage that I would even dare suggest such a thing.

'Is that why his cousin was so insistent in the club that night?' My attention moves to Fee, once Charles is suitably served the stink eye. 'I thought he was coming on to you, but maybe he was warning you off?'

'More like scoping me out,' I add quickly, not wanting to be drawn. 'He apologised later. It's all good.' It's so not all good, though Ben is the least of my problems having redeemed himself a little by doing what Remy should've done. *By telling me the truth.* And whatever his deal was that Saturday, at least he apologised. And he's not interested in me, thankfully.

'Let me tell you something.' Lips pursed, Fee leans forward as though afraid of being overheard. Maybe she doesn't realise Charles is just dying to spill the tea, aka spill the gossip, if he hasn't already started. He's not malicious, as far as I can tell. It's more like he just can't keep his mouth shut, especially in the office.

'I never liked that Amélie. She came to spin class a few times and behaved like a total bitch.'

A bitch she may be, but she also looks like a sleek thoroughbred. And I already know I'm the ass in this comparison.

'*Oui*, her family is not well liked,' Charles agrees.

'I understand why you've kept everything secret. I'm assuming that's all over now because you want to go public with your relationship.'

'*Non*. It is because *la chienne*, she is back,' Charles announces dramatically.

'The bitch,' Fee offers by way of translation.

'Remy tells me Rose is angry wiz him. But he cannot do wizout her, but 'e say she cannot forgive him for not saying 'e was engaged before.

'That's it, huh?' If only he knew. If only that was the issue.

'And 'e now wants the world to know they are in love.'

'Well, I for one, I do not *love* being called to his office multiple times a day,' I reply, dragging out the throw pillow from behind me and punching it into some form of submission.

'What was that?'

'Olga, she gave Rose Monsieur Durrand's account. She now works for 'im *exlusivement*.'

'Almost exclusively,' I correct. 'And yes, I am mad at him.' Sadly, not for the reasons they both think. 'And now he's driving me crazy, calling me to his office with all sorts of demands. He's got me delivering lunch and then an afternoon coffee every day to his office, even though he already has a fancy-assed coffee machine in there. Not to mention a hotel with a Michelin-star chef who would probably stoop to making him brains and eggs if he wanted.'

'Brains and eggs?' Fee's nose wrinkles.

'Best not to ask.'

'I wasn't going to. But I was going to say it's obvious he wants to make amends.'

'By ordering me to jump when he says so?'

'By getting you in the same room in the hope of making you remember the things you like about him.'

'*Comme sa bite.*' *Like his dick.* As Charles titters, Fee frowns across at him.

'He does order two of everything,' I say, refusing to be drawn. 'And insists I stay with him.' The first day, I refused to even sit down. He might've blocked out my time with Olga, but I didn't have to sit or eat. Or even talk. By the third day, it became clear he was intent on wearing me down so I decided I'd sit and eat my sandwich, because you don't make friends with salad, while just ignoring him. But even that didn't last long because the man is infuriating. He seems to take a perverse kind of pleasure in goading me.

'I think that's sweet,' Fee coos. I'm sure she wouldn't say so if she knew exactly what he'd hidden from me. But telling her serves no one, least of all me. 'But do you want to see him?'

'I don't know. It's complicated.' I get butterflies still when I'm on my way to see him, but then I remind myself of his lies, and the butterflies turn to pterodactyls that swoop and gnaw at my insides. When he's not in front of me, he's easier to hate. *Okay, dislike strongly.* And I think he knows that, or why else would he call me to his office multiple times a day?

'You were out for a long time yesterday,' Charles remarks, bringing my attention back.

'Yeah, his tailor was there. He wanted me to help him pick cloth for a bespoke suit or four. I suggested the green tartan but changed my mind at the last minute when he'd said if that's what I liked, then he'd order three. He'd probably wear them, too.'

305

'That is love,' he says through a wistful sigh. 'For I would not look ugly for anyone.'

I've had worse afternoons. I got to spend it ogling his broad shoulders and solid thighs while pretending not to be interested in his innuendo and wicked half-smiles. We kept the arguing to a minimum for the sake of Monsieur Veilleux, the elderly white-haired tailor. Which basically means Remy behaved as he liked, as always, while I refused to be riled. I, Rose Ryan, took the high road. While thinking low thoughts because, when Monsieur Veilleux commented on the increase in the width of Remy's bicep since his last measurement, he'd glanced over the man's head, shooting me the most suggestive look as he murmured something to the effect that he might need a little more space in the right sleeve as he anticipated that arm getting more workouts over the coming weeks.

The man has no shame.

At least his right hand isn't infidelity.

And I'm not going to admit to knowing which side he dresses on, even if Charles asks.

'Some people have all the luck. While you were watching a beautiful man being touched, I 'ad to add 'z final touches to a birthday party for twelve Pekinese.'

'That sounds like so much fun,' giggles Fee.

'Not when I tell you what the cake is made from.' His nose wrinkles with distaste as he stands to top up our glasses.

'Nope, you've got that wrong. My job is much worse. I have to look daily into the face of the man I have to remind myself I'm no longer allowed to love. The way things are going, Remy will be calling me to his office next just to pick up his dropped pen.'

'Yes, and you will bend over, and he will make like this!'

306

From the other side of the coffee table, Charles thrusts his hips lewdly.

And in a nutshell, that is how the rest of the evening goes.

'Rose, before you go . . .'

Week three post-Remy, I pause at the door following lunch number twelve, meeting number twenty-four, by my count, because there have been no accidental meetings in the hallways and mumbled greetings. No awkwardness, not beyond the tailor's visit, at least.

I let go of the handle and turn as though I'm about to face a firing squad.

Oh, Lord. I know what's coming. I bite the insides of my lips as I try not to smile.

'Yes?'

'I wanted to ask you about this.' He pulls on a drawer in his desk, reaching deep inside.

I can explain, maybe I ought to say, but I won't. Because I wouldn't know where to start. Plus, I wouldn't be standing here all calm and shit, instead I'd be garbling and red-cheeked because I've been dreading this moment since I woke up and realised what I'd done. But it's been almost three weeks since I placed the order.

I was hoping it might've gotten lost in the mail.

Angry girl music, a bottle of Sauvignon, and a credit card were my naughty companions following a particularly trying day at work where Olga called me into her office to tell me I'd be "taking care" of Remy exclusively while making it sound like I was to be his personal harlot. Then Charles wouldn't quit badgering me, asking what misdemeanour I'd committed to be summoned to her office. Like I said, a very trying day which ended when I basically went home and . . . got shit-faced. I woke on the couch in the morning, my emergency credit card unearthed from the depths of my purse and an email from an Etsy store congratulating me on my purchase of a twelve-inch chocolate penis, along with my selected upgrade of a dip-dye in edible purple glitter, which I'd presumed I'd chosen for old times' sake.

It's basically a *go fuck yourself* gift that you can eat. Or choke on, I suppose is closer to the sentiment. In fact, that's what I'd opted for the card to read, for the grand sum of an extra two euros. I even got a free bag of gummy dicks so I can gift someone with the words: choke on a bag of dicks. *Go on, literally.*

In my drunken state, I'd even managed to input Remy's work address correct. So, when he subsequently pulls out a plain brown box from the depths of one of his desk drawers, and settles it on the desk between us, I know what's coming.

Yes, the chocolate penis.

Is coming.

'This . . .' Something ripples across his face. I'm going to go with humour. 'Is from you, I believe.'

I nod, my lip-biting doing nothing to smother my smile. 'Don't pull it out on my account.'

His eyebrow quirks at my unintentional innuendo, his gaze lingering almost speculatively. This wasn't the exchange I had in mind when I ordered the man a purple penis, I'm sure. It isn't an angry anthem made in the flesh, or rather confectionary, and more like a reminder of how we got together. In the end, he avoids the cheap laughs.

'It's quite an art project,' he says, turning the thing in his hand as he examines it. 'Is it modelled on anyone anatomically?'

'Who knows,' I answer airily.

'It does have very impressive detailing.'

'Someone takes their work very seriously.

'And purple.' As his eyes rise to meet mine, merriment dances there. 'Like forget-me-nots. Not that I'm likely to forget.' As he speaks, he grazes a finger across his left brow where a sliver of a reminder lies. 'It'll be a funny story we'll tell our children when they're old enough, of course.'

My heart beats like a punchline—*ba-dum-cha!*—a dozen things going through my head. Who talks about children this quick? Children with Remy's green eyes and my dark hair, children with golden skin, and platinum futures. Children loved to infinity—and then I realise he's still watching me, and I have nothing but gushing to return.

'And don't forget glittery!'

His smile is so wide and so sudden, it's like I've just told him a joke.

'But perhaps next time, you might spare Madam Bisset's blushes by directing it be opened by me,' he says, standing the base against his desk.

'Oh, my God. No wonder she couldn't look me in the eye.'

'No, but she did look something else in the eye.'

'Maybe I should've chosen the chocolate assholes.'

'Pardon?'

'Forget I said that.'

'Where are you going?'

I turn and look over my shoulder. 'To apologise to Madam Bisset.'

'And what am I meant to do with this enormous erection in front of me?'

'I could tell you exactly where to shove it, but I don't think you'd be happy!'

30

ROSE

THURSDAY AFTERNOON, week four, I'm in the middle of helping Charles load a trolley filled with packages of deluxe doggy party favours into the service elevator when my phone beeps with an incoming concierge request.

'Lover boy?' Charles asks, his tone a little piqued, mostly because Olga suggested he supervise the doggy party planner this afternoon, even going as far as to hand him a pink poop-a-scoop. So I don't bite; we all have our limits.

'Apparently, he's left his gym bag at his apartment, and this flunky right here has to pick it up from the penthouse and deliver it to his office.'

'It is still more fun than my afternoon,' he grumbles, using his hands as though he were a balancing scale. 'A beautiful man 'oo wants you or puppies 'oo want to 'ump your leg.'

'You booked the dog walker to come along, right?'

He nods. 'Dog walker, party planner, Charles, and a poop-a-scoop.'

'It sounds like a joke.'

'Like my life.'

I leave a dramatically morose Charles to his afternoon and

collect the key card from reception; I gave him mine back after . . . well, just after, and take the elevator to the penthouse. At the door, I experience a pang of something like nostalgia, though choose not to indulge myself in the what-ifs and what could have beens, swiping the key and stepping inside. It's hard to ignore the temptation to snoop around a little, so I don't. I'm not sure what I'm expecting to find, though I know what I dread as the list runs through my head.

An empty bottle of wine.

Two glasses, one of them with lipstick.

Discarded underwear.

Condom wrappers.

A girl still in his bed.

I find none of those things, on the ground floor, at least, and I plan to have a little snoop-de-snoop to discover if what he says is true. Namely, that he is living here and not in the house he shared with *her*. And he is living here, according to yesterday's *Le Monde* newspaper discarded to the dining room table, the bottle of wine on the kitchen counter, along with the singular glass in the dishwasher, and the coffee stain on the fancy machine. They're all small signs but enough to make me feel oddly gratified as I begin to climb the stairs, halting halfway.

You're forty-seven floors up. No one is going to see you come.

No one but me.

The aural memory curls around my ear, causing a tiny explosion of fireworks deep in the pit of my belly. I know I'll be old and grey and in a nursing home and I'll still remember the way he held me against him. The way he carried me up this staircase as though I'd weighed nothing. I'll never forget the way he made me feel like a goddess.

I shake away the memory and the sadness that always seems to follow and make my way to his room.

What if he's here?

Shut up, stupid brain. Also, not helpful and not likely.

What if the room is filled with shiny balloons and rose petals leading to the bed and—

I should not have had that third coffee. Clearly, I'm high on caffeine. I push the door open, smiling to myself as I step inside, knowing that Remy isn't lying in the centre of his bed with a rose clenched between his teeth.

His bedroom looks exactly the same, little signs of my presence still lying here and there. A hair tie lies on my—*his* —nightstand, a pair of my shoes placed neatly in the walk-in closet, which solves the weeklong mystery of where I'd put them. The oversized T-shirt I'd wear to bed, for at least the first few minutes, has been laundered since its last wear. Laundered, folded, and placed on top of the pouffe in the centre of his dressing room. Like a reminder, I leave it all there, along with my shoes, a spare toothbrush, my travel-sized moisturiser, and spare deodorant. I can't bear to move them, and I suddenly realise I can't bear to be here anymore.

I glance around for the sports bag, ignoring the almost coffin-sized bag sitting on the top of the bed covers. But there isn't another bag anywhere. I unzip the thing flopping to the bed with a huff. This is it, confirmed by the sports shoes and a mask that resembles a teabag. If I don't put my back out, I'll be highly surprised, I decide as I pull on the handle and it hits the floor with a *thunk*.

It's a short elevator ride down to the executive floor, not really long enough to prepare but long enough to recognise the fizz of excitement.

'Don't be ridiculous,' I mutter to myself. 'You are not looking forward to meeting Remy Durrand, the man you thought you were in love with. The man you *can't* be in love with. Because that fact would make you an idiot—just look at the size of the bag he's got you towing around!'

And now I can add talking to myself to the list of my lovesick maladies.

Madam Bisset barely raises her gaze from her screen as I stagger in.

'Let me take that.' Two sets of arms rush to take the bag from me, but not before I drop it to the floor once again. 'I'm so sorry. I didn't even consider how heavy it would be.'

'It's not heavy. It's unwieldy. But I managed, as you can see.'

Remy moves it to the sofa before half sitting and half leaning against the long table, the other man taking a chair at the head of it.

'Rose.' I love how my name sounds on his lips; the rolling *R*, the husk in it. I strive to ignore it as he continues with his apologies. 'How could I have thought to ask you to bring this,' he asks himself, all self-deprecating good nature. *The man is no good for you,* I remind myself. Matterless, the words seem to bypass my brain, my response to the sight of him purely visceral. 'Thank you for saving me the trip. Everett and I are fencing this evening.'

I try not to imagine Remy in those tight, white fencing pants, mainly because there's a time and a place for those kinds of thoughts. Fencing has to be the ultimate posh-boy sport, or maybe that's polo. I can also claim to have had one other boyfriend who fenced, though that was more the stolen goods kind. Needless to say, he wasn't on the scene long.

'Cool,' I answer, starting as I mean to go on. *Disinterested.* I can't keep allowing him to seduce me into conversations because the next step is being seduced out of my panties. I'd be lying if I said I haven't enjoyed sparring with him. *Enjoyed. Obsessed over. Left his office feeling confused.* What I don't need, however, is to do it with an audience, as I note his security guard in my periphery. Even if the man was an audience to something that almost happened on that desk.

'I'm sorry,' he says again. 'I should've asked Everett to pick up my bag. You remember Everett, the head of my security team?'

'Hey.' The apathetic greeting is delivered over my shoulder on my way to the door.

'Nice to see not quite so much of you.' My steps falter, and though I think about turning around, I don't. Rise above, Rose. Rise above. 'I told you she can't stand to be in the same room as me.' The asshole chuckles.

This time, I turn, and I could kick myself because, by his expression, that's exactly what he planned on.

'Well, bless your heart.'

The man's gaze flicks to the other man in the room. 'That's like being told to go forth and multiply, right?' Quaint that he doesn't want to curse in front of me. In anyone else, I'd probably say it's good manners.

'You don't know me, and I don't even know you.' Subtext: I don't want to know you. I get that he's here to protect Remy, but seeing as my five-foot four proves no threat, I don't get why he's here now.

'Come on, Heidi, relax. Cop a squat,' he says, pulling out the chair next to him. 'Remy here's been jonesing for a little Rose all day.'

'Oh, so you do know my name.' I swing around to face him, the only thing rising above my blood pressure now. 'My *actual* name, that is.'

His eyes flick briefly to Remy. ''Course I do. Didn't he tell you I'm Team Rose.'

'This is what happens when you feed him carbs,' Remy

murmurs, his words delivered through a reluctant smile. 'Undying devotion bought for the price of a burger.'

'I wouldn't like to see how he treats his enemies in that case.'

'He's just jealous.' Rhett leans back in his chair, his hands clasped to the back of his head. 'Because you haven't had a burger since 2015. The man's a slave to his image,' he adds in an undertone that we're all meant to hear. 'Got to think about all those girlies who'll watch him lounging on his yacht. *Attention, beau gosse!*' he adds, his words pitched in a higher octave.

It means hottie alert. Something slithers in my gut. I tell myself it's not jealousy as Remy utters the man's name in a tone more weary than warning. Myself, I hope to appear unaffected.

'When are you gonna put him out of his misery?'

'I don't know what you're talking about.'

'Come on. You know it's only a matter of time before you give in. Look at him.' As though my brain has no sway in the matter, I find I do. Gorgeous, as always; broad in the shoulders and handsome in the face. The truth is, he could eat plenty of burgers without the consumption changing any of those facts. His shirt is blue today, the colour deepening the green of his eyes, and he wears his shirt sleeves rolled, the skin of his arms almost the same colour as the strap of his battered old watch.

Someone's been getting a little sun. Hanging out on yachts? Naked?

The slither of jealousy in my stomach turns to the size of an anaconda.

'Are you really gonna let him slip through your fingers because of an error in judgment? All men in love make mistakes. Love makes idiots of men.'

Love makes idiots of women, too. But am I an idiot in

protecting myself . . . urgh! Belatedly, my brain processes Rhett's insinuations. Let this hunk of handsome slip through my fingers? Like I'm the kind of woman who prefers pretty over substance—who would forgive pretty over substance.

'This has got nothing to do with you.' My words are icy, the look I send him arctic.

'I've told him he should just chuck you over his shoulder and drag you to the Gulfstream. A week of forced proximity on a luxury remote island somewhere would do you both the world of good.'

'I think you'll find that's called kidnapping,' I snap, my annoy-o-meter creeping into the red.

'He's fucking lovesick. In bits. And you've barely looked at him. You haven't even said hello.'

So I turn to him. 'Good afternoon, Mr Durrand. You're kind of quiet today. Could it be because you can't get a word in edgewise for him?' As I hoick my thumb in the security guy's direction, and Remy's responding smile is a little like standing in a tiny patch of sunshine.

'That's more like it.' I find Everett's smile however, more like a deluge of rain. 'I do love a good working relationship.'

'Yeah?' I snort my disinterest, at the same time as my hands turn to fists.

'Especially when the subordinate does as she's told.'

My head turns to him like the turret of a tank. 'Well, I don't work for you so you can kiss my ass.'

'That's not in my remit, Heidi.' Why does it sound like everything the asshole says is through a smug grin?

'Urgh! Do me a favour.' I rotate back to Remy. 'When you go fencing tonight, poke him for me.'

'And that's certainly not in *my* remit.' There's an almost playful curl to his words.

'Told you, Heidi. This is a poke-free zone.'

'Would you stop calling me that? Please,' I add with extra snark. It's really beginning to become annoying, as well as freaky. Is it a coincidence, or has he somehow intuited the name of my waitressing alter-ego? Unless . . . Oh, God. What if Remy told him about my waitressing gig? Only, Rhett's been calling me Heidi for longer. So how in the hell does he know?

'A Rose by any other name, and all that.'

'You are *not* quoting Shakespeare to me right now,' I retort with a tense laugh.

'Rhett, get out. And if you don't want to be pitched out of the window, I suggest you do it quickly.'

'Got it, boss man,' he says, drawing his long frame up from the chair. He saunters to the door, muttering something that sounds suspiciously like, *my work is done here, anyway.*

I bite back my retort of, *who's the subordinate now, asswipe?* Instead calling,' I hope your day is filled with people like you!' after him. I even throw in a little wave.

'You know he aimed to annoy you, Rose.'

'Then he was trying too hard.' Being in the same room is enough. 'Did you tell him about the place I worked before I moved here?' Remy maintains his even expression. Meanwhile, I am pretty disgusted with myself. When did I become a coward? 'At the strip club,' I add, almost choking on the words.

'Would you like me to?'

'Ha!' So he can think up some other god-awful name? No thanks. 'I've got to go. I've delivered your bag, patted your guard dog.' And now I need to leave because I can barely stand myself.

'I'll see you at lunch.' He makes it sound like a long-standing date, rather than an impersonal request through the app. 'A little later today. I have a meeting.' Worse than personal is high-handed. Does he think I'm his to command, in more ways than listed in my work contract?

'I won't be here for lunch,' I find myself answering. 'You can send me your request, and I'll get Charlie or one of the others to deliver it.'

'No, you will bring lunch.'

'I can't. I'm busy.' Annoyance builds alongside determination.

'We eat lunch together every day.'

'For no other reason than I have to.' The lie is out of my mouth before I can temper it.

'You don't mean that.' His lush lips firming, his eyes are suddenly more agate than emerald as he pushes off the table, sending my pulse skittering.

'It's true. I'm here in no other capacity than your employee.' Who reset my brain to uber-bitch today?

'Ah. So that's it? I hope you've been satisfied thus far by the scope of your work.' His voice is made for seduction, the rasp in it reminding me of the roughness of his hands. When I can't find the words to answer, he speaks again. 'I for one have been more than satisfied with how you've performed under me.'

'High praise,' I find myself murmuring, a dozen images of just that flickering through my brain. 'I wonder how many of your employees you can apply that to.' Because screw his work-based innuendo.

'It shouldn't matter.' His fingers skim my face in a shiver-inducing caress. 'The important thing to acknowledge is—

'That I always achieve the desired outcome?' Because let me tell you, I'm prepared to lie through my teeth right now.

'No, the important thing is that I undress you as my superior. Always.'

'Remy, don't.' As I step back, I wonder if this is what a withdrawal to an addiction feels like.

'Don't what? Want you so much I can feel it in my fingertips? Because I'm afraid I can't help it.'

'I'm going now.' Because, the truth is, I can see it happening all before me. I'll lean into his hand, and he'll kiss me. Next, we'll tear at each other's clothes, mouths greedy and fingers grasping. I can see it all, the images playing out like a movie in my head, so compelling, I can't stop them. But I can stop them from becoming reality, beginning with feigning an air of artificial boredom

'No, Rose.' His fingers find my chin, tilting my gaze to his. 'Don't look at me with indifference. I can take your anger but not your apathy.'

'I've promised you nothing.' My voice has a strength I don't really feel.

He nods, his fingers falling away before he pushes his hands into his pockets. 'No, but in time, you'll give it all to me.'

31

ROSE

'*ATTENTION, BEAU GOSSE!*'

For the second time today, I hear this phrase—hottie alert —though this time from Charles. I don't lift my head, stabbing my fork into my takeaway container instead. I can't even feign interest, my mind preoccupied with what happened in Remy's office earlier. Was the mention of children a cruel ploy? Was he upping his game, or could it be that he's serious about me?

I can take your anger but not your apathy. Why the heck does that sound sexy?

'*Coucou!*' Charles sings, though why he's impersonating a cuckoo, I'm not sure. 'Rose? Did you hear?'

'No boy talk,' I say, flicking him a look. 'Not today.' The grass tickles my legs as I point my toes, stretch out, the slight breeze plastering an errant wisp of my hair against my lips.

'Oh, but you'll want to see this one.' Fee's words sound delivered through a smile.

I slide the strands behind my ear before chasing the remnants of my couscous salad with my fork. I thought her joining us for lunch today might give me a break from

Charles. I'm thinking of getting him a T-shirt with *Team Remy* printed on it because whatever was said during Remy's *I love Rose* confession, it has plucked at the strings of "'is 'art," to quote my so-called friend.

'Oh, for goodness' sake, look!' Fee nudges me so hard, the much-chased grains fall off my fork and onto the picnic rug. A picnic rug for a picnic lunch on a tiny square of lawn at the rear of the hotel and tower complex. There are a dozen or so Wolf employees with the same idea, some sitting on a picnic bench, others lounging under the shade of trees.

'Okay, what? Where is this unmissable Adonis?' As I look up, I become aware of the powerful roar of a motorcycle, a beast of a machine all revs and no speed. 'Do you think motorcycle riders look sexy because of the way they're bowed over the machine?' There's something about it reminiscent of the bedroom.

'Because of all that power between the legs.'

That's not exactly what I mean, but yeah, I suppose.

The beast pulls up against the curb, the engine cutting out. A man is clearly in charge of the thing, though he's not really dressed for it. A tailored suit jacket hugs to his broad shoulders and powerful thighs as a jet-coloured helmet covers his head, the visor glinting in the sun.

'Men and machines aren't really my thing. Besides, he might look like Shrek under all that.' I guess some girls, or boys even, might make him keep the helmet on in that case because the picture he creates is pretty hot. For me, motorcycles conjure up images of denim and leather, beards and tattoos, not bespoke tailoring and shiny black shoes. Who knew these would be a good combination.

'What's wrong with men who ride?' If it were anyone else other than Fee asking, I'd accuse them of having a dirty mind.

'Nothing. If you like grease monkeys, I suppose.' The

words almost dry on my tongue as the driver dismounts, his hands rising to his helmet almost in slo-mo.

That's right, daddy.

Change my perception.

You take that thing off slowly . . . make it last.

'He knows how to play to an audience, am I . . . right?' The latter leaves my mouth as a squeak, the dark helmet exposing my very own personal Adonis. I mean, not exposing *him*—his fly isn't open or anything. Not that it matters because I'm still hit with the insane urge to make those around us avert their eyes because, Christ on a cracker, the suit, and the mighty beast combo looks so hot on him.

He places the helmet down on the bike, pulling wayfarer sunglasses from his inside jacket pocket; a must when you live somewhere that is sunny three hundred days a year. His shades hide his intentions as his purposeful stride in all his suit-porn glory heads our way.

'What is he doing here?' I protest while trying to compose myself. Placing the container down, I pluck at my skirt, shimmying it down my thighs. I was trying to catch a little sun, but now I'm just nervous. Nervous and a little excited at the prospect he's sought me out. Anxious that it might not be the case. *Maybe he'll just pass me with a casual smile, or even a studied disinterest.* Add in a little fear of the strength of my feelings and a little more loathing that I can't help myself, and what I am right now, sitting on a patch of grass is emotional soup.

The tension inside me disappears as the corner of his lip quirks; he's here for me.

'Ladies. Charles.' My internal organs seem to be attempting to rearrange themselves at the deep tenor of his voice. 'You picked a beautiful day for a picnic lunch.'

For the sake of your mental health, don't think about what's going on under that suit.

'Oh, would you like to join us?' Fee is already twisting her legs under her to free up the edge of the rug, but he's already shaking his head. The Remy of March would probably hunker down beside us, but the billionaire Remy? The demands on his time are just too great. It's just as well. Yet he seems to find time for me.

'Thank you, but no. I've already eaten.' His gaze flicks my way. 'Alone.'

Behold the field in which I grow my fucks. Lay thine eyes upon it and thou shalt see that it is barren. Which is just a fancy-assed way of saying, you're a big boy, you can eat alone. And a picnic lunch with friends is an appointment, even if my neck is suddenly prickling with discomfort. Or did I say I had a meeting? I can't remember.

'I wondered if I could have a word with Rose.'

It's a strangely formal request, but I guess he doesn't know my friends would probably drag my ass up and throw me into his arms if I refused. I'm proved right as they begin to fuss.

'I have to get back to the office.' This from Fee, who doesn't even work in an office.

'I—I 'ave to see a man about a dog. A Pekinese!' he exclaims, but we both know that party is over, Charlie boy.

'You can just wait right here,' I interject sternly, curling my legs under me to stand. 'Both of you.' It's not like they'd actually leave, anyway. They'd just find another vantage point.

I follow him to the shade of a nearby tree where I adjust the monogrammed scarf I have tied loosely around my neck, purposely ignoring how the sun crests his head, turning the ends of his hair almost copper.

'How was your meeting?'

You were just looking at it. 'Good.'

'And the rest of your day?'

'It's been pretty good up until now.'

At my answer, his lips quirk in the corner. 'Good until I appeared?'

I lift and drop my shoulder because I'm not sure I could even attempt to put together an answer that wasn't a lot of anger and half-formed thoughts.

'Then I'm afraid you're about to be very disappointed,' he murmurs, his mouth not quite giving into a smile.

'And you find that entertaining why?'

He tips his head back as though to watch the leaves above rustling in the breeze. The light shifts and dances, dappling his face. 'I'd like you to come to dinner with me tonight.'

'Ah, I get it. It's a joke.'

'No, I'm quite serious.'

'And I'm not interested.' My words are part incredulous huff, part *dude, I can't believe you'd even try.*

'Fine.' A ripple of disappointment moves through me. Was that it? He asks, I say no, game over, move on? 'Let me put it another way.' He slides off his shades, his eyes seeming to reflect the exact colour of the leaves above, the depths of his determination revealed in that intensity. 'Be ready for eight o'clock this evening because I'm taking you out.'

'In your dreams, maybe.'

His gaze moves over me, blood rising to the surface of my skin as though it were a physical thing. 'No, Rose. In my dreams we stay in. In my dreams, the only time we move from the bed is to change the room in which we fuck.'

The sound that next leaves my mouth was meant as derision. Instead, it hits the air as a gentle breath at his drawlingly dirty elocution. 'I can't stop you from imagining,' I manage eventually, 'but I don't have to go anywhere with you.'

'I anticipated as much, but you're wrong, of course. You

see, I own you.' He steps into me, forcing me to tilt back my head. But I won't cede any ground.

'Maybe between the hours of nine and five.' I look down at my hand, studying how my thumb slides over my fingernails as though checking for a rough spot. I'm conscious of the gawkers and refuse to satisfy any curiosity they might have by rising to the bait because that would suit him just perfectly, wouldn't it? Maybe I'd get angry, and he'd get a little cockier, then I'd push him, and he'd wrap me in his arms and press a punishing kiss to my lips. Where was I again? Oh yeah. I refuse to give in to him or provide the gossips and gawkers a sideshow along with proving the only work I do for him I do on my back.

'Perhaps you should reread your contract. I believe it reads *as required.*'

'Hours to be determined, up to thirty-five per week,' I parrot back. Read it? I've almost memorised it while looking for a way out of this job. *A way out you wouldn't have taken*, my mind whispers anyway.

'Even I don't have that kind of stamina.' His smile is disarming, contradicting his words. 'But I wasn't talking about your employment. I own you here.' Reaching out, he presses two fingers to my heart. It's not a sexual touch but a blatant one. To those looking on, I guess it could look like a quiet reprimand for the way I'm wearing my scarf as he flicks it, withdrawing his hand. A quiet reprimand or borderline sexual harassment, I'd lay odds that there's not one person looking on who wouldn't swap places. *If only they knew.*

'What are you doing?' I ask, stepping back. 'Do you want people to talk?'

'Yes, that's exactly what I want them to do. I want them to talk you into my arms. Dinner tonight. I won't take no for an answer. A car will pick you up at eight.'

'Then you'd better square in with Olga. If I'm working tonight, I'll need time off in the morning.'

'That sounds like a good idea. Perhaps I'll also block out my morning.' There's no need to guess what he means, his half smile pure sin.

'Don't get the wrong idea, Romeo. I'm just not working extra hours for free.' And I'm not working under you. Unless you ask nicely. No, I mean I'm not working under you for anything.

When he finally finds his voice, it's low and full of intensity. 'I realise you don't think a lot of me right now, but I want you to know that I'm going to do everything in my power to change that.'

'Good luck with that,' I huff. And with that less than satisfactory denouement, I make my way back to my friends. My smiling friends.

'What was that all about?' *Fee.*

'What did he say?' *Charles.*

'I've been ordered to dinner.'

'Ordered?' Fee repeats with a frown.

'Yup. So don't expect to see me in the morning. Close your mouth, honey,' I retort, turning to Charles, 'it's not like that. It's a working dinner.'

But only one of us will be working hard.

32

REMY

I DROP my bag in the entryway, still not quite believing I'd asked Rose to bring it to me. The thing is big enough to put her in! But it was another excuse to see her. One I just didn't think through properly. To add insult to injury, Rhett annoyed me the whole evening, completely throwing me off my game. I'm not sure the way he fights really enters into the spirit of things; he salutes like he ought to, engages as he should, but it's the constant running commentary of goading that sets him apart as far as things go.

As one of the original Olympic sports, he does the name of fencing no good. But he makes a worthy opponent, for someone who didn't take it up at the age of twelve. Even if he sometimes behaves as though he's twelve.

I head straight for the kitchen to examine what Marta left for dinner this evening. Chicken with tomatoes and tarragon, I can tell, before I've even opened the oven. I set the timer, pull out last night's open bottle of *Chapoutier Ermitage,* thinking I must've had more than one glass judging by the bottle unless Marta used it to cook. At two hundred euros a bottle, the dish better be good. Splashing a little into a glass, I take it into the other room, heading for the second floor to change.

I take the stairs two at a time, knowing there is only a few minutes between my tarragon chicken being ready and inedible. Wine glass in one hand, I use the other to unbutton my shirt as my mind fills with a dozen inconsequential thoughts.

My hair is still damp from the shower at the club, which means it's probably time for a haircut.

I'll have Paulette call George and book in for a trim and a straight razor shave.

I should invite Rose to watch.

Perhaps she'd like to learn.

Though after this afternoon, a cut-throat razor might not be the best thing to hand her.

I'm hungry, having worked up an appetite, and in a hurry to get to my meal before it spoils. The final button on my shirt loosened, push open the bedroom door, simultaneously raising the glass to my lips. If I hadn't been so preoccupied I might've registered the lights were on. And if I'd registered the lights, I might've realised that I wasn't alone.

'Amélie.' Her eyes widen with satisfaction at my tone. But she's mistaken if she thinks the husk in my voice is anything other than shock. '*Qu'est-ce qui tu fais?*' What are you doing?'

Here. In my bedroom.

With very few clothes on.

'I didn't like how we left things before,' she answers, raising the glass in her hand to lips.

'I thought you were out of the country.' Like the child who believes any attention is good, the key to success with her is indifference. Besides, I only know where she's supposed to be because I'd asked Rhett to keep an eye on her.

Because I trust her as far as I could pitch her across the room.

'Just for a few days.' She places one leg over the other, the opposite hand draping across her body, loosely clasping her hip. Some position, I suppose, she picked up from her modelling days.

'Well, you can go home now. Nothing has changed.' I don't bother asking how she got in here, mainly because I couldn't trust her answer, as I place my glass down on the dresser and consider how buttoning my shirt would seem like a weakness. But keeping it open might encourage her.

'But Remy, why does it have to end? You know I'm good for you. I don't place any demands on your time, but I'm always there by your side when you need me.'

'When I need the illusion of a partner, you mean? A life mate?' She nods gracefully, drawing closer, her walk something more at home on the catwalk. 'I don't need illusions any longer.' Were my illusions her delusions? I think probably not. We were never suited. This is more about a loss of standing, a loss of finances.

'Your little friend doesn't even speak French. I heard she used to work in a strip club.' She pouts as though pitying me my poor choices, her hand slides to the nape of my neck, her glass holding the other. 'She won't even fit into couture, Remy. How will that look at one of your mother's fundraisers?'

'You know, I always knew you were a bitch,' I murmur, trailing my fingers up her slender arm, 'but I didn't realise you were quite so unpleasant.' As I pull her wrist away, it drops to her side. 'Rose knows the meaning of an honest day's work. Something you wouldn't understand. Put your clothes back on.'

'Look at me—how can you possibly prefer her?'

'If you really need to ask, it's pointless asking me to

explain. Put on your clothes. And. Get. Out.' This time, I leave her in no doubt; it isn't a request. But just in case, I leave the room first.

'Where are you going?' she calls after me.

'Somewhere you aren't.'

I'll stay at the hotel, I suppose, as I have done many nights over the past two years. *No,* I decide. *I'll go down to the marina and stay on Le Loup de Mer. My yacht.*

33

ROSE

How does a girl dress for a night with a billionaire she wants to hate but can't? A night where there's to be dinner, for which she's negotiated overtime, along with a few hours off the following day. A sensible choice would be to don her uniform again. But she never was very sensible. At least, not when it comes to him.

'This is not some voiceover for a rom-com,' I mutter, examining the scant offerings of my wardrobe.

Included in the price of my flight out from the States was one twenty-five kilo piece of luggage, which contained workwear, a capsule wardrobe of weekend casuals. *pyjamas.* Underwear. Five pair of shoes. A fancy kimono that took forever to drop its creases. Going out dresses totalling three; one LBD, one floral cutesy number, one black lace with a nude underlay, super sexy, it also draws the eye to the girls.

I'm not sure I'm even convinced as I reach for the floral, feeding myself such excuses as the restaurant might be a little posh, and the LBD might be a little formal. Now the lace, though it provides full coverage from neck to knees, is the dress equivalent of an ostrich feather fan dance. *Now you see the boobs, now you don't.* I guess that makes my choice a little easier for this working dinner.

Well, I'm certainly *working it,* I decide as I examine myself in the mirror. The fabric of the dress works wonders for my shape, sort of sucking in and tucking up the usual things I don't like about myself. I tell myself my updo has the fashionable tousled look, one that says *take me to bed,* or even, *I just got out of it.* Either of those will do. Both are better than plain old big.

My phone rings a little after seven-thirty; a car is waiting for me downstairs. A Bentley, more specifically.

'*Bonsoir,* Mademoiselle Ryan.' The driver inclines his head, all deference and dapper suit as he opens the rear door. Well, I guess he just confirmed this isn't anyone else's ride. Lord knows there are probably as many Bentleys on the roads in Monaco as there are Ubers in most other countries. Relatively speaking, I mean. 'My name is Hénri. I am to take you to Monsieur Durrand.'

'Thank you.' I decorously slide inside, the buttery leather interior like an invitation to roll around in. An invitation I resist.

'Which restaurant are we going to?' From the back seat, I pitch my voice to be heard over the deep interior.

'I have instructions to keep the destination a surprise,' he replies, his eyes on the driver's side mirror as he pulls out into the traffic.

'Great. Super great.' Because that's not weird at all. 'I'll just text Fee and tell her if she hasn't heard from me in an hour to alert the authorities.'

'Pardon, Mademoiselle?'

'Nothing.' Catching the chauffeur's attention in the rear-view mirror, I smile and give my head a little shake. 'Nothing at all. But if we get anywhere near an airfield, I'm bailing at the first opportunity,' I mumble to myself.

The car drives west heading out of Monaco and in the direction of Italy, I think. I watch the scenery slip by the window; the landmarks unfamiliar to me as we make our way out of the city. The streetlights become sparser as the car begins to wind its way up the hilly vista, an area that has just been a backdrop for my Monaco experience so far.

The houses are more spread out up here, some more like estates behind imposing privacy gates. We slow in front of one such set of gates, gigantic wrought iron set back from the road. Palm trees sway in the breeze as they tower over high walls. This is either the kind of restaurant that's so exclusive it doesn't advertise its name, or it's not a restaurant at all.

Hénri murmurs something into the microphone, kind of like the one at a McDonald's drive-through. The gates swing slowly open, gravel crackling under the wheels as we follow the line of lush trees, lit by lanterns from below. Up ahead, the house—no, mansion—stands grand and imposing in the Belle Époque style. *Something else I've learned since I moved to Monaco.* A pale stucco front and mullioned windows, the building is all style and balanced aesthetic with Juliet balconies made of lacy ironwork. The car slows to a stop at the porticoed entryway. I'm not so green or uncultured to know I should wait for Hénri to open the rear passenger door. But when the door to the house doesn't open, I find myself glancing back at him.

'You must follow the path to the back of the house.' His smile is encouraging, his manner almost avuncular despite being around my age. My heels sink into gaps between the gravel, no doubt being destroyed, but a little farther ahead, the tiny stones give way to paving edged by lanterns. Though it's still light, dusk not appearing until late during the European summertime, leaves from the trees have darkened the sky above. As I round the house and the precisely trimmed greenery, breath catches in my throat, the space opening up to the most breathtaking view. I live pretty high above parts of Monaco myself, and the views are pretty spectacular, but there's a starkness about them. A modern austerity. But not here. Lush greenery frames an azure infinity pool drawing the eye to the view beyond. And what a view. It stretches out for miles, high above the whole of Monaco and out to the Mediterranean beyond. Mountains stretch left and right framing gardens that are a riot of colours. It's all so beautiful; it takes me a moment to remember why I'm here, but my feet begin to move again eventually.

Down a set of wide sandstone steps, the path splits in two; one way leads to the pool, the other to a pergola clasped in vines and divinely scented honeysuckle I can smell from here. I take the second option, drawn by the heavenly scent of the tiny blooms and the view. Oh, the view. Which includes a casually dressed Remy, which is a feast for the eyes. Dark loafers, navy shorts, and a light blue shirt, open at the neck, rolled at the sleeves, tan skin showing in all the places in between. *Riviera chic.*

His smile spreads rich and sweet like honey as I approach.

'You made it.' As I reach him, his hands find my shoulders, kisses pressed to each cheek. I try not to stiffen, and I think I manage mostly, until he pulls back, sweetness replaced with melancholy. 'When on the French Riviera . . .' The pause he left was long enough for me to understand his meaning.

'Greetings come with kisses.'

'But not always French ones.'

I find myself struggling to hide my smile and duck my head. In truth, it wasn't his greeting that was startling; it was

334

more his touch. The shock of his fingertips, the nearness of him. It somehow caught me off guard. Made me want.

'Please, sit.' He gestures to a refectory-style table; iron legs with a marble top, the table settings as fancy as any hotel. Ever the gentleman, he pulls out my chair before taking the seat opposite me. 'Would you like a drink? Maybe a cocktail?'

A waiter materialises as though out of air, and drinks are ordered; a G&T for him and a mojito for me, a *pot d'accueil,* or a welcome drink. We don't speak until the waiter withdraws.

'You look beautiful, Rose. I could've watched you all night, standing at the top of the stairs.'

'I think I almost stayed there,' I say, brushing off the compliment, 'the view is just like a peek at the heavens. It's cooler up here, too.'

'Too cool? Would you like the fire lit?' He points to the outdoor hearth that gets very little use, judging by its condition. It's filled with white stones, the mantel-shelf standing at least my height.

'No, honestly. I'm fine. It's kind of nice.' Nice. Urgh. Shoot me now. Will our conversation be so stilted the whole evening? Given the choice between arguing and playing nice, I'd definitely choose the former. The latter I can do with anyone. 'What's the story with the house?' I tilt my head back at the beautiful building behind us.

'What do you mean?' He brings his glass to his lips, his brows suspiciously high.

'Why are we here? Is the place yours? Does it have a big cellar, and have I been kidnapped?'

He shakes his head, kind of like you do with small children when they do something adorable. 'The house is mine, for a little while, at least. We are here for privacy and no. That doesn't mean we're hiding. As for a cellar, yes. But one with an extensive wine collection. Have you been kidnapped? I wish.'

'Well, I'm kind of confused.' And kind of wrong, I decide, as my lady parts decide to take an interest in the conversation.

'And I am kind of besotted.' I blush like a debutante with her first dance card at his words. My guess is it won't be the last blush of the night. 'But I draw the line at kidnapping.'

In front of us, the sky turns the colour of cotton candy and the sparse clouds like violets, as cocktails turn to our appetiser, and appetiser to entrée, or as they say in France, *entrée* to *plat principal*. I suppose it's kind of a simple meal, though every morsel is served with the greatest of care and is utterly delicious from the peppery salad that I could totally make friends with—wafer-thin slices of radishes and tiny sweet tomatoes in a heavenly vinaigrette—to the main event of *steak frites*. Steak with fries by any other name, though if you were served portion sizes like this back home, I'm sure there would be complaints. But the fillet is melt-in-the-mouth tender, and the fries such a perfection of crisp and golden that it's just as well there are less than a dozen on my plate. I think I could eat these until they came out of my ears. But by the time we reach the cheese course, I'm coming to realise the reason for the tiny serves.

'I chose a decent bottle of Beaujolais to pair with the cheese, or should we open the champagne?' The sky has long since turned to night, a chandelier hanging above us, fiery lanterns dotted around the garden.

'Are we celebrating?' Did I mean to purr? I don't think so, though the cicadas decide to join the chorus. At least, that's not how this night is supposed to go. It must be the cheese. I do love me some cheese.

'I think that's up to you.'

'I thought I was on the clock.' His laughter, deep and rich, resounds across the space, so much so that I find myself playing my response back in my head. *Nope, sounded correct; on the clock, not on the . . . you know what I mean.* 'What's so funny?'

A deep breath. A sigh. His gaze falling over me, trailing fire in its wake. 'Any night spent with you is cause for celebration.'

'Maybe you're just trying to get me drunk.'

'Tempting, but no.' His eyes, dark and glossy, dance with mischief.

'I shouldn't imagine you've ever had to get a woman tipsy to persuade her into bed.'

'I don't want a woman in my bed. I want you. Not just in my bed, but my life.'

I glance around me, wondering how I can change the subject, wondering if I really want to when he takes pity on me, changing the subject as the waiter appears with champagne on a silver tray accompanied by two tall flutes. *It's like he read my mind.* With a murmured thanks, Remy takes the bottle, the man drifting into the night like a ghost.

'Have you visited the casino yet?'

'Not yet,' I answer, sure he means the Casino de Monte-Carlo, an icon of Monaco. He presses a napkin to the cork before beginning to twist the bottle. The cork releases with a decadent hiss.

'You've done that before.'

'Once or twice.' The ends of his hair turn the colour of newly minted pennies as he reaches across the table, splashing the effervescent bubbles into a glass. 'I have a few other tricks I can show you sometime.'

'*Uh-huh.*'

He cuts a wedge of pale coloured cheese, coupling it with a torn morsel of bread. 'I once opened a bottle with my ski after a particularly exhilarating run, and another time with a sabre.'

When it becomes clear the cheese is for me, I open my mouth to accept it, a need sticky and sweet working its way down to my belly at his expression. I pause to chew as he takes his seat again.

'Explain, please.' I cover my mouth with my hand as I swallow, my gaze sliding from his. 'Let's go with the sabre first, because everyone carries one of those.'

'A little like purple sex-toys?' If this isn't a perfect example of how different we are, I don't know what is. Posh boys carry skis and sabres while girls from the other side of the tracks carry defence dildos. Only, the more I say it, the less it seems to matter to me. 'It was a wedding,' he continues with an almost disparaging shake of his head. 'In the wilds of Scotland somewhere, and there were these old cavalry swords hanging above the mantel.'

'And you couldn't resist,' I deadpan.

'More like I'd had too much to drink. Do you have a moral objection to casinos? It's just, you frowned when I asked.'

'Not really. I mean, it is a beautiful building and I guess I will go at some point.' If for no other reason than the inside is super swanky, so I'm told. 'Gambling doesn't hold any interest for me.'

'Really?' He picks up his glass, leaning back in his chair before proceeding to study me over the rim.

'Do you like to gamble?'

'Not in the ways you're thinking,' he answers cryptically. 'I think perhaps your objection to gambling comes from experience.'

'Not in the way you're thinking,' I parrot back. I pause as I debate the merits of telling this silly story.

'You look so torn, but that just makes me want to know all the more.'

'You're going to be disappointed.' I help myself to another wedge of cheese, eyeing the figs and choosing a grape instead. *Less messy.* 'When I was travelling, on my way to Australia from Europe, I had a layover in Hong Kong. The hostel I was staying in—you know, like dorms? Don't look at me like that —I bet you've never stayed anywhere less than five-star in your life. Anyway, I met a Danish girl in the hostel, and we decided to go to Macau where the casinos are.'

'There's a cheap bus, which is a bonus when you're broke. We wandered from place to place, munching on the complimentary snacks.' He looks less than impressed by that. 'Hey, it was no worse than some of the food we saw at one of the food markets. Shim Sham Poo or something.'

'Sham Shui Po,' he corrects with an indulgent smile.

'You've been?' He inclines his head. 'Well, the free food on offer was better than stinky tofu and those century eggs. Or even sea cucumber.' I shiver at the recollection.

'So you ate snacks. And then you gambled?'

'Cheap bus, free food, free bottles of water. All very important when you're living on a shoestring.'

'And you and your Danish friend were bought drinks by the casino's patrons, no doubt.'

'One or two,' I agree, though most men's focus lay elsewhere. 'Then after a few hours of wandering around, we decided to place a couple of lowkey bets, hitting the roulette table. Like you said, when in Rome.'

'Let me know when you're ready for those French kisses.'

'Ha. Right. Is that like, overtime?' I squint, he laughs, before I carry on with my story. 'Anyway, we had a couple of hundred dollars between us—'

'Hong Kong or US?'

I pull a face as though to say *is that even a serious question?* 'Which part of poor did you not get?' Or maybe it's more the case that he doesn't understand what poor is.

'So, you had thirty dollars,' he murmurs indulgently.

'Thirty we were willing to waste,' I reply, feeling the definition is important. I had money at that point; more money than I'd ever had in my life thanks to the windfall from mom's mysterious relation, but I also had a plan. Travel. Get worldly. Move back and take the hotel management world by storm. While even the best-laid plans go belly up, I still had a blast.

'Did you try the blackjack tables or the slots next?'

'We stuck to roulette,' I answer loftily. 'Flipping a coin every six or seven hits, placing a red or a black with no expectations and no seriousness. Within thirty minutes, our thirty bucks became two thousand dollars. Hong-Kong dollars, but it was a lot of money to a traveller on a budget.'

'It must've taken you a long time to save for a trip around the world.'

'Actually, a distant relation died and left me a little money. It was a godsend, really. Plus I worked as I travelled. Fruit picking, waitressing, that kind of stuff.' Remy nods as though understanding, but how could he? I carry on. 'To us, the money was a fancy dinner and night in a hotel instead of a backpacker's place. Maybe not Monaco fancy,' I say, reaching for my glass. 'Stop laughing! I'm not talking about the kinds of places you stay in. Hell, the places you own.' It suddenly hits all over again how different we are. How we'll always be so.

'What is it?' His expression falters, his laughter dying away. There's no sense in making us both feel sad.

'I was just thinking that, back then, a fancy dinner was a place that had linens and plates.'

'I don't know, there's a certain charm in eating food from a stick,' he replies, referring to the Hong Kong street markets. I guess we do have some experiences that are similar. 'And drinking beer at rickety tables with plastic tablecloths.'

'Slumming it, were you?'

'Gaining a little life experience, the same as you. So, you had your night in a hotel,' he asserts, getting us back on track.

'Not at that point.' I take a sip of my champagne, placing my glass down. 'We had to go back to the hostel in the city to grab our things. We ate dinner in Macau and headed for the bus back to the mainland. But while we were waiting, we got to thinking.' I tap my index finger against my chin for effect. 'If we made two thousand with two hundred dollars, what could we make with two thousand?'

'You were bitten by the bug.'

'Well, we were definitely bitten.'

'And what was the outcome?'

'We shared a can of cola on the way home. Gambling is for suckers,' I say over the sounds of his guffaws.

Remy's mirth settles, his eyes dark and glossy in the ambient light. 'Some things are worth taking a risk on, you know.'

'I suppose this is when you tell me I need to take a risk on you?' My cynical response was in the place of a hundred things I could've said. Things I'd rather have said. But I'd just be creating problems for another day. Yet his answer still blows me away.

'No. Take a risk on love.'

34

REMY

'Don't.' Her expression falters from teasing and testy to disquiet. I hate that she's unhappy, that I made her unhappy, but I can't envisage a time when I'd give up. Give up on us. 'Don't do that. Don't blur the lines.'

'Rose, we don't have lines. You have a demarcation zone and barbed words like wire.'

'And why is that?' she answers fiercely.

'Because I'm an idiot. And arrogant. And I thought I could take care of this before it ever got near enough to hurt you. You remember our first time here in Monaco? Remember how I said I'd never had another woman in my bed? It's true.'

'Because you never lived there,' she almost whispers, her eyes looking anywhere but at me.

'It doesn't matter. The penthouse, the house with Amélie, the hotel—none of those beds have seen another body next to mine. Since March, I have been faithful to you. As ridiculous as it might sound, I never wanted anyone else, though I had chances.' More recently, Amélie. At one time, I might have taken her up on yesterday's offer, if for no other reason than to teach her how little she meant to me. But not anymore. 'I was faithful to the idea of you. The woman who looked after me. The angel.'

'I'm no angel.'

'To me, you are. So, when you arrived in Monaco, it was like a sign. I'd already moved out of the house, though in truth, Amélie was rarely there. The place is like a palace, and though we lived under the same roof, we never lived together. But the day I saw you in the hallway, I moved to the penthouse, like I was wiping the slate clean.'

'Except you didn't, not really. You just swept your problems under the carpet.'

'For a little while. I thought she'd come back, and I'd tell her. That I'd buy her off, I suppose. I fully intended to tell you, but at the point where I could say the ties between us were truly broken. The problem dealt with.'

'Instead, it came and bit you in the ass.'

'And I deserved it. I'm only sorry that I hurt you.' Reaching across the table, I cover her hand with mine, something unfurling inside as she allows me. 'We punish ourselves sometimes, I think, with the kind of love we think we don't deserve. But I want to deserve your love. I want to be worthy of you. Don't say anything, please. Just listen because I've had a very, very beautiful idea. Don't look so worried. I'm not going to drop to my knee with a ring. Unless you want to,' I add quickly.

'If you drop to your knee, I'm out of here.'

I find myself laughing as I top up our glasses. '*Mon petit hérisson.*'

'*That* sounded like something that requires a trip to the pharmacy to cure.'

'I called you my thorny hedgehog.'

'Oh, yeah. That's super endearing.' But she's smiling. 'You want me to take a risk on love, and then you liken me to a

343

spikey rodent? My mother was right. Trying to understand men is like trying to explain what colour the number nine smells like.'

'Men are not so complicated.'

'Yeah, I've heard that, too,' she replies cynically. 'You have two settings. Hungry and horny. If you haven't got a hard-on, I'm supposed to feed you a sandwich, right?'

'Would you like to know which of those I am now?'

'Nope,' she retorts as she reaches for the cheese, plucking then throwing a grape my way with the words, 'Just in case.'

I'd like to say I suavely caught it, but unfortunately, it glances off my nose, making us both laugh.

'Thank you, but I'm not hungry. Do you have anything to help the second state?'

'You mean Pennsylvania?' Cupping her chin, she props her elbow on the table.

'That's a strange word for an erection, but I can go with it. Same with the glittery penis.'

This time, she groans, her hand moving from her chin to cover her eyes. 'I might've been drunk when I ordered that.'

'And when you hit me with it?'

Her fingers separate as she shoots me a glare. 'Frightened.'

'I know. But it's all been worth it so far, no?' A quirk of her plush lips is her only answer. 'Can I show you something?'

'If it's hard or purple or sparkling or currently in your pants, then the answer is no.'

'Take a risk.' I grasp my glass by the rim and round the table, holding out my hand. 'Bring your glass, if you'd like.' My stomach tenses as the tips of her fingers touch mine. *Dieu*, her dress appears as though it were painted on, like someone took a delicate brush to her skin to detail the intricate swirls of lace. My gaze is drawn to the golden sheen of her toned legs, farther still to her red painted toenails. 'Rose, are you wearing my shoes?'

'Don't be ridiculous,' she answers. 'My feet are much smaller than yours.'

But she's smiling. And those sandals with heels the height of the Eiffel Tower are the ones I bought. Which begs the question, what else is she wearing under that dress?

'I can hear you thinking. Stop it.'

I tuck her hand into the crook of my arm. 'If you can hear me, the decent thing to do would be to tell me.'

'It's impolite to ask a lady about her undergarments,' she murmurs primly, and through a smile. My laughter resounds through the courtyard.

'*Bon*. Let us go into the house.'

We begin in the *salon,* working our way through the dining room, the small library, and into the family kitchen; the commercial kitchen already being occupied by the catering staff.

'This is like an entertainer's dream,' she says, running her fingertips across a silver vein in the marble as she wanders around the space. 'I asked you if this place was yours. You didn't answer.'

'I know.' I fold my arms and lean a shoulder against one of the cabinets as I watch her marvel at the place. She liked the library, which she called the den, and the grand staircase. But it's this room she likes best, I can tell. 'Do you like it? The house, I mean.'

'It's like something out of *Cribs*.'

'*Pardon?*'

'You know, like MTV. Lives of the rich and fabulous.'

The gaze she slides me over her shoulder can only be defined as provocative. I push away from the cupboards and come up behind her, our bodies almost touching, my lips coasting her ear. 'I am the rich, you are the fabulous.'

A tremor runs through her, though she tries to hide it by stepping away and raising her glass to her mouth.

'You didn't answer.'

'Yes, of course, I like it,' she says, turning to face me now.

'You haven't seen the upstairs.' I don't miss the tiny catch in her throat and the way her eyes darken, though I force myself to turn. 'This way.'

We pass the cinema room, the entrance to the gym and the indoor pool, none of which I mention as she follows me up the stairs.

'The tiling looks original.'

'Yes, most of the features are. It's unusual in a property as old as this.'

'This staircase has probably seen a lot of debutantes.' Brides, too, I almost answer. 'See how it curves at the bottom?' she says, tipping her head over the bannister as she points. 'That's the kind of place where kisses are stolen.'

'Well, I missed that.' Too busy watching her climb the stairs, too engrossed in the flare of her hips and the sinuous arch of her lower back

'How many lives must these walls have seen.' The moment is oh, so perfect as she reaches the top of the stairs and turns. 'Love affairs and heartache and every emotion in between.'

I was going to wait. I fully intended to show her around the upper floors, to tell her the stories my mother told of her childhood. Of how she sat at the top of the stairs listening to music drifting up from the *salon*, along with the faint scent of my grandfather's Gauloises cigarettes and the chink of glasses. I was going to wait until she'd seen it all. Until I'd explained all. But now I can't.

'Would you like to live your life within these walls?'

'What?' Her word bubbles with laughter, like vintage champagne. 'Sure. Who wouldn't?'

I take the next few stairs seemingly in one, taking her hands in mine. She doesn't need to know this is the house my mother grew up in, or how my father sold it from under her when their marriage turned sour. She doesn't need to know my connection to it, which really isn't much of a connection at all now that I've found her.

'This house is yours. Please let me finish.' The words fall from my mouth, my fingers tightening on hers to make her still. 'It's yours because you love it. And because I love you. You said once that your childhood lacked the permanency of a home, but that it never lacked love. Fill this house with love, ma Rose. Make it a happy home.'

'Remy, please be serious. I can't take a house from you.'

'You cannot refuse me. If you cut me out of your life tomorrow, I'd still want to give you this gift. Because I can. Because you deserve it. Because of all you've done for me.' And because, contrary to my words, I believe this is the home where our story will truly begin.

'I don't know what to say. Except you're crazy. Just because I'm wearing the shoes you bought me'—*don't look down, don't*—'it doesn't mean I'm going to accept a house.'

'The shoes come from a different place. Everything in those bags did.' I incline my head. Sometimes, the truth only comes with a little difficulty. 'They came from the place of, I'll admit, wanting to annoy you. But more than that, each item wrapped in tissue and ribbon, every single thing, I harboured thoughts of seeing you in. The dresses, of course. The shoes, the underwear, the watch. I hoped I'd see you in those the most.'

'Do you have a thing for wrists I don't know about?'

347

My cock twitches; the sweetest of percussion. 'I have a thing for your wrists.' Along with my answer, I rub my thumb over those dainty contours. Who knew this part of the body could be so erotic? This part of *her* body. 'But in truth, I hoped to see you in the watch and nothing else.'

'Same with the shoes?' she says, her words sieved through a soft chuckle.

'What can I say?'

'Nothing. Best to say nothing at all.'

I allow her hands to fall as I step away. 'Go. Take a tour of your new home.'

'Stop that.' But she's still smiling as I step down one stair. 'You're not going to come with me?'

'*Non*. I can't be in the same place as those wrists and a bed.'

'Really?' Her smile is small and wry but threatens to blossom.

Bringing her fingertips to my lips, I kiss them then utter, '*Irrésistible*.'

'You're ridiculous.'

I am ridiculous; ridiculously in love with her.

There's a bottle of champagne on ice waiting in the kitchen, our glasses replaced with new. This is the magic that happens when you treat staff well. I pop the cork and pour out two glasses, not exactly savouring mine as I try to drown the unfamiliar unrest running through me, though not because I expect she'll refuse me because I know she will, just like she fights me for everything. She's worth the fight. Worth the work. So why am I restive? Because every molecule of my being wants to go to her.

Eventually, I hear her heels in the hallway.

'Well, she's a stunner,' she says, leaning half in and half out of the kitchen, her hand wrapped around the doorframe.

'She's a she?' I ask, taking her glass to her.

'Yep.' She takes it from my hand, leaning her shoulder against the doorframe instead. 'Definitely. You should buy her, but for you.'

'She's already mine.' Rose watches me from over the rim of her glass, almost as though she's examining the meaning behind my words. *She does well to.* 'And I'm gifting her to you.'

Another decorous sip, and she twists, placing the glass on the countertop. I watch almost in slow motion as she steps into the room, into me, her arms feeding around my neck. The height of her heels make her taller than usual, her soulful eyes turning liquid gold as I take her hips in my hands.

'I'm not doing this because you want to buy me a house—'

'There's no *want to* about it. It's happening.'

Undeterred, she carries on. 'I'm doing this because I've had the best evening and because no one has ever said such perfect things to me.'

'I'm not the first man to say he loves you. As long as I'm the last, I'm fine with that.'

'You're certainly the first to want to buy me a house. And Remy? I'm not saying it back.'

'You're not saying you'll buy me a house?' I ask, being deliberately obtuse, making her shake her head in a long-suffering fashion.

'Do you want this kiss or not?'

Out of the hundred things she could've said. The hundred denials, explanations, or promises, this answer I like infinitely best.

'Want. Definitely.' A feeling I've become familiar with since opening my eyes to her in the hospital in March. I'm not a perfect man, and I never will be, but I'll try to be perfect for her.

Her eyes seem to search every inch of my face before she tips up onto her toes. I meet her halfway, my lips slanting over hers. *Dieu, it feels like it's been a lifetime.* Her lips are lush and sweet with the taste of champagne, and twice as intoxicating. But this kiss isn't about me as she tastes and teases me, dancing her tongue between the seam of my lips.

'I've missed this.' Her admission is barely a whisper and tears at the centre of me.

'I'm so sorry.'

'No. No more. Just kiss me. Kiss me properly.'

If there ever was a better direction, I've yet to hear it as I curl my hands around her hips, taking possession of this kiss, making it deeper and wetter and more passion-filled than any kiss in a kitchen has a right to be.

'Kiss me again,' she whispers, her voice taut as she tightens her arms around my neck. 'Don't stop.' But I have no plans to, not as my hand spans her ribs to feel her breath tightening. I press my lips to her jaw and curve my thumb under her breast, the lace rough to touch as I slide it against the underside of the plump flesh.

'I've missed the feel of you.' The admission sounds as though dragged from the depths of my chest as she bows, pressing into my hand. I press my palm to her breast. My fingers. Soft swipes and pretty pinches, I alternate the sensations until she arches into my hand with the sweetest of sighs. My kisses traverse her jaw until I reach her ear. 'But I'm not going to fuck you.' She convulses against me; a revolt against my declaration or a want without words.

'Why does that word sound so much more from your lips?'

'No matter how much I ache to.'

I don't answer. Can't. My hand slides to the curve of her rear, pressing her against me with a growl, a growl countered by a soft moan. Heat rushes through my veins as I stagger forward, pressing her hard against the doorframe.

'Maybe I'm not going to let you.' Despite her soft words, I hear the invitation and see the provocation in her languid gaze. A second later, a low groan rises from the depths of my chest as she sucks my bottom lip into her mouth, sinking her teeth mercilessly into the flesh as though she'd keep me there. Lips pressing hard, tongues thrusting, my hand moving to the hem of her dress as she tilts her head, giving me access to the skin of her neck.

A crash like cymbals sounds from beyond the kitchen, a curse following. I don't think I'd have noticed any of it had Rose not stilled beneath me. But now that she has, I see that I'm ruining my own plans.

'I can't decide if your skin is softer here,' I whisper, my fingers skimming her inner thigh. 'Or here.' I press the most teasing of open-mouthed kisses in the hollow below her ear, making her shiver.

'You're a tease, Remy Durrand.'

'There's pleasure in lingering. I'd like to show you again sometime.' Sometime not now as I pull away. Her lips are slightly swollen and kiss pink, even if currently quirked mockingly. 'Perhaps you'd let me linger in your kitchen again?'

'You never give up, do you?'

Taking her palms in my hands, I move my shoulders in the tiniest of shrugs. *Not until I get what I want,* I hope it says. 'This house is yours, and I hope one day you'll invite me to be here with you.'

'And in the meantime?'

'I wait. Until you're ready to say you love me.'

Until you're ready to confess what your heart already knows.

———

Hénri takes Rose home after a much more sedate kiss at the front door, the kind that left her giggling and complaining about being watched and feeling like a schoolgirl. Like a lot of things between us, our high school dating experiences wildly differ. While she speaks of chaste good-night kisses behind hedges and places her mother couldn't see, I can only recall the young mathematics teacher who didn't last at the school very long, though long enough for me to lose my virginity. Willing chalet girls during ski holidays who were possessed with what seemed like at the time, a world of experience, and weekends of sneaking local girls into the school grounds during term time. Our experiences may be very different, but Rose and I, we are not. We both want.

'Kissing you goodbye isn't what I want,' I'd told her, brushing away the fallen strands of her hair. 'I want to be able to kiss you good night every night.'

'So you give me a house?' Her voice held more than a note of cynicism, but her gaze was soft. 'Maybe you should get a tent and pitch it in the garden.' Her laughter vibrated through my chest, and I wanted nothing more than to keep her there. To take her upstairs, fall into the bed. Fall into her.

It will happen. Just not tonight. Tonight, I gave her a lot to think about, and I hope she climbs into bed tonight and dreams of our future.

The caterers leave, and the housekeeper retires for the evening while I top up my glass and wander out into the garden. Below, the lights of Monaco glint and gleam like fireflies, the sea beyond as motionless as dark-coloured glass. I wonder when exactly I should mention to Rose that her house comes with staff. That should be an interesting conversation. Maybe one that ends with a little more fulfilment than a fumble in the kitchen.

Perhaps I should see it as delayed gratification. But she was so hot under my fingertips, and she'd watched with the kind of intensity that made my vision go hazy with need. There will be other times, I tell myself. A lifetime of moments; happy ones, angry ones, years spent in bed making it up to her. Because I envisage I'll be the one at fault. As I am now. Because I can't help myself.

À chaque jour suffit sa peine. Trouble for another day.

For now, I go to the marina.

The night is still mild as Hénri drives me to *Port Hércules* with instructions to collect me in the morning. On the quayside, I find myself whistling as I weave my way between the parked Ferrari and Aston Martins as I head to the pontoon where *Le Loup de Mer,* the three-hundred-and-fifty-foot super yacht registered to The Wolf Group, is moored. I'd grown up on boats, or rather yachts, and owned quite a few of them myself. If you want to live the life of the profligate rich, you have to have the toys. Meaning yachts to party on, high-powered motorcycles to race, and cars to cruise in. An apartment in every uber-cool city and the girl on your arm. It's a life you bore of before long. That's when I sold up and bought a piece of an island, where I learned to sail and to build instead of destroy. I tell myself I could have those days back, but the lure of business is still too great.

But still, I enjoy owning the toys, even if this one is more a tax break, and *Le Loup* is the largest boat I've ever owned. So much so that she's not the kind of vessel I could operate myself, requiring both crew and captain. She's a status symbol; an indicator of wealth and power, rather something you can take out on a sunny Sunday afternoon. Polished oak floors and designer bedrooms. A saltwater swimming pool, a jacuzzi, and space to lounge until your heart is content all on one deck. She has a formal dining room large enough to seat twenty and space to entertain, whether that be dancing or gathering around the baby grand piano or seated at the cocktail bar. Sleek, yet grand and imposing, she really is ridiculous but a good way to fox the taxman. And the place I'll be sleeping for the next few nights.

The vessel is moored at the very end of the wharf, stern to, which is reversed in, I suppose, with the port side almost parallel with the pier wall. I approach the passerelle, the gangway, and though I don't have the prerequisite footwear, I don't intend to go barefoot once on board. Boat rules are barefoot or boat shoes, but as I'm heading directly for the master cabin, my bespoke Berluti's will have to do.

I take a moment to watch the moon riding high as I contemplate how much more open Rose was this evening. It's taken almost a month to get her to see how much I regret hurting her. A month for us both to realise how much I love her. I suppose the old adage is right; absence does make the heart grow fonder. Not that, strictly speaking, she's been physically absent from my life, but I've felt the loss of her in my bed each and every night. Lord knows, or perhaps I should rather invoke Everett's name, I've tormented her with my presence enough to drive her over the edge. But my plan is about to come full circle because tonight she looked at me with such a softness that I can believe she truly loves me, though she might not yet have said so.

The thought alone is enough to make a man feel as though he could fly, I reflect as I take a step onto the passerelle, my hands gripping the aluminium railing. As far as thoughts go, it's not so bad to be the last thought I ever have as the metal beneath my fingers vibrates, a rending sound filling my ears, reverberating into my flesh. I don't have another moment to process what's happening. One second, I'm gripping the barrier, the next, the LED lighting under my feet blurs. My head suddenly feels like it's been cleaved in two as I follow the railing into the water. Colours around me meld. Blue. Grey. White. The moon like a smear of paint up above.

Death is only dangerous in a life lived without love.

A flash of cruel clarity quickly followed by another.

I would've been happy living a life that simply lingered between her kisses.

I see colours no more. There's not time to be philosophical as I sink into the dark, empty void, the bitter taste in my mouth not water but regret.

35

ROSE

I NEED to be inside you.

His voice is somewhere between a breath and a groan, his hand sliding up my thigh.

Oh, yes please. My voice is breathless as I grasp the edge of the sink, grounding myself as my body begins to tremble.

My whole body.

Aching.

Shivering.

I want him so badly I can almost taste it.

His eyes track up my body, his gaze full of heat and promise.

Rain on mullioned glass. A house with honeysuckle and a view. Children playing in the pool, their hair lightened and skin kissed by the sun, kisses in the kitchen, arms wrapping around my waist as I rinse a glass at the sink. The scent of bergamot and spice and the musky scent of his skin. The feeling of happiness radiating from my chest, so bright and so large, I feel like I could burst.

Bees buzzing around pink honeysuckle.

Buzz Lightyear lying in the grass.

Buzzing.

Incessant buzzing. Like a bluebottle flying around my ear.

I come up from my pillows until I'm sitting up, ramrod straight in bed. Amber's whisper drifts from my ear. *Rich or poor, a good man is his own reward.*

My phone is ringing—it's already in my hands, but that isn't what's dragged me from sleep. I blink, brushing the hair from my face as my mind begins to whir. It can't be Amber because she wouldn't be at my front door. Unless I'm about to be faced with two emergencies. *One on the phone, one in my face.*

Throwing back the covers, I prod my phone as I note the time. It's not even four thirty yet. The number is local but not one I recognise.

''Lo,' I croak, my feet already trotting across the cool floorboards. I guess I can add champagne to the list of things that make me sleep like the dead.

'Thank Christ. It's like waking the fucking dead.' I bustle along the hallway, pulling the shouty voice away from my ear as it then commands, 'Open the fucking door.'

'Who is this?' The words are out before my mind grasps that there's only one man alive who would speak to me in this tone. *Everett.* My brain skips from one name to another as I unlock and pull open the front door. A fist instantly squeezes my heart as I take in his creased T-shirt and the way his hair is literally standing on end. But more than that it's his forbidding expression. 'What's happened. It's Remy, isn't it?'

'I'll tell you on the way.' I step into the communal hallway when his large hand cups my shoulder. 'It's best you put some clothes on first. We don't want to worry the rest of Monaco.'

'Not until you tell me what it is,' I reply as I try unsuccessfully to shake his hand off.

'He's okay.' His eyes are soft and kind, but tired too, as he gives my shoulder a little shove. 'Go on. I'll wait here.'

I nod and step back, and I'm still nodding as I skitter along the hallway to my bedroom because if he's making jokes, it can't be all that bad, whatever it is.

'You can start now,' I yell, stabbing my legs into a pair of jeans because, despite my internal reassurance, I'm freaking the fuck out. My whole body shakes, the only thing stopping my ass from hitting the floor is stumbling to the bed.

Get a hold of yourself, I intone, reaching for my abandoned bra and almost simultaneously whipping my nightie, *okay, T-shirt*, up and off my head.

Inhale.

Stand.

I shove my phone into my back pocket, grabbing a hair tie from the top of the chest, and a clean sweater from the drawer beneath. I make my way out into the hallway, still pulling it on.

'Talk now. Tell me, please.'

Rhett frowns, his gaze cutting to the slice of skin between my waistband and sweater. I yank it down.

'There was an accident,' he says.

'Up at the house?' The door slams behind me, and I realise I haven't brought my key.

'With Amélie? Was he there this evening?'

'No!' My head rears back at his suggestion, almost as though he'd dealt me a slap. 'The other house. The one up in the mountains.' I wave in the vague direction that the house may or may not be. 'I don't really know where the hell it is. But tell me, what happened?'

We pause at the elevator, and Rhett pokes the call button. 'All I know is I got a call from the crew of *Le Loup* to say he was dragged out of the water at the marina at one thirty this morning. They said he was unconscious and that he was in an ambulance on the way to the hospital.'

The elevator doors slide open and almost close again as I try to process what he's saying. It's like I understand the words, but the whole moment feels surreal. Like I'm here but not really part of it.

'But he's okay? You said.' And also because he has to be.

'I've seen him.' The words seem to leave his chest in a whoosh of air. 'He's alive and he's talking, but he looks like death.'

I nod as though I understand, but I *so* don't. What I do know is that looking like death is something I can deal with. But being dead . . . *no.*

A shiver runs through my entire body. Someone isn't walking across my grave so much as breakdancing on it.

'What was he doing at the marina?'

'He didn't tell you?' I wonder if anyone has ever told him his frowning system seems to be a whole other language on its own.

'Tell me what?' I ask.

'That he was staying there.'

My attention is pulled as the elevator door jerks, trying to close against the bulk of his shoulder, but I don't have the bandwidth to comment.

'At the marina?'

'On the yacht.'

I knew he had a yacht. I think. I guess he has a lot of things he hasn't spoken of. Like houses.

'I wonder why?' I realise I've spoken aloud, but Rhett doesn't offer any response. It strikes me as strange because, tonight aside, Remy hasn't exactly gone out of his way to give me any space since we broke up. His "win her back" strategy has been a full-on frontal attack. *Apart from setting up Charles.*

He wouldn't have moved out of the building, deferring to my wounded sensibilities. Not when he was calling me into his office multiple times a day. I guess that's why he insisted I go home alone, not because he couldn't trust himself but because he wasn't going the same way.

'But he's okay, isn't he?' I ask again, sending out a plea to the heavens, *please, please, please let him be okay* as my stomach clenches, unease stirring like the silt from the bottom of a river.

'He came around.' He nods grimly. 'And he looks like shit, but he asked for you.'

'Who's with him now?'

'Come on, stop that.' In an uncharacteristically tender action, he reaches out, obliterating a fallen tear with his thumb. 'He was being sent for a CT scan when I left.' I step into the elevator at his urging. 'How can I put this?' He eyes the panel before selecting the button for the subterranean parking lot. 'As he left, he impressed upon me very strongly the idea that he'd like you near.'

'That's crazy formal,' I reply through a bubbling, wet-sounding laugh. I use my sleeves to wipe away more tears.

'You got the crazy part right, at least,' he says as we make our way out of the elevator and into the underground parking lot.

The car journey is fraught. Filled with tension. At any other time, I might've made some retort, some quip about bats and exiting hell when Rhett begins weaving the black Range Rover in and out of the sparse traffic at some speed. If it weren't for the thought of Remy being in the hospital alone, I might even have managed, but I don't speak, my fingers gripping the sides of the seat as Rhett gets us to the hospital at warp speed. We're shown to a waiting room shortly after, the kind they put families in when they have something terrible to tell them.

'How long had he been in the water?'

The chairs make the back of my thighs itch through my jeans. I try not to squirm, but as I raise my head, I'm struck by the full force of Rhett's gaze. I'd never really noticed before, but his eyes are grey, a potent mixture of gunpowder and broken glass.

'We don't know. What we do know is Hénri took him to the marina a little before one a.m., and that he was found floating face down by one of the deckhands around twenty minutes later.'

Oh, God. I think I'm going to be sick. People die from being in the water for that kind of time, or suffer life-altering brain injuries. What if he—

No, I refuse to consider the possibility that anything other than a full recovery is waiting for him. Rhett said he'd asked for me, so if he's speaking . . .

'Did you call his mom?'

'She's in the Bahamas. He doesn't want her called.'

'Well, thank you for coming to get me.'

'He's got a nasty gash on his head,' he answers, disregarding my words. 'And a concussion that's making him talk shit. There was some discussion of brain injuries after he was resuscitated.'

'Resuscitated?' The gravity of his words suddenly sinks in. That means he stopped breathing. For all intents and purposes, he died. What if that had been it for him? What if I never got to tell him that I loved him because of my stubborn pigheadedness?

'Resuscitated, yes. Keep up. They're worrying about other shit now. He hit his head, stopped breathing, and nearly drowned.'

'Your bedside manner sucks.'

'Good thing I'm not a doctor then.'

'You're tellin' me!'

'Stop crying, Heidi.' Though his voice is gruff, it's not a command.

'I'm not crying. You are.'

'We'll all be fucking crying if he doesn't get well and get his arse out of here soon,' he mutters with an unhappy huff.

'He's not just your boss, is he?'

'I'm talking about these chairs. Christ, they're uncomfortable.'

I angle my head and keep my watery smile to myself when the door opens, and a young doctor in blue scrubs steps in. I jump from my seat like a jack-in-the-box as Rhett stands more sedately, the pair shaking hands before he introduces me as Remy's girlfriend. By his manner, I assume he and Rhett had spoken earlier.

'The CT scan results are back,' he begins without preamble, 'and they are good. No skull fracture, as was the concern. No swelling, and no signs of haemorrhage or a hypoxic brain injury.'

'I'm sorry,' I find myself interrupting because I don't speak doctor. 'What exactly is that?' I get the no swelling and a haemorrhage is a brain bleed, both of which I'm super relieved to hear about.

'A hypoxic brain injury is when the brain goes without oxygen for a period of time. It's often associated with serious head injuries.'

I feel relief, but more than that, I'm confused. 'Was he knocked out before or after he fell in the water?'

'That is the question,' he says with a very Gallic shrug.

'How did he fall in the water in the first place?' My gaze

flicks back and forth between the men, my mind brimming with questions.

'We think he was getting onto the yacht and the railing gave way,' Rhett supplies. 'Maybe he hit his head on the way down.'

'It is possible that he was knocked out as he hit the water from that height, water being an incompressible liquid.'

'He means it can be like hitting concrete,' Rhett adds. 'Except for the gash to the back of his head. That had to have come from something else.'

'Like debris in the water?'

'I do not think so,' the doctor answers. 'There was some force to the impact to cause that kind of laceration.'

'Force?' I feel like I'm wading through glue, yet my thoughts won't stick.

'Whatever he hit his head on, or whatever hit his head.' This from a stern-faced Rhett.

'Do you think he was attacked, or that he bumped his head? That he almost drowned?' Do I sound a little hysterical?

'To the latter, the short answer is yes.' I can almost feel the blood leeching from my face and reach out to steady myself by grabbing the back of a nearby chair. 'This, in addition to the initial head injury, could have caused what we term a secondary brain injury from cerebral hypoxia. In other words, lack of oxygen to the brain. It does appear, however, that the chill of the water may have assisted Remy's brain injury in the minutes he was immersed. It may have resulted in an increase in peripheral vasoconstriction, or a narrowing of the vessels in his limbs, shunting his blood and providing an increase in the flow of blood and delivery of oxygen to his vital organs.'

Brain injury. Almost drowned. That's almost all I hear. 'But he's okay, right? Rhett said he'd spoken to him?' My head swings between the two. I know I keep asking the same question but I've yet to receive a definitive yes.

And I need one, desperately.

'While we might not be able to say what exactly happened, it may, in time, come back to him. But what we can say with absolute certainty is that he is a very lucky man. Thanks to the vigilance of his crew and their knowledge of Expired Air Resuscitation, the care performed was enough to trigger Remy to cough the water from his airways and begin to breathe on his own. We're extremely lucky they found him when they did. We will be admitting him for observation. I am still concerned that his period of immersion could cause aspiration pneumonia, and that is why we will need to observe him for a while yet. But if you'd like to see him now, you may.'

I can't speak for the knot in my throat and the fear in my belly. I manage to nod because, yes, I'd like to see him right now more than I ever have.

His skin is the colour of wax paper as I stand at the doorway. The lights in the room are low, and his eyes are closed, his head resting against a pillow, the head of the bed almost upright.

'He looks awful,' I whisper as I make a path to his bed, almost surprised to find his hand is warm to the touch. My gaze slips over my shoulder to where Rhett stands like a guard at the door. *Where were you when he fell into the water?* I quash the thought immediately.

'I think we'd all look pretty shit after what he's been through.' Rhett answers in his normal register. In other words, loud.

'Shush. Can't you see he's sleeping?'

'He won't be sleeping for long.' His expression twists. 'Not in here, at least.'

'It doesn't mean you have to talk like a foghorn,' I retort . . . like a foghorn.

'Ah, there she is.'

At the sound of Remy's voice, I pivot.

'Hey, there.' Tears prickle against my lids, but I refuse to let them fall. 'You know, we really ought to stop meeting in places like this.' I tighten my hand on his as though crushing his fingers might make him understand my fear. My love. 'Like, *really*.'

'You mean in hospital.' He winces as he turns his head my way. His eyes are rimmed red and swollen, a spectacular bruise forming on the left side of his face.

'Yes.' I choke back the threatening deluge of tears. 'Let's meet somewhere else next time you want me to hold your hand.'

'Like dinner?' His mouth kicks up in the corner in an attempt at a smile.

'Dinner is better. Only don't turn up looking like this. Because you really look like shit.' I choke a little on the words.

'Are you saying you wouldn't have taken me home in March if I looked this terrible?'

I throw my arms around him as best as I can and smother my tears against his hospital gown as I shake my head. 'I would've been frightened of breaking you.' His chest vibrates under my ear as he laughs, the sound turning to a groan just as quick. 'Get me some clothes, and I'll take you home and show you exactly how unbreakable you make me feel.'

'Jesus,' comes a grunt from behind me. 'I was gonna tell you to get a room, but you've already got one. I'll be outside. Give me a shout when you've stopped with the dirty talking.'

With that, the door opens and closes in very quick succession without either of us looking once Rhett's way.

I straighten and dash the backs of my hands across my cheeks. 'If you had died, I would have been very, very angry. And you know what else?' I take his hand in both of mine, pressing my face to his until his features become indistinct. I can't believe I almost lost him. He would've died without knowing the strength of my love. 'I would've been very, very sad because I love you too much to let you go, you stupid ass.'

If there are better ways to express it, I can't find the words. But it doesn't matter, not as his smile becomes the flame of a lit wax candle. Mainly because *wax* is still the colour of his skin.

'Your hold was fortifying. I feel like a battery recharged. Where are my clothes? We need to leave.'

'I don't think so.' More tears, this time through smiles.

'I'm alive and the woman I love loves me. If that's not cause for celebration, I don't know what is.'

'The only bed you'll be seeing me in is this one. As for battery, you look like you've experienced the wrong end of assault and battery.'

He has no time to complain as the door to his room opens, and two nurses file in.

'I'm just going to step outside to speak to Rhett.' I press a kiss to his forehead as he raises my hand to his lips.

'Tell him to go home,' he murmurs, exchanging my kiss for his. 'I'll speak to him in the morning.'

'It is the morning,' I answer, pulling away. But he doesn't let go of my hand. 'Okay, I'll tell him, but I don't know why you think he'll listen to me.'

'Remy says to tell you to go home,' I say to Rhett as I close the door to room behind me. 'He says he'll see you in the morning. He also said thank you.'

366

'That's it. The bastard's dying, then?' From his position leaning against the opposite wall, Everett grins. The expression is absolutely disreputable thanks to the dark stubble on his chin. 'Because if he said thank you, I'm fucked.'

'Okay, so that was a little artistic license, but I read it in his expression, anyway.' I shove my hands into my pockets and tip forward on my toes. This feels . . . strange. Between Rhett and me. Like we've called a truce. 'Does stuff like this happen to him often?'

He frowns, his head angling. 'What do you mean?'

'Well, in March, I found him on my doorstep after a motorcycle accident.' I slide my hands from my pockets, linking my fingers instead. 'You know about that, right?' He inclines his head briefly, though offers nothing more. 'And now this. He fell off his yacht. Does that not seem weird to you?'

'Why should it?'

'Because it is weird,' I retort, my tone firmer.

'You're all right, you,' he states quite abruptly, pushing off from the wall.

'Well, yeah. Because I'm not the one who's been admitted to the hospital. Oh. I get it. Was that supposed to be some kind of praise?'

'It's the best you're gonna get.' He folds his arms across his chest, and I notice his biceps are the size of hams. *Meat arms to go with his meathead*, I think uncharitably. Whatever. One conversation does not make us friends. 'I didn't think you'd stick around.'

'Oh, nice.' I drag my gaze from his noticing a nurse exiting a nearby room with a tiny old lady hobbling behind her. 'I get it. You thought I was just out for what I could get. A gold digger.' I glower, my gaze moving back to him.

'Nah.' His mouth turns down in a show of distaste. 'I just

thought you'd have more sense. When you found out, I mean.'

'About Amélie?' My innards suddenly feel like they've been filled with wet cement. 'So, still not a compliment. You think I'm stupid—stupid for staying with him?'

The man closest to him gives me this advice now? What the heck is that about?

'No. He's a good man, on the whole. And no one's perfect.' His wide shoulders ripple with a shrug. 'I just thought, well, people like us. People who've known real poverty, we're pretty good at protecting ourselves. In some ways, we're like the rich, though it's usually self-preservation and not greed that makes us put our needs first. That and maybe experience.' His shoulders lift and drop, and he makes a show of stretching his back. 'Anyway, I'm gonna go and get a few hours kip. Need me to bring you anything when I come back?'

'Like what?'

'A coffee? A rope?'

'To escape or to strangle him?'

'Maybe to tie up the bad guys. You know, in case they try to bum-rush his room.'

I lower my voice and incline my head, speaking under my breath. 'Because you think someone did this to him?'

'I don't get paid enough to think.'

'Bullshit.' My answer is nothing more than an incredulous laugh. 'You wear the same kind of suits as your boss.'

'And I look better in them than he does.'

'You really are a piece of work.'

'It takes one to know one, Heidi,' he retorts with a cheeky wink. 'He's all yours. Try to be nice to him.'

As I watch him saunter down the hallway, the door to Remy's room opens as the two nurses slip out, pink-cheeked and giggling. One turns to follow Rhett's direction, the other's gaze collides with mine, causing the colour in her cheeks to deepen.

Girl, I know.

Gripping the doorhandle, I fix a smile on my face. If the ills of the world can be solved by salt, I'll stick to sweat and seawater because I've cried enough tears.

I'm just going to love him from here on in.

36

ROSE

I SPENT the next thirty-six hours on a chair next to Remy's bed. No way was I leaving him alone. I also figured it was the best use of company time. In order to lead the company, Remy needed to be well. In order to be well, he needed rest, and he was more inclined to rest while I was near. Though I will admit he wasn't thrilled with my company when I told the next doctor who came into his room that this was his second concussion this year. The news created a flutter; there were questions, warnings of traumatic brain injuries, talk of keeping him in the hospital for a longer observation period, and mutterings about the odds of the occurrence of aspiration pneumonia, almost as though it were some kind of side order dish. They spoke in English, maybe garnering that they'd get the unvarnished truth from me, rather than an imperious mouthful and denunciations of *charlatan* and *impostor* from the grump in the bed.

'You fuss too much,' Remy complains, his eyes appealing to the ceiling for deliverance.

'And you're a very bad patient. Do you think this is my idea?' I ask, my hand flying out to indicate the wheelchair by the side of the bed. The wheelchair Rhett's currently sitting in.

'My legs work perfectly.'

'So does your mouth, unfortunately,' I reply in an undertone.

'Not even two days together and you two are already bickering.' The wheelchair wheels squeak against the hospital floor as Rhett attempts a spin in the tight space. 'Are you sure you're cut out for spending more time together?'

'I can't wait to get her alone to kiss every inch of her skin. To taste her from her lips to the tips of her toes as I whisper my want of her at all the places in between. Does that answer your question?'

'A little too graphically,' he retorts with a twist to his mouth.

'It must be the concussion speaking.' Remy grins.

'You don't need a wheelchair. You need a muzzle.' My cheeks sting, no doubt pink.

'I don't need a wheelchair, period.'

'Well, according to the hospital's insurance policy, you do. So get your cutie-patootie butt in that thing, and let's get this show on the road.'

Rhett stands. 'I think I was just a bit sick in my mouth.'

A nurse wheels Remy to the entrance of the hospital to where Everett has brought the Range Rover around. I try not to hover around him as he climbs into the car, but honestly, it's hard.

'Got everything?' I ask, ready to close the passenger side door.

'I think I left my dignity in there.' With a sniff, his gaze lifts above my head to the hospital building.

'Remy, I love you. You're probably going to get sick of me saying this because the thought of you—' I stop abruptly. He

371

needs to hear this less than I need to say it. I think he's pretty sick of being reminded of his own mortality. I take a deep breath. 'So, I love you. I'll thank the heavens every day.' He reaches out to where I'm gripping the door, his fingers lightly brushing mine. 'But I have to tell you, you are a pain in the ass.' Eyes narrowed, he can't seem to stop his reluctant grin. 'Love you!' I slam the door shut before he can say anything else.

'Have you had any more thoughts?' At the back of the car, I keep my voice purposely low as Everett loads Remy's bag into the trunk.

'About what?'

'You know—the thing we were talking about. Remy's so-called accident.'

'Did we have a conversation about this?' His expression is blank as he reaches up and presses a button, the tailgate gliding closed.

'You know we did. Out in the hallway.'

'I think your imagination is playing tricks on you. Remy slipped from a passerelle with a defective rail. It's been investigated and the cause determined as just that.'

'And the huge wound he has on his head? The one that looked like he'd been hit *with* something, rather than the other way around? There was no blood on the gangplank thing—you told me that.' He'd mentioned it in passing, then looked like he wished he hadn't.

'Gangplank?'

'The thing he fell off.'

'Why do pirates not visit strip clubs?'

'What?' The mention of strip clubs barely registers. A second later, my stomach fills with dread. 'Pirates? Why are you talking about pirates?'

'Pirates don't go to strip clubs because they already have

all the booty.' There's an air of resignation in the shake of his head. 'A gangplank is for pirates, love. It's a gang walk or a passerelle to those in the know.' His eyebrows ride high, his attitude infuriating. 'Also, *Le Loup* is in water. Water and blood are both liquids, and seeing as water was the larger source, it would've washed any blood away.'

'Why are you being such a dick?'

'Why are you playing Miss Marple?'

'Because if it was what you think it was, that means someone tried to kill him.' I throw my thumb over my shoulder in the direction of Remy sitting in the passenger seat. 'And I want to know who it was.' So I can repay the favour.

'It feels like you're shouting. You're not shouting at me, are you?'

'This is called whisper shouting. You must never have had a girlfriend.'

He laughs; I assume it's some lame-ass inside joke. 'I didn't say it wasn't an accident., but we can't really know either way. Not unless Remy remembers something.'

'Who was it, do you think?' Because no way I'm buying that, even if he is folding his arms and doing that whole *big boy swinging my dick thing.* 'Was it Amélie?'

His expression twists. 'What would she stand to gain from murdering him? She's not the one named in his will.'

'Don't look at me like that, and don't say shit like that to me.' Not unless you want me to have a coronary. 'It totally could have been her. A woman scorned and all that.'

'All right, Velma. Keep your hair on.'

'Velma? Like as in jinkies?' My incredulity, or maybe my anger, makes him smirk. 'What in the Sam Hill is wrong with you?'

'Look, she wasn't in the country when this happened,' he

asserts, beginning to tap off the points using the fingers of one hand. 'She hasn't got the kind of upper body strength to inflict that kind of damage.'

'Ah, so you do think his wound isn't consistent with a fall.'

'Like a rabid poodle with a bone,' he mutters. 'Look, she has nothing to gain from killing him.'

'But she has motive. Jealousy. And she could've hired an accomplice.'

'You know who else has motive, and means, and all the other shit? Ben.'

My shoulders slump. He could have a point. 'Except Ben was the one who explained the whole Amélie situation to me.'

'So?'

'So, if he wanted to hurt Remy, he could've helped drive me away. Okay, so not physical pain, but the emotional stuff.'

'Look, the fact of the matter is, Ben is at the end of a very long list of people who'd like nothing more than to see Remy at the bottom of the marina.'

'What are you talking about?'

'Shit above my pay grade,' he snarks. 'That's business out here. It's dog eat dog, and well, wolf eats everything.'

'You're saying Remy has enemies?'

'I'm saying get in the car.'

'Sure, *dad*,' I snark folding my arms across my chest and not going anywhere. *Ass.*

'Look, you leave the investigating to the big boys and just get him well.'

'Do I look like a nurse to you?'

'I'm not the one looking forward to a sponge bath. By the way,' he adds, his eyes dropping to my feet. 'Your knickers are showing.'

My gaze drops to my waist. *Nothing.* But then a flash of

yellow at my feet causes panic to flare as I take in the cotton and lace of yesterday's panties, which appear to be peeking from the ankle of my jeans. Jeans that were both taken off and shoved back on in a hurry.

Rhett's chuckle follows him to the driver's side of the car.

'You think you're so hardcore,' I whisper-shout after him, whipping the offending panties out from my ankle before shoving them in my pocket. 'You're not even apple core.'

Urgh!

'How about a bath?'

Rhett brought us to the house, my house, as Remy called it. *The honeysuckle house.* It'd seemed like a good idea at the time. Out of the city, the air is fresh and the pace less hectic. and more importantly, his office isn't at the end of an elevator ride. I agreed it might be the best place for him to rest. But I guess it shows what I know as he barely looks up from his laptop. We're camped out in the den—at least, that's what I'm calling it when I pretend this house is really mine—for the fourth day since his discharge. He can't seem to settle anywhere. The light is too bright in the kitchen and for some (stubborn) reason, he doesn't want the drapes closed in any of the other rooms. He sniffed at my suggestion we sit in the shade of the pergola and snarled when I said Rhett might bring him his sunglasses and a hat next time he visited.

Basically, I'm living with a monosyllabic teenager. I guess I wouldn't be fun to be around after what he's just been through. But if I thought he was hard to understand before, right now, he's downright baffling.

I put down the magazine I'm reading and flop to the opposite end of the grey sectional sofa to face him directly.

Elbow bent, I rest my cheek on my hand. 'You know you're not supposed to use electronics for any length of time for the first week.' So the doctor said, though I won't invoke his name because we *all* know he's just a charlatan . . .

He probably got his medical license in a Paris flea market, right?

'I'm just dealing with emails. A business doesn't run itself.' He doesn't once look my way. Not even a glance.

'So, that was no to the bath then?'

This time, our eyes connect over his open laptop. 'It depends where your motivation is coming from.'

'What do you mean?'

'Is it a desire to get me naked, or a need to look after me?'

'Do you care either way if I get a little handsy?'

'I'm not sure I'd recognise the difference.'

'Well, ouch.' This isn't a slight on my nursing skills but rather something else. Something we've probably been dancing around.

'Remy.' Since when have I begun to say his name so carefully? 'You're recovering from a second concussion—a second mild traumatic brain injury the doctor called it. You—we've—got to be careful.'

'That's exactly what I mean.' His mouth firms, his eyes almost burning a hole in his screen.

'I can see you're in pain.' I find myself chewing on the inside of my lip, but I can't keep myself from speaking. 'And you're taking the pills, so I know your head still aches. The doctor said it would take up to two weeks. You need to rest your brain and your body, avoid driving, strenuous mental activities'—I point at this laptop—'and physical activities, too.'

'I know. I read the leaflet, too. But I'm tired of being treated like porcelain.'

'You've only been out of the hospital for four days!'

'I've been out of your bed for much longer. I want to feel your love, Rose. Not just hear you utter it as you press a kiss to my forehead when you hand me a glass of water, or we turn in for the night.'

'Is worrying about you, looking after you, not showing love, too?'

'You confuse it with pity.'

'That's unfair, and you know it.'

'It took this accident for you to admit your feelings—'

'You think I told you I love you because I felt sorry for you?'

I know I shouldn't be raising my voice, I know all about neurological fatigue, pain, and the possibility of overstimulation because I've spent hours on the internet trying to prepare myself for what to expect. Yet, this is no whisper-shout.

'I knew you loved me well before you told me,' the arrogant ass retorts. 'Are you glaring, or do you have something in your eye?'

'Yes, it's called murder.'

His gaze runs critically across my face, almost examining me. 'It isn't conceit. I knew it when I saw how much hurt my foolishness brought you. But now I've heard it from your own lips, I want nothing more than the evidence of it. I crave it like a physical thing. I'm not breakable, Rose. And I want you like I've wanted nothing else.'

I realise he's right in that sickening instant. I've been treating him like an invalid, scared to touch him, maybe even afraid he wouldn't be the same man. Frightened that he was almost taken from me. Fearful because I hadn't told him what he meant to me.

'Do you know, you even recoil from my touch in your sleep?'

I find myself on my knees in front of him. Why? Because sitting next to him on the chair, I'm frightened I might somehow hurt him. Jostle him? I don't know. He's not the only one who's scarred from the incident.

As he lifts his laptop over his head to put it on the chair, I slide my arms around his waist. We don't speak for some minutes—I don't know what to say. Not as his fingers sift through my hair. Not as they move to loosen the knots in my back. I just stay there listening to the sounds of his breathing and feeling his touch.

He's alive, and he is well. I'm not going to break him with the strength of my love.

'The lengths a man will go to get your face in his lap,' he murmurs almost carelessly.

'*Not* even funny. And also not even a little bit subtle.'

His deep chuckle echoes under my ear. As do the signs of his discomfort, the way his body goes taut, and the tiny stifled groan I'm not supposed to notice.

'You'll injure yourself.'

'A risk I'm willing to take, though I'd rather the fault be yours.'

I pull away, sitting back on my heels. 'You want me to hurt you?' I ask, deadpan. 'You know, there are names for people like you.'

'I want you to fuck me, and if I die in the course of that fucking, you can mention in my eulogy that I died visiting my favourite place. That I went with a smile on my face.'

'Nobody's dying. And nobody's getting laid. How about a compromise?'

'As long as this compromise does something about this.'

He takes my hand, pressing it to the part of him that's clearly defined through the fabric of his shorts.

Pleasure licks at me at the unexpected contact, my mind already awash with plans. Yet I blink back, almost owlishly, as though not quite sure what he's asking. But I can't hold onto my grin as I answer, 'Oh, I think I can manage that.'

37

ROSE

THIRTY MINUTES. I asked him to give me thirty minutes before following me upstairs.

Sure, I could have lifted him out of his shorts and taken care of him on the sofa, but that's not what he asked for. Seeing the outline of him right before me was more than a little tempting. *His hands in my hair, his eyes glazing over at my touch.*

Could have. Would have. *Gladly.* But he's right. We've both been scarred by this week. We need to come together, and we need to heal.

Also, in coming together, we might even *come* together.

If we're lucky.

So, I flit around, carrying things to and fro between the master bedroom suite and the adjoining bathroom, which has the kind of styling you'd see in a home magazine. A copper bathtub sits in the centre of a room that's a very handsome mix of modern and heritage stylings. The dark, sleek tiling is contrasted by pale marble vanities, the black and copper-coloured veining tying the look together.

I don't have time to admire the gilt-framed mirrors or the

shower that's the size of a squash court because I have plans, the first of which involves stripping off to treat myself to a super quick d-i-y trip to the spa. *Slather and shave in record time. I've been kind of preoccupied the past few days.*

Dumping my clothes into the laundry basket, I pull out my beautiful kimono robe, grateful Remy's housekeeper thought to pack it. When Rhett sauntered into the house the first afternoon we were here, I'd flinched, noticing the familiar suitcase in his hand. He'd dumped it down, along with a masculine looking leather weekend bag, and announced he'd visited our apartments and packed us both clothes to save us the trouble.

Great!

Actually, not great at all. I'd almost choked at the thought of Rhett selecting clothes for me, of him thumbing through my underwear drawer. Worse still, of him finding the Pussy Pounder 2000.

Like I'd ever live that down.

I couldn't even use a lethal weapon defence, not without opening a whole other can of big-ass worms. But as it turns out, Remy's housekeeper had packed my bag, and very thoughtfully too, because she'd included my gorgeous kimono. One of my first gifts from Remy.

The silk is heavenly against my skin, and it's so glamorous, I feel like a silver screen goddess in it. As I slip it on, it makes me want to float around my boudoir. But again, timing issues.

I twist up my hair then carry a couple of fluffy towels into the bathroom, my insides bubbling with nervous anticipation. The good kind of nervous. The excited kind. The kind of nervous that makes a girl feel like she's balanced on the precipice of something great.

'Are we having a Wiccan gathering?'

I pivot at the deep sound of Remy's voice to find him

standing at the open doorway, the shape of him framed by the light from the bedroom.

'Well, I am all about the glow,' I reply, eyeing the dozen candles I've placed strategically around the room. I think it looks kind of sexy, and the smell of scented oil rising up from the hot bathwater is heavenly. I place one towel on the floor next to the bath, the other folded over the lip of the tub near the top. *To make it more comfortable for his head.* 'But any more nonsense from you,' I add, moving to the vanity to ostensibly tidy my hair in the mirror, 'and I'll offer you up as a sacrifice.'

'I thought you needed a virgin for such dark arts. I'm sorry to say that ship sailed more than twenty years ago.'

'You have *not* been having sex for twenty years.'

In the mirror, Remy smirks as he sidles up behind me. Maybe because slack-jawed isn't a good look. But he lost his virginity at the age of fourteen? Yikes.

'You know what they say.' His arms envelop my waist as he presses his lips to the place my neck and shoulder meet. 'Practice makes perfect. No complaints because you, ma Rose, get to reap the benefits of my early corruption.'

'Is that so?' I try to suppress a shiver.

'I'm not sure about so, but it is a promise. And one I intend to keep.' Flames dance in the mirror, sparking off the copper bath, bringing out the highlights in his hair, his eyes like green glass. 'We're bathing together, are we?'

I turn my head as though only just realising there's a tub full of water behind us. I'm not distracted for long as his mouth returns and I gasp as his hand slips between the gaping sides of my robe. He holds the soft fullness of my breast in his hand, and I find I have to stifle a whimper as his thumb lightly brushes the already hardened bud of my nipple.

'I love how sensitive you are,' he whispers in that velvet

voice of his, clever fingers beginning to tease. A soft swipe, a firm pinch, a kiss, a whisper of breath blowing the soft hairs on the nape of my neck, and the line between kindness and cruelty melts my body against his. He presses his whole length against me, hard and unyielding.

'You're spoiling my plans,' I complain, even as I'm pulling his head closer to press my breast into his hand.

'Shouldn't we at least get a little dirty before our sins are washed clean?'

He finds his answer in a sensitive spot under my ear, a place that seems to be inextricably linked to the point pulsing between my legs. I arch, my hand slipping between us to feel his want of me, our joint moans resounding through the heat-filled room. My arm curved around his neck, I pull his mouth down to meet mine in a kiss, a kiss that can't claim any kind of finesse. We're greedy, teeth clashing and tongues swiping, need colliding with need. It's a kiss that's wet, hot, and long overdue. A kiss that would easily lead to other things as his free hand slips to my thigh.

'What are you doing?' I still his hand with my own. I feel his smile curving against my shoulder and his lack of restraint pressed at the small of my back.

God, I want it. Want him. This infuriating and frustrating man who will cause me a lifetime of strife and trouble. This man who offers me his love. I want him so badly my heart is fit to burst.

'Taking a little visit to the promised land.'

I almost laugh. 'More like trying to distract me.'

'If by distract, you mean fuck then yes, I am guilty.'

My gaze slides to the tub as I give second thoughts to my plan, even as I offer him more skin to kiss. It's certainly big enough for both of us. But it would be awkward. And just . . . not how I want this to be. Instead, I turn in his arms as I reach for the hem of his T-shirt. 'You've got an answer for everything.' I pull the soft cotton up and over his head.

'That's what my mathematics teacher said the year I turned fourteen.'

'Your teacher?' My scandalised tone is more an act of subterfuge to hide my distress at the sight of his torso. Even in the darkened room, I can make out at least a half dozen shades of blue, green, and red, the contusions and bruising healing at different rates along his sides. It's not the first time I've seen his bruising, and I know his back to be much worse, but it still catches me off guard that his beauty is so marred. I won't acknowledge his hurt or his suffering. I want only to help him heal. Help *us* heal.

'Have I shocked you?'

'I'm . . .' I nod my head a little, stalling for time. 'I'm never ever roleplaying with you.' His deep burst of laughter resounds through the space, a moment later a groan of discomfort taking its place. 'Remy.' I press my hand to the side of his face. 'Let me love you now.'

I help him with his shorts, sliding the waistband down the long line of his thighs, and watch as he sinks into the scented water, the discomfort easing from his face inch by warm inch. His elbows hook over the sides as he tilts his head back and closes his eyes.

'Is it good?' I'm almost reluctant to speak as I press my knees to the folded towel next to him.

'*Oui. C'est bien.*' His eyes close, the heat in the room turning his lashes into spiky half-moons against his cheeks.

'*Français*? I hope you're not trying to trick me like you did back in March.'

'Ah, March.' The word rolls from his tongue like a favourite dessert. 'Where it all began.' His voice has the kind of quality to it that suggests he's edging towards sleep. He dips his hand into the water before dragging it down his face. 'You were my last thought, you know.' His eyes are still closed, his words spoken so quietly, it's almost as though they weren't meant for my ears.

'Your last thought? You mean the accident?' If that's what it truly was as I take the noise from his throat as one of assent. 'Do you remember what happened?' I ask, taking care to keep the intense need to know from my tone. I know what he said to the police, thanks to Rhett's translation. It seems the meathead understands French better than he speaks it. But at least he speaks French. Unlike me.

'I was . . . happy. Happy to be with you that evening. Happy to be given a second chance. One minute I was almost on deck, and the next.' He pauses, his chest moving with a deep inhale. 'The next I was in the water, my head feeling as though it had been split. My life didn't flash before my eyes, though my mind did find you.' His hand reaches out, covering mine where I grip the edge of the tub. 'Worse than the pain was the sorrow. I had lost you, and the bitter taste in my mouth was one of regret.

'No regrets. We're here now.'

Remy sighs as I trail my fingers down the centre of his chest, over the hard, ridged planes of his stomach, taking care to avoid the places that might make him flinch. Air leaves his chest again as I trace the same path back, grazing a swirling pattern across his skin. A drop from the faucet hits the surface of the water, cicadas in the garden beginning to sing their night-time chorus. I register the sounds, but I don't really hear them, aware of little more than the silky-soft feel of him and his deep, even breaths. His knee appears quite suddenly through the mound of bubbles, a surprising glimpse of his wet, bare skin. My insides draw tight. He's a little battered and bruised but so beautiful. And he's all mine.

His head angles my way, his glittering green eyes now almost midnight.

Midnight eyes that watch me with such intensity. Such love.

'You feel so good.' His voice is all husk and want.

'I think that's supposed to be my line.' He rests his knee against the side of the tub, the position not so much a suggestion as a dare. A dare I ignore, for now, as my touch continues to steal and swirl against the narrow path of hair from his navel down.

'*Embrasse-moi.*' His words are more a growl as he reaches for me. His hand wet on the fine silk of my robe darkens a patch of peacock blue to black as his forefinger circles my nipple. A teasing touch, yet one of such touch of intent.

'Kiss you or . . .?' *Or kiss it.* Something thrums deep inside me, a desire so acute it cleaves.

'Give me your mouth, Rose. Bring yourself to me.'

'So you can pull me into the water?' I reply. 'I don't think so.'

'Would it be so bad? There's space for two.'

'But there isn't space for what I want to do.' His responding smile is like sin itself. 'Close your eyes,' I whisper. 'You wanted to feel my love. So *feel.*'

He doesn't answer but rests his head back against the folded towel as I continue to touch and tease over the coarse hair of his thigh and knee, from fingertip to bicep, to where his hair is beginning to curl at his nape in the heat of the room. I follow a bead of moisture making a path down his neck. Acting on a moment of instinct, I lean forward and lick.

'I couldn't resist,' I whisper, sinking my teeth into the fleshy part of his ear. *And my breasts to his arm.*

'I think you're trying to kill me,' he whispers, his hands tightening on the sides of the bathtub.

'You can suffer a little time not being in charge,' I murmur, aching at the brush of silk and the feel of his hard flesh beneath.

'Oh, I suffer. *Certainement.*' Certainly.

Breath stutters from his chest as I trace the flat circle of his nipple, an achingly perfect moment building between us. He's affected by my touch, and I'm affected by his response, from the tiniest of tremors and inhalations to the way the taut muscles in his jaw flex. Blood sings in my veins and pulses between my legs, and as I inhale a soft breath, Remy reaches across his body, drawing the robe from my shoulder with his wet hand.

'This is silk.' My protest is half-hearted as his gaze brims with heat and unspoken promises.

'If it shrinks, it will be all the better for it.' The backs of his fingers graze my newly exposed nipple. 'The view will be all the better for it.' As he sits forward, the water moves almost soporifically, clinging to his skin. I don't blame it. His head bends to mine, his lips a teasing glance. 'You are so beautiful.' His voice is low and husky, and almost filled with wonder. 'A picture of such delicious dishabille.' His touch echoes my own, the feeling so delicious, I'm almost swept away.

I push my hand into the water, and he gasps as I draw my fingers down his length from tip to hilt. As I take his hardness into my hand, I consider pulling out the bath-plug to better see the whole of him. The water ripples, his body undulating, his expression the most heavenly mixture of pleasure and pain.

'Does that hurt?' I already know the answer as his sharp bursts of breath disturb wisps of my hair.

'It is the sweetest of agonies, and I never want it to stop. I want to laugh with happiness,' he says through a groan as I tighten my grip, 'but it hurts too much. Not in the fun way. I want to dance around the room, throw you down on the bed and sink into you.'

Ideas for later, I suppose, yet my thoughts fall away like blossoms in a breeze at his sexy stream of consciousness, his hands falling to the sides of the tub, grasping the rim as I work him.

'Yes,' he grunts. '*Plus fort.* Harder.' The sounds he makes are almost unravelling.

He groans again as my hand tightens, his next breath is a long, measured exhale, almost like he's preparing himself. An instinct that's proven correct as scented bathwater suddenly spills onto my robe as he pushes himself to stand. I sit back on my heels and just marvel at him. The width of his shoulders, the supple curve of his bicep and the long line of his thighs. The ladder of his abdominals and the trail of glistening hair that leads to his jutting cock. There are just so many delectable spots. And I want to investigate them all.

He reaches for the towel, his long legs bending at the knee as he steps from the bath. I stand, my reflection wanton in the mirror opposite. Cheeks pink, eyes dark, the silk dripping from my shoulder, exposing me. Wordlessly, I take the towel from his hand and begin to pat him dry. His shoulders and arms, moving down, ignoring the part of him that extends as though inviting touch. I slip behind him, tending gentle touches to the bruises, pressing my mouth to his heated skin as though my lips could heal.

His body trembles as I trace a finger across his hip, moving in front of him once again.

He's a feast for the eyes and, boy, do I feast. I touch. I handle. I kiss until his masculine groans become strained, and I drop to my knees. My palms against his toned thighs, I press the most gentle of kisses to his crown.

Above me, his face half in shadow, half washed in the glimmering light, he tips back his head with a curse.

'Rose.' My name is a thing with thorns as I slide my lips down, down, over him, hollowing my cheeks for the return. His skin is hot to the touch and he smells so heavenly, a mixture of bath oil and man as I take the weight of him into my hand.

His responding moan is taut and desperate, his body seeming to vibrate with restraint as I work him, as I lick, suck and swirl, need twisting inside me, the heady sensations unspooling like silk.

'You look so beautiful on your knees.' His accent thickens, his words like velvet as he brings his hands to my head, almost in gentle benediction. 'And you suck me so well.'

Desire builds in my veins, demanding more. More kissing, more sucking, more of this man inside me as I begin to work him harder, his hands directing me, sliding the fallen hair from my face, punctuating his shallow thrusts with a whispered catechism of, '*yes, yes, yes.*'

His chest rises and falls rapidly as he suddenly slides his hand under my arm, encouraging me to stand. '*Tu vas me faire jouir.*' My insides begin to pound at the knowledge of the one word I'm able to pick out. *Jouir. Come.* His thumbs stroke a path along my cheekbones, his whisper fervent. 'I need you.'

As though to emphasise the point, he flexes his hips, pushing against me. 'I've dreamed of this all week while you slept so peacefully next to me.' His mouth is just a breath from my ear. 'Now it's time for to make these dreams real.'

Bedroom, I think as I turn, when Remy twists me back, my hands falling to the marble vanity.

'Do you remember the mirror, Rose?' His hand spans my collarbone, his touch skating across my nipple, barely touching. *It throbs all the same.* 'You were so beautiful. I knew then I would never get my fill.'

My cheeks heat at a sudden deluge of memories; the scarf around my neck. The way it fluttered against my skin. How his gaze lingered and burned.

'This is pretty.' Pleasure spirals through me as he toys with the edge of my robe, the woman reflected back a dark, desirous thing.

A woman half undressed, half falling apart.

'It was a gift. From you.' My answer is no more than a whisper as his hand moves across my bare breast to the other. His forefinger and thumb pinch the hardened bud over the silk.

'I know. I wanted to bring a little brightness into your life.' His eyes rise to mine, his thumbnail circling. 'Who knew it would be the other way around. That you would be my brightness.' His gaze dips once again. 'So, so, lovely,' he whispers in the space between his kisses. 'But not as lovely as you.'

His hands glide around my waist, loosening the knot of the belt. The silk flutters against my legs as he slides it from my shoulders, his mouth following his touch in a shiver-inducing caress.

'Do you have any idea what you do to me? What I want to do to you?'

'Please, I need you, Remy.'

He stills. His hands on my body, his lips on my skin. 'Tell me again.'

'I need you,' I whisper, pressing back against him.

'Now I know I'm no longer dreaming.'

His touch slips down my body, pausing to make a slow circle around my navel, two fingers sliding to where I know

I'm already wet. He pushes them inside and I writhe against him, desperate to be filled.

'I want to fuck you with my tongue. Fill you.'

My answer is in the way my legs almost buckle from under me as he begins to create some kind of magic against the swollen bud between my legs. I whimper, bucking up into his hand, unable to get close enough. I feel wired yet hollow all at the same time

'You are so wet, ma Rose. Just for me.' With those whispered words, Remy pulls away, rubbing my arousal between his fingertips, the moisture glistening in the light. My eyes reflect back in the mirror, dark and wanton as he brings those digits to my lips, painting me with my own arousal.

38

REMY

'WHAT ARE YOU WAITING FOR?'

The tip of her tongue darts out to taste, a graze of her teeth following, her arousal still sticky and sweet between my fingertips.

What did I do to deserve her? To deserve this?

The answer that echoes through my head is that I don't. But it doesn't stop me from taking her. From tasting her. From sampling the very essence of her from her own delectably kiss-swollen lips. The warm air in the bathroom swirls around us as I feed my fingers into her mouth, her tongue flicking, her lips devouring.

I turn her as she whispers my name, but I can't stop kissing her, the sound like honey on her tongue. *Or maybe that's the taste of her.* 'Take me to bed, Remy. Make love to me.'

As she takes my hand, I know I'd follow her anywhere.

Moonlight spills across the floor of the darkened bedroom, slicing across the room and highlighting the hypnotic sway of her hips and a heart-shaped ass just begging to be squeezed. The cicada song filters through the window; a bird calls, another answers as I turn at the edge of the mattress, tipping her chin. My hand falls oh-so naturally to the curve of her hips as I close the distance between us, bringing my mouth to hers.

'You are so, so very beautiful,' I whisper as my thumb brushes the curve of her waist. A press of lips, a glide of my tongue, a whispered word, as I work my way down the side of her neck until she melts.

I lower myself to the bed, pulling her into the space between my splayed knees. Kiss her collarbone and the rise and fall of her breasts before taking them in my hands to lavish them with attention. The brush of my thumbs, a soft pinch. The caress from the tip of my tongue and she's leaning towards me like a flower seeking the sun.

'Please, don't stop.'

I couldn't, not even if I wanted to. Not as her hands clasp my shoulders, her eyes glistening yet unfocussed as her sweet breath brushes my cheek.

We would make such beautiful babies. The thought comes unbidden as my hand sweeps over her stomach. Everything stills—the thought, my hand as it slips between her legs—as I attempt to process this.

I find it's . . . not wholly unwelcome.

Filling her. Fucking her. Her body ripe with our child.

Something primal washes over me, a surge of need as old as time. I wrap my hands around her thighs, bringing her heat over me, above me, causing her to suck in a sharp breath.

'Is this okay?' Though I ask, I know the answer anyway. It's in that gasp and the way her body tilts to meet me as we work together to centre ourselves on the bed. My hands at her hips, my cock is poised at her entrance, swollen and thick. 'I'm yours, Rose. Yours to love.'

Her reaction is in the visceral. Her tremble, the languid vowel sound she makes as she rises above me on her knees.

My chest tightens, pleasure spiralling in the instant our bodies meet as she rocks against me, pressing her wetness along my length. The sensation is so sublime, this slow, teasing ride of delight, trapped between her pussy and her hand. It's the kind of torture that depletes brain cells as a volley of nonsensical words burst from my chest.

'You and your sexy French mouth,' she whispers, dipping to press her mouth to mine as the tight buds of her nipples brush my chest. 'Your mouth does things to me.'

'My mouth would like to do things to you,' I counter, propping myself up against the mattress on my elbows. 'Why don't you come sit on my face, and I'll show you exactly what kinds of things.' It takes her a moment for my words to sink in. I know the exact instant they do because I feel her desire and her indecision fluttering around me. '*Tu es délicieuse. You're delicious.* And I'll take you however I can get you.' I buck up into her, gently at first, then much less so, her resultant moan a little ragged around the edges. '*Jouis sur mon visage, Rose,*' I purr, tapping my forefinger to my chin.

'I'm not asking you to translate.' I hear the husky sound of her response, her wilful denial. Before I can translate, before I can invite her to come on my face, the image of Venus rises above me, hands sliding into her hair.

I forget everything.

The flare of her hips is an enchantment.

The sway of her breasts a bewitchment.

'I need you inside me, Remy.' Pleasure swirls as she wraps my base, my eyes almost glued to her body accepting mine. To where she takes my cock inch by slow inch as our joint moans sound in the air. She's so hot and tight. The angle so much more this way. And the view . . .

If I last more than a few minutes, it will be a miracle.

'*Tu es si belle,*' I whisper again and again. 'You are so

beautiful.' Her hands fall to my shoulders, our pace punctuated by long, slow kisses. Moonlight slides through the shutters, dappling her with light and shade like the perfect symbol for my love for her. Moans layer, her tight breaths over my tortured rasps, our eyes watching, our fingers touching, our hearts brimming full.

With a groan, I coax her body upwards, my hands on her hips, my hiss a counterpoint to her cry as I bring her down hard. As our bodies collide, need floods my veins, heady and sweet. My hands cup her ass, rolling her beneath me, the movement as easy as the rolling tides.

Is the feeling in my chest relief? Whatever it is, I'm greedy for it as I kiss her again and again, my cock still seated deep within, our soft sighs and moans an expression of hard need. As I withdraw, we both give a taut moan at the sensation, her thighs pressing my hips as though to hang on to it. But I'm not going anywhere as I anchor myself to her, our fingers twisting, hands pressed into the bed.

'*Je t'adore. Je suis amoureuse de to.*' I begin to build a slow, easy rhythm, lost to the tide of her body pulling me in.

'Tell me,' whispers my soft-eyed supplicant.

'I adore you. I'm in love with you.' I fuck my promises into her, this thing between us building into something wild and frenetic. My need to possess her is overwhelming. She cries out as I go deep and whimpers when I deliver shallow thrusts, hungry for it all, raising her hips as she meets me thrust for thrust.

My cock throbs with need, her cries reaching a crescendo as I begin to pump and flex, fucking her harder and harder as though I could make her feel my love this way.

In one crystalline, brilliant moment, my mind empties. This moment, the feeling of her around me will be forever burned into my memory and my skin. I'm lost to all but the pound of my heart, the throb of my release, and the latent pulse of hers.

Tu me manques, I type into my new phone, the old now sitting at the bottom of the marina, I suppose. *I miss you.*

I miss you, too, comes her almost immediate response.

Then you should be here with me. Looking after me. Tending to my fevered brow.

You don't have a fever.

That's besides the point.

Or else you'd be back in the hospital. Probably with pneumonia. And a chest drain.

Rose, come home. I can't help but smile as my thumbs slide over the phone. Home. Come home to me.

I've got to work. You know that.

You work for me. Your time would be better spent here with me. For the good of the man you love. For the good of the company.

Bossy AF. Her reply is accompanied by an angry faced emoji.

Tu me manques more properly means you are missing from me. When you're not with me, it's like a piece of me is missing.

Sickened by my own neediness, I throw my phone across the sofa, the message unsent. This is the first day since my accident I've been left to my own devices. Left to myself. Left to my own thoughts since Rose went to work.

C'est ridicule—it is ridiculous that I'm effectively paying her not to be here with me. But I promised I wouldn't interfere, and as she so solemnly pointed out this morning, I'm not currently a resident of Wolf Tower . . .

'Aren't I?'

'Nope,' she'd said, stepping from the circle of my arms to finish getting dressed for work. 'You've got to live there to benefit from the services.'

'But I am the owner.'

'Stop looking at my ass,' came her reply as she caught me doing just that.

'If I'm no longer a resident there, what is my residency status here? Am I your guest? Your housemate? *Vivre en amoureux*?'

'What was that last one?'

'Your live-in lover.'

She'd turned as I'd answered, her feet now secured. She'd walked back to the side of the bed, clad in only her panties and heels, and wrapped her arms around my neck.

'Do you always get dressed so tangentially?'

Her lips had quivered as she tried to restrain her smile. 'I was trying to distract you from the fact that I have to go to work.'

But we both knew she was going nowhere for quite some time as I'd rolled her between my body and the mattress.

'Nice to see you've got a smile on your face.'

Rhett pulls me from my daydream, my smile slipping not as a result of his interrupting my reverie but rather because I realise I was daydreaming.

Imbécile.

'Are you camped out at this place indefinitely now?'

'Until she asks me to leave,' I reply, realising she hadn't truly answered my question about my status here.

'Who asks you to leave? Have you given the house back to your mother?' Dropping the paperwork Paulette requires signatures for, his hands grip the back of the sectional sofa as he frowns down at me.

'No, I gave the house to Rose.'

'Jesus, can I not leave you alone for five minutes?'

My ribs ache as he drops to the opposite end of the sectional sofa, jostling me, my aches exacerbated by the rigours of sex. Something I have no intention of telling Rose.

'You might not have fractured your skull, but you must've broken your fucking head,' he grumbles, frowning across at me. 'So, you gave her a house. Not just any house, but your grandparents' chateau. Hasn't it been in the family for years?'

'It was. Until Emile sold it before I was born.'

'But you bought it back last year, right?'

Because I could.

'It's just real estate. Bricks and mortar.' And a place we'll make beautiful memories, I hope. Because since my balls had decided Rose and I would make beautiful small humans, I haven't been able to shake away the thoughts of her swollen with our child. I've no idea what to do with these thoughts, except dwell on them some more.

'I suppose you can always take the cost out of her inheritance.' His gaze flicks around the space, the action casual. I won't hold my breath for the punchline though I know it's coming. 'Because you must've told her about that by now. Right? And that you don't exactly know how she comes to be in your life.'

'I no longer care why. I'm just grateful that she is.'

'Near-death experiences will turn a man a little philosophical, so I've heard. You'll get over it.' I imagine his words are supposed to sting like an insult. But he should have learned long before now that I really don't care for the opinions of others. Rose being a recent exception to this fact.

'I had an email from the investigator. He says he's had a couple of breakthroughs. He wants to know if you want to meet face-to-face or if he should just courier the intel over.'

'Neither. Pay him his fee but tell him I no longer have need of his services.'

'You don't really mean that.'

'Bring me these breakthroughs, and I'll burn the envelope without looking.'

'No worries. We have this magical transportation of image and text these days. It's called email.'

'Even easier to delete.'

'You just don't want to know the truth, in case it proves to be inconvenient.'

'Don't take me for a fool. I don't need proof of Rose's innocence in any of this, so if you came here to goad me, you're wasting both of our time.' She even thinks the money she went travelling with came from the death of a distant relative—she offered up the information without the slightest concern, without an ounce of artifice. She's guilty of nothing but naiveté.

'I came to see how you're doing, arsehole.' He inhales and spreads his fingers wide on his thighs. 'I also came to tell you the CCTV footage came back from the marina.'

My head twists, and is followed by another painful twinge. 'Did it show anything?'

'Not much. People milling around. A few drunks. The sight of you making your way to *Le Loup*, but the angle isn't right to show you boarding.'

'What aren't you telling me?' I've known Rhett too long for him to begin hiding things from me now.

'There was a figure. A man. Walking in the direction of the yacht before you arrived. He had something in his hand that we think might've been a crowbar.'

'Or perhaps an umbrella.'

'It would be an odd thing to be carrying around in the middle of summer, and at that time of night. Plus, the footage shows him leaving around the same time you were found in the water. He wasn't carrying anything at that point.'

I still for a moment, my mind processing the implications before I realise I've raised my hand, my fingers hovering above the wound on the back of my head. I lower it again, noting Rhett's curious look. I have no intention of telling him that I still suffer from headaches, or that my concentration is poor. I'm told the symptoms will last another week. *Or perhaps much longer*. I push away the residual negativity caused by my doctor's earlier visit. If there's one thing I know, it's that sheer will gets a man much farther than most people recognise.

'It could be someone taking a tool to their boat, then leaving without it.'

'Possible,' he agrees. 'But not probable. Not that time of night.'

'And the passerelle?' I know he will have arranged divers to search for it.

'No outward signs of tampering to the sunken railing. No signs of an abandoned crowbar, either,' he adds with an unhappy huff. 'But then, if I was going to crown you one, I wouldn't drop the weapon into the same body of water afterwards.'

'If you wanted to commit murder, you mean.'

'And make it look like an accident.'

We both fall silent, retreating into our individual thoughts. Though one of us not recently suffering an attempt on their life has less to think about, evidently.

'Benny boy called with a million questions.'

'He's been to the house.' I resist the urge to shrug. 'You know he likes to think he knows all. Sees all. Everything has an angle with him.'

'Yeah, and they're all obtuse,' he comments dryly. 'I told him fuck all. What about you?'

'I spoke to him through the gate intercom. I told him I wasn't well enough for visitors.'

'Good call. I bet he loved that.'

'Ben didn't hit me with a crowbar,' I assert, knowing Rhett's mind as I do.

'I wouldn't put it past him,' he mutters. Then he adds, 'Your bike was found.'

'What?' I wince, a pain splitting my head as I turn it too quickly, pressing my fingers to my temples. I'd much rather talk about my motorcycle than my cousin. 'The Ducati? From March?'

'Unless you've lost another motorbike I don't know about.'

'Where was it found?'

'In the same state at the back of a chop shop. It seems someone decided the Ducati was a little too pretty to break up. It had been resprayed, a pretty good job, by all accounts.

'I'm delighted,' I answer deadpan, expecting him to get quicker to the pertinent points.

'The plates have been swapped, and it's ready to go.'

'Ready to go where?'

'Wherever they offload it, I suppose.'

'You mean to say it's been found but not recovered?'

'I know it was your favourite toy for all of five minutes, but you got the insurance money for it, right?'

'That's not the point.' And, yes, it was a new toy and one I liked a lot. But that's not what this is about. 'I'm not in the habit of letting people steal from me.' It's usually the other way around. Not that I'm a common thief. More an uncommon one. In fact, a chop-shop is an apt analogy for how I do business.

'Consider it the price of information. The investigator had set up a meeting with the head honcho crim. But if you're not interested . . .' He allows his words to trail off, like a carrot dangling from a piece of string.

'I told you, I no longer care.'

'But this has nothing to do with Rose,' he says with such gravitas that my mind ceases to whirr. 'Two accidents in five months, or two attempts on your life? You already know which my money is on.'

'Tell me,' I demand. 'Tell me everything.'

'The owner of the shop isn't your run-of-the-mill criminal. He's not some thug for hire and is mixed up in some pretty heavy shit.'

'I don't give a fuck who he is or what he does. What I want to know is what happened.' Has someone tried to murder me twice?

'In which case, you don't want to put the investigation on ice, right?'

I narrow my gaze at some cost.

'It doesn't have to be about her. Or it might. But do you really want to leave it to a third successful time to find out?'

'Bring me the information. All of it.' Better it's in my hands than anywhere else.

'That's more like the twisty fucker I know.'

I shrug off his words. Even that hurts today. I'm left to ponder my decision for the rest of the afternoon, and though I know Rose has nothing to do with any of this intrigue, the echo of Rhett's voice takes up space in my consciousness.

No one tried to kill you before she came into your life.

You still don't know how she came to be in the will.

The fact that she found you that night could mean she's in on the whole thing.

It's all bullshit of course. And I can see he barely believes it himself, but I understand his reservations, because he doesn't know Rose like I do.

39

ROSE

THE DAYS PASS and as the doctor suggested, Remy's health improves steadily. Headaches lessen, dizzy spells dissipate, and the lethargy he suffered from seems to disappear almost overnight. Which means he's back to work and no longer complaining about me doing the same.

Honestly, I did get his point. The company pays my salary, and he owns the company, so in effect, he pays me. But that doesn't mean he gets to say where I'll spend my days. There are a whole host of managers between him and me. Besides, I have colleagues to think about. Even if one of those colleagues would dump me in a heartbeat should Remy suddenly decide he prefers dick.

But things at work are good. It seems Olga has decided to stop being a mega-bitch to me, which certainly makes the days more pleasant. As for the accident itself, Remy remembers little about it, and the couple of attempts I've made to discuss it with Everett have fallen on deaf ears. I thought we'd reached a kind of understanding in the hospital, but I guess not because he still insists on being a pain in my ass every time I see him.

DONNA ALAM

It's a little after seven when my phone rings. I'm expecting Remy home around now and wonder if it's him as I hop down from my stool and hurry across the kitchen, swiping it from the countertop next to the fridge.

Amber's number flashes up on the screen.

'What are you doing up?' I know it's later and I mentally calculate the time difference, coming to the conclusion that it's three a.m. in Sydney. *Late or early?*

'I'm on baby duty,' she answers. 'Byron has a meeting in the city tomorrow at sparrow's fart.' Sparrow's fart is Aussie speak for early morning. 'I don't want him up half the night with the baby. I like him a little too much to risk him falling asleep at the wheel on the freeway.'

'You're sure embracing the language,' I say, a smile leaking through my response as I make my way over to the island bench, hopping back up onto one of the velvety high-back stools.

'I am raising my own little Aussie and living in a house full of the ratbags. I figured if you can't beat them, join them,' she says, using the insult as a term of endearment. I think.

'How is beautiful baby Beryl?'

'You know that's not her name,' she replies fondly.

'Maybe not. But you know it's going to stick.' Given the whole family is already calling her Beryl and has been almost from the day she arrived. Byron had even sent a photo to my phone last week of her blowing spit bubbles, the accompanying text had read: **Beryl loves bubbles as much as her mum.**

But I think I'll keep that to myself right now.

'We won't let it, will we Ruby-Roo?' From somewhere nearby, a baby coos.

Mattie, Edie, and Ruby. All the "e"names together, and individually, all very cute.

404

'Because Ruby-Roo is such an improvement on Beryl.'

'Ruby's a lovely name,' Amber retorts.

'Oh, agreed. It's so pretty it doesn't need the additional kangaroo suffix.' Even if it's a little cutesy.

'Ah, listen to Auntie Rose sniping, Rubes.'

'Urgh. I give up. But I will say you're taking these early mornings very well.' When we travelled, Amber was not a fan of early mornings, as I recall.

'I've had four months to get used to it. Besides, I can't complain when I get to wake up to this gorgeous smiling face, can I, baby girl?'

'I'm assuming you're not asking me.' Not in that babying tone, at least.

'What are you up to?'

I lean back in the chair and stare at the crystal chandelier that wouldn't have been hanging there back in the day. In fact, I'm pretty sure this kitchen wouldn't have looked anything like this. I'm not just talking about the fancy cabinets and appliances but how airy and light the space is.

'I suppose I'm partaking in a little self-care,' I reply, swinging my feet.

'So, you're drinking.'

'I also have snacks.'

'Cheese?'

'Camembert,' I confirm, twisting my barely touched plate a little straighter.

'That's it?'

I eye my cheese and wine party for one debating the merits of telling the truth. 'I also have a little Roquefort that can be described as *plus fort,* or in other words, it smells to high heavens. But I'm told it tastes almost celestial.'

'Nice,' she responds. 'What else?'

'I have a bottle of Cabernet Sauvignon, aired for, oh, at

least three minutes.' No need to tell her that selecting a bottle from the cellar was not a fun experience. What if I picked a thousand-euro bottle, or something that wasn't really wine at all? Because other than the usual wine terms—Pinot, Merlot, Chardonnay, Sauvignon, rosé, rouge, and blanc—I don't really know what the labels say at all.

I need to take French lessons.

I also need to get over myself. So what if, back in the day, olden day Rose would've been a scullery maid and not the lady of the house. I decide I'm not sharing any of this with Amber today. Not the cellar, not the house with twenty rooms and a legion of staff—okay, a housekeeper, a cleaner, and a gardener don't quite amount to a legion, but it's still a lot— and not the shitty stuff that happened to me today.

As far as Amber is concerned, I'd planned on staying with Remy in *his* house during his period of convalescence, that we'd enjoyed the arrangement so much, I haven't yet moved out.

'You wine philistine.' She giggles. 'Byron would have an absolute fit to hear that. He's already drawing up a list of wines he wants you to bring when you visit. You know, so he can prove to the world that Australian wines really are the best.'

'I don't know. I've had some pretty tasty wines out here.'

'Don't let him hear you say that,' she says with a chuckle.

'Anyway, a year out here and maybe I'll be cultured enough to hold my own at your dinner table.' I'll also have saved enough for a business class flight. *Because I pay my own way.*

'Our table? If you can cope with chicken nuggets, you'll do,' she replies, obviously referring to the little Phillips people. 'Now, go ahead and pleasure me with more of your cheese porn, please.'

'That sounds *so* wrong.'

'I didn't say anything about dick cheese!'

'Amber,' I whisper, faux-scandalised. 'Not in front of the baby!'

'With Byron for a dad, her first word will probably be fuck.'

From different time zones, we set off laughing.

'Tell me what cheese you're eating, *please*. Oh, next time you visit, I'll take you to this tiny boutique dairy I've recently found. Edie went there for a school trip last term.'

'To eat cheese? That doesn't sound very educational.'

'To see how it's made, but mostly she was just pooped on by the cows on the farm.'

'Oh, man. I can't imagine how she'd have taken that.'

'She'll probably still be having nightmares when she's twelve. Cheese!' she demands. 'Breastfeeding has turned me into a cheese beast.'

'Well, I have a little Pélardon,' I say, moving it around my plate. 'It's a goat's cheese from the Languedoc. Plus, a small bunch of grapes—'

'For decoration, of course. What about crackers?'

'*Mon Dieu!* The French don't eat their cheese with crackers They eat it with bread.'

'Good. You passed the test. And, oh my God. *Une baguette, une baguette!* My kingdom for *une baguette!*'

'I thought you said if you'd seen one baguette, you'd seen them all.' Talk about innuendo.

'Taste is a different experience altogether,' she answers a little primly. 'And the smell is almost heavenly.'

'Unless the baguette is in sweatpants that haven't been washed in three weeks.'

'I'm talking about bread. French bread. I love, love, love a trip to the *boulangerie*!' The bakery. 'And the *patisserie*.' Also known as the bakery not for bread.

'Ew, stop with the sex groans. You're in charge of an impressionable child, remember?'

'Airy macarons, mille feuilles, and the dacquoise I ate in Pierre Hermé in Paris,' she continues, completely ignoring me as she runs through her list of patisserie porn. 'Oh, hazelnut meringue! Chocolate ganache, and Chantilly crème—seven layers of delicate deliciousness that just melts in the mouth!'

'I got the bread from *le marche*,' I admit. Basically, the grocery store.

'That bread is no substitute! Get thee to the boulangerie!'

'I'll take it under advisement.' I usually ignore the aroma as I pass the boulangerie nearest to the office. My ass needs less carbs. Besides, it's not like I have to do the grocery shopping myself these days.

'It's got to be dinnertime there, right? And you're eating cheese all alone?'

'Remy will be home soon. Dinner's cooked'—though not by me—'but I decided I couldn't wait.'

'No, sweets. In French terms, you've just switched the courses around a little.'

'I like that idea. It's better than stress eating any day.' The explanation rolls off my tongue before I can bite it back.

'Stress eating? Is it the job? The boyfriend? Do you have too much glamour in your life these days?'

'Do you know French women don't get fat?' I say airily instead, flipping over the book I've placed next to my plate. The title in a bold font reads:

French Women Don't Eat Cake

And Other Reasons French Women Aren't Fat.

I wasn't going to say anything to her but find I can't help myself.

'They don't? Maybe I should apply for a passport.' Amber's answer is accompanied by a snort. 'This baby weight is proving a little harder to shift than I imagined.'

'*Puh-lease.* You are hot!' And still slim. I've seen the proof on Facebook. 'Also, you cooked a whole human in your goddess bod.'

'Let me tell you, it still looks like I'm cooking something in there. Maybe a cake.'

'Well, French women don't eat cake,' I grumble, flicking through the pages.

'Then they're living very, very boring lives. What exactly is this about?' Her tone turns a little militant. 'There are women who would kill for your figure. And men who'd kill to get their hands on it.'

'Easy for you to say when you don't have to shove your fat ass into an evening gown soon.'

'*Ohhh!*' she trills. 'Who's having a party?'

'Remy's mom.'

'Is she nice?'

'I've no idea.' But if she's half as nice as Amber's mother-in-law, I'll be happy. Sally Phillips must be the gold standard.

'You're going to her party, but you haven't met her?'

'Apparently, she's been busy.' Too busy to be told about her son's accident while she does whatever she's doing in the Bahamas. 'So I'm told. And it's not a party. It's a benefit gala.'

'That sounds kind of scary as far as first meetings go.'

'It gets worse. Remy's ex has been her right-hand woman through the planning.'

'Far out!'

'I think the word you're looking for is *fuck*.'

Fuck is as good a word as any to use right now, even if my

bestie doesn't know about the whole business-deal-fiancée-fiasco because I figured it'd be something easier explained face-to-face, at a time when it doesn't smart quite so much. We'll crack open a bottle of wine and tell war stories about how we were both pursued by gorgeous and determined men, men who hadn't the sense to wait for us to turn up first. Gorgeous men who had pasts that lingered and hung around like a bad smell. Or maybe that's just my take on things, I think as I glance at the book once more.

'Yes, totally. Fuck her. You'll look ravishing, and you'll have the man on your arm. And she won't.'

Or maybe I didn't confide in Amber because I couldn't bring myself to explain it all.

'Anyway, French women do eat cake. That's just the title of some book from a few years ago.'

'Yeah, I know. I just found a copy on my doorstep.' Not here, but back at the Tower. I'd gone to collect some clothes after work to find a wrapped package lying next to my door. I thought maybe a neighbour had dropped it on the way past because mail isn't delivered this way. But when I'd picked it up, I saw it was addressed to me.

'You found a copy on your doorstep? Is it, like, a failed Amazon delivery?'

'Nope,' I reply with a bitter sounding chuckle. 'It was addressed to me, gift-wrapped, and lying on my welcome mat.'

'You do not have a welcome mat.'

'You're right, I don't.' But I think I might get one for this place. You know, while I'm pretending it's mine. Something totally kitsch and maybe just a little bit tasteless. 'But if I did have a doormat, that's where the book would've been.'

'And your theory as to who left it there is what?'

'I don't know.' Not for sure, at least.

'Have you made any enemies at work?'

'I'm not super close with my boss, but I don't think she's the subtle type.'

'I can tell you have your suspicions, so go ahead and say it. You think the ex left it for you, right?'

I squish a wedge of camembert between the cheese knife and the plate feeling more than a little mutinous. I can't believe I'm allowing her to put me off my little cheese platter, but it's like the tasty fun has been sucked out it. 'Yeah, I think so. If not her, who else?'

'Fat is a feminist issue, so they say. But it sounds like, in this case, fat is an issue of insecurity.'

'Don't ever go into counselling, babe.'

'I'm not talking about you, dummy. You are gorgeous, even if your brand of self-deprecating is a little old.'

'Amber, the woman looks like a Victoria's Secret model,' I answer, uncomfortable with how plaintive my words sound.

'So? You think skinny girls don't have insecurities? Believe me, anyone looking at you would never believe you think your ass is fat. We all have our issues. While you're cursing her skinny ass, she's probably cursing your curves. The grass is always greener, even when it's really not.'

'You must really be sleep deprived.' Because she's not making sense. No one who looks like Amélie could be in any doubt of how attractive they are.

'*You* are every bit as gorgeous as she is, I'll bet. You are everything you're trying to convince yourself you're not.'

'I own a mirror, Amber.' I'll never be in the same league. 'I don't have blonde hair, and I will never fit into a size two dress unless I get a bad case of dysentery.'

'You don't want to be a size two. You want to be you. Remy wants you to be you. If he'd wanted you to be her, he'd be dating her—or some clone of her. The bitch is trying to get in your head, and what's more, you're letting her.' In the background, Beryl, I mean, Ruby begins to fuss. 'See, even Rubes here knows you're being an idiot. And she's not happy about it.'

We chat a little more as Amber feeds the baby. We keep our voices low as she tells me what's going on in Riposo Estates, regaling me with tales of her little ones. Man, I miss their antics and their cute faces.

'Oh, goodness!' Mid-sentence, Amber stretches the exclamation out over several syllables and an almost jaw-cracking yawn.

'Why don't you go back to bed?'

'Because it's nearly time to get back up again.' But her protest is half-hearted, and we begin to say our goodbyes. I top up my half-empty glass and contemplate throwing the cheese in the trash when Remy appears in the kitchen with a genuine smile on his face.

If he wanted her, he wouldn't be looking at you like you're the winning lottery ticket, idiot.

I give myself a mental shake and slide my napkin over the book. Yes, napkin. Because this is the kind of house that brings out the napery in me. But concealing the book means we don't have to have this conversation, and if we don't have this conversation, I won't end up sounding super needy. Independent girl for the win. Or at least the appearances of.

Remy slides his arm around my shoulders, his forefinger at my chin as he tilts my face to his. 'I've missed you.'

'You just saw me at lunchtime.' Because he still hasn't given up using the app. We eat lunch together most days now that he's back at the office. Sometimes we even go *out* to lunch. A novel experience!

'You're lucky I call for you in the afternoon.' His words end in a playful curl, and there's a certain light in his eyes.

'Hmm. I'm not sure if it makes me lucky or unlucky.' I bite back my grin, the book and Amélie forgotten for the moment.

'I couldn't stop thinking about your lips, ma Rose.' He kisses me again, this kiss full of intent. 'And where I wanted them.'

'Could it be you wanted them here?' I turn his face, pressing my mouth to his stubble-brushed cheek.

His eyes linger on my lips as he replies, 'I was thinking about a place a little lower.'

I laugh softly as I kiss his chin. 'How about that?'

'Also very charming, but I promise you that wasn't the place I was thinking of when I considered faking a headache during this afternoon's board meeting.'

'How did that go?' I ask, wrinkling my nose at this mention of it. This is the first board meeting since he broke up with Amélie. Though the official story is she broke up with him, her father must know this isn't true.

'Well, Monsieur Pastor, her dear devoted father, made a few barbed comments, but no one cares for his opinion these days. I'm making us all far too much money. You started dinner without me,' he murmurs, indicating my plate.

'I couldn't wait. But when you're ready, you can eat.'

'I love a woman with an appetite.' My heart gives a little twist, almost as though squeezed. 'Only, what I want to eat isn't in the oven.' His green eyes gleam as he pops a wedge of my cheese into his mouth. 'Though I'm sure ,' he says, leisurely rubbing my thigh, 'we could put it on the stovetop if it needs warming up.'

'Remy Durrand.' I take his angular cheeks in one hand and squeeze. 'Are you suggesting my derriere should be hotter than it is already?'

'You speak of the impossible.' He takes the back of the high stool in his hand, swinging it around until my whole body is facing him. Unfortunately, the motion skims my elbow against the book, knocking both it and the napkin to the floor.

'Let me get that.'

'No, it's fine,' I answer , but he sweeps both items up from the floor. As he rights the cover in his hand, he frowns down at it.

'*French women don't eat cake.* Perhaps someone should tell my mother.'

'She's a little round, is she?' I curse my hopeful tone, but Remy answers without an ounce of concern.

'She's like a coat hanger.'

'Angular? Like, slim?' Urgh! I could cut out my own tongue right now.

'I suppose.' Confusion flickers in his expression, or maybe it's something else. It's probably the kind of dick-shrinking unhealthy to quiz a man how his mother looks in her underwear. 'But I meant she's a fan of padded shoulders. It's like the nineties never left.' Both his tone and smile are wry. Then he asks, 'Why have you got this book?'

'Me? I, erm. Well, I suppose it's not really my book.' Because there's no way I'm admitting where I found it or who I think it's from because I may as well go and tell him that his ex thinks I'm fat—hell, I may as well point it out to him myself!

'It looks like a stupid book anyway.' He skims it carelessly onto the island when it lands with a *thunk*. 'Everything in moderation.'

'Except burgers,' I counter, recalling that day in his office and his disgust of that particular foodstuff. Weirdo. Who doesn't love a burger?

'Everything in moderation.' His mouth lifts in a slow grin. 'With the exception of sex.' His hands grasp the back of my chair, caging me in. 'How do you feel about christening the kitchen?'

'Something tells me you're not talking about drinking champagne,' I reply, lifting my arms to circle his neck.

'We could drink champagne, then fuck. Or we could fuck, then drink champagne.'

'Those are my choices?'

'There is a third choice,' he whispers, pressing his stubbled cheek to my mine.

'My guess is it still involves fucking.'

'Ma Rose,' he says, pulling back a little, his expression thoroughly scandalised. 'You have such a dirty mouth.'

I laugh a little. 'We can't all sound seven kinds of sexy when we say *fuck*.' No hard fricative, no base kind of tone. He draws the word out, making it all length and temptation.

'I say *fuck* different to everyone else? Don't answer that. Just let me fuck you right now.'

'Did someone feed you red meat this afternoon?' We'd had sex this morning and even fooled around a little in his office over lunch, though nothing more than some tentative petting because, despite the newly installed lock on his door I'm still paranoid Rhett will walk in. And this time I'd be forced to kill him. He's annoying enough as it is without giving him something else to taunt me with.

Remy straightens, pulling me up with him until I'm on my feet. 'Meat? Feeding? I believe there's a joke in there somewhere.'

'But you're too much of a gentleman to say.'

'Ma Rose, if you think that, then you don't really know me at all.' His hands skim up my arms, breaking my hold, and before I have a chance to comment or complain, he spins me around, putting my back flush with his chest. 'If you want my opinion, that book belongs in the trash.' My heart stills. Have

I outed my fears somehow? But as his silky words follow the path of his touch from my thighs to my hips, my thoughts turn to other things.

'Beauty curves. In life. In art.' His touch feathers my ribs and the sides of my breasts as, in the darkened window, I watch him trace the bow of my lip. 'There is a mystery in this curve. A magic even. And here . . .' His hands slip between our bodies, pressing the cheeks of my butt. 'Venus, thy eternal sway. All race of men obey.'

Something tightens in the pit of my belly as he presses his palm to the centre of my back, his gaze nothing but serious.

My hands fall to the kitchen counter, my expression one of surprise reflected back at me. Surprise, excitement, anticipation, our darkened likenesses coloured by the watermelon sky beyond.

I allow him to fold me over until the pale marble is cool at my cheek and stifle a tremulous moan as his hands climb the sides of my thighs, gathering the fabric of my dress without another word. His thumbs hook into the sides of my panties before he peels them down my legs. The oven hums, the central air quietly ticking over, sounds I barely notice over the deafening noise of his zipper opening.

His smooth crown bumps between my legs, but he doesn't check if I'm ready for him.

Does he know I'm already soaking?

A dark pulse begins to throb between my legs, his grunt disturbing the soft hair on my neck.

Did he feel that?

Does he know I throb for him?

My breath hitches and holds as he slides into me, my fingers curling against the countertop as though I could hold onto the sensation. Of being taken. Of being filled. Of being worshiped and used and every sensation in between.

'*Je t'aime,*' he whispers. *I love you. 'J'adore te baiser.' I love fucking you.*

His words are their own filthy kind of reverence, the slide of him between my legs an absolution I can get nowhere else. My head empties of all thoughts of French women, cake, and bitches who play games as he fucks the fears right out of my head.

40

ROSE

'Hey, do you know why my full salary went into my bank this month?'

From the doorway to the bathroom, fresh from the shower and wrapped in a towel, the downy fabric secured low on his hips, Remy barely pauses in the action of rubbing his head with a smaller one. 'Most likely paid leave on compassionate grounds.'

'I don't remember seeing that in my contract.' I straighten the perfectly white bed linens over my legs as I force myself to concentrate on his face rather than the bronzed perfectness of him, yet somehow my mouth still races ahead. 'Are you still going to sunbathe naked here?'

'What?' His one-word answer brims with laughter.

'Naked sunbathing. You know that I know you don't have any tan lines. And that tan,' I say, circling my finger in the air to indicate the deliciousness that is him, 'didn't come from a can. Or a tanning bed.'

'No man is that vain.' His expression twists in a perfect expression of derision.

'Shows what you know,' I reply, picking up my iPad to log

out of my banking app. I've known some very vain douches in my time, but least said on the topic, the better.

'So, I was wondering how you're going to top up that tan without the benefit of a secluded balcony.'

He drops his hair drying towel to the bottom of the bed, his forefinger held aloft. 'I heard, where and when will you be getting naked.'

'Sure, you did, but the question stands.'

'I'll consider it,' he replies with a smirk.

'Be sure to report back. In the meantime, I'll buy some binoculars.'

With a taunting glance, he pulls the towel loose from his waist, dropping it like a statement.

'You have no shame,' I announce, sounding more encouraging than prim.

'No shame, but ample cock. No need for binoculars.'

'I wasn't maligning your excellent . . .' No finger waving now to indicate said area. Nope, this time, I use a hand. 'Equipage.' *Cockage?* 'I was thinking more about watching the watchers watching you.' Or something. And now the conversation is totally off course. 'And I know my compassionate leave officially amounts to five days. I received way more than that. And about the email detailing my pay increase? Well, I just don't want it.' I can't quite believe I'm saying this. A few months ago, I would've walked across broken glass for a raise, yet here I am, turning one down.

Lowering his naked self beside me, he takes my hand in his. 'No one privy to your pay increase will breathe a word of it to anyone.'

'That's beside the point, Remy.'

'Is it? That's what you're worrying about, isn't it? What people will think. What they'll gossip about.' He doesn't say it, though I hear them anyway. *They'll say you earned it on your back*. 'You need to stop worrying about other people's opinions. To have interest gives them power, and power is not something you give. It's something you take.'

'That's easy for you to say.'

'It's just all a matter of practice.'

'I don't need a raise. Can you see how uncomfortable it makes me feel?'

'An increase in pay is a drop in the ocean of what's due to you.' I open my mouth to speak but catch myself at his entreating look. 'There are some things that I can't tell you yet —I will tell you. I'll tell you everything when the time comes, and I know it's a lot to ask, but I need you to trust me. To have faith.' His hands tighten on mine, as his gaze dips to where our fingers meet, as though he could gather strength from the sight. When his head rises once again, his green eyes glitter with intensity. 'I want to look after you, Rose. Like you've looked after me. I want you to let me love you like you deserve. Your pay increase stands. You're good for the company.'

'I'm good company, or good for the company?'

'You're excellent company, and you're good for me.'

'These things you aren't telling me? Are they . . . are they going to hurt me?'

'I want to say I won't let you be hurt, but the truth is, nothing worth having comes without a little hurt. So instead, I'll say this to you. If I ever do or say anything that may be construed as hurtful to you, something that leaves you confused in the interpretation, I promise you I mean it in the way that will hurt or offend you least.'

'You're going to try not to hurt me.' But is that enough?

'I promise you with my life.'

Yet I still have to push away a sense of foreboding

The Omega watch store on Place du Casino is busy for a Wednesday afternoon, filled with boomer-aged German tourists. I don't have an appointment, but I'm only picking up, so I won't take up too much of their time.

I spot a space as a rotund sixty-something moves over to peruse the watches in a different case, smiling as I approach the counter to muscle my way in.

'Hi, Yuri. I dropped off a repair last week. I wondered if it was ready to pick up.' So far, I've bought five watches from Yuri, though obviously not for me, meaning we're on pretty good terms.

'Oh. I'm not sure.' Her black brows wing up, her expression disconcerted. 'Was it the older watch with the brown strap?'

'Sounds like the one.' I smile to cover the pinprick of discomfort I'm currently experiencing. She's not sure, but she knows it has a brown strap? I hope to God they haven't lost Remy's grandfather's watch. I mean, it's not like he's asked for it since he took a tumble into the marina, but that's doesn't mean to say he won't at some point. He's been wearing a Rolex Daytona model lately that I know costs fifty thousand euros because a client ordered a similar one last month. Meanwhile, I took it upon myself to get his old watch fixed. I thought it would be a nice surprise, but if I've got to tell him it's now lost, I'll be more than mortified.

I also won't be buying him a new one. Not at a Rolex price bracket, anyway.

'Can you wait just a minute? I'll go and ask Pierre.'

'Sure.' I move over to the side of the store as the boomer returns to the same case. Holidaymakers seem to have flooded the principality, and though I haven't been here very long, I've tired a little of the place. The cafés are so busy it's almost impossible to get served these days due to the numbers of summer day-trippers bussed in from other parts of the Riviera. They come to take selfies in front of other people's parked Ferraris and Bentleys. Or maybe I'm not so weary and just more partial to the place in the mountains I now call home.

The peace and seclusion.

The man who finds me there.

Remy hasn't mentioned ownership of the house again. He seems satisfied that I call it home. Which is exactly what it feels like, and I love the way he smiles when I say so. We've slept in the same bed together every night since he checked himself out of the hospital. I want to smile so wide when I think about it because sleep isn't the only thing we do.

It's almost like we've found a new religion and become a couple of zealots, because we just can't get enough of each other.

I know all relationships have a honeymoon period, but this is kind of insane. I've even gone as far as making an appointment with Doctor Google to try to diagnose the reason for my own sexual insatiability where Remy is concerned. I can't say it was all that much help. But in all seriousness, it's like everything between us is heightened since his accident. Heightened because every feeling is just a little more, every declaration of love a little more fervent. We know what we nearly lost, and we're making up for what might never have been. Quite honestly, when I dwell on the strength of my feelings for him, it becomes scary.

To think I almost lost him.

My attention is drawn to the door as the wave of German nationals file out. There are still one or two people being served at the glass counters. A couple buying a graduation gift, I decide, and a younger man buying a watch for his girlfriend. At least, these are my imaginings.

'Rose?' I lift my head at the sound of my name. *Oh.* Yuri's troubled expression doesn't look very promising. 'I, erm, don't know how to tell you this,' she says, producing a clear plastic pocket containing Remy's watch.

'You have it! For a minute, I thought it was lost.' I pull a face, conscious of the inadvertent slight I've just delivered. 'Crazy, right?'

'Actually,' she lowers her voice, drawing closer as though to impart a secret. 'We couldn't officially repair it. Because it's not a genuine Omega watch.'

'What?' The word is a tremulous chuckle. 'That can't be right.'

'I know it's vintage. I can definitely tell you that,' she says, turning the thing in her hand. 'But it doesn't have a serial number. The workshop says the mechanics aren't authentic, either.'

'Yuri.' I draw closer too, so as not to be overheard. 'The watch belongs to Remy. It has to be genuine.' I know she knows who I'm talking about because I saw her talking to Charles in a nearby coffee shop, and I *know* he can't keep his mouth shut about anything.

'I don't know what to say.'

'How am I supposed to explain this to him? It's his grandfather's watch.'

'At least you can tell him it's fixed.' Her hands open, and she gives a tiny shrug. 'I mean, it hasn't had an official service or anything, but because you're one of our most valued customers,' she means the concierge service is, 'Pierre asked the workshop to see what they could do.'

'Well, I guess that's something.' I find myself nodding as I resolve not to mention any of this to Remy. I mean, it's not like this is his only watch. He has at least a dozen more back in the closet at the penthouse and can probably afford a hundred more. As awkward as this knowledge is, I don't have to pass it on and embarrass him. I got his grandfather's watch repaired, which is what I set out to do, so I'm calling it a win.

Yuri takes my credit card to ring up the invoice while I take a look at the new season's wares. I'm not looking for myself, but more in a professional capacity when something sparkly catches my eye. A diamond-encrusted Deville Ladymatic.

'It's beautiful, isn't it?'

I look up at the deep voice and straighten, a little embarrassed. 'Did I just make a noise?'

'You did. Like a magpie about to peck the glass and flee the scene.'

'Well, I do like sparkly things,' I reply, adding a little confusion to my embarrassment.

'Carson Hayes.' He holds out his hand for me to shake. He's tall and blonde with swimmers' shoulders; the kind of all-American golden boy movies love to depict.

'Rose,' I offer, meeting his hand briefly.

'Could I ask you to do me a favour?'

I eye him like a very sensible eight-year-old who's just been offered a peek at some puppies. 'That all depends.'

'Well, I have to buy a gift, and I'm really terrible at it.'

'Oh? Well, sure.' I am, after all, kind of an expert these days.

'All ready for you now.' Yuri appears once again, holding out a glossy bag and my card. I sign the tiny slip of paper and turn back to Carson.

'How old?'

'I'm thirty-two,' he answers with a cocky half-grin.

'Not you. How old is the person you're buying the gift for?

Also, gender. Though I guess you're buying a gift for a woman.'

'And what makes you say that?' *Now he's trying to be cute.*

'Well, you were looking at the women's watches,' I reply, pointing out the case behind us.

'You're right. It's for my grandmother. It's her birthday.'

'Happy birthday to her!' I smile widely, covering the hope that he was about to say his girlfriend because I've no time for cute. 'Well, I'm kind of on a schedule, so shall we?' I turn and wink at Yuri. Maybe I should ask for a commission, but I guess one good turn deserves another.

'Does she like silver or gold? What about the one with the blue face?'

'I think the dial is too small,' he says, frowning down at the glass case. 'Did you get what you were looking for?' His words are so mild in their delivery that I know he overheard. Whatever. What are the chances he overheard everything? Not high, I'd guess. Besides, it's not like he just caught me slipping diamonds into my pockets.

'Yep, I totally did, thanks.'

'Did I hear you say you work for The Wolf Group?'

I play back my earlier conversation with Yuri. Did I mention the company name? I don't think so. I don't even think I mentioned the word *concierge*.

'I do,' I answer carefully. 'But I don't recall saying so.'

'Busted.' He smiles all white teeth and *aw-shucks* false embarrassment. I bet it works for him plenty. But not today. Not with me. 'I overheard you mention Remy,' he continues when I don't answer. 'Also, the issue with the watch.'

I feel myself frown. Damn.

'Well, this is a watch shop, sure,' I answer, refusing to admit anything else.

'Exactly. You were picking up his watch.' And if I'm not admitting anything, I guess he's playing along, too.

'Do you know Mr Durrand?'

'Oh, it's Mr Durrand now.' He smiles again, but I'm tiring of his repertoire.

'Well, he is the boss. Now, shall we get back to this watch?'

We browse a few more minutes, and I recruit the assistance of Yuri, and it isn't too much longer before she's ringing up a five-thousand-dollar sale. *Lucky grandma.*

'It was nice meeting you, Carson. I hope your grandmother has a great birthday.' I make to turn when he speaks again.

'I hope you don't think I'm being too forward, but would you allow me buy you a coffee to thank you for your help?'

'Oh, no. That's fine. You really don't have to do that.'

'But I'd like to. Not just to say thanks but because, well, I also think you're very pretty.'

'Thank you.' Accept the compliment, then move on. 'And I'm sorry, but I'm already seeing someone.'

'Lucky him.' He pulls out another smile, this one a touch more insincere. 'Let me give you my card. Just in case.'

Nothing like suggesting to a girl; *I hope your relationship fails!*

He pulls out a tiny silver case, handing me an embossed piece of finery. Business cards. How old-school. It reads,

CARSON HAYES III
COO HAYES CONSTRUCTION

'Who are Carson Hayes the first and second?' I muse.

Oops, I probably should've mused a little quieter, judging by the quirk of his mouth.

'My grandfather and my father,' he answers equably. 'You should ask Remy about us.'

Should I frown a little fake confusion for the sake of propriety? *Remy? Who could that be again?* We're hardly a secret anymore, but there's something a little strange about this exchange. In the end, I say nothing, mainly because he speaks first.

'Well, Rose, I'm sure I'll see you around.'

'Absolutely.' Though, not if I see you first. 'Monaco is a small place.'

With that, I shove the damn card in the bag with the watch, give the man my own version of a disingenuous smile, and get out.

41

ROSE

FRIDAY MORNING, my email inbox yields another surprise: an appointment this time.

'Charles, do you know anything about this?'

He lifts his head from his screen, swinging around in his ergonomic to face me. '*Bien sûr.*' Of course. 'I make the appointment for you wis Glenna. Please confirm the time. Fee is driving me to your new house to watch the magic 'appen.'

'It's not my house. It's Remy's.' But Glenna Goodman? *The* stylist in Monaco? Olga recently hauled my butt over the coals for being unable to get an appointment for one of the residents. 'Did he put you up to this—Remy?' Is this another gift?

'He asked.' Only Charles could lift and drop his shoulder with such an attitude. 'You have a gown to buy for the gala next weekend.'

'I can shop for myself.'

'H&M won't do, *mon petite canard,*' he answers, full of condescension as he makes as though to tap my nose.

'I'm not your little duck,' I retort, knocking his hand away. 'I'm perfectly capable of picking up a gown for next Saturday.

428

In fact, I found a cute little vintage designer store in Monaco-Ville last week.'

'And?'

'I tried on a couple of dresses that might work.' Maybe. With a little alteration. 'Plus, there's a rent-a-gown place in Nice that Fee told me about. You can go to the store to try the dresses on or order online for delivery.' So Fee said.

'But your . . . ' he says with such distaste, indicating my chest. No, not indicating but rather rubbing the air in front of them as though they were drawn on a whiteboard he's trying to scrub clean.

'They're called boobs, Charles. Or breasts. You can use your big-boy words.'

'I only say you need the help.'

'I must need psychiatric help,' I mutter, swinging my chair away from him. 'Some friend you are.' I begin to tap the keys of my laptop a little viciously.

'You will see,' he answers, unconcerned.

'Anyway, what do you mean you and Fee are coming?'

'What I said,' he replies without turning. 'You will need moral support. And Fee and I want to see the magic 'appen. Glenna normally only styles for rich or royalty. You should be grateful.'

Maybe he's right. Instead, I feel railroaded.

I don't hear from Remy that morning so I assume he's too busy for lunch today. Instead, I grab a sandwich and work through, trying hard to ignore my grumpy mood. *More money. A house. A driver to take me to and from said house. What's next? An elephant on a gold chain? A magic carpet?*

With the last of those thoughts, I find myself sitting back in my chair with a wry grin. My life *is* a fairy tale—this is my once upon a time and maybe even my happily ever after. There are a lot of things to fight in this world; discrimination, gender equality, homelessness, poverty, and food security. As I sit, I realise, each of these has touched my life in some way. I've lived hand to mouth as a child, and as an adult, there have been times where I almost didn't have a roof over my head. I've been touched and spoken to in ways no person should have. I am literally complaining my diamond shoes aren't a good fit.

If my Prince Charming wants me to see Monaco's most selective stylist, then I'll make sure my underwear matches, open a bottle of champagne, and pretend I damn well enjoy it.

Pretend to enjoy it. Pretend, pretend, pretend.

Glenna Goodman and I, well, we don't hit it off exactly. She complains about having to travel out to "the sticks", as she puts it, and is mighty unimpressed when I don't have someone there to help her wheel her wares into the house, despite having an assistant all of her own who followed her car here in a black Mercedes van brimming with fashion goodies. Tall and austere looking, she is, as you would expect, the kind of effortlessly stylish that reminds me of an older-era Lauren Bacall.

'Usually, I spend the day with a new client getting to know them better, getting a feel for their lifestyle,' she says in drawling, laconic tones. 'How do they spend their day? What kind of movement their wardrobe requires?'

'I don't have a very physical job,' I reply, just in case she thinks she's getting me into something with elastic at the knees. 'The most strenuous aspect of my day might be picking up something from Gucci for one of my clients. I slide Marco, Glenna's assistant, a sympathetic smile.

'I meant how often you're required to move from the office to meetings, to functions in the evening.'

'Oh.' I nod, eyebrows riding high on my forehead. 'My mistake.'

'May I top up your champagne, Glenna?' Fee asks from the sofa. I'm not sure if it's a sense of awe or fear that has her sitting so primly; straight-backed, knees together, hands placed carefully on her lap.

'No, thank you,' Glenna answers. 'One glass is sufficient when I'm working. I'd also like to take a look in your closet while I'm here. To see what we have to work with.' Her eyes flicker over me, from my ballet flats and skinny black jeans to the silver-blue square-necked blouse I'm wearing. I can almost sense her disappointment.

'Actually, Glenna, right now, I just need something for the gala.'

'As I understood it, Monsieur Durrand required more outfits for your perusal?' She turns to Charles, who begins to speak in rapid French, the older woman deigning to nod in several places.

'I explained you do not have your full wardrobe at this house.'

'Yes, that's true.' I shrug; whatcha gonna do? There's no way I'm letting this woman get a hand on my drawers. Also, Monsieur Durrand can "require" all he likes.

'Then this selection will have to do for now. Perhaps at a later date, we can book in your shopping consultation. I am available in Monaco, of course, but also for trips to Milan or Paris, as you wish.'

I wish not to go shopping with you anywhere, least of all for a little continental hop to shop. Plus, with me, you're more likely to get a lift on the back of a bicycle than a Gulfstream even if I own neither. When I don't reply beyond a benign smile, she gestures to Marco, who begins to unzip a dress cover lifted from a gleaming gold-coloured garment rack, glossy shoeboxes sitting underneath, a dazzling array of brands. Dior, Louboutin, Manolo Blahnik, Chanel; the stack of labelled boxes goes on and on. I'm handed a garment of tissue-thin silk and gestured into something that looks like a windowless sound booth, which is actually Glenna's portable fitting room.

Have van . . . will bring the kitchen sink!

Inside the box, I slip into the dress, happy I'm not flashing my (matching) underwear as originally feared. I pull up the concealed side zipper and take a look in the mirror. I look like I belong in a box of Valentine's chocolates picked up at Bergdorf. There is also the possibility it might cut off circulation to my heart because it's so tight.

'Oh, pink.' Fee is the first to speak. *Diplomatically.*

'Well spotted,' I find myself answering.

'No, this is not the dress for you,' Glenna decrees. 'The Valentino.'

And so it goes. I try on six dresses in colours of a kid's painting palette. A red from Valentino. A yellow from Givenchy. A blue from YSL. A black from Off-White. If you'd asked me a month ago if I'd enjoy an evening of trying on designer wear or statement dresses, I would've said hell yeah! Until I came to Monaco, I'd never even been close to this kind of luxury. But right now, I'm hot, and I'm antsy, and I'm beginning to think I just don't have the body type for designer dresses. Too tight in the chest, or the arm, the waistlines too long. According to Glenna, some of these can be altered in the right dress. But we've yet to find "the one".

She's not taking it well . . .

'Marco!' she snaps. 'The Chanel. Not the orange but the white.'

White and I are not friends. White is an invitation to spilled spaghetti sauce and splashes of red wine and sitting through a dinner with a napkin tucked in your neck.

Stylish, yes?

'I'm . . . not sure,' I begin as the woman turns her gimlet glare my way, but I won't be browbeaten. Doesn't she know who the customer is here? But as Marco's arms begin to slowly retract the offer, I see the look on his face. I hear you, my friend. There are better ways to spend a Friday evening. 'Okay.' I make a grabby hand in his direction, my words unenthusiastic. 'Pass it over.' What's one more wrong dress added to the total?

The dress flutters over my head, my arms gliding effortlessly through the armholes, the fabric settling at my waist where it falls to the ground in luxurious swathes.

I suck in a breath as I pull up the zipper, tightening the braided silk belt before I dare to take a peek at my reflection. And 'Oh, my God.'

'Oh, that sounds exciting,' says Fee from beyond the box.

'I knew 'zis would be the one,' Charles bursts out. 'Let us see, Rose.'

But I'm too busy looking at myself, though I think the actual word is admiring.

I run my fingers along the ribbon-like wrap-around top. The neckline is low, the cowl cut somehow both minimising and bringing attention to my chest. It's not exactly white in colour, maybe more oyster, and there's something almost Grecian about it. Whatever the style, I've never had a dress make me feel like this. Look like this. And as I step out from the box, Glenna's smile is immediate.

'This,' she announces. 'This is why I love my job. Darling, you look *divine*.' Her voice seems to drop a whole octave on the last word. 'Marco, the shoes.' She snaps her fingers. 'Not those ones, *stupide*!'

I'm handed a pair of matching sandals by her red-faced assistant. Spike heels and leather fashioned into silver ropes. I put them on, and the dress is pinned at the hem, and all the while, I can't restrain my happiness. Glenna makes another few suggestions from her golden rack of gorgeousness, and as the dress is such a success, I find myself eager to try them on.

'That's gorgeous,' Fee marvels, fingering the ruffle of a blouse by a French designer, Jour/Ne.

'Why don't you splurge?' I suggest. But she just wrinkles her nose and shakes her head. While she's not looking, I add it to my pile of purchases. Remy might be picking up Glenna's exorbitant appointment fee, along with the dress, but the other things I'll buy. Including my gift to Fee.

Glenna sweeps off in her low-slung Jaguar a little while later following delivery of double air-kisses to all and an almost emotionally charged *au-revoir*. Probably because she earned a fortune in fees and commission tonight. Marco hangs back to exchange numbers with Charles, but before he leaves, I ask him if he has anything in the van that might be a little more masculine. And he does; boxed gift sets containing a tie and a matching pocket square. I take two of the exact same design. While Charles might be currently enjoying a little flirt with Marco, I know he'll *just die* when I tell him Remy and he are tie twins.

As everyone leaves, I deposit the last glass to the dishwasher when my phone buzzes with a text. A text from Monsieur Baguette, as I've saved Remy's number in my phone.

Did you buy anything nice?

One or two things, I reply. **If you're good, I might show you when you get home.**

If I'm very good, do you think you might take them off for me instead?

Mr Durrand, what kind of girl do you think I am?

There follows a series of short replies.

A smart one.

A stunning one.

Delectable from head to toe.

Not really a girl at all, but all woman.

A willing woman, I hope.

Also, mine.

That volley of texts. Those simple characters typed into his phone, the knowledge they bring, causes a series of tiny explosions of delight deep inside.

I missed you today, I type back, which is a pretty lame reply, compared to his.

I've missed you, too. But I'll see you soon.

Any idea how long? Are you hungry at all?

Forty-five minutes. I had dinner earlier, but I'm sure you can guess what I'm hungry for.

I'll see what I can rustle up ;)

A winky face. What am I, twelve?

A shimmer of anticipation washes through me as I place my phone down, and my eyes fall to the gift boxes of ties. And a spark of inspiration hits. I know just what my man needs after a hard day at the office.

Me!

42

REMY

CLOSING THE DOOR BEHIND ME, I resist the urge to call out *honey, I'm home*. I find myself smiling at my own ridiculousness, but if home is where the heart is, she is it.

I twist my head to my shoulders, left then right, the satisfying click of joints and stretch of cartilage easing the tension in my shoulders as I slide my jacket off. A fresh bowl of lilies sits in the centre of the Art Deco era occasional table, their scent sickly sweet and reminiscent of funerals. I make a mental note to ask the housekeeper not to order them again as I quickly sift through the mail.

Nothing of note. Also, nothing for Rose. Perhaps I should ask Paulette to sign her up to some circulars; mail in her name to tie her to the building that has already won her heart. She loves this old place, and I love seeing her here. I love us being here. Together.

'Rose?' I drop the mail to the table, suddenly noticing the absence of noise. There is usually a hum of a TV from the den or the newly installed flat screen in the kitchen, music playing somewhere, the shuffle of her feet as she dances to the beat. Though the lights burn bright in the hallway, the rooms I pass are dark and still. Salon, formal dining room, sitting room, music room, library, or den; I duck my head into each, just in case, as I make my way to the back of the house when I notice light coming from the kitchen. But there's no sign of Rose.

My fist clamps around my heart as I take the treads of the second staircase two at a time. I've had a particularly trying day. One where I might have, possibly, once again faced my own mortality, if not for the vigilance of a member of staff. I had a meeting in Turin, Italy—just a forty-minute helicopter flight away—but when I arrived at the helipad, I found my usual pilot arguing with a new member of the maintenance crew. It seems the engineer noticed an irregularity with a lubricant that had been used for the rotors, and used for quite some time, as I understand. It wasn't an irregularity but an error, an error that hadn't been picked up at the one-hundred-hour maintenance check just last week. The engineer was trying to make the pilot understand the potential for an accident, while the pilot could only see that the previous week's maintenance report as proof of all was well. An error, not a case of tampering. *Probably.* Though still a potentially costly one, and not just in terms of possible repair expenses. An unsuitable lubricant causes erosion, which would have, at some point, resulted in a mechanical failure. Possibly in midair.

Needless to say, I did not fly to Turin in my own helicopter but in a hire. An investigation is underway, but it appears to be a case of human error on the part of the old engineer. Words that are easily said. Words that have no effect on the chill currently creeping up my spine.

A low light shines from under our bedroom door as I push it open, my heart rising to my throat.

'Rose?'

No answer, not as I push the door wide and—

'Honey, you're home.' I hear her before I see her, the warmth in her voice thawing my internal chill.

'There you are.'

She lifts her chin, an act of courage, not of enquiry, as the colour in her cheeks reflects the blush pink colour of the velvet chair she's lounging on. Her toenails are painted a similar shade, her nail polish one of just three things she appears to be wearing.

Pink nail polish. A man's tie. A white shirt that I believe is mine.

Home. *I am home.* I step farther into the room, pushing my hands in my pockets as I will my heart to still. She's here. She's okay. She's my home, and no matter what, she always will be.

'Have you been looking for me?'

Only my whole life, I almost answer because how do you look for something you didn't realise you needed. But I do need her. I've needed her all along.

'What have we got here?' I make a path to the ottoman as she points her toes, my gaze crawling from there up the length of her toned legs. In one hand, she holds a crystal tumbler by the rim, something tawny contained, as her other draws soft circles against the silky pile of the chair arm.

'I bought you a present. From Glenna,' she adds, in response to my slight frown. 'Only you wouldn't know who Glenna Goodman is.' Her eyes are beguiling, even as she raises her brows.

'Ah, the dressmaker.'

'Not even close,' she says with a tiny laugh. 'I'm not sure a dressmaker would make one of these.' She toys with the thin end of the tie she's wearing looped casually around her neck. The outer side lies down the length of her torso, pointing like an arrow to the heaven between her legs.

'And what is that?' My tone is pondering as I bring my

hand to my chin. 'Do you think someone needs direction? Is it perhaps a subtle hint?'

'It's a gift.' She arches a little in the chair, the cotton of my shirt exposing the bud of her nipple. She is a gift, from the way her dark hair gleams in the candlelight and the way it licks at her skin. Her gift is in the heat of her gaze and the way she lowers her lashes as though to conceal it.

'What are you doing?' There's a tremble in her voice as I wrap my hand around the back of her knee, desire, not nervousness, I decide, as I take a seat on the ottoman between her legs.

'I'm following directions,' I murmur, pressing my mouth to the inside of her knee, keeping it there with a deep inhale. I know the scent of her intimately now, like a favourite perfume, the taste of her beckoning. Her sharp gasp twists at my insides as I reach out and drag my finger down the red silken path, her held breath becoming a sigh as I lift her knee and hook it over the arm of the chair, spreading her for my gaze. *Pink, and lush, and ripe.* I take the glass from her hand and bring it to my lips. *Cognac, the good stuff.*

'I was supposed to be doing something nice for you.'

I watch her over the rim of the glass. Rose with the soft skin and the raw kind of beauty. Only she would think I deserve good things.

'Oh, Rose, I do love you. But nice is the least of the things I'm about to do to you.'

'Here.' Rhett drops a large envelope to my desk, sinking into the chair on the opposite side. I don't normally work from the chateau, but when Rhett called to say he had a package to drop off, I decided speaking with him away from prying eyes would be preferable.

'What is it?' I narrow my gaze at him, not entirely sure why I'm asking as a fist tightens my innards.

'The information from the PI. It came by courier this afternoon.'

Pulling open a drawer in my desk, I drop it to the darkness it deserves. 'I assume you haven't opened it.'

His brows pull down. 'What do you think? You asked me not to, so I didn't. Even though I think you're being a colossal arsehole in not opening them yourself.'

'For the final time, not that I have to explain myself to you, but Rose had nothing to do with what happened back in March, and whatever she was to Emile, I've already decided I don't want to know.' She isn't my sister, and whatever fucked-up thing he thinks she's guilty of, he's wrong. I know it. And I have plans for the content of this envelope. At some point, Rose will need to know the truth. Or at least some of it.

'There's a story behind this, and you know there is. You don't leave that kind of money to some woman you've never met. Someone you've no connection to. But I was thinking.' He sits suddenly forward in the chair, his fingers at his darkly stubbled chin. 'Could she be some other debt. Maybe that fucker Ben's half-sister. Someone Emile might've felt honour bound to look after?'

'Emile had no honour,' I reply, slamming the drawer shut. 'And whatever is in that envelope is of no interest to me.' At this moment, at least. All the same, I make a mental note to take it into the office to be locked in the safe with the rest of the investigator's work.

'Not even what happened to your motorbike? You were still pretty pissed off last time we spoke.'

'Was that supposed to be provoking?' I ask in a drawling

tone as I relax back into my chair. But Rhett just stares back, his expression inscrutable. Fuck him and his poker face, even if he's right. I'd owned that bike less than a week, but more than that, I don't like the idea that it now belongs to someone else through my own stupidity. With a sigh, I give into the urge. 'So, did he talk, this hardened criminal of yours?'

Rhett curls his hands around the arms. As one corner of his mouth kicks up, I know the answer. 'Nah. The PI offered him money, but the fella got a Bobby big balls complex as if he was some fucking Don.'

'Extortion?'

'Pretty much.' He shrugs.

'So that is the end of the road.'

'The end of the road where you fell off your bike. Or you were pushed? Did you fall off a damaged passerelle, or did someone take a crowbar to your head?'

'Yet, I'm still here.' I spread my hands, though I feel less than magnanimous.

'Yep, here you are even after the bike and the boat, and even after someone used the wrong lube and you were nearly fucked dry.'

The helicopter, of course.

'And by fucked dry, you mean fucked dead.'

'What's there to smile about?' he asks, both annoyed and perplexed.

He doesn't need to know I'm thinking about Rose remembering the way she complimented my cursing, my mind slipping to last night, and how she'd enjoyed the other ways I'd used my tongue. I'd devoured her as she'd writhed between my face and the velvet chair, taking her pleasure, taking all I had to give. She'd crawled over to me then, her movements as sinuous as my shirt was wrinkled, her fingers at my shirt, my belt, feeding my cock between her legs. And as my tongue traced the rise and fall of her breasts, the pointed tips, she'd stripped the day from me, kissed away my dread. Scoured my thoughts of what might've been. Of what is.

Am I three times lucky? Or three times almost dead?

She'd taken me on a slow ride to heaven as I'd realised I'd never ever feel her enough, be inside her deep enough, be enough for her in this or any other life.

Rhett's voice brings me back to the moment all at once. The helicopter.

'You could've been killed.'

'So, you heard.'

'Some head of security I would be if I hadn't. Do you think the lads don't report back to me?'

'I want you to double the security of the house.' My answer takes the conversation in another direction but not as a diversion. It's more a gut reaction.

'Okay.' He sits straighter in his chair. 'But fuck the house. You need close personal protection because some fucker is trying to do you in.'

'Maybe.'

'Corporate or personal, d'you reckon?'

'I'll leave that discovery to you.'

'Thank the fucking Lord.' He smiles like the devil himself, his voice like the action of rubbing his hands together. 'Want to tell me why? I mean, it's not like I haven't been telling you to pull your head out of your arse for months, but why the change of heart?'

Because I have something to lose now. Because these no longer feel like coincidences. 'A precaution,' I answer instead. 'I want someone watching Rose, too.'

'Ha, that last one might be problematic. She'd take to close personal protection like a dog losing its balls, I assume?'

'I'll talk to her about it.' Or not. 'We could keep it remote for now.'

'A tail you mean?'

His tone isn't lost on me. 'I want her protected, not watched.'

'Yeah, sure. Because those aren't the same.' He pauses, the look he sends my way almost penetrating. 'Is there something you're not telling me?'

My gaze slides to the window and the expanse of blue beyond. 'It's just a feeling I have.' A sense of foreboding, I suppose. A sense that all is not well.

'That's hardly surprising, given what's happened to you lately. Normal people might even seek some counselling.'

The look I send him could best be described as withering. I don't need help. How I feel is not superstition, and I'm not at all sure it's suspicion, either. Could it be a fear of fragility, rooted in how I'm still keeping the truth from her?

I twist my laptop to face me, opening up a new email.

'Fine. Don't answer. I'm just the hired help, after all.'

'Just do it, Rhett. Please.' As my gaze flicks his way, his expression reflects his surprise.

'Yeah, no problem. But we're upping your security, yeah? Because, I tell you, these midnight meanders through the marina aren't gonna do you any good.'

I consider it as I type out an email to the head of my legal team to schedule an appointment for reasons both private and personal.

Security for me has been, up until now, concentrated on securing my estate, my property, and my information, not close personal protection.

Of course, I'm mindful of those who might like to exact revenge for business decisions that have affected them, events that they may deem unjust or unfair. And there have been threats. But no action. And in Monaco, I've always felt safe. I've required close personal protection only while travelling and only ever as a precaution. But it seems all of that should change.

I have someone now I don't want to lose.

Someone I would like not to cause any more pain.

Any more pain than I have to.

I close my laptop and look up as I answer, 'Yes, I think we should.'

43

ROSE

'I GOT you one of those disgustingly healthy green juice things, and a protein bowl.'

Pushing the door closed with my butt, I slide the key card to Remy's office into my pocket, my nose almost in the brown paper bag. I'm so hungry my stomach thinks my throat has been cut. 'I also got you extra chicken,' I sing, my words heavy with meaning as I smile to myself thinking about what he'd said last night. We were in bed, legs tangled in the sheets and chests still heaving, when he'd made a very un-Remy like comment about his testicles being drained.

'I figured a little extra zinc might . . .' My words trail away as I look up and realise not only is Remy not sitting at his desk. He's also not alone. 'Oh, I'm sorry. Miss Bisset wasn't at her desk.' I take a step backwards. *Abort! Abort!* 'I didn't realise you were busy. I can just come back later.'

'Rose.' Remy stands from the ultra-modern couch setting, gesturing me closer. 'I don't believe you've met my mother, Josephine.'

Ah. That would be no. And here comes the meeting I've been dreading. His mom smiles as she glances my way, but

445

not before I see the particularly eloquent look she gifts Remy. They've been talking about me. Oh, boy. That's a conversation I would not like to hear about.

Here goes nothing.

How did you meet my son, Rose? Well, you see, I scraped him off the pavement in San Francisco. He had a head injury, and I screwed him so hard I think I might've made it worse because apparently, he's in love with me.

Crazy, right?

'No,' I squeak. 'I have not had that pleasure.' I put down the bag containing our lunches, mourning the fact that my chicken pesto wrap will be mush before I get to it. 'It's so lovely to finally meet you,' I positively gush. 'Remy's told me so much about you.'

'You have that advantage over me, my dear,' she says, proffering a dainty hand. A dainty hand with buff-coloured nails and a grip like a WWE wrestler. Her voice, like her person, is very refined. Perfect English with just a tiny inflection of an accent. 'My darling son has told me nothing about you. In fact, it was only this morning I heard he'd been in the hospital.'

Someone's in *trou-ble!*

And for the record, what Remy has told me about his mom I could write on the back of a postage stamp and still have space for my signature.

'Yes, that was frightening. But I did suggest someone contact you, right?' My gaze flicks to Remy, his eyes sparkling with mirth. Yeah, I know. Brownie points for Rose. Or maybe brown nose points. 'But you're all healed now, right, babe?' With the exception of those empty testicles, maybe.

'Yes, absolutely.' The corner of his mouth hitches, but if he asks me if I've seen the movie, I'll give him a concussion myself. Urgh, babe! Where the heck did that come from?

I make my way to him—strength in numbers, right—and his hand rests against my waist as he kisses each of my cheeks. It's a very warm yet "dialled down for the audience" kind of greeting before we sit.

'Remy tells me you're from Kentucky, Róisín.'

'Yes, ma'am.' Originally, at any rate. I cross my legs at the ankles and slide them to the side with my hands clasped in my lap. No low-class fidgeting here.

'Are you any relation to the Kelly family?'

'Not that I'm aware of.' Yes, because Kentucky is such a small place that all the people with Irish names are related. Sheesh!

'That's a beautiful watch, my dear. Is it Piaget.'

'This? Yes, it is.' I clamp my lips together in a closed-lipped smile, resisting the urge to admit the watch was a gift from Remy. It's almost a compulsion; someone pays me a compliment, and I follow it up by telling them where the thing came from, along with the price. Though, admittedly it's usually more along the lines of: you like my skirt? Thanks! It's from Forever 21. I was in the sale—a steal at ten bucks. And look, it has pockets!

But look at me right now, all full of good grace and stuff.

'And you work for the group now, here in Monaco.' She doesn't address this as a question, but Remy answers it anyway.

'Yes. Rose and I met in America.' He turns to me, his eyes lingering on my lips before his attention returns to his mother. 'We met a second time when she came to work for the company.' His hand tightens on mine and whatever he says next, I don't understand. It's not French. Well, not like any French I've ever heard.

His mother nods just once in return, like a monarch blessing him with her assent. She is, quite honestly, beautiful.

Her olive skin is almost ageless, and her dark hair sleek and well behaved. I know for a fact the blue shift dress she's wearing is from Eudon Choi's new line, and those are definitely Choos on her feet. *And not a padded shoulder in sight.*

Josephine Durrand might look like a lady who lunches, but I sense under those designer labels lurks a will of steel.

'Benôit tells me you're staying at Chateau Margaux. I would've thought that old place would be a little out of the way for you, Remy, and not very in keeping with a bachelor's lifestyle.' Her gaze turns my way, her meaning clear. *Hear that? My son is single.*

Excuse me? We live in a chateau? Isn't that the same as a palace? Or a manor house, at least?

'You shouldn't listen to what Ben says,' Remy replies.

'You're not staying at the chateau?'

'I'm not single.'

'Well, you'll forgive me for saying that you were engaged last time I was in Monaco.'

Oh, dear Lord.

'Mother, you know the agreement I had with Amélie Pastor. You were party to it in its inception, as I recall.'

'Yes, I was. And you know why. The Wolf Group is your birthright. But Amélie told me last month that things had changed. I saw her in Milan,' she says, waving away the details. 'She said that a fondness had developed between you both.'

'The only thing Amélie has ever had a fondness for is my money.'

'Remy, that was crass. Aside from being very uncomplimentary, it is beneath you to speak in such a way.'

Hmm. Seems like she's one of those rich people who doesn't like talking about money. I bet *she's* never had her power cut off.

As though sensing my discomfort, Remy presses his thigh to mine as he answers. 'But it is the truth, nonetheless.'

'Our families have always been so close. We are of the same world.'

I . . . am not of the same world. I'm also tapping out. No way am I sitting here to listen to his mother sing the praises of another, no matter how lukewarm.

'Maybe this is a conversation you should both have alone.' I begin to stand when Remy's fingers tighten on mine.

'Stay. Please.' His gaze runs warily across my face before his attention turns to his mother once more. 'I was never in love with Amélie, not for a minute, and I can assure you the lack of sentiment was returned. I'm not sure why she would tell you otherwise. And Ben is wrong. I'm not living alone. I'm living with Rose.'

Ho-boy. Talk about happy families.

In the mirror, she stares back at me, dramatic eyed and voluptuous. The satin clings to her breasts and hips before flowing to the floor, elongating and slimming and making her look like she belongs on the pages of a glossy magazine.

'Hello, gorgeous.' I finger a glossy braid running along the side of my head in a style the hairstylist had called *a crown of curls and braids*. I'm so pleased I'd allowed Charles to persuade me to book an appointment, rather than d-i-y it tonight.

'I don't know who you are, but I like what I see,' I whisper to my reflection. And then, because I promised Amber I'd send her a selfie, I do. Pulling a ridiculously over-the-top-duck-pout in the mirror, I take the snap, knowing it'll give her a giggle. Then I take another more serious photograph as proof I ever looked this way.

Grabbing my clutch from the dresser, I make sure the contents of the plastic envelope from Omega is in my clutch before slotting away my phone.

Remy has yet to see my dress. It's not like I've hidden it from him, but we just happen to have separate dressing rooms. You know, like *one does*. I giggle, not sure if it's a reaction to the way that sounded in my head, or because I feel so lucky, or if it's because I'm loving the way I look, or that I'm giddy at the thoughts of seeing Remy's reaction. Probably every one of those things.

I make my way out to the bedroom, not really expecting to find him there. I also don't expect to find him waiting for me at the bottom of the stairs as I reach the halfway point of the staircase.

Waiting. For. Me.

One hand on the polished bannister rail, and in the other, I've gathered my dress, holding it up and to the side as I attempt a graceful descent. Which is pretty difficult, considering the sight of him sends my insides aflutter.

Dust motes dance like fairies between us, his face made up of shadow and the piercing green of his eyes. But as I draw closer, I see the love shining there. This beautiful man loves and desires me, and whatever happened in my life before and whatever happens going forward, this moment feels as perfect as the lustre of his blue-black satin lapels as they catch the dying rays of the sun.

Oh man, I knew he'd look good in a tux, but I didn't expect it to make me want to strip him out of it *tout de suite*. I restrain the urge to say so as I reach the bottom stair but one, trying for something a little more dignified as I smooth my hand across his shoulder.

'Don't you look dashing.' This is such an understatement. He looks like James Bond's better-looking brother with his hair swept back from his face and the angles of his cheekbones and strong jaw smoothly shaved.

'And you . . . you have stolen my breath, my thoughts, and my words.'

As he leans toward me, I press my hand to the centre of his chest. 'This lipstick might promise twelve hours of staying power, but I'm still not sure it'd withstand a make-out session with your rakishly handsome self.'

'Rakishly handsome?' he repeats, his tone playing up to the role, the lift of a singular brow a perfect complement to my assertions. He's Rhett to my Scarlett. Darcy to my Elizabeth. Jacob to my Hannah, and I am crazy, stupid (in) love.

'Yep, you're so deliciously right yet so deliciously wrong.' I lower my voice as though there are people around who might hear. 'Because I know what's going on underneath that fine suiting.' I trail my hand down his chest, my gaze following the path of my fingertips. As I reach his belt, he lifts my hand to his lips.

'And you say I'm the wrong one.' His eyes sparkle as he presses a kiss to the back of my hand. He's still holding it as I take the final stair, somehow finding myself twirled into the curved space at the very bottom of the staircase.

'I don't need to ask you for a kiss, because this is the place kisses are stolen.' His words are an echo of my much earlier ones. The first time I'd visited this house, I'd spoken of debutantes and brides, of the love affairs and lives the four walls of this house must've seen. The realisation that he remembers, as though he'd plucked my words from the air and kept them close causes, a tiny explosion of delight inside of me.

In an achingly perfect moment, his lips glance across mine. 'You look so beautiful, Rose.'

'No one ever called me beautiful before you,' I find myself admitting.

'That's a little hard to believe.' He twists an artfully curled lock of my hair, brushing it against my neck. His mouth follows his fingers and I sigh, my head rolling to the side as his lips press to the curve between my shoulder and neck. One kiss becomes two, two becomes a trembling sigh with my back pressed against the bannister in an attempt to keep myself upright. 'My beautifully tempting Rose. Perhaps you were waiting for me to bloom.'

And bloom I do, under his wandering hands and his lips, and under his beguiling attentions there, at the base of the stairs. And when he finally withdraws, my lipstick is right where it ought to be, though my wits are rolling about the floor like marbles.

He presses his palm low on my spine, leading me to the front door when a sudden realisation hits

'I almost forgot.' I turn to him, finding myself once more in the circle of his arms.

'Do you want to test your lipstick again?'

'First, the places you kissed weren't wearing lipstick. Second,' I say, sliding my hand into my clutch, 'I thought you might like this.' I place his grandfather's watch in his palm, folding his fingers over it.

'You had it repaired?' His expression is a mixture of surprise and something I can't quite identify as he looks down at it once more.

'They had to replace the strap, but it's almost the same. And the mechanism underwent some kind of repair.' *With genuine parts.* I push away the thought. There would be nothing to gain from telling him what was discovered in the store.

'This is . . .' He pulls me to his chest. 'I have no words.' His expression shines with such appreciation as he strips off the Rolex and discards it to the table in the hallway to wrap the new leather Omega strap around his wrist.

'It's wonderful, Rose. Thank you. I can't believe you've done this for me.'

I feel ten feet tall, and as we begin to move once more, I make a silent vow.

This house will never before have witnessed a love like ours.

44

ROSE

THE GALA IS BEING HELD at the *L'Hôtel du Loup*, the imposing building that sits almost at the heart of Monaco. Built at the height of the Belle Époque period, it's well regarded to be the epitome of timeless grace and elegance.

Hénri brings the car to a halt outside of the grand entrance, my door immediately opened by a liveried valet.

'This looks like it's going to be *trés* fancy,' I whisper as Remy settles my arm in the crook of his. The clip of my heels is muffled by the lengthy red carpet leading into the hotel.

'Oppressively so,' he agrees before adding, 'but I feel like I should temper your expectations.'

'Don't tell me I got all dressed up for an evening of snooze.'

'Just don't expect too much.' His mouth twists a touch sardonically.

'Will the food be good, at least?'

'As best as can be expected when feeding hundreds at the same time.'

'And there'll be champagne?'

'Rivers of it.'

'And I'll have you,' I add, tightening my grip. 'All my needs sound taken care of. I'll be as happy as a clam.'

Remy nods his greetings to a couple of matronly looking women and shakes the hands of at least four couples on our way in, yet he doesn't stop to chat. Instead, he murmurs exactly how he intends to take care of *my needs* when we get home this evening. How he'll take his time unravelling my braids before kissing me from the tips of my toes to the top of my head and some very particular places in between.

'If you're trying to make me blush, it's working.'

'I'm just giving you something to look forward to. That's all.'

'I'm not going to be able to look at your mother without wondering if she can read my thoughts.'

'Well, she is remarkably astute,' he agrees.

'That's not helping!'

I find myself coming to a halt at a pair of giant doors that lead into a ballroom the length of a soccer field. The gilded domed ceiling gleams from above as crystal chandeliers glitter and glasses chink, the space already filled with guests; men in tuxedos and women in a rainbow of colours. An orchestra plays from a raised gallery at the front of the room, and the space is heavy with the scent of fresh flowers and a hundred perfumes.

'It's like stepping back in time,' I find myself whispering, awestruck. As a college kid, I'd worked a few weddings at fancy hotels, but I've never seen anything like this. European glamour and wealth meet history in one space.

'You haven't been to the hotel yet?'

I shake my head as I answer. 'I've been to the kitchens. And the foyer. But that's about it.' And Remy owns this magnificence. The realisation is like an anvil to the head. I mean, I know he doesn't own it all—the group has shareholders and a board to placate. But oh my God, I thought Wolf Tower was a lot to get my mind around. But this? This is crazy.

'Rose? You've gone a little pale.'

'I'm fine.' I shake my head and inhale. It feels like I'd forgotten to do that for a while.

Remy is rich. So rich he tried to give you a house—a chateau, no less. You'll get over it.

Because he's also very good looking. And very sweet, if not a little bossy.

He's also the man you love.

And he puts his underwear on one leg at a time, just like everyone else.

Pep talk over, I tug on his arm. He tilts his head to my ear. 'Are we late?'

'Last in first out. That's usually my plan of attack.'

'We forgot to look at the seating plan on the way in. Unless we're just doing a lap of the room before bailing,' I say hopefully because now that we're actually in the ballroom, nervousness is beginning to creep in.

'If it were any other night, we wouldn't have even made it to the car. Because that dress . . .'

'Stop looking down my cleavage.'

'Ma Rose, a dress like that is an invitation to imagine peeling you out of it.' His half smile could best be described as enigmatic. 'But our table is here.'

Of course we'd be front and centre. The ball is named after his family, after all.

'One thing.' I find myself glancing down to where he covers my hand with his own, my spidey senses instantly tingle at his tone. 'I probably should've told you earlier, but Amélie will be here.'

'You did say. She helped your mom with the planning, right?'

It's not like she's the ex who's been invited to our wedding. *Not that there's any sign of a wedding.* But only a petty bitch would demand "it's me or her", and not only am I not petty, I'm also pretty certain I'd be the one on the bus home if I did pull this stunt, given his mother's lukewarm reception to meeting me in Remy's office.

'But what I didn't say is that she'll be seated at the same table as my mother. The same table we are seated.'

'Oh, boy.' My laughter is hard, his fingers tightening. 'Were you banking on me not noticing the gazelle in the room?'

'What do gazelles have to do with anything?'

'It really doesn't matter.'

'If you'll let me explain—'

'But what does matter is that you really are a piece of work.' I nail a smile to my face as I begin to scan the space for an exit, other than the one behind me. I'm not leaving—at least, not yet—but this is something that requires a discussion in private. Somewhere without an audience that run into the hundreds.

'Do you remember when I said that I would never set out to hurt you intentionally?'

'Oh, so this was an accident? *Right.*'

'This is not my doing,' he replies, turning us in the direction of a side door and into another room. No, not a room; more a narrow hallway with staff to-ing and fro-ing, turning their bodies sideways as they pass, barely sparing us a second glance.

I'm pleased, at least, he had the same opinion about privacy.

My hand still secured in the crook of his arm, he leads me left into an alcove very much like the ones I've read about in historical romance novels. A seclude alcove. A dark curtain. A window seat. A place to canoodle without anyone seeing.

There will be no canoodling today. But there will be answers.

'I swear to you I didn't know.' He stares down at me, his green eyes angry. 'Not until Everett sent me a text when he saw Amélie's name on the seating plan.'

'And you didn't think to tell me then?'

'No, because I spent the rest of the afternoon trying to track down my mother to correct the fuckup.'

'Yeah, sure.' I resist the urge to fold my arms across my chest because there's no way I'm spoiling the fall of this gown. 'So you went around town looking for your mother?'

'I asked Paulette to find her, and when I spoke with her this afternoon, she agreed it would be tactless for Amélie to be seated at the same table. She was under the impression the event planner had moved her to another table.'

'And?'

'It seems she moved herself back.'

'Which means what, exactly?'

'Apart from the fact the woman has a screw loose, I'm not sure. Unless you want to cause a scene.'

Which, I'm sure, would go down so well for me. 'You should've told me, Remy.' Yet another incidence of his high-handedness

'And give you a chance not to come?' he retorts.

'And that would be my decision to make, not yours. You get that, right?'

'Monaco is a small place. You're going to come across her sometime.'

'And I would've preferred it to not have been tonight,' I counter, trying very hard to stay calm in the face of this overbearing asshole side of him.

'All right, lovebirds. Break it up.'

At the sound of Everett's deep . . . ly annoying voice, I find myself growling at the ceiling. 'I feel like breaking something.'

'Not me,' he says, pointing at the earpiece dangling from his ear. 'I'm working.' His gaze slides to Remy. 'And not him, he's got a speech to give.'

'I suppose that leaves Amélie then.'

'I reckon you could take her. Let me know if you're gonna throw down, and I'll start offering odds.'

'Rhett,' Remy murmurs wearily. 'Don't encourage her.' But he's smiling, even as he watches me roll my shoulders.

'All right, slugger. Your table awaits.' Rhett flourishes a bow, the kind suited more to a seventeenth century gent.

'You smell nice,' I say as I pass. 'What is that? Chloroform by Tom Ford?'

'I don't need to knock them out, Heidi. I have to beat them off.' He mimes something that looks a little like baseball but not quite. Cricket, maybe?

'There's a joke in there.'

'Please don't look too closely,' Remy adds as we reach the hallway again.

'I'm not sure I'm talking to you.'

'I think you're annoyed at the wrong person.'

'I appreciate you tried to sort this out, but you can't make my decisions for me. You get that, right?' He doesn't offer an answer, though a muscle begins to tick in his jaw. 'Besides, do you really think I'm so petty as to throw some kind of tantrum and make you come on your own?'

'I wasn't sure what your reaction would be.'

'Then you don't really know me.'

'I know you enough to trust you with my heart.'

My anger drains away, my throat suddenly tight as I tip up onto my toes and press my lips to his smooth cheek. 'Then let me look after it. And let me make my own decisions.'

At the table, Remy has been placed to his mother's left, my own seat almost facing his, as is often the way at formal dinners. Not that I have much experience from this side of the table. The guest side, I mean, not the proximity.

'Will Rhett be close by?' I ask, placing my clutch on my chair, not yet ready to sit.

'Rhett's working this evening.' I guess my face must reflect my surprise as he adds, 'He once told me he would rather take a vow of silence than sit through one of these things.'

'He couldn't keep his mouth shut if you wired his jaw.' But I know what he means. 'I think the least I'm going to need is a drink to get through this myself.' I glance behind me, hoping for a passing waiter. As I glance back, Remy is doctoring the place settings. 'What are you doing?'

'You need a drink to get through this, which we'll take care of very soon, and I need you near me,' he says, placing my name card next to his. 'There. Let's go and find the champagne and make some ridiculous bids on some useless items.'

I don't know about useless, but there are some pretty swanky things on offer in the silent auction part of the evening. Around the periphery of the room, stations have been set up with items to bid on. Rather than a traditional auction model of public bids and a banging gavel, this is much more sedate and civilised. Remy and I are given numbers to use, rather than our names, and we wander from station to station, examining the lots and placing anonymous bids.

A spa day here at the hotel.

A hot air balloon ride.

A cooking class with a Michelin starred chef.

A tasting session with a leading sommelier.

A piece of art from a Paris gallery that's a little depressing.

A golf lesson with a PGA star

Electric items: iPads, laptops, new phones, and other tablets and gadgets.

Jewellery.

A day for twelve on a superyacht.

Sailing lessons.

Tickets to an upcoming opera.

Plus, an afternoon appointment with Glenna Goodman, which seems to be causing a bit of a stir. The list goes on and on and on.

'What about the necklace?' Remy suggests, pointing at a diamond pendant in a glass case with its own security guard.

'No thanks. I'm thinking more about the cooking class.'

'Sounds good.'

'Not for me. For you. That way you can dazzle me with more than just a cheese sandwich.'

'A Croque Monsieur is a French classic. Besides, my cooking skills are not how I aim to dazzle you.'

We wander a little more, placing a bet here and there. I have no expectation of winning anything tonight, considering the net worth of the room's inhabitants. Eventually, we wander back to our table, and as the evening begins, there is one chair unfilled.

Amélie's.

Dinner is served, candelabras burn, crystal gleams, and china chinks. And of course, champagne bubbles and flows.

The conversation is mostly in French, though the man to my left, an elderly industrialist I'm told, involves me in conversation lots. Ben sits at the far side of the table, remote but friendly, I suppose. I guess I should be pleased he hasn't tried to cultivate a friendship between us, given what happened in Wolf Tower that day.

Remy introduces me as his girlfriend throughout the evening, translating for me where he can in French, Monegasque, and Italian. *The show-off.* And even more surprisingly, his mother makes a point of apologising for the misunderstanding with the table placements. *Albeit in a cool way.*

All in all, I'm having a good night, especially as Amélie's chair remains unfilled.

'It must cost a fortune to run an event like this,' I muse as my glass is filled with champagne once again. The remains of our sumptuous dinner have been cleared and people have begun to drift away to speak with other friends or join in the casino games being run in adjoining rooms.

'Yes, it's very expensive, as I understand it. It's largely my mother's concern.'

'What does it cost to get a seat at one of these tables?'

'Four thousand euros,' Remy answers without missing a beat.

'What?' I almost choke on my bubbles. 'Wow. Why don't people just donate to the foundation and cut out the middleman?'

'Then they don't get to be seen doing good, decked out in their finery and quaffing champagne.'

'Rich people are weird.'

'Does that include me?' he asks, full of good humour.

'No, honey.' I press my lips to his cheeks. 'You're so rich

you passed by weird a long while ago. You get to be classified as eccentric.'

'Lucky me.' After another halting conversation with the little old man industrialist, I turn to Remy's voice once again. 'Do you dance?'

'What, you mean like that?' I tip my glass in the direction of the couples waltzing very properly around the room, the orchestra now playing "The Second Waltz", if I'm not mistaken.

'There will be other dances later in the night, if you'd like. Though I'd hoped we'd be home by that point.'

'Doing the no-pants dance?' He shakes his head indulgently as I add, 'I can dance, and I can *dance*.' My words are heavy with a comic kind of meaning. 'One I learned in a class. The other . . .'

'Yes?' he asks, his lips wrapped in some semblance of a smile.

'Probably underneath the bleachers,' I admit. 'But not with the math teacher.'

'Not everyone learns to dance these days.'

'No, some of us just stumble our way through it and hope we get better at it each time.'

'I was talking about *actual* dancing.'

I begin to giggle, so much so, my cheeks begin to sting. 'I guess not everyone's mother forced them into a summer of cotillion classes in the seventh grade. God, I hated every minute of it,' I confess. 'The dress. The shoes. The stuffy atmosphere. But, yes, I learned to dance. What about you?'

'Also at school.' He scratches his head with his forefinger, his eyebrows riding high. He seems bashful, almost. It's a look I like on him.

'Are you going to tell me she was very thorough?'

'I wasn't about to say a word.'

463

'She should've stuck to teaching math. Maybe you should ask me to dance,' I add. 'On the floor, I mean. Here.'

'You're giving in far too easily for me.' He narrows his gaze playfully.

'What's that supposed to mean?'

'With you, it's almost as though your opposition is a pleasure all on its own.'

'Then Remy Durrand, I will never dance with you.'

'Never?'

'Waltz,' I qualify because I'm not giving up the other kind. 'Unless you ask. Nicely.'

To my amusement, though mostly my delight, he pushes back his chair and doffs a courtly bow as he addresses me. 'Miss Ryan, would you please honour me with this dance?'

'I'd be delighted,' I reply, beaming as I place my hand in his.

'And if you'd be so kind to permit me, I'd like to fill your dance card later. And by dance card, I mean—'

'I know exactly what you mean.'

As the orchestra strikes the first chords of "It Had to Be You", Remy rests his hands in places I'm sure Miss Pierce, leader of the cotillion class, would never have stood for. And as he leads us smoothly into the moving throng, I'm certain his touch is the only thing that grounds me.

We dance and we dance, until my heart is light and I'm breathlessly giggling.

'What's so amusing?' he asks as he leads me back to our table.

'I was just thinking of that saying. Dancing is the vertical expression of a horizontal desire.'

'That's just what I need to hear when I'm about to ask my mother to dance.'

'You're a good son.' I angle my head to look up at him.

'Besides, the waltz is a perfectly proper dance. No one watching you move so elegantly would ever guess what a beast you are in the bedroom.'

'Beast?'

'Totally in a good way. You're safe to dance with your mom.'

And it does my heart good to see her smile up at him as he offers her his hand. It also makes my pulse skitter as he glances back on the way to the dance floor, sending me a smouldering look.

I thank the waiter as he fills my champagne flute and ask him for water for the table before flicking open my purse and pulling out my tiny compact for a quick makeup check. As I sense someone behind me, I shift very slightly to the left, assuming it's the waiter with a fresh carafe when something gold flickers in my mirror.

My spirits sink just a little, and I slide my compact away. As my attention lifts, I come face-to-face with Amélie as she lowers herself into Josephine's chair.

She's a vision in gold, her dress covering every inch of her lithe body, clinging to her like a second skin from her neck to her wrists, where a diamond sparkles on the fourth finger of her left hand.

Deluded bitch.

Actually, I revise my first impressions. She looks like an Oscar statuette.

For the porn industry.

A brunette fills Remy's seat, a blonde sitting in the chair next to Amélie. I guess what we have here is the high school bully and her slightly drunken posse.

'I don't believe we've been introduced formally,' she purrs, her mouth more pout than smile.

'No, I don't believe we have,' I reply placidly. 'I also don't believe we need to be.'

Her blonde friend at the other side of her rattles off something fast and French under her breath, but I get the general gist.

'I don't know whether you know,' I say, addressing the blonde, 'but *Américaine idiote* pretty much stands on its own in English.'

Now who's the dumb bitch?

Go ahead, glare all you want. I don't give a flying fuck . . .

'What a gorgeous dress.' Amélie's comment seems sincere, but she's not finished yet. 'And such an improvement on the one you were looking at in *Deuxième Amour*.' I find myself frowning as she turns her head over her shoulder, addressing her friend. 'That's the place in Monaco-Ville I was telling you about, Colette. Second Love, it's called in English. The store that sells used designer wear.'

My skin prickles as her attention returns, this time with a sneer.

'I don't know why you're looking so superior. You were obviously in the same place as I was.' Apparently. Though I don't recall seeing her.

'Yes, but she was dropping off,' her bitch of a friend replies on her behalf. 'She wasn't thinking of buying other people's used clothes.' She says *used clothes* as though I was trawling the bargain bins for something in the colour herpes.

'I donate the resale value to charity,' Amélie adds with careless shrug.

Sure. And I sell smack to kids at the local playground.

'Well, bless your heart,' I say, going all Southern on her skinny butt. 'I guess that's easy to do when you're buying the stuff with someone else's credit card.'

'Yes, it is nice,' she purrs. 'And I'm sure Remy doesn't mind picking up the cost.' Her hand coasts down the long line of her sleeve from shoulder to wrist. 'Especially when he gets to rip those clothes off me any time he wishes.'

'Bat. Shit. Crazy,' I mutter under my breath.

'What did you say?'

'I said your parents must be so proud.' I pick up my glass, despite telling myself I'd take it easy on the stuff, but when you're swimming with sharks, you do what you can to not act like chum. Taking a decorous sip, I set it back down. 'Well, apart from the fact you weren't able to seal the deal with him, so there's very little chance of him ripping anything off you. Except maybe that fancy black credit card out of your cold grasping hand.' I throw in a tiny shrug, kind of an *oops, sorry. Not!*

'You don't know what you're talking about.'

I sigh, allowing my gaze to roam over her. 'I know you just don't have what it takes.'

'*Je t'emmerde, salope,*' she spits. Basically, fuck you, bitch.

'Well, I tell you, *Emily,*' I say, getting a kick out of her ripple of indignation. 'The way I see it, I am the only bitch between the pair of us who is getting fucked. By Remy at least.'

Leaning across the brunette between us, she makes as though to grab my hand, her words low and furious and in French and really not making a lot of sense. Until they do.

'He will tire of you, you are *vulgaire.* Cheap! You have novelty value only. You want him for his money—the house and the jet. The dress that you wear! But he will come back to me.'

'I guess that's where our opinions differ. The fact that Remy is rich doesn't interest me,' I reply, sliding out of my chair. I'm so serene and so cool and proud of the way I'm handling myself because what I really want to say is, *bitch,*

467

please; I don't live in no house. I live in a chateau! 'The fact he's hung like a horse and fucks me like the Energizer Bunny however, does.'

So that wasn't exactly serene or cool and worse, as I turn, I find myself face-to-face with Remy's mother. Her hazel eyes as wide as saucers while, behind her, Everett looks like he's about to explode. With laughter.

'I'm sorry you had to hear that, Josephine.' I tilt my chin a fraction higher than it's been all evening. 'But it's true. Or at least it was in the beginning. I also happen to love him. And sure, the house is very nice, and it keeps the mystery somewhat alive that I don't have to wash his sweaty gym gear or his underwear, but I know I'd love him as much if we were living in a hovel. I'd just have to teach him to do his own laundry, I guess.'

With a nod in her direction, and though I may live to regret it, I take the arm that Everett offers.

'Did you see her face? That was fucking hilarious, Rose.'

'Stop. A compliment *and* you used my name. Are you trying to kill me?' I keep my eyes straight ahead because if I look at him, I might be tempted to sneak a peek at the table behind us, and I'm not sure that will do me any good.

'What happened to Remy?'

'He was waylaid by one of the journalists from *Monaco-Matin*. Publicity for a good cause and all that.'

'Okay, so where are *we* going?' I ask, still tottering alongside him.

'We're going to dance. I reckon one quick spin around the dance floor and the Weird Sisters will have pissed off elsewhere.'

'The Weird Sisters?'

'You know, double, double, toil, and trouble. Fire burn

468

and cauldron bubble. Get a black Amex card, then firm and good is the charm.'

'Pretty sure those weren't Shakespeare's words. Anyway, I thought you were working tonight.'

'I'm working it.'

'Ha. Not with me, you're not.'

'Nah, you're the job. At least until lover boy gets back.'

'Does that mean I get to boss you around?'

'Nope.' At the edge of the dance floor, his hands move into the proper position; right hand high on my back, his left hand holding mine. It's a hold much more proper than Remy's earlier one.

'Ooh. Someone knows how to dance,' I tease as we join the revellers on the dance floor.

'The Army teaches a man many things.' As I open my mouth to speak, he adds, 'And most of them are unfit for discussion in polite company, Heidi, so don't ask.'

Urgh! And back to Heidi again. 'It's the braids, right?'

'Something like that.'

'You know, you're like the kid in grade school who annoys because he doesn't have the emotional maturity to say he likes a person.' Oh my God, the man's face is priceless as he glowers down at me. 'That was a joke, Everett, not a dick. No need to take it so hard.'

On the downside, he doesn't speak to me again once—not for the whole song. And as I'm deposited back to the table, or rather dumped, Remy still isn't back.

'Journalists,' his mother offers with a shrug, breaking her conversation with the man to her right. 'They can be so demanding. I'm sure he won't be too much longer.' She smiles kindly before returning to her tête-à-tête, leaving me to check my phone, as a girl does to fill in the time.

Since I last checked, I've received a text from an unknown

number. There's a video file attached. My thumb hovers over the file as I debate the merits of playing versus pressing delete, knowing in my heart and in my head that no good can come from pressing play.

A corrupted file?

A ruined phone?

It's not enough that curiosity killed the cat as I press play anyway.

45

ROSE

I TAKE a sip of my drink and use the napkin it was served with to catch a tear at the corner of my eye, hating myself a little more as I hit play for the second time. Out here, in the hotel cocktail bar, Ella Fitzgerald croons quietly from concealed speakers about the wayward ways of a wayward town where love is bought and sold.

Love that's lightly spoiled, she sings.

It's something that sounds painfully familiar right now.

I turn up the sound on my phone, angling my body in such a way no one could mistake my desire to be left alone. Left alone to watch and listen this time.

The screen fills with the image of Remy's bedroom; the one at the penthouse, which is strange enough, but not quite as strange as the sight of Amélie standing at the end of the bed in nothing but her underwear. A lace balconette bra, her long legs encased in matching black stockings. The tiny triangle of her panties. *Probably a thong.* A wine glass dangles from her hand, her expression one of extreme self-satisfaction.

The sound of the door pushing open.

Footsteps on the hardwood floor.

Her smile as Remy says her name, his tone low and husky.

His shirt is open, the ladder of his abs ripple in the light as he turns and sets down his own wine glass, his own expression giving nothing away as he watches her cross her legs at the ankle, cocking one hip. She drapes her arm across her body, all long legs and lithe beauty.

The sound cuts out, replaced by the hum of static, though her mouth moves as she lifts the glass to her lips, eyeing him expectantly over the rim.

She nods gracefully, probably in response to something he says.

Come closer.

I've missed you.

Take your panties off.

Get on your knees.

Let's fuck.

My mind swims with a dozen suggestions, a dozen more answers as she struts across the room to him.

Just once more.

Once more to add to the total

I won't tell.

A whispered word. A pout. She's sliding her arms around his neck, her fingertips at his nape. Her last glance at the camera is a triumphant one as Remy's fingers trail up her slender arm.

Then the screen goes black, jumping back to the starting frame.

It's just seconds long. A minute? Two tops.

How long does it take to ruin?

Ruin a night.

Ruin a relationship.

Ruin an appetite for good liquor.

Or maybe not as I throw back the remains of my margarita.

'Well, if it isn't the girl who likes sparkles.'

Despite positioning myself as I have, it seems some people can't take a hint.

'I'm sorry?' Flipping my phone face down, I turn my head over my shoulder, not quite in the mood to give a fuck about appearances.

'Rose, right? You helped me buy my grandma a gift at the Omega store?'

'Oh. Right.' I allow my eyebrows to relax as the man rests his forearm on the marble bar top.

'You wouldn't let me buy you a coffee, but maybe you'll allow me to buy you a drink.'

I glance at my glass and decide why the hell not. After all, I'm not the one who's been cavorting with my ex in my skivvies. Though maybe cavorting is stretching it some, because despite the protestations of my mystery sender's second text (that's my mystery sender also known as Amélie, I'd guess) I don't believe for one minute that the clip cut where it did in deference to the intimacy between them.

I'm not only saying I don't believe they were screwing. I'm also saying I believe the whole thing to be a setup. Fake. Total bullshit. But that doesn't mean I'm not very, very pissed. Because I am.

Je suis hors de moi. I am very angry. Énèrvee. Pissed off!

'I think I would like that. Carson, right?'

Drinks are ordered, and I turn from my self-imposed timeout to spend a while with a cute guy who wants to talk to me. And talk we do. He tells me he's in construction, but I guess he means property development. There aren't many construction workers who wear fifty thousand-dollar watches and smell like oud wood, as far as I can tell. He tells me he studied architecture at Cornell but that he doesn't practice, instead taking an interest in the family business.

'So concierge, huh? You must have some crazy stories.'

'Crazy stories from crazy rich people?'

He brings his beer—the very unfancy Kronenbourg 1664 —to his mouth as he nods.

'Rich people like you, you mean?'

'My family is wealthy,' he says, setting down his glass again. 'Me? Not so much.'

'Says the man wearing handmade shoes.' I tip my head forward, glancing down at his feet. 'Called it.'

'These were a gift,' he protests and, as though uncomfortable, hooks his feet around the legs of the barstool.

'Mm-hmm.' I slide him a sceptical look.

'Okay, so I've got money,' he says with a chuckle. 'It doesn't make me a bad person, does it?'

'I don't know you well enough to decide.'

'Well, I think we need to do something about that.' He clinks his glass against mine, and I suddenly realise he thinks we're flirting. *Damn.*

'You know I've got a boyfriend, right?'

'Yeah. A boyfriend you've left at the gala, I'm guessing.' He tips his glass in the vague direction of the ball room. 'I'm right, aren't I?'

'Maybe.'

'Want to talk about it?'

'Not particularly.' An ache creeps up the back of my throat, though I swallow it down.

'Come on. We were getting along so well. Don't go cold on me now.'

'I guess you were headed to the gala, too.'

'The monkey suit gave it away.' I nod as he straightens his

cufflinks, then his sleeves. 'I have a ticket, but I didn't even make it into the room.'

'Oh?'

'I couldn't bring myself to.' A smile flitters across his face. It doesn't last very long.

'At four thousand euros a ticket, I'd at least made sure I was there for the dinner.'

'Was it worth it?'

'Was it worth four thousand euros?' I shake my head. 'If I were you, I'd go help myself to a couple of bottles of champagne.'

'Where are your bottles then?' He hooks his arm over the back of his stool with a grin, glancing across the bar to where my clutch lies.

'That's different. I didn't pay for my ticket. But then you already guessed that. Probably even back at the Omega store.'

'You can't blame a guy for wanting to take a pretty girl for a coffee.'

'You were a couple of months too late for that even then.'

'Because of Remy Durrand.' The way he says the name of the man I love tells me all I need to know.

'So you did hear.' At the store when I'd mentioned Remy's name to Yuri. I wonder what else he heard as I take another sip of my drink. I set it down, not quite meeting his gaze.

'Yeah, I heard. It seems we're both sitting out here for the same reason.'

'I doubt that very much,' I reply, staring at my glass still.

'We're sitting at this bar because he's in there and not out here.' He taps his forefinger against the bar top to emphasise his point, and though he might be right, I'm not about to agree. 'My guess is you've found out some things about Remy that aren't in keeping with the man you think you know.'

'If you're trying to get me to agree, to say anything against him, you're wasting your time.'

'Well, honey, I don't need to hear your reasons to hate him. I have my own.'

'I don't hate him,' I reply through a deep sigh. 'Just the opposite.'

'Then I don't envy you. He must be a hard man to love.'

'You're wrong. Loving isn't supposed to be hard. That's why they call it *falling* in love. Because it happens so fast, it's impossible to do anything about it.'

'Falling in love might be easy. Staying in love with a man who treats you wrong sounds like the definition of insanity.'

'I shouldn't be here,' I suddenly decide because this feels wrong. It's not the act of sitting in a bar with a man, chatting. But rather sitting with a man who seems intent on telling me who the man I love really is. 'Thank you for the drink.' I slide my clutch from the bar, taking out a few euros to leave as a tip. 'But I think I'll get back to the party.' And Remy. Because this text isn't going to sort itself out.

'Wait.' His fingers curl around my forearm and I find myself staring at them. 'Remy Durrand is not a good man. Maybe you haven't found that out yet, but you will.'

'You're mistaken if you think I need some kind of protection. Remy would never hurt me.'

'No,' intones a deep and familiar voice, 'but he would hurt the man who's touching you.'

I try not to turn, to look at Remy, but the pull of him is too great. It's unfair that anger looks so good on him, his eyes the colour of stormy seas. Meanwhile, my twelve-hour lipstick is likely long gone, and the tears I've tidied with the napkin have probably ruined my smoky eye.

'Well, if it isn't the cunt of Monte-Cristo.'

My head whips to the amiable man I've spent the last

thirty minutes with. His fingers tighten on my arm, the sudden venom in his tone a shock to me.

'I'd say it's good to see you, but we'd both know I'd be lying, Durrand.'

'Let go of her, Hayes.' Remy's command is so cold I think it might've been less frightening if he'd actually yelled.

'Maybe I don't want to. Maybe I'm tired of having things taken away from me.'

'This isn't business, Hayes. If you have something to say to me about business, you should make an appointment. Not lay your hands on the woman I love.'

'Hear that, sweetheart? The man with *no* heart says he loves.' Sliding from his stool, he brings his mouth to my ear. 'The man is a fraud, just like the watch he wears. You can't trust a thing he says.'

'Let go of me, Carson. We were just having a drink.' I'm not sure who needs to hear this; the man who has my arm or the man staring daggers at him.

'You have my card,' Carson murmurs. His grip relaxes, but he doesn't immediately release me. 'If you need me, I'm only a call away.'

'She won't be needing you.' Remy's declaration is filled with menace as I take a step towards him. 'I'll be seeing you, Hayes,' he adds as I brush past him without the slightest intention of being the bone these two dogs are baying for.

'What the fuck was that all about?' One grip is exchanged for another, Remy's question a low growl in my ear.

'What does it matter?' I retort, trying to pull away. After the drama, my heart is now smarting. I dash the back of my hand against my cheeks, reluctant to let him see the manifestation of my anger.

'Rose, what is it? Did he hurt you?'

'Him?' His head jerks back at my tone, almost as though

I'd dealt him a slap. 'Carson Hayes hasn't hurt me. You, however . . .' My gaze rakes over every painfully beautiful inch of him.

'What are you talking about?' This isn't an appeal for information but more a deflection. A swerve. 'One minute, you were dancing with Rhett, and the next, you were gone. How the fuck do you know him?'

'He was in the store when I got your watch fixed. Not that it's any of your business.' I steeple my hands over my nose, the tips of my fingers at the very corner of my eyes, blotting those building tears. 'I helped him choose a watch for his grandmother's birthday.'

'Carson Hayes doesn't have a grandmother,' he growls again. 'His grandfather has a succession of women in his life younger than his grandson.'

'How very Riviera,' I snipe. One walk along any marina on the Côte d'Azure and you'll see rich old men surrounded by a bevy of beautiful and much younger women.

'And you just happened to see him in the store, but you didn't think to mention it to me?'

'Why would I mention it? I mean, it's not like *I* had a fiancée hiding somewhere, is it?' I retort, using the same tone. 'You don't get to make me feel like shit, Remy Durrand. Not when I was doing something nice for you. I'm not the one who owns liar pants.'

'What?' His brows draw down over angry green eyes. 'Why weren't you there for the speeches?'

'The speeches? Or *your* speech? Urgh!' My feet start to move again to put distance between me and this situation. Me and this fuckup.

What's the big deal?
Like I speak French!

I don't get far as he spins me around, pressing me against a nearby door, my palms flat against the wood.

'Listen to me, I don't care about the speech. I just want you to tell me what this is about?'

'I'm sorry I wasn't there, but while I know you like an audience, I'm pretty sure I've seen enough of you today.' I snatch my hands away, sliding out between his body and the doorframe. I'm so angry right now, I can't even think. I need a moment alone to process how best to approach this fucking text.

'You can't leave.'

'Pretty sure that's what I'm doing,' I mutter, sweeping down the long corridor to the elevator.

'Tell me what I'm supposed to have done,' he roars after me, bringing my feet to an immediate stop. I swing around.

'You lied to me again. You were with *her* in the penthouse. Drinking wine, half undressed, her in her fucking underwear!' My fists pound his chest, and I wonder how I got here—got to be in front of him when he was behind me just a moment ago.

One giant leap for Rose.

One angry blow for Remy.

One aching heart.

'When are you going to stop hiding things from me?'

46

REMY

My fingers loop her wrists as she stares up at me, her eyes bright with recriminations and tears. I want to wrap her in my arms and squeeze my love into her. Make her understand this is who I am. That I don't know how to be *other*. That I will always seek to protect her. That I'll do anything in my power not to hurt her, even if that includes hiding things.

Motorcycles, yachts, helicopters. Money, motivations, inheritance. Where would I even begin to explain? Tell of the secrets I keep? And how could I describe to her the magnitude of my dread when I'd returned to the table to find she was missing. And then to see her sitting with Carson Hayes, a man whose legacy I have ruined?

She could never understand. Not in a million years.

'Perhaps you're right. Perhaps I should've told you, but I didn't see what that would achieve.'

'It might've stopped me from feeling like shit.' Her voice is husky with emotion, laced with pain. 'She sent me a video, Remy. She was in your bedroom.' Her fists unfold, her forehead and fingers pressed to my chest as though she's not sure if she'd like to hold me tighter or disappear.

I underestimated Amélie's level of cunning. I should've known a revenge fuck wasn't on her agenda. *Just revenge.*

'There was nothing to show. I didn't touch her.' Surely, any recording would reveal just that? My mind flits back to that evening. Lingerie. Wine glasses. My shirt already open. I can see how it might've looked, but the evidence is hardly damning.

'It doesn't mean it doesn't hurt.' Her words are muffled against my chest, and though I long to wrap her in my arms, it feels safer to keep her manacled.

'She wasn't there by invitation, and nothing happened, I swear it. It happened the day I asked you to bring me my fencing kit. I got home that evening, and she was there. A few words passed between us. I told her to get dressed and get out, yet I left first.'

Her gaze rises to mine. 'You just left her there?'

'It seemed easier. I haven't been back to the place since. She was the reason I was staying on the yacht.'

'Why didn't you tell me any of this?'

'I didn't see how it would be helpful, or what it would achieve. I have no interest in Amélie Pastor.'

'What about me? Do you have any feelings for me?'

'I love you.' My reply is instant and vehement. 'I would do anything for you, you know that.'

'Then you have to start telling me the truth.'

'Come with me.' Without letting go of her wrists, I move her in the direction of the elevator. When the doors open, we step inside, and I swipe my card against the sensor, keying in the number of the top floor.

'Where are we going?'

'To somewhere I can show you my truth.'

'I sense that's a euphemism.' She huffs unhappily, unfolding her purse from where it's pressed between her ribs

481

and the inside of her arm. The action pulls my attention to the angry rise and fall of her breasts. 'What are you doing?' she asks as I take the tiny purse from her hands and slip it into my jacket pocket.

'How could you think for one minute I would want anyone but you?' My gaze drinks her in, bold and possessive

'That's not why I'm angry.' She angles her chin, her gaze burning defiantly.

'Isn't it? Not even for a minute?' I step closer, my hand pressed against her ribs, just as her purse was. She feels so delicate here, her ribs the fine lines of an artist's brushstroke. And I should know because I've catalogued every dip and curve of her.

Her chest expands, but I don't give in to the temptation, keeping my eyes on her face. 'When I saw you with Carson Hayes, I would've happily ripped off his arms for touching you. Tell me you don't feel the same way about Amélie.'

'This is about you keeping things from me.'

'Everyone has secrets, Rose. We even hide the truth from ourselves. But this, this is something else.'

'It isn't jealousy, Remy.'

'Isn't it? Not even a little bit? Because right now, I myself am feeling very covetous,' I whisper as I trace the slope of her shoulder, my finger sweeping down her bare arm. She shivers as I reach her hand, her breath hitching a little as I press it between us to where I'm rock hard. 'He touched you, and you're mine. I want you to feel that possession, Rose. I want to obliterate his touch with mine.'

'Except you don't own me.' In the soft light of the elevator, her gaze is burned honey, her words a soft barb.

'I own you here.' I press my lips to the rise of her breasts. 'As you own me.'

As her fingers tighten around my cock, the elevator doors

slowly open, which is probably good timing, considering the placement of the security cameras.

Six steps and we're at the door to my suite. Two more and we're inside, the door slamming closed. Our mouths immediately fuse, her hands grasping and frantic as she grapples with the lapels of my jacket, pushing it from my shoulders.

'Let's go inside.'

'No.' Her response is immediate and adamant. She gives up on my jacket, her hands at my chest now instead as she backs me up against the wall. I'm so sorry I hurt her but so ready to make this about something else when she drops to her knees in the foyer, her fingers plucking at my shirt and my belt.

As much as I want this, my conscience gets the better of me.

This is my fuckup. I've made her hurt. I don't deserve—

'Rose, *non*. Come here. Let me touch you.'

'Fuck you, Remy Durrand.'

The clink of my belt and the roar of my zipper, and any protest I might have is swallowed as her cool fingers wrap my cock. I hiss out a quiet curse as she squeezes just the right amount.

'You let her touch you.' In the dark, her words are a recrimination, her dress a shimmering pool in the moonlight.

'No.' My denial is a carnal, needy groan. 'I pushed her away because she wasn't you.'

'Not in the video. In your office that first day. I didn't even know who she was, yet you let her kiss you. You didn't even look at me. You *wouldn't* look at me.'

'I'm sorry.' My apology is slurred as she runs her thumb over my crown. I sound drunk—drunk on her. 'I was protecting you.'

'I'm a big girl,' she taunts, her breath a hot brush against my flesh. Her mouth is so close, and I ache for her. 'I can look after myself.'

My second curse isn't so quiet as she takes me to the back of her throat and holds me there. My back bucks from the wall, pleasure twisting my insides. I am stuck between a rock and a soft place, quite literally, as she works me between her fist and her lips, her tongue the epitome of wickedness.

'*Suce-moi. Suck me, Rose. Fais-moi jouir. Make me come.*'

My thoughts are wicked, my demands probably making very little sense as I tangle my fingers in her hair, plucking out the pins, desperate to own her from the ends of these strands to the rasp of her breath.

'Are you looking at me now, Remy?' Her mouth glistens, and her eyes shine.

'*Je te vois.*' I swallow back my groan as she sweeps her thumb across my wet head. 'I see you.'

'What do you see?'

'The woman I love making me beg for mercy.'

'Mercy you don't deserve.'

My moans are deeper, rougher, every inch of me burning, trembling, yearning as she bends to take me in her mouth once again. She sucks me with a breathtaking urgency, her moans rocking through me and disintegrating my brain.

'Please, I need you.' If I don't do this now, I'll be nothing but an impression burned into the wall. A flash of heat and I'll be gone.

Hands under her arms, I bring her mouth to mine in a kiss that's hard and unforgiving. I suck on her tongue like she sucked me, then run my teeth down her neck as I whisper my litany of dirty promises in French and in English and God only knows what else. Our positions reversed, I gather her dress, pushing it upwards. Tan legs, the very apex of her covered in a wisp of cream lace. I rest my hands in the dip of her waist as I press my face against her and inhale. Slowly, I slip her panties down her legs, her legs trembling as they travel. I pull down her zipper as I rise, the satin soft fabric at her chest beginning to gape, the reveal not quick enough for my senses. I bring my hands to the neckline.

'If you rip this dress, so help me, I will never take you in my mouth again.'

'Don't make promises you have no wish to keep,' I tease softly, pinching her nipple over the silk.

'Conceited man.'

'I'll buy you a dozen dresses.' I press my words to her neck. 'A hundred. A thousand.'

'But it won't be this dress.'

I find myself smiling, the picture of her already burned into my memory. 'You always look so beautiful, ma Rose. In a pretty dress on the stairs, on your knees full of me. Pressed up against a wall, your mouth wet, and clothes half undone.' She shivers as I run my tongue across the rise of her chest, peeling away the remains of her dress until the round fullness of her breasts are revealed.

She is the picture of a modern-day Venus; no virtue and all want.

Her breath hitches as my thumbs trace the soft undersides of her breasts, the pads sliding up those heavenly slopes. She rolls in her bottom lip as she turns her cheek to the wall, refusing to give in to her sigh. But as her nipples tighten, and I brush my mouth over them, our movements suddenly become frantic. Wild. My jacket hits the floor, my tie pulled open, my shirt half unbuttoned as my fingers slide between her satin thighs. As her legs widen to accept my touch, I fill her with my fingers, again and again, her pleasure in the tenor of her cries and the sweetness coating my fingertips.

Without any real cognisance, I lift her from the floor, slam her down on my cock, and press my wet fingers into her mouth.

'I want no one but *you*.' I punctuate my words with my thrusts, desperate to fill her everywhere as her dark eyes silently beg. 'You fill my *thoughts*. You fill my *head*. I have *carved* your *name* across my *heart*.'

Her body begins to jerk against me, the hot clasp of her unravelling as I hold her between the wall and my cock. Her entire body trembles against mine, pulses around mine, her fingernails digging into my shoulders as though to prevent her fall. But fall she does, the pitch of her cries frantic as I follow her. A bolt of white heat lances through me, almost wiping the strength from my legs as it blesses me with a moment of clarity. I want to protect her. Keep her. Make her whole. But I can't do any of that without her owning a part of my soul.

Her dress lies across a chair, her shoes abandoned to another room somewhere, and my own clothing discarded in a heap. We've fucked. We've made love. We've whispered promises and chanted prayers. We should be sleeping, yet we aren't.

And I can't get the image of Carson Hayes out of my head. *His hand on her*. It's not just that he touched her. It's the way he looked at her. The way he looked at me.

'What did Hayes whisper to you in the bar?' Though I keep my voice even as I ask, she still stiffens against me.

'I don't remember.'

'You're a very bad liar, ma Rose.' I run my fingers through her hair, as much for my reassurance as for hers. She sighs, settling her hand between my chest and her chin.

'He said you're as fake as the watch you wear.' Her eyes don't meet mine, though she traces the contour of my wrist above the leather. 'I didn't want to tell you.' Her chest expands against mine with a deep inhale. 'But your grandfather's watch is apparently a fake.'

'I know.'

'You do?' She pushes up, her shock evident even through the tangle of her hair. She bats it away.

'Of course.' I bring her fingers to my lips, placing a kiss against her knuckles before smoothing the hair from her brow. 'My mother's family were successful merchants going back to when Monaco really began. But my grandfather wasn't really motivated by money, so I'm told. Unlike me, I can hear you thinking.' I pull a lock of her hair to accompany my teasing tone.

'I didn't say a word.'

'Money isn't a motivator for me, you know. Not really.'

'That's because you have lots of it. Money motivates the poor. Power motivates the rich. Besides, what's not to like about being rich? It's like being Batman. You get the car and all the gadgets, the ear of Gotham City's mayor. You get to do what you want, be who you want, and then there's the really cool suit. Only yours is custom made, and you don't look like a toy in it.'

'Sounds like you've given it some thought.'

'You were telling me about your grandfather.' Her smile is a cynical quirk; it's time to move on.

'Yes. I suppose he had a philosophy, though one that I didn't really appreciate until I met you.'

'You're not going to tell me he was a time traveller, are you?'

'*Non*. He was a man of his time. One who believed the only luxury in life is time. Because time you cannot get back.'

'Ah, so the fake watch was worth nothing.'

'And time is worth everything.'

'And that's why you wear it? As a reminder?'

'Perhaps.' But I don't need to be reminded anymore. Because now I have her.

'I'm sure Carson will be very disappointed to find your fake watch has meaning.'

'You're on first-name terms already?'

'Calm your farm. I barely know the man.'

'I know him better. Trust me when I say this is an acquaintance you don't want to cultivate.'

'You stay away from Amélie,' she murmurs, 'and I'll see what I can do.'

'Rose, I'm being serious.' I push up onto my elbow to better look at her. Dark hair splayed across the pillow; her eyes clear. 'Stay away from him.'

'What is it between you two?' she says, settling back into the space between my shoulder.

'It's just business.' And a small matter of blackmail that his grandfather brought on himself a long time ago. Though he is now old and wizened, I have no sympathy for him. Men who prey on the weak are the lowest of the low.

What is more personal than blackmail and perhaps attempted murder?

'Speaking of business, you missed my mother's big announcement earlier.'

'I'm sure she won't mind. In fact, I'm sure she won't even have noticed.' Her body has begun to relax, her breathing to slow.

'She's donated her share of The Wolf Group to her charity.'

'Really?' At this, she rouses as she asks, 'Did you know? Before the announcement, I mean?'

I shake my head, my mind flipping to the standing ovation she received and the way she seemed to be almost lit from within. 'I'm generally not kept in my mother's confidence.' Or she mine.

'How do you feel about it? I mean, I guess that would've been your inheritance, right?'

'I'm proud of her,' I admit. 'I already have enough.' Enough for several lifetimes over. 'Go to sleep, Rose.' I press my lips to her head. 'We can talk in the morning.'

'That sounds ominous,' she says through a yawn.

Ominous? No.

Life-changing? I do hope so. Because I'm coming to realise that man should desire his life to be blessed with few things. He should want health, comfort, and to arrive wizened and grey to his own death, his heart filled with love.

47

ROSE

THE ROOM IS STILL DARK when I wake, the silver drapes drawn closed. God knows what time it is. Well, God and my phone, but only one of them will tell me the exact time. *If I knew where it was.* Remy had watched the video file sometime last night, tossing my phone as though it had offended him, and not the bitch on the screen, as he'd muttered something unintelligible, his tone one of supreme disgust.

I wonder where he is. I can't hear the shower or much of anything. Just the quiet hum of the central air circulating the room.

Wherever he is, he won't be long, I'm sure. And while we might be over last night, I also know it won't be the last conversation we ever have about him hiding the truth from me. But it has to get better. Maybe he can learn to open up in time? In the meantime, I guess I'll always have making up to look forward to.

I roll onto my back, pushing the bird's nest of hair from my face; half unravelled braids and bits of professional backcombing, along with the knots from Remy's fingers. It's going to take me an age to untangle, not to mention give me a sore head. *Problems not for now*, I think, as I stretch out along the bed, my fingers pointed to the wall behind me, my toes towards the bottom of the bed as I savour the delicious aches last night have left me with. I was so angry. Angry with her, angry with him, and so sick and tired of feeling like a puppet on a string. But I got my payback, even if I was on my knees. I made him dance to my tune. And then, he made me dance to his. So I ache. It's like I've had the best kind of workout, the only kind of workout, as I stare at the pale ceiling with a wide grin, studying a chink of light from a gap in the drapes as it dances off the glass light fixture.

'A smile. You must've had pleasant dreams.' His assertion is accompanied by a soft, husky laugh. Meanwhile, I commando roll across the bed, grabbing the sheet as I go.

'One of these days, you'll give me a heart attack,' I complain, curling my legs under me as I push myself up against the pillows. 'What time is it?'

'Early still.'

'Then why are you up? And dressed?' I rub my palm against my eyes and take a second look at the tall, dark, handsome, and infuriatingly sexy man sitting in the chair at the end of the bed. 'Your shirt is all creased.'

'It's also missing a button,' he says, dipping his chin and glancing down. The recollection of how it happened is a hitch in one corner of his mouth. 'I was going to send it to the laundry overnight but then you fell asleep in my arms, and I just didn't want to be anywhere else.'

My heart does a little leap. 'Beautifully answered.'

One hand slides over the flat planes of his stomach, and I consider ruining a few more buttons before we're through.

'Thank you. And also true.'

'So it's to be a walk of shame through the hotel for us? Or

are you going to smuggle us out in the service elevator? Or maybe send someone to fetch clothes?'

'What? And risk someone coming across your purple friend? What was it again? The pussy pounder?'

I bury my face in my hands with a groan. 'Never ever say that again.'

'Pussy?' he asks blandly. 'Or pounder? Or was it the coming across it that you have a particular objection to.'

'I have never . . .' My words trail away as he begins to chuckle, and I crack my fingers to peer out at him. 'Are you done?' I ask, my tone very slightly piqued. 'And like I'd even keep that thing in a drawer. It's stowed away in my suitcase, thank you very much.'

'I should think so. Weapons are supposed to be kept secured.'

I launch a pillow at his head, which he bats away easily.

'One more thing.' He holds his forefinger in the air. 'Would you care to explain why I'm listed under your phone as *Monsieur Baguette*?' I notice in his other hand he holds my phone.

'Have you been going through my contacts?'

'No. Why, do you think I should?' He glances at my phone, then back again, his expression bland.

'If you want to look, you should ask.' Because if you're thinking about Carson Hayes and getting all jealous again, I might just enjoy setting you on your ass. Again. 'And if you do, you should also be prepared to hand over your own phone.'

At this, he reaches into his pocket, pulling out his own phone. It lands on the sheet next to my legs with a quiet *slap*.

'Feel free,' he offers. 'I wasn't looking through your contacts, by the way. I was looking for your phone by calling it. Or at least, someone called Mr Baguette was.'

I pull another pillow from behind me, this time to hide behind. 'Let me know when you're finished tormenting me.'

'*Mon petite hérisson.* You're just too much fun not to.'

'Calling me a prickly hedgehog is not endearing.' I lift my head from the pillow, intending to repeat this louder for his hearing, when I squeal as his hand clamps around my ankle, pulling me flat against mattress.

'I intend tormenting you until my very last breath.' He climbs over me, his clothed body caging my semi-covered one. I notice he has his shoes on. 'All this silken skin just begging to be kissed.'

'Why do you have your shoes on?' And why am I not just going with this?

'How much do you love me, Rose?' His face above mine is so close his features are blurry.

'Enough to turn a walk through the damned hotel in last night's clothes into a victory lap.'

'Rose, I've already been out this morning. In these clothes. Without giving a damn for who saw me or what they thought.'

'Where'd you go?'

'First, tell me how much you love me.' Though his mouth delivers the summons playfully, his gaze demands.

'This sounds suspiciously like you've done something wrong,' I counter, cupping his face as I narrow my own gaze. 'Like you're trying to get me to say I love you so when you tell me what you've done wrong, you can remind me of my earlier declarations.'

'*Mon Dieu,*' he appeals to the ceiling. 'I already know you love me. I'm asking you how much.'

'I'm right, aren't I? You're trying to trick me.'

'I might've done something a little crazy, yes. Something a little out of character. Something that requires your love *and* your encouragement.' His lips play at smiling, not quite giving in.

'I need you to move.'

'Afterwards. First answer me.'

'No, Remy. First I need to pee.'

My heart pounds in the silence as he stares down at me, but *ohmygodohmygod, I really need to pee. Like, now!*

He nods and flips over onto his back, blowing out a harsh breath as I roll from the bed, trying to drag the sheet with me but eventually giving up and making a dash for the door. I do my thing, brush my teeth and my hair, thanks to an excellent amenity kit . . . which I'd ordinarily pop in my case, along with all the miniatures. Except, I don't have a case. Or clean underwear. Or even suitable daytime clothing. But what I do have is a hot hunk of man in the other room waiting to torture me some more. So, I slip on the white robe hanging on the back of the bathroom door and step out into the bedroom.

Light now floods the room. The bed is still a mess, though Remy isn't in it. Instead, he's kneeling on the floor. Kneeling on one knee, more specifically. I clasp my hand to my runaway heart as he curls his finger in a *come-hither* gesture.

And I hither—I hither like a screw drawn to a magnet.

'I couldn't sleep,' he begins, his mouth twisted in such a way that I feel like I'm waiting for the punchline. But he's on his knees, right? In front of me. So, if this is a joke, he'd better be ready for a throwdown. When he takes my hand in his, I swear, I no longer need to breathe.

'I tried to think of how I'd lived my life before you were a part of it, and I couldn't. I couldn't remember how I filled my days and my nights without you. Then I knew. My days and nights going forward? I need you in them. Forever and always.'

I'm smiling so wide right now, my insides set to dance mode.

'Then I started to wonder how I could do this. How I could ask you *this* question. Should I take you out on the yacht, then on to the speedboat to a secluded cove. Get a ring and put it in a fancy shell and drop to my knee on a beach. Or should I drop it in a glass of champagne. Or maybe I could propose as we jet to Bora Bora. So many thoughts revolving around my head. How does a man choose? How does he know the woman he loves will say yes?'

'Well, usually, it starts with a question.'

'And I'm getting to it.' His teeth gleam as he presses them over my knuckle in a silent threat. 'So, I couldn't sleep, and I'd glanced at my wristwatch wondering how long I'd lain there. And I remembered.'

'The only luxury in life is time.'

'Because you can't get it back,' he adds, echoing his earlier words.

'So, I kissed you and crept from the bed. I made a call. And visited a jeweller at five o'clock this morning.'

'You must've been very persuasive.'

'Aren't I always, Roísin Samira Ryan?'

The way he says my name. I melt! No one has ever made it sound so perfect. I find myself dashing away happy tears.

'Don't cry. At least let me ask you first.' He pulls a ring from the pocket of his shirt, the diamond setting roughly the size of a quail egg. I'm exaggerating, but it is big. And sparkly. And oh, so beautiful. A platinum band with delicate filigree accents.

'Do you like it?' I nod as he twists the band between his forefinger and thumb, sunlight dancing across the stone's facets. 'I do, too. As soon as I saw it, I knew it was the one.' *Because there's something rose-like about it* he doesn't have to say.

495

'I love you more than I love my beautiful Chanel dress,' I find myself whispering. 'More than my Piaget watch. More than our gorgeous home, and more than the car sitting in the garage I'm not supposed to know about yet. Because they're just things. Beautiful things, but I've lived without them before. You I love so much, Remy. It's you I couldn't live without. Now, please get to the point and ask me to marry you.'

And so he does.

———

'It's so beautiful!' Fee tilts my hand to the light, marvelling at the ring on my finger.

'*Si belle*,' Charles agrees, albeit with a slight frown. 'And you are not . . .'

'Santa Claus?' I ask as he makes a fat-ist gesture with his hand.

'What?' Fee asks, her head swinging to Charles.

'He's asking if there's going to be a shotgun wedding.' My mouth twists. 'What do you think, Charlie?'

'I think nothing. I say nothing. I see nothing. I speak—'

'Too much,' Olga says, striding into the office. 'So, you will be leaving us soon?'

'Nope. Unless you know something I don't.'

'I only know a rich man will not want his wife running around after other rich men. Or women, for that matter. It is not done.'

'Well, I'll let you know when I'm a rich man's wife. But for now, I'll be at my desk, like always.'

I'd find it hard to describe the look she sends my way before her door slams.

'She's jealous,' Fee whispers. 'Charles told me she used to have a thing with Remy's dad, Emile?'

'Really?' I'm not sure why I'm pulling a face. Pot, meet kettle much?

Charles glances up from his laptop and sort of shrugs. 'I only know I saw her wis him once.'

'That doesn't necessarily mean anything, does it?'

'It depends on what she was doing on 'er knees.'

I roll in my lips to keep myself from laughing.

'That is so bad,' Fee whispers, her gaze sliding to Olga's office door. 'Oh, bloody hell!' she says, glancing at her watch. 'I'm going to be late for my afternoon spin class. I just wanted to pop in and offer you my congratulations!' she squeals a little again, throwing her arms around my shoulders and giving me one heck of a hug. 'Let's catch up soon, yeah? And you can tell me all about your wedding plans.'

'Sure!' Not that there's much to tell so far. All I know is Remy's keen to get married sooner rather than later, and I'm all for that. We've even talked about the idea of honeymooning in Australia so I can introduce him to Amber and her little tribe and, of course, Aussie wines.

'Urgh,' I find myself complaining as my phone buzzes with a text. 'I have to schlep out to Monaco One.'

'Why?' Charles looks up and pulls a face. 'It is too 'ot outside today for shopping. Go to a mall not outdoors.'

'I can't. I've got a pickup at Max Mara for a client.'

'Too bad. You will get big hair, but you can bring me back a bubble tea? Kiwi, please.'

'I'll think about it,' I reply, grabbing my purse from my desk drawer.

As I'm on my way out of the office, my cell rings with a withheld number.

'Hello, Rose speaking.'

'Rose, this is Benoît. Congratulations! Remy just told me the good news.'

'Thank you.' My smile spills from my words as I glance down at my ring again. I'm just so happy! Maybe I should get engaged every day. 'What can I do for you, Ben?'

'I wondered if you'd have time to meet me for a coffee this afternoon.'

Really? *Pourquoi?* Or in other words, why?

'Oh, I'm sorry.' And I hope that sounded sincere. 'But I'm at work until five and we have dinner reservations for seven.'

'Maybe I could visit before you leave?'

I feel my expression twist. Remy has been pretty clear about his feelings about Ben. I think he's still smarting a little he took it upon himself to explain Remy's involvement with Amélie, even if his cousin was trying to do him a favour, I'm sure.

'I'm not sure that would be a good idea,' I hedge. 'By the time I get home, the turnaround time isn't great. You know, with us living outside of the city these days.'

'Ah, yes. I forgot. Why don't I meet you at the restaurant, then? It would save me the drive. It really is quite important.'

Not so important that he'd try to save himself the inconvenience of a little drive out of the city.

'Look, I'm on my way to Monaco One now. Can you meet me there?'

'Perfect. The café near the apartments? Say, thirty minutes?'

'Sure.'

I hang up and make my way to the mall, reaching it in plenty of time to visit Max Mara first. When I get to the café, Ben is already sitting at a table in the far corner. He stands as I approach and, his hands resting on my shoulders, he presses his lips to my cheek. *Once, twice.*

'I ordered,' he says, pushing a tiny espresso cup and saucer across the table towards me. '*Café crème.* That's right, yes?'

I nod even though it isn't my go-to order. As I bring it to my lips, I repress a shiver at the bitter taste. 'What was it you wanted to see me about?' I ask, bringing the large Max Mara bag under the table and placing my purse on the floor next to it.

'This is quite difficult for me to say.' He sits straight in his chair, his lips firm. 'But I feel I must. You see, I came across some information recently, and I didn't really know what to do with it.' His expression is troubled as he glances up. Is that . . . sympathy? 'I was going to ignore it, but then Remy told me this morning that he had proposed, and you had accepted.'

'You've kind of lost me.' I bring the bitter beverage to my lips again, Ben's next words taking some time to comprehend.

'Remy hasn't told you the truth, Rose. About how he came to find you. About why you are here. About everything. Your relationship is built on a lie—a mountain of them. You deserve better than that.'

The coffee turns sour on my tongue as I watch him angle his head, his eyes filled with pity. I don't have a reply. Just a sickness washing through me.

'Of course, you should see the truth of it,' he says, reaching for a dark document wallet behind him. He begins to unpack the contents, the items dropping to the table in a blur. Some I understand. Some I can't make sense of at all. What I do know is, the document and photographs and emails are about me.

Paperwork detailing my name. My old address. My hours at The Pussy Cat.

An email trail between Rhett and someone who works for a company called BDT Security Solutions.

Photographs—dozens of them. One a close up of my face. I'd painted freckles against my cheeks with an eyeliner. I'm wearing my blonde wig with the braids over my own dark hair. As I flip the image over, there's a name in an unfamiliar hand scrawled on the back.

Heidi.

Instinctively, I know this is Everett's writing.

More photographs. Some grainy, taken from a distance, so perfect. Like the one taken in The Pussy Cat. I have a tray in one hand as the other removes a customer's hand from my ass cheek as I smile. You'd be forgiven for thinking I was enjoying myself. Another at the grocery store, my coat wrapped tight around me as I buy bread and milk and a newspaper.

But maybe this isn't all about me. There's a photograph of a couple; a glamorous blonde and an older man with his arm wrapped around her. He's wearing a dark suit and a crazy tie while she wears a tiny dress with spaghetti straps, fashions from decades ago.

'I don't know who this is,' I whisper, pushing the image back across the table even as I realise my denial is ridiculous.

'That's okay.' My skin crawls as he leans forward and covers my hand with his own. 'I don't know if this is all about you. But what I do know is Remy hasn't been honest with you. This is you, no?' He holds up a photograph. I'm wearing my Pussy Cat uniform of knee-high socks and stripper heels. My ass practically hangs out of my shorts, and my boobs sit almost under my chin.

I'm smiling in this one, too. A smile that says *I need the tips.*

'You are Heidi?'

'Just stop it.' I begin to gather the photographs, the emails, and whatever the fuck the rest of this stuff is. 'Put it away. I don't want to look at it anymore.'

'You don't want to know who you're marrying? Why he's marrying you?'

'I don't want to look at it in here,' I grate out. 'For Christ's sake, let me think.'

But thinking is something I'm beginning to struggle with. More than anger and upset, more than pain and embarrassment, I feel sick. Dizzy. Like I'm wading through glue.

'I don't feel well, Ben.' I reach for my cup, my hands knocking it over in the saucer.

'It's okay. You've had a shock,' he says, examining the dregs in the tiny vessel before righting it. He waves away someone from behind me. I suddenly very much want to ask them to stay because, though his manner is mild, the word *sinister* rings through my mind.

Sinister. Sinister. It's all I can think. But I can't say it.

Because nothing will come out of my mouth.

'I can see you find this all very upsetting. Let me put everything away and take you to Remy. I'm sure he can explain, okay?'

Yes. Remy.

I need him.

48

REMY

'Rose?'

The house is dark. No music. No dancing. No tuneless singing.

The kitchen is empty. The outer kitchen, too. Then I remember we're going out for dinner. Everyone has the night off.

Except for security, but I won't go there yet.

Because that would be admitting something is wrong, and I refuse to let my mind run with such thoughts.

'Rose?' I take the stairs two at a time, my heart lodged in my throat when I realise it's dark up here, too. Our bedroom door rebounds from the wall as I open it. The bed is made, clothes scattered across it. *Her clothes.*

Underwear. Shoes discarded on the floor. Cosmetics lying spilled.

I move to her dressing area to find coat hangers empty. Clothes lying dropped on the floor.

'*Merde.*' I turn and swipe my hand through my hair. Pull at the ends. My reflection in her mirror shocked yet not at all. Didn't I deserve this? 'Fuck! Fuck it all.'

I seem to take the staircase in one leap as I drag my phone from my pocket and dial her number.

'Pick up. Come on, pick up!' It cuts out. I dial again, and this time, the automated message informs me that the subscriber is unavailable.

I send her a text—more than one—panic invading my chest until it aches.

Where are you?

Please call.

Talk to me, Rose.

I check the rooms once more as I make my way to the office she doesn't use.

The desk lamp is on, the low light illuminating a mess of paperwork.

Photographs.

Documents.

Things she would never have seen if it were up to me.

I step closer, my heart filling with cement because what I'm looking at is betrayal.

My betrayal of her.

My phone is still in my hand. I hit call.

'Rhett. She's gone.'

'Who has?'

'Rose has left. I don't know how, but she's seen everything.'

'How the fuck can that be? *You* haven't even looked at everything.'

I didn't want to. Like a child, if I'd closed my eyes, I wouldn't be party to it all.

'I'm looking at it all now.' All of it as I begin to sift the things I know and the things I'm now learning about.

'I'm on my way.'

The phone cuts out.

49

ROSE

MY HEAD ACHES and my limbs feel like they don't belong to me, my feet numb yet tingling.

'Remy?' I push myself up to sit, the sensation under my palm as hard as stone.

'Good. You're awake.' A figure swims in and out of focus in the gloom. 'I worried for a moment that I might've given you too much.'

'Ben? Is that you?' He steps away from the corner, his arms folded across his chest, his expression grim. I feel like I should be wary. Like something important has happened, but I can't think what.

'How are you feeling?'

'Like I've had the flu.'

That's a benzodiazepine for you. It can take you to heaven or make you feel like hell.'

'Benzo . . .' I can barely wrap my mouth around the word.

'Easier just to say roofied.'

Oh my God. 'By who?' But even as I'm asking, my mind is whispering the answer.

Sinister.

'I'd like to tell you it'll all come back to you, but it doesn't usually.' His voice is even, as though we're talking about the weather or the soccer results as he pulls out a chair from the darkness. Darkness, yes. We're in a room. Windowless. But the air is cool. There's a lamp plugged into the corner on my right, and though the light spilling from it is poor, it still hurts to look.

'That happens sometimes, too,' he says, crossing over to the lamp and tilting the shade. 'Sensitivity to light, headaches, a lack of memory. It sounds like you got all the unfun stuff from your trip.'

'Why did you do this to me?'

'Quite simply because I need you incapacitated for a little while.'

'Why?'

'I'll tell you, but you need to understand first that if I do, there's no chance of me letting you go. There will be too much at stake. So, the choice is yours, Rose. Do you want to know all? Know everything?'

'No,' I answer immediately. 'Don't tell me. I don't want to stay here. Let me go, Ben, and I promise—I promise you on my life—I won't breathe a word to anyone.' Images begin to swim through my head. The girl in the blond wig. An old photograph.

'Do you promise you'll leave? You'll go far, far away and never come back to Monaco?' His words are earnest, his expression as solemn as any I've ever seen.

'I promise—I'll go. I'll leave.' I'm not entirely sure why I need to leave, but I'm pretty sure the first place I'll go *to* is the police precinct. 'I won't cause you any problems if you just let me leave.'

'You're either much stupider than I thought, or I dosed you a little too hard. *Non*.' His earnest expression falls like the curtain falling at the end of a play. 'Maybe you think I am the stupid one.' In two steps, he's towering over me. In one frightened heartbeat, he's crouched in front of me, his hands on my knees. 'You're going nowhere. So, I'll tell you everything.'

'No! I don't want to hear.' I recoil from his touch, cold tendrils of dread wrap like vines through my insides, filling my veins with ice water—the sensation seeming to wake me the fuck up.

'Of course you do. Fear lurks in the unknown, Rose. Better to face your future. Make friends with it. Accept it, I think.'

'My future is not here with you.'

He smiles indulgently. I almost expect him to reach out and ruffle my hair.

'How long do you think that Austrian man kept his daughter underground?' My heart jolts, my spine stiffening. 'Years, certainly. You see, I'm going to keep you here for as long as I see fit. Or until I get bored of your company. Whichever comes first, I think.'

'I don't want to hear this!' Like a small child afraid of the dark, I screw my eyes closed, my hands pressed tight to my ears. 'You're not keeping me here.' I kick out, pushing to stand when he's suddenly towering over me, his hand at the back of my head, yanking me by my hair.

'You will listen, *salope*.' His breath is as hot on my cheek as my knees are weak. 'You remember the coffee shop?' He smiles as I try to nod.

Sinister, sinister, my smile screams out.

'I'll give you the abridged version. Emile fucked your mother for a time, and she must've been a very good fuck because, almost thirty years later, he left you shares in the company. You! Who did nothing to deserve or even earn them! Bad enough that he promised me the running of the company, bad enough that he left Remy the majority share, but he has to go and leave an interest to you. All this time, you've been fucking your brother. How do you feel about that, *ma chérie?*'

'That's not true. I know it's not.' Even through my denials, I feel like I'm going to throw up. It can't be true—it can't!

'And the worst of it is, Remy has known all along. Beautiful, tortured Remy.' Ben pouts, his brown eyes sad. 'Sleeping with his sister. So wrong.'

'I-I don't believe you.'

'No?'

'No.' Remy might be a lot of things, a lot of things I don't yet understand, but he isn't that. He isn't that kind of corrupt, I know, as the image of him flickers to life in my head.

His broad shoulders blocking out the sunlight, his face smiling down at me, shining with such love.

But that's not a reasoning I'll share as, from my scrambled brain, one thought rises above the morass.

'If I am Emile's daughter, then I wouldn't just deserve a share. I would be owed it.'

Like a child thwarted, he huffs unhappily. 'It was a slip of the tongue. Good catch.' 'You're not his child. Remy made sure of that, though not before he'd fucked you first.' Suddenly, his face looms closer, spittle hitting my face as he rants. 'You're just the child of his whore of an ex!' He releases me, but not before pushing me back down against the stone bench.

'This has got nothing to do with me. I never met Emile—I don't even want his money.' Money I know nothing about. 'Please, Ben. Let me go.' Tears track down my cheeks, my head feeling like it's been split in two. And I'm scared. So scared.

'No, you don't need the money because now you have

Remy.' His head tilts to the side, his eyes feral. 'Or you did. And now you'll have me.' His fingers trace my cheek and I do everything in my power not to move, not to show how repulsive I find his touch. 'One way or another.'

'No, Ben. Not like this, please.'

'It's not ideal, of course. But it shouldn't have come to this, you know. I saw you first. In the office on your first day. Remember I told you that?'

'At the club.' I try to nod and wince and try to swallow my fear. My mouth is so dry. Whatever he used to knock me out has left me with a terrible taste in my mouth. 'You said I looked like a fish out of water.'

'That's right.' He seems pleased that I remember, his hand retracting from my jaw. 'I didn't even know who you were then, but I wanted you. It's just a shame I was already off my head when I saw you.' His eyes fall to my chest as he readjusts my jacket by the lapels. 'I think I frightened you off a little.'

'No, that's not it—'

His sharp gaze rises, his expression sardonic. 'You don't have to lie to me, Rose. After I behaved the way I did, there was no turning the clock back. You were never going to see me in a favourable light. I could tell you were already smitten with *him*. Before my error, I could've courted you., and you might have fallen for me. But he hid you from the start. He acted unfairly. He always did, even when we were kids.'

I bite my tongue from yelling that's not true—that the brute in front of me is just a pale facsimile of the man I love. That he's crazy if he thinks for one solitary minute he ever had a chance. 'You weren't interested in me. Not really.' I almost choke on my words.

'Oh, you're wrong.' I screw my eyes tight shut as his lips brush my head. 'But I blew my chance thanks to a little too much cocaine. So, I didn't bother trying afterwards. At least,

508

not romantically.' His voice turns cold, and I stiffen as his hands feather my shoulder, brushing the sides of my breasts, the touch testing yet blatant.

And sickening.

'You told me about Amélie. Why would you tell me the engagement was fake if you didn't want me to fall in love with Remy?'

Disappointment ripples across his face, a look quickly replaced by distaste as he drops to the chair, his legs wide and relaxed, his arms dropped negligently to his thighs.

'You really aren't very bright, are you? Staying with him after he lied to you, still defending him after the proof I showed you this afternoon? The way he's lied to you again and again, yet you still would go back to him?'

'I thought you were sincere when you didn't hit on me. When you didn't hang him out to dry.' I try to remember what he showed me in the café; the photographs, documents, but my brain feels like an Etch A Sketch that's been shaken to the max.

'I believe you Americans call it playing the long game. Though I did think about fucking you, about getting you so drunk that afternoon that you couldn't say no. But driving you farther away wouldn't have helped my cause. And you might've told Remy, and excuse me for saying so, but one fuck wasn't worth spoiling my plans. You're not worth dying over.'

'Then why am I here, Ben?' I ask plaintively. My bottom lip begins to wobble. This is like something you see on TV, not something that happens to me.

'Because I thought you'd be smarter. But you're not. You're just a dumb bitch sucked in by a rich man. And also because of bad luck.' He suddenly stands. 'The announcement of your engagement on top of his mother pledging her shares of The Wolf Group to charity. My plans had to be accelerated. Your shares would become his,' he snaps, pointing both hands left, then right. 'His mother's shares going to an outside party. Where did that leave me?' he asks manically, pointing at himself this time. 'I'll tell you where. Farther away from controlling the company than ever.' The echo of his low-pitched anger reverberates around the dank space.

'I don't understand. Josephine's shares were never going to be yours. She would've left them to Remy if she left them to anyone.'

'Josephine's shares are not the issue. The issue is Remy getting his hands on your stake through marriage, making him more powerful. The issue is, that in killing him, his shares would then go to you.'

'But we're not even married yet.'

'Ah, not so nice now, Rose, huh? But I know what you're thinking. Why not kill him before you're married? Why not do so before you'd even met him because then you'd just be a small stakeholder and his shares would be mine. Well, let me tell you, I. Have. Fucking. Tried!'

'The motorcycle and the yacht.' Blood cools in my veins; he's not just crazy. He's a murderer.

'And a couple of other times besides.' He waves away the admission like batting off flies before linking his fingers behind his head as he stares at the ceiling as though the answer to all his problems are painted there. 'Had that *connard* done his job back in March, Remy would be dead by the side of the road, and I wouldn't have had to trash your bedroom to make it look like you packed with the hounds of hell on your heels.'

'How can my share of the company be worth all this? Keeping me here? Making yourself a criminal—a murderer?'

'It's all a matter of perspective. Alone, your shares are worth nothing. But pair them with Remy, and he becomes unstoppable. And unfortunately, *ma petite*, the point has come where I can't try to kill him anymore. For a little while, at least. But I can stop him controlling your stake. You're not married, and therefore, your shares aren't his. You'll go missing, driven away by grief of discovering his lies.'

'He won't believe that. He won't stop looking for me.'

'Good. If he's otherwise engaged, that leaves more for me. You'll stay missing, and probably presumed dead after five years have passed, and your shares, according to Emile's will, shall be divided between Remy and myself. Except, he'll already be dead by then.'

'When his estate will go to Josephine.'

'You underestimate the strength of our bond. I'm almost certain Remy will leave the company to me. There is such hubris and pride tied to the Wolf brand. He won't want it to go to charity.'

'No, it will all go to his mother,' I hedge. 'Not you. And then when Josephine passes, it'll all go to charity.'

'Oh, I don't think so. A widowed, childless woman, stricken with grief. She'll need someone to lean on. Someone like me. And in time, she too will die, you're right. Maybe sooner rather than later. Maybe not.' He affects a shrug. 'But her charity wishes might not come into effect by that time, by my design or from sheer gratitude. Who is to know?'

'You are crazy. This is so wild and fantastical; ifs and buts and maybes. And for what? Money? Haven't you got enough —more than you could spend in a lifetime?'

'It's not about money, you stupid bitch. It's about power! It's about being promised something, about being groomed to run the largest company in France, only to find it ripped from your grasp at the very end.'

'That's it? Jealously? You drug and bring me here. Tell me I'm going to end my days here, and for what? Because you're not happy your cousin got the better toys?' I find I'm on my feet, angry that I'm caught up in this web of envious macho bullshit.

'Oh, Rose. Don't worry,' he replies with a gleam. 'You're the toy of Remy's I'm looking forward to playing with the most. In fact, you're the toy I intend to break first.'

50

REMY

'No, Remy. Stop for a minute. Just think.'

'I am thinking,' I growl as I stalk across the home office towards him. 'I'm thinking I should tear off your balls and shove them down your fucking throat. You should've had her covered by full-time security.'

'Remote, you said. Until you'd squared it off with her. So that's what she's had. A fucking tail.'

'Then why wasn't there anyone tailing her today?' My hands ball in his shirt as I push him up against the door.

'We hacked into her planner.' With his words, Rhett twists, coming out from under my grip. We're too evenly matched for there to be any kind of victor, not that it matters when all I can see is red.

'Explain.' I rake a hand through my hair, my thoughts in disarray. How the fuck did she get into the safe? What prompted her to look? Why the hell has it come to this?

'It was supposed to be a way we'd know where she was during the week. When she was tucked up safe in the office, and when she was out and about and needed to be watched.'

'Protected,' I correct. 'She wasn't under suspicion.'

Rhett flicks a sardonic look at the desk, contradicting me. It's covered in documents and photographs; items she wasn't supposed to see yet.

'Clearly, that hasn't worked,' I say, bulldozing on. 'Because she's fucking missing, and she shouldn't be!' I roar even though beyond the red, angry haze, I know this is as much my fault as it is his. I wasn't ready to talk to her about her security, conscious of her life having already changed in so many ways since we met. I've found it hard enough to admit to myself that I might be a target. I didn't want her to know, let alone have to admit the possibility that the danger might extend to her.

Bottom line, I was hiding things from her again.

Ducking the hard conversations.

And now she's gone. The desk might be covered with *why*. The question now is *who?*

'Jared's going through the CCTV footage from here,' Rhett shoots back. 'Pierre and Jon are at Wolf Tower going through the stuff from there. Her phone is off but we're onto the network to see where and when it was last used.'

I hear, but I can't comprehend, my mind awash with a million thoughts as I begin to sift through the intel I'd paid to be collected over the preceding months. Including the latest instalment I'd refused to acknowledge.

Idiot.

I trace my finger over a photograph. *Place Massena* in Nice, a well-known landmark and familiar to me, stands as a backdrop to a couple holding hands. The man I know, the woman I do not, though I can easily guess her part. So much time and energy has been spent wondering how Emile might've met Rose or her mother in the US, when in fact it had happened in France.

There are other snapshots of proof. Employment contracts. Wage slips. Details of her mother's immigration to the US.

She was here, long before Rose was born, I think, flipping over a business card that, it seems, belongs to Carson Hayes. A fist with vice-like grip twists my innards.

'She's with him. With Carson Hayes.' My low growl reverberates through my insides. 'I saw the way he looked at her. I know the way he hates me. He has to be behind it.'

I turn to find Rhett's hand on my shoulder.

'Listen, there are a dozen things that might've happened. Don't go off half-cocked at a rustle in the wind.'

Without answering, I rip his hand away as I make a path for the front door.

I feel like someone has punched a hand into my chest and pulled out my heart while I wasn't looking, the tattered remains discarded to rot on the ground. And I know I've brought this on myself. I know I should've told her about her inheritance, about the secrets I've kept—all of it. And now I look like a monster who proposed for power, not for love. And worse than that, as the final pieces of the puzzle slot into place, I realise the link between my life and hers.

The reasons Emile left her a share of the company.

Money touched with blood and innocence.

If she never wants to take possession of it, I will forever understand.

I stride out into the hall without giving Rhett or the mess I leave behind another thought, snatching up the car keys from the table. My shoes crunch against the gravel, the car alarm chiming as I approach it. I climb into the driver's seat, my head whipping around as the passenger side slams.

'You're a hot-headed arsehole,' Rhett asserts, yanking on his seat belt. 'But you're not going alone.'

'I don't think it's wise. The way I feel right now, I might kill him.'

'That's precisely the reason I am,' he mutters. 'Put your fucking belt on.'

The tyres spray gravel as I swing around the turning circle and head for the gate.

'All right, Lewis fucking Hamilton! I'd like to get there in one piece,' Rhett complains, invoking the Formula 1 racing driver's name as he hangs onto the interior door handle. 'I'd also like to know why we're using my car.'

'Because yours isn't in the garage.' The gates are already swinging open as I approach them.

'Watch the fucking paintwork,' he yells as I scrape through.

But the Range Rover's paintwork is not my concern as I swing out onto the road, my destination Fontvieille on the coast.

I only have thoughts for Rose

ROSE

'Where are we, Ben?'

'Nowhere anyone would think to look for you,' he says, closing and locking the door behind him. In his hand, he has a bottle of wine and a couple of glasses—plastic glasses—and a loaf of bread. *A boule, not a baguette.*

I'm still sitting on the stone bench where he left me, though I have investigated the place in the time he's been gone . . . doing whatever he was doing.

'I don't mean where we are exactly. Just, what is this

place?' This windowless room that smells like earth and seems like the kind of place you'd put someone you want to forget.

'It's a cellar in a house I bought recently.'

'I'm assuming Remy doesn't know about it.' Even as I ask, my heart constricts, and I send out a silent prayer that he does.

'You assume correct. And like so many properties out here, it's owned by a shell company operating out of the Cayman Islands. Completely untraceable. Here.' He passes the bread to me, pulling out a lump of wax paper wrapped cheese from the pocket of his jacket and handing that over, too. I tamp back the bitter disappointment as I place them down on the bench next to me, quickly sitting on my hands again. My knuckles and fingernails are stained earth-brown from feeling my way around the gaps in the door, then along the walls and floors where they meet, frantically looking for something that might help my predicament.

I become aware of my engagement ring digging into my thigh, its presence suddenly the comfort I need as I swallow over my hammering heart, not sure if it's scarier being here alone or with Ben

Ben, who is completely nuts, it would seem.

'I'll bring better food tomorrow. And blankets. You'll forgive my hasty preparations,' he says, using a small corkscrew attached to his keys to open the bottle of wine.

'Is that one of those Swiss Army knives?' He nods and I watch as he scores the seal before beginning to push the screw into the cork, as I aim to look either thirsty or thoughtful and not at all interested in where he puts his keys when he's done.

'You'll come to see it's not so bad being with me.' Ben

angles his head, and I become aware of how close I am to him right now. I immediately lean the opposite way.

'Yeah, sure. A dank basement is totally the kind of place a girl wants to live.'

'Better than dying in it,' he murmurs, dragging the toe of his shoe along the earth packed floor. *All the better for burying you in*, the movement seems to say.

'How am I going to use the bathroom?' This isn't a question. More a demand.

'When I'm sure you can behave, I'll take you. A couple of times a day, I should imagine.' And he'll be visiting me twice a day for what? I push away the thought. I'm *not* rotting away in this place. 'I'll bring you a bucket tomorrow,' he adds. 'For when I'm not here.'

I bite back my answer to that. Now is not the time nor the place, no matter how scared I am. No matter how a scream seems to be clawing its way up my throat.

I can't stay here.

I can't wait to be rescued.

What if Remy takes one look at the space where my suitcase was and decides I'm not worth chasing?

No. That won't happen, I tell myself. You don't declare your love for someone and then let them walk away. He'll want to hear me say the words myself. Not that I'm going to say anything like that. I'm going to listen to what he has to say. Listen to his reasons, his explanation. Listen to his love.

But what happens if he never finds me?

What happens if he never looks?

My chest begins to heave, my sight going dim as everything narrows in focus.

The dirt floor. The door. The walls as they close in.

Oh, God. Is this a panic attack? Drugs? Am I dying?

'Rose?'

At the sound of my name, my head lifts to Ben who watches me with a kind of peeled eyeball kind of intensity that's chilling.

'Breathe,' he says, still watching me. 'Everything will be okay. Unless you don't co-operate and then it'll be like hell.'

He turns his back on me and splashes a little wine into the plastic glasses, handing one to me. I knock it back immediately without giving thought to what my dirty fingernails say. I don't consider how the liquid could've been doctored, or the taste, or bouquet. I just throw it back, desperate for something to take away this sick feeling of dread.

Sinister. Sinister.

'Please let me go, Ben.' My voice is small; my fear, by contrast, immense.

'I've already explained why I can't. After the lengths I've gone to, things must be so.'

'Remy will know I haven't gone anywhere. He-he'll get someone to check the movement on my passport.'

'Boats come and go from the port all of the time. You could've crossed over the border into France and gotten lost. There are all kinds of places you might go. All kinds of things that might happen to you, Rose.' The menace in his softly delivered words rings loud and clear.

'He won't stop looking for me. He loves me.'

'Except you left him after you discovered how he'd lied to you.'

'I don't care about any of that. You can have the shares. Everything! I just want to go.'

'I can't let you go. It's better for you that you stop asking.'

'Please.' Tears trip and spill down my cheeks, my fear an

all-encompassing thing. It's not a walk where you can't see the end of a dark alley, or a swim in the ocean where you lose sight of land. This isn't the fear of the unknown. There's no need to hypothesise what lies at the end of this for me.

Because I know.

51

REMY

Was she forced?

Did she leave on her own?

She left the gala without a word, though not really. She only went to gather her thoughts and came back at me, all guns blazing.

'Are you listening to me?' Rhett's voice brings me back to the moment.

'*Oui*.' Twisting the wheel to a hard right, I cut across the early evening traffic.

'Much fucking good you'll be to her dead. What about her friends? Could she be with them?'

'She wouldn't have taken a suitcase for a coffee,' I grate out.

'They might know where she is, though. Where she's likely to be.' He begins to type something out on his phone.

Shouldn't I know better than them? Because the closer I get, the less certain I feel. The deeper my dread grows. The harder I grip the steering wheel. The more likely I am to grind my molars to dust.

Please, Rose. Tell me where you are. Tell me you're okay.

'Try her phone again.' My gaze cuts to Rhett, moving back

to the road instantly. Not for safety's sake but because of what I see there.

Pity.

'I just did. It's still off. Watch the . . .' His arm shoots out, finger pointed, as I swerve around the motorcyclist. 'Fucking hell. I'll be grey before we get there.'

'What have you got in the trunk?'

'What do you mean?'

'Guns. Weapons. Firearms.'

'Remy, man.' He blows out a breath, rubbing a hand across the top of his head.

'I want to know where I stand, Everett.'

'On fucking trial, by the sounds of things.'

'I'm not losing my head. Just preparing.'

His phone chimes with a text. 'Right, according to one Castain, Charles, she left work around three this afternoon to go to Monaco One. She didn't go back to the office. Apparently, he's still waiting for a bubble tea.'

'Did she have a meeting?'

'No, she was picking a jacket up from Max Mara. What time did you last speak to her?'

'At lunchtime, a little after noon.'

I need to be inside you. Her response had been something between a breath and a groan as I'd trailed my hand up her thigh, bringing with it the hem of her skirt.

Ah, but not in the office. Her laughter was pure tease as she'd pressed herself against me. My whole body had ached and trembled, the need to be deep inside her always so powerful.

'And she was okay then?'

I nod once, rather stiffly. 'She was fine.' As fine as a charcoal illustration drawn by an old master's hand.

'Less said about that, the better,' he mutters as we pull into the private complex near Larvotto Beach, slowing for the boom gate.

'You'll need the security code, or the plastic policeman will pop out of his box to quiz you with his clipboard.' He means the security guard, of course.

The window buzzes as it lowers. I lean out and enter the code.

'Have you got a place in here?' he splutters as the gate begins to rise

'I've got places everywhere.'

I park in one of the visitor spots and climb out, ignoring, for now, the options a gun might bring to my hand. I know this complex well, having lived here a decade ago. I already know he lives here, and my guess is he'll be at home right now. He doesn't strike me as the kind to be interested in happy hour drinks straight from the office. More like sundowners on the deck, I decide, as I approach the back of his townhouse, Rhett's footsteps sounding from behind.

I open the low gate to his garden and stride up the path.

'You know this isn't the front of the house, right?'

Without answering, I slide open the glass patio door.

'Fucking great,' Rhett complains. 'We're adding breaking and entering to the list of your felonies today.'

'Door was open. No breaking required. And no felonies to report today.' *Yet.*

I stride deeper into the house, not giving a fuck that I've invaded someone's home as need consumes me. A need to find him. A need to find her. A need to know what is going on.

Then he's in front of me, dressed in board shorts and a T-shirt with a towel in his hands.

'What the fuck are you doing here? In my house?' It's almost as though the realisation that I am standing in his house seems to hit him as he speaks. 'Get the fuck out!'

'Sit down.' With the five points of my fingers at his chest, I push him into the chair that's conveniently behind him. Convenient for him, at least.

'Fuck you. Get the fuck out of my house.' He's immediately back on his feet, squaring up to me.

'I said sit down.' I push him again, and Rhett chuckles from behind me. I see it the moment he realises I'm not alone.

'Where is she?' My voice sounds calm—too calm for these riotous feelings curling and twisting inside me. I need reassurance that she's okay because I'm heading towards violence.

'Where's who?'

'Rose. I want to know where Rose is.'

'She had the good sense to bail, did she?' he crows. 'Well, good for fucking her is all I have to say.'

'I'll give you one more chance to tell me where she is.'

'Remy.' Rhett's tone is a warning, my fists already balled.

'I don't know where she is, and I wouldn't tell you if I knew.'

'Listen, pal.' Rhett is suddenly between us. 'We have other places we need to be. But the fact of the matter is, we just want to make sure Rose isn't in danger.' His tone turns conciliatory, his manner, too. 'She's gone missing, and there was a lot of mess at the house. We think she might've been abducted.'

My veins flood with ice. I'm worried, yes. But I hadn't considered the possibility, not truly, and was taking the blame squarely on my own shoulders. *I fucked up, so she left*. But now I see the danger. Now I see he might be right.

And if he is, Carson Hayes isn't the man I'm looking for.

'Well, I'm sorry for that,' Carson answers. 'She seems like a good person. But I've been in Turin all day; took a flight out early this morning. Knock yourself out, check the flight manifest if you don't believe me. She wasn't with me. And kidnap seems more your skill set.'

For a moment, I think he's talking to Rhett—there's no mistaking he's military—as though he's inclined to undertake such acts in a professional capacity.

A coldness settles around my shoulders when I realise he's addressing me.

'What the fuck is that supposed to mean?'

'Acquiring companies by less than fair means. And by acquiring, I mean stealing. Blackmail. Threats. I can see kidnapping being added to the list real easy.'

'What about rape?' I say, stepping into him, close enough to see his gaze flare. 'What about sexual assault? Abuse of power? Are those on the great Carson Hayes' list?'

'What are you talking about?'

'Not what, who. Just ask your grandfather.'

And with that, I plant my fist squarely in his gut.

'Got it.' Outside, Rhett ends the very brief call he's just received, staring at the phone in his hand a beat longer than is normal.

'What you said in there? You think—' I swallow and start again. 'You think she hasn't left? Left me, I mean? You think she might've been taken? Kidnapped?'

'Remy, mate, we need to look at this from all angles. But, I dunno, it just seems too convenient that she's seen all the stuff from the safe, then pissed off. I reckon she'd be more likely to wait and speak to you about it. She might then run you over in her car, but at least you'd know.'

'So who, Rhett? Where?' Blood burns in my veins. 'I need answers, and I pay you to get them.'

'And we're getting there,' he asserts, not accepting the barb. 'But do you wanna tell me what that was all about?' He lifts his thumb in the direction of the Hayes' townhouse.

'You know how I got my hands on Hayes Construction.' I press my palms to my thighs and bend at the waist as I try to control my breathing. My heart hammers in my chest, my head feeling like it might burst at any minute.

'Blackmail,' Rhett asserts. He knows. He was party to it. 'But that in there? That was personal. I saw the way you looked at him. I heard the way you wanted it to be him.'

I huff out a desultory laugh. 'What is it you said? The apple doesn't fall far from the tree?'

'Stop speaking in fucking riddles.'

'The paperwork I didn't want to look at. I was keeping it until I told Rose about the shares. About everything. What a fuck up that would've been.'

'Not your finest plan,' he agrees. 'But I say again, want to explain?'

'It seems as though, as a young girl, Rose's mother, Noorah, worked for the Hayes family as an au pair.'

'Oh, fuck.' He forces his hands through his hair, intuiting where this is going.

'Presumably, her Lebanese heritage would've meant she spoke French. She would've been on a Lebanese passport, too.' Not living in the US. Not travelling on a US passport.

'It seems she met my father in Nice, at a time he was an up and coming hotelier.' And that is as much as the investigator seemed to discover about their relationship. 'She lived in France for two years before going home before she turned twenty.'

'And there the story would end, if it not for the small issue of intimidation,' Rhett says.

'But I wasn't the first Durrand to have that bastard Hayes

over a barrel. Emile got there first.' But as for my involvement, my intimidation of Carson Hayes senior and my plans to crush his company, several months ago, while in the midst of an audit, a certain recording was found. Carson Hayes labouring over the body of an unconscious woman.

'The girl in the video,' Rhett asserts. 'She was Rose's mum.'

'Rose's mother and my father's girlfriend. And the year she left France is the year The Wolf Group was born.'

Created from the proceeds of my father's blackmail.

Born and built on her suffering.

Suffering I used once again to blackmail Hayes.

'Fuck.'

'That about sums it up.'

He doesn't have time to absorb the information as his phone buzzes with a text. His eyes flick over the information contained.

'What is it?' I demand. 'Is it Rose?'

He nods tersely. 'CCTV at the house shows her in the driveway just after four this afternoon.' His head rises, his eyes hard. 'Ben was driving.'

'Ben?'

'She was in the passenger seat. He parked at the side of the house, in the courtyard.'

'Where the CCTV coverage is poor.' He nods again. The orange trees growing near to the house have partially obscured the view of the camera there, including leading in and out of the house. 'I should've gotten the tree surgeon out earlier. I'm sorry, Remy.'

I wave away his apology as unnecessary at this point. 'What else?'

'Footage shows him leaving via the driveway ten minutes later. Just him, though. There was no sign of Rose. He even stopped to talk to the gardener on the way out. The bloke says there was no one else in the car. Just him.'

'Or that's what he wants us to think.'

'Yep. Then, at four thirty a taxi pulls up. Same place. Drives out again, soon after. The windows were tinted so it's hard to say if there was anyone else in it but the driver. We ran the plates. They were fake.'

'Ben? I can see him helping her to leave.' Yet I don't really believe she has. 'But this level of fucked up? It's beyond him.'

'You're blind to Benny-boy's antics. You think because you knew the knobbly kneed kid, you know the man. You don't know half of what he is.'

'And you do?'

'I've been keeping an eye on him long enough. You might say he's been a side project. Kind of a hobby.' His expression twists, though he knows he has my attention. 'You wouldn't have listened if I'd told you I found out that he'd he recently bought a crowbar on his Amex card.'

'If you knew, why was Rose not receiving around-the-clock security?' The ice in my voice matches the drop of my temperature, my blood running instantly cold.

'Because he had a hard-on for you, not her. If I'd thought for one minute—'

I wave away what's coming next. Recriminations. Blame. None of this is of interest.

'What next?'

'Apart from the crowbar,' he muses, scratching the stubble on his cheek. 'Fuck!' His spine straightens, the soldier in him suddenly very obvious. 'As far as suspicious shit goes, how about this? Last month, his shell company completed a sale on a tumbledown shack a few kilometres outside of Menton.'

I release a volley of French curses that just aren't enough. 'Fuck. Fuck. Fuck!'

'Watch the rims,' he complains as I lash out with my feet.

'Fuck the rims!'

'For all your language capabilities, there's nothing quite like *fuck*. Is there?'

'There will be nothing quite like Everett soon.'

'You can try, but you're too angry to be much more than a happy place for my fist. Cool head, boss man, if you don't want things to go tits up. Get in the car.'

I throw him the keys.

Tits up is not an option.

ROSE

'Can I have more?' I hold out my plastic glass. Please, sir. This little waif would like a drop more wine. At least, I hope that's what my expression says as I channel a little Oliver Twist.

'Of course.' He twists from the waist, bending to grasp the neck of the bottle from where he's placed it on the floor. As he does so, I peer behind him, hoping to see where his keys are.

Really, Rose? You're going to fight your way out of the creepy cellar with the use of a tiny bottle opener? Or maybe the can opener? The nail file?

But I have to do something because I can't stay here to pee in a bucket.

'Thank you.' I smile as he tops up my glass.

'Not too much, *ma chérie*. Not after the drugs.'

Yes, you look after me. So you can kill me at your leisure.

'I'm starving. May I have a little of the cheese?'

He puts the bottle down on the floor between his feet, twisting at the waist to reach for the meagre provisions. Bread tears and wax paper rustles as I put my glass down on the bench. As he turns back, passing over my dinner, I fumble and drop the bread.

'Butter fingers!' I bend quickly forward, the bread bouncing away like scree down a hill. But I'm not interested in the bread.

Not as my heart pounds against my ribs. Not as the scream jammed in my throat turns to a growl as I clasp the neck of the bottle, everything slowing and playing out frame by frame.

His expression morphs.

His hands reach.

The slow spin of the bottle in the air.

Red wine spilling from the neck like blood.

His head rearing back as I spin.

His eyes closing as I smash it against his temple.

From slow to fast, the sounds played out in stereo. His low cursing, my nails scraping the stone bench. My feet slipping on the dirt. The jangle of the keys as I try to jam them in the lock.

'Fucking bitch.'

I cry out as he yanks me back by the hair. I land on my twisted elbow with a sob. The pain is jarring, my fear amplified, making me feel physically sick as he throws his keys in the corner and makes his advance.

'I warned you. I said there would be no escape.'

'I'd rather be dead than stuck here with you.'

But they're just words. Words I don't mean. But I don't get the chance to retract them as he towers above me quite suddenly.

'That can be arranged.' His eyes burn with a mixture of hatred and hunger. 'But not before I take what's owed.'

Then he's on his knees in the dirt, his fingers biting into my legs, pressing them down, pushing them open with his own. He presses one knee against my thigh, the pressure reverberating through the bone. As he catches my pummelling fists, his body crushes mine to the ground, stones piercing my back as we grapple. But then my wrists are in one of his hands.

'I like a girl with a little fight.' His breath smells of wine and desperation, but I don't answer. I can't find a suitable retort, not as I continue to fight.

It's fight or get fucked.

Fight or be killed.

Body bucking, my shoe comes off as I try to pound him with my heels, choking out a strangled sob as his hand slips under my shirt to squeeze.

'But not this much,' he grates out, that same hand moving to my neck. He grabs me, his grip tightening and making it hard for me to breathe. The more I try to inhale, the tighter his grip gets. Panic and pain fill my chest and my head. I feel like I'm about to burst. There literally isn't space for anything else inside me but this and fear as I claw at his hand, claw at my neck.

And then it's not so hard to breathe anymore because the room begins to go dark.

Pain follows darkness immediately. My throat feels crushed, and I'm gasping, swallowing, desperately trying to inhale, desperately trying to breathe.

Just breathe.

Just breathe.

Just breathe.

Slowly, my focus begins to shift away from the pain in my chest and neck and my head, my lungs expanding, my body working as it should. But this shift brings me to another terror as I become aware of his fingers at the button of my pants. Something digging into my spine. The popping of buttons,

DONNA ALAM

another fierce squeeze. But I have bigger issues than his groping hands. Like staying alive.

'I warned you,' he hisses, spittle hitting my face. His mouth is wet and unwanted, the front of my blouse rending, the waistband of my pants digging into my hips. 'I warned you.'

I push ineffectually as he lowers his head again, his excitement a hot breath at my ear, a grasping between my legs.

A bang, loud and clear, resounds through the space, my ears beginning to ring.

And then my hands are hitting nothing but air, the weight of him no longer there.

I roll into a ball, tears changing direction as they roll across my cheeks, fat and wet. Scuffles. Yells. Curses. I roll again, this time onto my hands and my knees as dirt flicks up my arm.

My attention turns to the light spilling from the open doorway—not daylight—an electric light, flickering across a beast on the floor. A beast that roars and pounds. As it beats a man's head into the ground.

'For fuck's sake, Remy.' The silhouette in the doorway sounds like Rhett. I cough out a very, very grateful laugh. One I'll remember not to tell him about later.

He pulls at the beast, still yelling. 'He's not worth the fucking paperwork.'

The beast rolls and roars, and then I'm in his arms.

He smells like bergamot and spice.

And copper and dirt.

He feels like home.

EPILOGUE

REMY

THE BABY REACHES OUT, catching Rose's finger between five fat little digits.

'You're a natural.' My voice breaks the connection between their gazes; a mutual appreciation society that isn't taking applications for new memberships. But that's okay. Rose and I have our own kind of club. One where I've promised her my undying devotion and truth above all else.

I promised her the truth yet, still I lie.

'I don't know,' she muses. The smile she sends my way is a burst of happiness to my heart that I will always try to deserve. 'This baby looked very much at home in your arms earlier.'

'Beginner's luck,' I answer, tipping back my head as though to study the precision in the weaving of the grass roof. We're on the island of Sumba in Indonesia on a resort I'd helped build with my own hands a few years ago before The Wolf Group fell to me.

'I don't believe that. You'll be a good dad,' she answers. 'I can tell.'

But how can she, given the hand I was dealt?

Few sons are like their father. Few are better. Many are worse.

I thought I came into the last category. That I was worse than my father. I wish I could say I take comfort in the discovery that I'm not. With all my heart, I wish I could say that my sins outstrip his because then Rose's mother would never have suffered as she did.

I hope the bastard is rotting in hell. I know Hayes the older rots from the inside out now that his grandson has distanced himself. He isn't cut from the same cloth as the elder. A fact I'd begun to realise in the course of our dealings, dealings where he'd also expressed an interest in helping Rose raise funds for her own charity foundation. In a strange turn of events, Rose and my mother have become firm friends in the course of the venture.

'Do you want to hold her?' Rose asks, bouncing the tot in her arms.

I shake my head. 'The view from here is too beautiful to spoil.'

She rests in a chair framed by the window; the wooden shutters open to the view beyond. Blue skies. Coconut palm swaying in the breeze. Bougainvillea winding its way around the pergola, brilliant pink against a wash of blue sky. The ocean laps at the sand a few short metres away, and the sun hangs like a brilliant jewel in the sky. And that's not even the best part of this view.

Rose is.

She wears a gauzy white cover over a jade-coloured bikini. Her skin berry-brown and her hair piled haphazardly on top of her head. She is Venus. Juno. Made of hills and valleys and curves as abundant as the love that pours from her heart.

She is a prize I won't ever deserve.

But she's mine anyway.

That terrible day, when we'd arrived at a building that

wasn't the shack we'd anticipated, but a modest house at the end of a long track no one would ever happen across by accident, I knew I wasn't afraid to die, should it come to that. I was only afraid of living a life without her.

The windows were boarded up, the heavy doors locked. Everything about the place screamed abandoned. We found Ben's car stowed out of sight in a nearby outbuilding, Rose's suitcase in the back, a length of rope and a hunting knife in the trunk. The sight sent a shiver down my spine. That she might leave me tore me in two. That she may have been forced to leave, that she may have been murdered because of me, left me in a purgatory filled with helplessness and rage.

Would I ever hold her again?

Steal a kiss from her at the bottom of the staircase?

And then, the sight of her on the dirt floor.

Her voice no more than a pained whisper as she fought.

Fought him off. I had a gun in my hand—I'd used it to break the lock—but I didn't think to use it because I'd wanted to kill him with my bare hands.

He was going to keep her there, she told the police, for reasons that made no sense. For revenge, for madness? I don't think a sane person would ever understand—could ever understand. That's not to say Ben is insane, though his legal team have begun to prepare this as a possible defence. As I understand, his premeditation will prevent any chance of this. We're told to expect he'll go to prison for a very long time.

However long, it won't be enough.

Some days, I regret not killing him with my bare hands.

Other days . . . well, I regret it those days, too.

'Remy.' I look up at the sound of my name. 'Don't look back, remember? We're not going that way.'

But how can I not dwell there when I will bear her grief forever? I'll bear it because I can't bring myself to tell her what happened to Noorah, to her mother, because it would only serve to break her heart. It isn't about the money or business; it's about protecting her from the impotent pain of not being able to change the past.

She had little recollection of the photographs and documents Ben showed her that afternoon. Benzodiazepine has the nasty habit of not only rendering a person unconscious, given enough, but it also robs the memory. Which is why it's often the date-rape drug of choice. Ben himself had little interest in the information the safe contained, except as a red herring to serve her disappearance. He thought he'd learned all he needed to know.

Then later, far from being abhorred by my lies, Rose listened as I'd explained how I'd looked for her in San Francisco—the misunderstanding that we can now look upon as fate. She understood how I'd needed to know the truth of who she was and how she came to be inheriting. It was never about the money, and she understood that. Her inheritance was never going to affect mine.

The fact is, my father raised me to mistrust everyone and everything around me.

Then he died and left me a secret of his own.

I became obsessed with knowing the truth. Obsessed until I met her, when my obsession took the path to love. I was able to truthfully say to her that, by the time the final package arrived from the investigator, I didn't care where she'd come from. I proposed, she accepted, and I'd planned to tell her about her inheritance following our wedding night, when I'd also tell her my wealth was now hers. Had she chosen to discover the truth, we could've faced it together. Opened the package together.

Instead, after all that had happened, after I'd discovered the horror of it, I'd told her a half-truth. I said that our parents were romantically involved a long time ago. That Emile left her shares in the group because of that connection. I then set out to make sure those who knew the truth would never tell. I trust Rhett with my life. Carson Hayes III carries his grandfather's shame. He has pledged to support Rose as she directs her inheritance to the benefit of others. To fight discrimination, homelessness, and poverty. All matters close to her heart.

Going forward, I'll carry this alone. I'll make it up to her the only way I can.

By pledging her my eternal love.

'You've changed your mind?' she asks as I stand and take the chubby babe from her arms. 'See, no one can resist the charms of baby Beryl.'

I press my lips to the top of my fiancée's head. 'I'm returning Ruby to her parents because you and I have plans.'

'That sounds ominous,' she says, her words ending in a playful curl.

'Almost as ominous as marrying me in the morning.'

'There's still time for me to escape,' she teases, chuckling as I reach the door when Ruby grabs my bottom lip, cooing delightedly.

'Not for you,' I murmur, though the words don't quite come out that way as I peel baby fingers from my lip. 'These lips belong to Tante Rose.' I press a kiss to Ruby's chubby fist. 'She's going to need them later when I tie her to the bed.'

'Is that a fact?' Her voice is pitched lightly, though I'm conscious of the way her eyes flare. Of how she presses her thighs together as she stretches out in the chair.

'It's a promise. There's no escape, ma Rose.'

'As if I'd even try. Don't let Byron pour you a drink. Hurry back.'

'I'll be gone only long enough for you to make a list.'

'A list of what?' she asks, a little bemused now.

'A list of all the things you want me to do to you between now and tomorrow morning.'

'You mean between now and our wedding ceremony?'

'Exactly. The way I look at it, the next fifteen hours will be the only time in your life you get to be fucked by someone other than your husband.'

'Are you trying to manage my expectations, Remy Durrand? I don't believe I'm looking forward to a lifetime of missionary with the lights off.'

'Who knows what will happen after tomorrow.' Except that I will love her always. That she will always be my home. 'We should put the next fifteen hours to good use. The kind of use that encourages unrestrained debauchery.'

'Then what are you waiting for?' she asks with a smirk. 'Get baby Beryl back to where she belongs. It's time we started baby making of our own.'

'Ma Rose, I would like that very much.'

ACKNOWLEDGEMENTS

To the usual cast of wonderful characters, my mahoosive thanks, but especially to Elizabeth (the keeper of the rear) who was at the beginning, the middle, and the end of this one.

Thanks to Lisa for her encouragement and medical skillz, and to Michelle, the Bo-Peep of the Lambs, and excellent cheerleader.

To Michelle C & Annette (good cop and also good cop) for trying to get my bum in some kind of order. I'm a work in progress.

Thank you to the Lambs for hanging out in my corner of Romancelandia. You rock my socks! Also, thank you to you lovely people who pick up this book, the girlies who read my stuff religiously and those giving a Donna Alam book their first whirl. You both amaze and humble me. I just don't possess the words to say exactly how much.

Also, thanks to COVID and 2020 for giving me serious brain drain, along with a new "colleague" in the form of my daughter. How come it's *my* office yet I have to make the coffee?

ABOUT THE AUTHOR

USA Today bestseller Donna is a writer of love stories with heart, humour, and heat. When not bashing away at her keyboard, she can often be found hiding from her responsibilities with a book in her hand and a mop of a dog at her feet.

Get to hear all the news by joining her newsletter or come say hello in her private reader group, Donna's Lambs.

Keep in contact

Donna's Lambs
Donna's VIP Newsletter
mail@donnaalam.com
www.DonnaAlam.com

Printed in Great Britain
by Amazon